O9-BUD-382

AFTER THE RED RAIN

BARRY LYGA
WITH
PETER FACINELLI
AND
ROBERT DeFRANCO

Little, Brown and Company

Hachette Book Group
1290 Avenue of the Americas, New York, NY 10104
Visit us at lb-teens.com

Little, Brown and Company is a division of Hachette Book Group, Inc. The Little, Brown name and logo are trademarks of Hachette Book Group, Inc.

The publisher is not responsible for websites (or their content) that are not owned by the publisher.

First Edition: August 2015

Library of Congress Cataloging-in-Publication Data

Lyga, Barry.
    After the red rain / by Barry Lyga ; with Peter Facinelli & Rob DeFranco. — First edition.
        pages cm
    Summary: "Set in a future world of environmental collapse and mass poverty, where a mysterious boy named Rose discovers he possesses inhuman powers that can irrevocably change the lives of everyone on the planet" — Provided by publisher.
    ISBN 978-0-316-40603-1 (hardcover) — ISBN 978-0-316-40604-8 (ebook) — ISBN 978-0-316-40606-2 (library edition ebook) [1. Science fiction.] I. Facinelli, Peter, 1973– II. DeFranco, Rob. III. Title.
    PZ7.L97967Aft 2015
    [Fic]—dc23

                                                                          2014036677

10 9 8 7 6 5 4 3 2 1

RRD-C

Printed in the United States of America

*Is it strange to dedicate a book to one's coauthors?
Then call me strange, for I can think of no
better dedicatees than my coauthors. Rob and
Peter, thank you for conjuring Rose and his quest,
and for inviting me along.*
—*Barry*

*For Kristen, Fiona, Enzo, Lola, and Massimo.
Love you dearly.*
—*Rob*

*To Luca Bella, Lola Ray, and Fiona Eve. "Think left
and think right and think low and think high. Oh, the
thinks you can think up if only you try!" —Dr. Seuss*
—*Peter*

PROLOGUE

The Last Days of the Red Rain

The clank and rattle of what he thought of as The System had long since faded into mere background noise to Gus. Or maybe he was just going deaf. He was certainly old enough—beyond old enough—for it. In any event, it didn't matter. He was the only one tending to The System, so he was the only one to talk to. And he'd gotten bored with himself a long, long time ago. Stooped and twisted with age—nearly fifty years, if he remembered correctly, an almost unheard-of longevity—he limped around the chamber with only himself for company.

The System was a series of belts, tubes, pulleys, and wheels arranged in a circuitous route through a large chamber. It began at an inclined chute at one end and wended its clacking, whirring way through the chamber to the opposite end.

The System was all about bodies.

Tall, short, thin, fat, young, old, frail, robust, every color and shade decreed by Nature or by God—take your pick. The bodies wound through The System day and night, hauled along as machines snapped and plucked at them, stripping them of clothing, jewelry, and all the other accoutrements of the living world. They entered The System as they'd died; they left it as they'd been born: naked and alone.

Gus monitored The System. He attended to its needs. Though he had his suspicions, he didn't know where the bodies came from or where they went. Long ago he'd decided that it was best simply to be grateful he wasn't one of them.

This day, a sound came to him, pitched high above the muted rumble of the machinery. At first, he thought it had to be his imagination. Then he thought it must be his ears finally giving up the ghost after so many years of abuse. He scrabbled at one ear, then the other, with his little finger, digging around.

The sound persisted. High-pitched and abjectly terrified and definitely alive, not mechanical.

He peered around the chamber, seeking the source of the sound. In the echoing confines of The System, it was difficult to pinpoint a specific noise. Especially with ears fading, as his were. Standing still, he listened intently. Rotated and took a few steps. Paused again to listen, willing the sound to become louder.

Miraculously, it did. It rose to a bloodcurdling howl.

Gus rushed to the tunnel that opened up into The System. The noise had come from there, he knew it.

He gaped at what he saw.

Gus had worked The System as long as he could remember. Most of his life, really. Decades. He'd never tried to count the bodies that came through, and even if he had, he would have given up on tallying them long ago.

But this, he knew, was the first time he'd ever seen a living one.

A baby.

A tiny, defenseless baby lay on a series of grinding cylinders that bore the bodies into The System. She—for she was naked—squawked and squalled, waving one pudgy fist in terrified indignation, kicking her chubby legs.

She was stuck. As she'd slid down the chute, her left shoulder had been caught in the gears of the machinery. It pinched there, purple-going-black, and she howled.

Sometimes bodies got stuck like this. Gus had tools to break them loose. But such tools were for dead bodies, not living ones, and he froze for an instant, unsure what to do.

She cried out again, her face going purple now.

There was no time to hit the emergency shutdown switch—she would be ripped to shreds before then. And besides, hitting the switch would mean questions, and Gus understood that it was best not to have questions when he had no answers.

Wincing in sympathetic pain, he tugged at her, gently at first and then, finally, with all his strength when *gently* didn't suffice. With a yowl of pain, she came free from the machine, leaving behind an inch-wide strip of flesh from high up on her neck to her shoulder. Bright red blood spilled, and Gus nearly lost his grip on her as it flowed down to his hands, making her slippery.

"Shush, shush," he cooed, almost by instinct. A baby. When was the last time he'd seen a baby?

A *living* baby, he amended.

"Hush-a, hush-a," he tried, and still she wailed. He couldn't blame her.

He knew what he should do. He knew his job. Bodies came into The System, and bodies went through The System, and bodies left The System. His job was to make sure everything ran smoothly. And while he'd always assumed the bodies would be dead and had always *seen* only dead bodies...no one had ever specified dead.

He should put her on the rolling cylinders and let her leave The System as everyone else did, to go wherever they went.

She screamed and whimpered, and her blood spilled. Gus chewed at his bottom lip.

It had been so long since he'd cried that he didn't even realize

3

he was doing it until the first fat tears splashed onto her round, little belly.

"Hush-a, hush-a," he whispered, bouncing her lightly. "Hush-a, hush-a. That ain't gonna heal on its own. Sorry, no. But I think old Gus can do what he can do."

He carried her to his workbench and swept his tools aside. The bench was dirty and scarred with age, but better than whatever lay beyond The System. He set her down and began rummaging in his toolbox, muttering to himself.

"Fishing line, fishing line..." He hadn't fished since he was a boy, and even then the rivers had been dead. But the line came in handy for a number of tasks, so he always kept a supply. He dug it out now and then found a needle from the kit he used to repair his clothes.

"This ain't gonna feel so good right now," he warned her, threading the needle with the fine, light filament, "but it'll feel better later, I promise."

He took a deep breath. He held her down and began to sew.

PART 1

SIXTEEN YEARS LATER,
DEEDRA AND THE BLUE RAT

CHAPTER 1

Deedra wouldn't have seen the blue rat that morning if not for her best friend, Lissa.

"What are you thinking about?" Lissa asked, and Deedra realized she'd been staring up at the bridge that crossed the river on the edge of the Territory. The bridge that *used* to cross the river, actually. Halfway, the bridge had crumbled—when the river ran low, you could still see chunks of concrete, sprouted with spider legs of steel, resting in the water where they'd fallen. She and Lissa had hiked out from the center of the Territory toward the border, maneuvering past the Wreck. Now they stood on the shell of what had once been a train car, or a truck or some kind of vehicle, turned on its side and rusting into oblivion. From here, they could see the whole putrid shoreline of the river.

Deedra shrugged. "Nothing," she lied, and held up a hand to shield her eyes from the nonexistent sun. On a good day there would be maybe a half hour of direct sunlight, usually in the morning. The rest of the time, like now, the sky clouded over, steeping the Territory and the wider City in gray murk.

Along one edge of the bridge, some long-ago vandal had spray-painted WAITING FOR THE RAIN. The words were black, except for the last one, which had been sprayed bloodred.

"You're thinking of climbing the bridge," Lissa said knowingly, and Deedra couldn't help but smirk. Her friend knew her too well. Deedra was the risk-taker, the climber.

One time, years ago, she'd found a bird's nest out by the bridge. Birds were rare, a nest a rarer wonder still. It was up high, built of bits of wire and cabling and trash, more a web than a nest, caught in the spot where a fallen beam crossed a jutting bit of concrete. She had to figure out how to climb all the way up there, using a bunch of broken packing crates and some discarded lengths of wire to fashion a sort of flexible ladder. It swayed and dipped when she so much as blinked, but she made it, coaching herself along the way under her breath: *You can do this, Deedra. You can make it. You can do it.*

In the nest were four perfect little eggs. They were delicious.

"You're thinking of the *eggs*," Lissa said even more confidently, and Deedra groaned.

"Okay, yeah, you got me. I was thinking of the eggs."

"Lucky day," Lissa said with a shrug. "You're not going to get that lucky again."

Probably not. The odds of finding anything alive and edible in the Territory were slim. The rations they earned from working at one of the Territory factories were synthesized in laboratories, using DNA spliced from extinct species like turkeys and asparagus. Such rations kept them alive, but scavenging for something to eat could make the difference between simple survival and quelling the rumble of a never-full belly. Plus, it tasted a whole lot better.

The bridge was Deedra's personal challenge to herself. She swore to one day climb its supports and reach the top. "Who knows what's up there?" she asked, focusing on it as if she could zoom in. "I've never heard of anyone going up there. There could be all kinds of—"

"No one's ever gone up there because there's nothing worth seeing," Lissa said drily. "If there was anything worthwhile up there, don't you think the Magistrate would have claimed it already?"

Deedra shrugged. "The Magistrate doesn't know everything. No one ever even comes out here."

"Who can blame 'em?" Lissa hooked her thumb over her shoulder at the Wreck: easily a mile—maybe two, who was counting?—of old automobiles and other such vehicles, jammed together at angles, piled atop one another, packing the route back into the heart of the Territory. Picking a path through the Wreck was dangerous—any of the precariously positioned cars could tilt and crash down at any minute. Pieces of them—weakened by rust—had been known to drop off without warning, crushing or slashing the unwary.

"I can't believe I let you talk me into coming back out here," Lissa grumbled. "We get one day a week out of L-Twelve, and I'm spending it out here. You're going to get me killed one of these days."

"Not going to happen."

"Give it time. Oh, look!"

Deedra followed Lissa's pointing finger, then watched as her friend carefully clambered down from their vantage point to the ground.

Lissa was smaller than Deedra, with a mountain of wild jet-black hair that would have added two or three more inches to her height had it not been tied back in a tight, efficient ponytail. Like Deedra, she wore a gray poncho that covered her torso and arms, with black pants and boots underneath. A breathing mask dangled around her neck— the air quality wasn't too bad today, so they were bare-facing it.

She reached down for something on the ground, cried out triumphantly, and held up her prize.

Squinting, Deedra couldn't tell what it was, so she joined Lissa on the ground. Lissa held up a small, perfectly round disc. It was just the right size to be held with one hand. It had a similarly perfect hole in its center, and its face was smudged and scratched, but when Lissa flipped it over, the opposite side was clean and shiny.

"What is it?" Deedra asked.

"I thought you might know. You're the one who scavenges every free minute."

Deedra examined the disc. On the smudged side, she could barely make out what appeared to be letters: Two *D*s, with a *V* between them.

"I don't know what it is."

Lissa suddenly exclaimed with excitement. "Wait! Let me try...."

She snatched back the disc and poked her finger through the hole in the middle, then held it with the shiny side out. "See? It's a mirror! You put your finger through to hold it and look at yourself in the shiny side."

Deedra's lip curled at the sight of herself. It was something she usually tried to avoid. Her muddy-brown hair was down around her shoulders, even though it was more practical to tie it up while out scavenging. Even around her best friend, though, she couldn't abide the idea of exposing her scar. It was a knotty, twisted cable of dead-white flesh that wended from under her left earlobe all the way down to her shoulder, standing out a good half inch from her body. She flinched at her reflection and turned away.

"Sorry," Lissa mumbled. "Sorry, wasn't thinking—"

Deedra immediately felt terrible. The scar wasn't Lissa's fault. "Don't. It's okay. And I think you're right." She took Lissa's wrist and turned the disc so that it reflected Lissa instead. "It's a mirror. Very cool. Check out the pretty girl."

Lissa chuckled. She tucked the disc into her pack, which she'd slung over one shoulder. Already, it bulged with junk she'd scavenged on their careful slog through the Wreck. Lissa was a good friend but a terrible scavenger. She kept *everything*. Deedra had tried to tell her: *Save your pack for the trip back. It's less to carry that way, and it means you can save your space for the very best stuff you come across.* But Lissa never learned. She wanted it all.

The wind shifted and they caught a whiff of the river, which made them gag. Lissa slipped on her breathing mask. "Disgusting. We're not getting any closer, are we?"

Deedra shrugged. She'd come out here for one reason. And, yes, getting closer was a part of it. The river formed part of the boundary with Sendar Territory. Deedra and Lissa lived in Ludo Territory, under the auspices of Magistrate Max Ludo. Ludo and Sendar were part of the City, which—as far as anyone knew—didn't have a name. It didn't need one. It was the City.

Ludo Territory was under terms of a peace treaty with Sendar... but even long-standing peace treaties had been known to change without warning. So being out by the river was at least a little bit dangerous, and not just for the risk of breathing in the toxic brew.

Still, she wanted to climb the bridge. And today would be the day.

"Check it out!" Lissa cried, pointing.

Deedra turned and saw—right out in the open—an enormous rat. It had to be at least a foot long, standing three or four inches tall, and it had paused to scratch at the loose gravel on the ground.

"I see dinner," Lissa singsonged, and rummaged for her slingshot.

"Uh-uh." Deedra held out a hand to stop her. "Not that one. Look closer."

The rat stood still, shivering. It bore blue tufts of mangy fur.

"Mutant," she told Lissa. "You eat him, he'll be your last meal."

For weeks now, drones had swooped low over the Territory, warning everyone about the danger of the hybrid rats that had begun edging into the Territory. *Citizens should not harvest and eat blue rats*, they'd boomed. *Hybrid rats are a dangerous food source.*

"Citizens should not eat anything I don't give them," Lissa said, aping the Magistrate's voice. "Citizens should not blah blah blah."

"You want to risk it?" Deedra asked.

"Not a chance."

"Didn't think so."

Deedra picked up a nearby rock and tossed it at the rat. It landed in front of the rat and off to one side. The rat stared for a second, totally unafraid, then loped off toward the river.

"I'm going to follow it," Deedra said casually.

Lissa wrinkled her nose. "Why?"

"Maybe it shares a nest with normal rats."

"And maybe you just want to get closer to the bridge."

Deedra shrugged with exaggerated innocence but didn't deny it.

"I was wrong before," Lissa said. "You're not going to get *me* killed—you're going to get yourself killed. Go have fun doing it. I'm going to check over there." She pointed off to an overturned truck in the near distance. "Meet back here in ten?"

"Make it twenty." She didn't want to climb the bridge and have to come right back down.

They separated. The smell from the river grew more intense as she got closer, following the blue rat as it scampered away. She slid on her own breathing mask. It got twisted up in her necklace, so she paused for a moment to disentangle the pendant before slipping the mask over her mouth and nose.

The rat stopped and looked back at her. Deedra picked up a crushed tin can and hurled it. The rat ran a little way, then turned around again. Deedra stomped after it, scooped up the can, and threw it again. She chased the rat nearly to the water before it disappeared into a pile of scrap and garbage.

The chase had taken her around to the far side of the abutment. A collapsed chunk of pavement leaned against the column. The pavement was nearly vertical, but she thought she could use the cracks in it as handholds and scale her way up to the bridge itself.

She could hardly believe her good luck. She had thought she would have to climb one of the other abutments, which didn't have nearly so many handholds.

"You're my hero, ugly mutant blue rat," she called. The rat, if it heard her, didn't bother to answer.

She tied her hair back to keep it out of her eyes as she climbed. "You can do this," she muttered. "You can do this...."

It was hard going, but she fell into a rhythm soon enough, using her legs to push herself up rather than pulling with her arms. That was the trick—using the bigger, stronger leg muscles for movement and the smaller arm muscles for balance and direction. She'd gotten about twenty feet up and was pretty pleased with herself. Below and off to her left, the river glimmered, oily and slick. Sometimes, in the rare sunlight, it was almost beautiful. Not today.

She kept a tight grip with her right hand and wiped sweat from her brow.

Stop daydreaming, Deedra. Get moving. Lissa will be waiting.

With a heavy sigh, she reached for the next handhold, flexing her legs for distance.

And the pavement under her right foot crumbled and peeled away.

Deedra gasped as her whole right side listed, suddenly hanging out in open air. Her right hand hadn't reached the new handhold yet, and her entire left side was already protesting the strain of holding her up. She flailed for a handhold, for a foothold, for anything at all, but her motion made her position only more precarious.

She glanced down. The ground swam at her.

It was only twenty feet, but the ground was studded with chunks of concrete, sharp bits of steel, and heavy rocks. If she dropped, she could easily bash her head open or break her back.

Her right hand slapped against the pavement, seeking purchase. She lifted her head; looking at the ground was stupid when she needed to find a handhold instead.

Across the river, something caught her attention. It was so unexpected that she actually forgot her situation for an instant.

Something—some*one*—was across the river, in Sendar Territory.

Running toward the river.

It was another girl.

■ ■ ■

Deedra flattened herself against the pavement and reached straight up with her free hand. She had to twist into a contorted, painful position, but she found a grip. Planting the heel of her loose foot against the wall, she stabilized herself.

Deep breaths. Deep, deep breaths.

When she looked into Sendar again, the other girl had made it to the opposite shore. At that distance, she almost disappeared into the background clutter of crumbled concrete, twisted steel, and broken glass.

If not for the coat she wore. It was long, down to her ankles, and from Deedra's position, it looked like a very dark green. Deedra had never seen a coat like that.

Maybe you should worry less about the coat and more about not dying.

It was at least an additional forty or fifty feet to the bridge, but she figured she'd risked enough for one day. Time to retreat back to the ground. Live again to climb another day.

And besides . . . it would be a chance to scope out the stranger.

With some difficulty, she managed to retrace her steps, finding by feel and memory the handholds and footholds that had gotten her this far. She inched down the incline and then dropped the last three feet to the ground.

She came around the bridge abutment for an unobstructed view of the river. The other girl was standing on the shore. Very slim, but tall and broad-shouldered. The weirdest girl she'd ever seen, for sure.

The girl started to undress. Her body, so different from Deedra's, came into view—those broad shoulders, a surprisingly flat chest, then a concave belly tapering down to slender hips, and . . .

And this was no girl. Not at *all*.

It was the prettiest, most exquisite boy Deedra had ever seen.

She shook her head to clear it, blinked her eyes. The pollution had to be affecting her sight. No man could look like that. It *had* to be a girl.

She looked again.

No. Still a boy.

Like no boy she'd ever seen. He seemed more chiseled into existence than born. His skin was unblemished and smooth; clean, unlike everyone else's. Even her own. He was slender, but not emaciated like most people. Healthy. Vibrant. He didn't stoop or slouch—he stood straight and tall after slipping out of his pants.

She couldn't help herself—she stared at him as, naked, he carefully folded his clothes, wrapping them in the coat. Then he stepped into the water.

The river was only a couple of feet deep at this spot. He waded in up to his knees, then his waist. Fording the river with his clothes held well above the water, he began to struggle as the current grew stronger toward the center. He'd started out with a good, strong stride but was growing weaker as he waded farther and farther in.

Deedra started fidgeting with her necklace, running the pendant—a circle with a Greek cross jutting out from it—back and forth along the chain. *Stupid kid. If he would just ditch his clothes, he could swim across easily.*

But he wasn't going to do that. And with each step, it was clear that he was getting more and more exhausted.

He wasn't going to make it. He would be swept downriver. And if

15

he managed not to drown, he would wash up on one of the piers down by the Territory of Grevan Dalcord.

The Mad Magistrate, they called him. Max Ludo could be unfair, corrupt, and pigheaded, but at least he didn't execute criminals by sewing rats to their faces and letting the rodent gnaw its way free. That was the sort of thing Dalcord was known to do. Ludo Territory was technically at peace with Dalcord, too, but everyone knew it was only a matter of time before the Mad Magistrate launched an attack. It was inevitable.

The boy in the river was about halfway across, but making no further progress. The current was too strong.

She found herself running to the water's edge. There was something in her hand, and she realized as she ran that she was dragging a long, old piece of rebar, still straight except for a little crook at the end.

The boy was looking around, not panicked, but concerned, as the water began relentlessly shoving him downriver. She shouted, "Hey!"—it was all she could get out as she ran—and waved her free arm to get his attention.

He noticed her just as she got to the water. She heaved the heavy rebar with all her strength. It flopped—*splash!*—into the river, throwing up a sheet of filthy, grimy water. For a moment colors sparkled and hung in the air, distracting her with unexpected beauty.

Him, too. He stared at the kaleidoscope as the water tugged him farther away.

"Stop staring and grab this!" she yelled.

That snapped him out of it. He tucked his clothes under an arm and reached out for the rebar, but he couldn't find the end of it no matter how much he flailed.

She took a deep breath and planted her feet and groaned, levering the far end of the rebar out of the water. She couldn't hold it very high—just right at the level of the water. Just close enough?

Yes! He managed to grab hold of it. She braced herself, expecting his weight to overcome her muscles and drag her in. But he didn't. He must have weighed next to nothing.

"Don't let go!" she shouted. She took a precious second to reposition and replant her feet. The shore was mostly wet gravel and trash. She gouged at it with her heel until she'd dug a little ramp to brace herself against.

"Hold on!" she called to him, and when she looked up, he'd begun pulling himself along the rebar. He still had his clothes tucked under one arm, so it was awkward going, but he was making progress.

She heaved, pulling the rebar hand over hand.

They were close enough now that she could make out his expression. He didn't look terrified. Just... uneasy. The strain of keeping his grip seemed to bother him more than the idea of what would happen if he let go.

It felt like hours to haul him in—her groaning, fiery shoulders would *swear* it was hours—but it had to have been only a few minutes. Just as she thought her muscles would give out, his body emerged from the water down to his knees. She tried not to stare anywhere in particular as she found a final burst of power that allowed her to pull him even closer.

Once his knees cleared the water, he let go of the rebar without warning, and she stumbled backward down a slight grade. She yelped in surprise, then swore loudly, collapsing on her back. The mask slipped away from her face, and the reek of the river stabbed at her nostrils. Stones bit into her; she lost her breath.

When she managed to struggle up to a sitting position, she saw him there, on his back on the rocky ground, gazing straight up. He wasn't even breathing hard.

He stared at the sky, and she stared at him. Even up close, he was still perfect. She'd thought that maybe he only seemed so flawless at a distance, but here he was in front of her, and his pale skin was just as unmarked. Which was unusual because everyone had brands identifying their Territory. They were usually burned in along the left shoulder/neck area, but since Deedra's scar made that impossible, her own brand—in the shape of some kind of water creature that was the symbol of Ludo Territory—was on her right shoulder.

The boy had no brand. Not on either shoulder. Still naked and utterly self-possessed, he simply sat up and stared at her, studying her.

She couldn't imagine why he would want to. Why anyone would. Only once, long ago, as a child, had anyone told her she was beautiful. One of the caretakers at the orphanage where she'd grown up. But that had been a cruel joke. The truth was as obvious as her own skin: The hideous, mottled scar commandeering the left side of her neck, trailing down to her collarbone, made her nothing more and nothing less than ugly.

It was time to go. She had helped him. Fine. But for all she knew, he could be crazy. Or even—and it just occurred to her, in a rush of terror—a spy, sent to infiltrate Max Ludo's territory. Magistrates were supposed to keep out of one another's Territories, but that rule only applied to what could be proved in a Citywide Magistrates Council. If the Mad Magistrate thought he could steal some of Ludo's rations or encroach on the area to alleviate his own overcrowding, well, why not do it?

Wary of the incline, she took a careful step back and would have turned to run, but at that moment—as if he knew she was leaving—the boy twisted on the ground, rising with a smooth, easy motion into a crouch. His eyes—a deep and almost succulent green—met hers and locked; she couldn't have moved if the entire river had suddenly risen up behind him and threatened to devour them both.

He froze her.

Not with fear or worry. No. It took a moment, but she soon

recognized the kindness and curiosity in his eyes. No sudden flinch of realization, no moment of recoil and disgust.

Her hair. It was still in a ponytail and he could see. Could see the scar.

Even though there was nothing but gentleness in his eyes, she still found herself reaching back and fumbling to let loose her hair and drag it around her left side.

And still he said nothing. Just watched.

"Thank you," he said, "for helping me."

His voice...it was somehow deep and light all at once, pleasant and alive in a way she didn't know voices could be. It was like a piece of him, set loose to drift in the air. Without even realizing it, she took a step toward him.

"You're welcome." Her own voice was clumsy and raspy, a stupid, harsh thing, not effortless like his. "Are you all right?"

He nodded, still completely unself-conscious about his nudity. Her neck and cheeks warmed again as she forced herself not to stare. With no particular urgency, he began to pull on his clothes, finishing with that peculiar dark green coat.

"I've never seen someone cross the river," she said, lamely. "Why would you leave Sendar Territory?" Glorio Sendar wasn't a great Magistrate, but she wasn't bad, either. Journeying from Sendar's territory to Ludo's was like trading a weekday ration for half a weekend ration. Same difference.

"I'm not really from there," he said. "I've been traveling. For a long time."

"What about your family?"

He simply shrugged. His expression didn't change at all.

"I'm an orphan, too," she whispered. For no reason, her eyes began to water, and she wiped at them angrily. She'd been alone her entire life. Being parentless, familyless, was nothing new. Why did it suddenly feel so powerfully wrong and painful?

She took a step closer to him—within reach now—and the boy flinched, jumping back.

Deedra flushed and turned partly away.

"I'm sorry," he said immediately. "I didn't mean to...I wasn't..." He groaned, clearly upset with himself. "Look, it just might be safer if you keep a little ways back."

He took another step back, as if to prove his point.

She had no idea what he meant. Was he worried about something from the river infecting her?

"I'm not afraid," she told him. "As long as you don't drink it or soak in it for too long, the water won't make you sick."

He frowned as though he didn't quite believe her. They gazed at each other for a few moments. She sucked in a deep breath and risked it: She held out her hand.

"My name is Deedra."

With a reluctant little nod, he shook her hand, then immediately pulled back, as though he'd pushed luck as far as he was willing. "I'm Rose."

Deedra blinked. "Wait, isn't Rose a girl's name?"

Rose shrugged. "It's mine."

She smiled and had no idea what to say next, and then the world took the necessity of speech away from her.

A drone buzzed overhead, its speakers blaring, *"Citizen Alert! Citizen Alert! Seek shelter! Seek shelter!"*

■ ■ ■

The drone had come from nowhere, sweeping in, its blast of sound doubled in volume as it echoed off the surrounding sheets of steel and glass from the nearby Wreck. Deedra hissed in a breath and clapped her hands to her ears, shutting her eyes reflexively against the assault of sound. The drone whizzed closer by, blasting out its warning again, nearly driving her to her knees.

Shelter. She had to find shelter.

She opened her eyes and looked up just in time to see the drone banking by the nearest abutment, cutting a sharp left to avoid crossing the Territorial boundary. Bleating out its warning again, it zoomed north.

Deedra looked around for shelter and realized in the same instant that the boy—Rose—was gone.

His sudden disappearance stunned her into paralysis. She forgot about shelter and stood rooted to her spot. How in the world had he disappeared so quickly? Where had he gone? She spun around, thinking maybe he'd ducked behind her or run off in that direction, but no. Nothing.

Not even a path of disturbed gravel where he would have run.

"Deedra!"

It was Lissa, screaming to her from near the Wreck. Deedra was shocked to see how tiny Lissa looked—in the mad rush to pull Rose from the river, she'd run farther from the Wreck than ever before, closer to the river than she'd ever dared.

"Come on!" Lissa shouted, gesturing wildly. Overhead, the drone cried out its warning again, this time farther distant and not so painfully. Deedra unfroze her legs and ran at top speed toward Lissa, who kept motioning for her to hurry. As she got closer, she saw that Lissa was propping up an old sheet of corrugated metal against a block of concrete. A decent enough shelter, in a pinch.

Lissa crawled in as Deedra neared her, throwing herself under the metal sheet as the drone's alarm faded into the distance.

Under the impromptu shelter, it was dark and the air—even filtered through her mask—tasted of rust. Deedra panted, catching her breath, as she curled into the tight, unyielding space with Lissa.

"Just like home," Lissa joked.

"I would laugh, but I don't have enough room."

They giggled, then suddenly stopped at a sound in the distance.

"Was that an explosion?"

"Could have been a…" Deedra broke off. She didn't know *what* it could have been. She just didn't want to think it was an explosion. Especially not when she was stuck out here at the edge of nowhere with only a sheet of metal between her and who-knew-what.

They held their breath together. Deedra counted to thirty in her head, straining to hear.

Finally, she blew out her breath, an instant after Lissa did.

"I don't think it was a bomb. There would have been another one, right? It could have been something falling over. Back in the Wreck."

Lissa shrugged. Given their close quarters, Deedra felt it more than saw it.

They waited. It was impossible to tell for how long. Eventually a drone buzzed by calling out the all-clear. They struggled out from under the makeshift shelter, untangling themselves from each other.

"That was fun," Lissa said, pulling down her mask. She inhaled deeply, coughed, and grimaced. "Not worth it."

Deedra pulled down her mask, too. The air smelled and tasted awful, but it was—for the moment—better than the hot, humid air in her mask. She turned away from Lissa, looking back down toward the river. From this vantage point, she could see a whole stretch of the riverbank and the bridge abutments. Rose was nowhere to be seen. She couldn't even see a place where he might have sheltered.

"What are you looking for?"

"A boy."

Lissa snorted. "That's pretty ambitious scavenge, Dee."

"No, seriously. There was a boy. Down there, by the river. A boy named Rose."

"Rose? Like the . . . what do you call it? Like the flower?"

The flower . . . *Oh, right*, Deedra remembered now. Flowers. They grew out of the ground, like weeds. She'd seen images of them, but never one in person. No one had, as best she knew. At least since the Red Rain. In fact, some people weren't even sure they existed at all. They were just mutant weeds, really. Weird flukes of nature, like the blue rat.

Or like me, she thought, and stroked one finger along her scar without intending to, only half-realizing it.

Lissa slapped her hand away from the scar. "Cut that out. It's not like you can make it go away."

Easy for Lissa to say; she didn't have to live with it. Deedra shook her hair into place over the scar with a long-practiced jerk of her head. "He was down there. He . . ." She sighed. "Never mind. He's gone."

"We should be gone, too. Just in case they alert again."

She was right, and Deedra knew it, even though it rankled her. She'd really wanted to climb the bridge today. And now she also wanted to know what had happened to Rose. Where had he gone? And just as important: Where had he come from *before* Sendar Territory? Why cross the river?

Lissa tugged at her poncho. "Let's go. It'll take a while to get through the Wreck."

They began to make their way deeper into the Territory, carefully retracing the path they'd taken through the Wreck.

"What do you think it was this time?" Deedra asked, trying to take her mind off Rose. For some reason, she had difficulty not thinking about him, in a way she'd never experienced before. "Another gridhack?"

"Nah. Another false alarm, I bet."

Deedra shrugged. The wikinets—the Territory-wide public-information system—would report later on the cause of the alarm.

Maybe. Sometimes a Citizen Alert would be sounded, then canceled, with no reason offered, leaving everyone to wonder if it was just a glitch, a test, or something classified.

In the end, it didn't matter, she realized. One way or the other, when the drones said shelter, you had to shelter. There was no other option.

Danger meant shelter. Somewhere out there, she knew, Rose had run. She hoped he'd found shelter. She hoped he would continue to.

She didn't know why she hoped these things. But as she picked her way through the Wreck with Lissa, she realized when she thought of Rose, she was smiling.

■ ■ ■

From his perch above the claustrophobic crush of ancient metal and glass, in a hidden nook high up on a ruined bridge support, Rose watches Deedra thread her way into the distance through the Wreck with the other girl.

"Deedra," he says quietly. Then, drawing it out, testing it, tasting the syllables: "Dee-dra. Deeeee-draaaaa."

He purses his lips and begins to whistle.

PART 2
NEW GROWTH

CHAPTER 2

They never learned the cause of the Citizen Alert, and by the next day, it was forgotten, just like dozens of others over the years. It had probably been another gridhack attempt. They were happening more and more these days. The Magistrate said they were cyberattacks from Dalcord Territory, preparation for an invasion. Deedra wasn't sure she believed that, mostly because she didn't want to believe it.

Fortunately, she could believe what she chose to believe. The first time she'd logged into the wikinets—as a child at the orphanage—she'd become lost in a bewildering array of points, counterpoints, narratives, and counternarratives. Caretaker Hullay had assured her that the contradictions didn't matter.

"Which one is true?" Deedra had asked. "I don't understand."

"History is still up for debate. No one really knows for sure. Any of them could be true. You have to decide which one you believe."

"But I don't want to *believe* one of them. I want to know what's actually true."

And Caretaker Hullay had indulged her with a patient smile, this one fraying and brittle. "Whatever *you* believe, that's the truth."

The idea of an all-out war among the Territories terrified her. So when the grid was hacked and the power went out, there was nothing to do but stay safe and wait it out. The power would come back. It always did. And in the meantime, she refused to believe war would come.

Sometimes it helped.

Days passed, and the abrasions on her palms from trying to climb up to the bridge slowly faded. Soon the only reminders she had of the day by the bridge were the weird finger-mirror (Lissa had given it to her as a gift) and the curiously powerful memory of the boy.

Of Rose.

She didn't know why, but he stuck fast in her memory, embedded there like pebbles in soft tar. She could remember every detail of him, from his green eyes to his lithe, limber form....

To the way he'd simply vanished.

Which was to be expected. That was the world—good things didn't stay for long. And good people were rarer than good things.

Several days after the Citizen Alert, she crawled out of bed from underneath her roach netting. Her little unit was four floors up in a smallish building. Her vid blinked at her, which meant a news blip. She'd already maxed out her bandwidth ration for the month, so only news blips could come through. No great loss—other than vidding with Lissa, the wikinets were really only good for conflicting news reports about the Antarctic War.

AIR QUALITY: TENTATIVE, the blip read. MASKS ADVISED.

Deedra sighed. She rummaged in her cupboard for a fruit disc, chewed it down, and swallowed the gummy blob with water that trickled straight from the tap. *Masks advised.* There were more and more mask advisories. The air was getting worse. Sometimes she wished she could just stay inside on days like this, where the air was at least partly cleaned by scrubbers. Even when the grid went down, it was still better to wait it out for the hour or two it took to re-establish power. Why go outside?

In fact, WHY GO OUTSIDE? was the slogan emblazoned on billboards all over the Territory, showing Max Ludo's smiling face with a word balloon asking the question. REMEMBER, another balloon proclaimed, IT'S SAFER INSIDE!

It *was* safer inside. That's why Deedra never went anywhere without the knife she'd assembled from a piece of sturdy, jagged glass and some thick tape. She tucked it into her waistband at the small of her back.

"Yeah, safer inside," she muttered, pulling on her poncho. "But then again, it's more boring, too."

■ ■ ■

The factory was a ten-minute walk from her unit. She met up with Lissa halfway there, and they fell into step with a group of slow-moving citizens headed the same direction. On a tentative air quality day, no one was out on the streets who didn't have to be; most people stayed indoors, heeding Max Ludo's advice.

For people like Deedra, though, there was no choice. It was either go to the factory and work for her food, water, and bandwidth rations, or stay home and miss out. She didn't have the luxury of a family to backstop her.

"What are you doing out on such a bad air day?" she asked Lissa. "You could stay home." Lissa had a brother, a sister, and two parents. Between the five of them, they were able to stockpile rations for rough days.

"Who knows what kind of trouble you'd get into without me around?" The lower half of Lissa's face was obscured by the mask, but her eyes crinkled in a smile. "If I'm not here to keep you grounded, you'd start climbing something and wouldn't stop until you broke through the cloud cover."

The security gate at the factory groaned open as they approached. **LUDO TERRITORY PRIDE FACILITY NO. 12,** its official name, was stamped in now-rusting letters over the gate. But everyone who worked there called it L-Twelve.

It was hard, dirty work, but better than some of the other "Pride Facilities" throughout the Territory. The food-processing facilities were grimy and stank of rejected genetic combinations. The furniture facility's air lingered with enormous motes of dust.

At L-Twelve, they built air scrubbers. Good, solid tech, designed to make the world a little better. To literally help people breathe a little easier. She was contributing here. Making a difference. The more air scrubbers, the better the air. The better the air, the better the world, right? She usually thought the addition of the word *pride* to the name of the factory was nothing more than propaganda, but when she thought of what she was actually building...Sometimes she *was* proud.

The building itself was a low, flat rectangle cobbled together of cinder block, brick, and metal sheeting. Once through the gate, they had to wait in line as each worker's brand was scanned. It was the only way to be sure you got your earned ration for the day. It was a small thing, the matter of a brief moment in front of a camera, but it rankled Deedra.

Because the camera was mounted on the left, to scan everyone's brands. And her brand was on the right. Every day, she had to turn around and go through backward.

She did it again today, feeling as conspicuous as ever, even though she'd been doing this for four years, ever since the orphanage shut down, putting her out into the Territory on her own at twelve. With so few people having children now, there was no longer a compelling need for the orphanage.

Just as well. She'd been miserable there. Now she took care of herself.

On the factory floor, they swapped out their personal masks for work masks, designed to filter out the particles thrown into the air by the machinery. L-Twelve's innards were a single, wall-less space, subdivided only by the serpentine meander of conveyor belts studded at regular intervals with tool holsters mounted to the side. Deedra's usual workstation was open, as was the one next to it, so Lissa and Deedra hurried to get to them first.

"Yes!" Lissa hissed in triumph. A ten-hour workday went a lot faster next to a friend.

They quickly scanned their tool holsters: powerdrivers, cliphammers, hex wrenches. "Is the Little Magistrate in today?" Lissa asked under her breath.

Deedra stripped off her poncho. It was too loose to wear around the conveyor belt, where it could be caught in the gears. As she bound up her hair—taking care to wind her ponytail down to cover her scar—she looked up and off to the right.

L-Twelve was two stories tall, but completely open from floor to ceiling. Except along the perimeter, where a series of offices jutted from the walls like misplaced bricks. One extra office was suspended in the very center of the factory, connected by a series of catwalks. It was positioned so that it was impossible to look into it from any angle on the floor, though the resident could see out to the floor however he liked.

That was the office of Jaron Ludo. Only son of the Magistrate. No older than Lissa or Deedra, but already in charge of the entire factory. Some days, he just stayed home and let his second-in-command or his personally selected floor monitors run things. It's not like anyone could tell.

Except for Deedra. She'd realized one day that this particular workstation sat under an air duct from Jaron's office. She couldn't hear anything specific—just muffled noise. But early in the day, before the machinery started up, she could hear enough to tell if Jaron was watching that day. She tried to get this workstation whenever possible, though she'd never told Lissa how she could detect Jaron's presence, only that she could. A little secret, just for herself.

Now she shrugged. She'd been listening since taking up her position. "Yeah," she said at last. "He's in today."

"Great," Lissa muttered.

Deedra didn't share the hatred of Jaron most of her fellow workers fostered. He was just doing his job, like she did hers. "You'll have to be on your best behavior," she joked.

Lissa said nothing for a moment, her expression frozen. Then she blinked and shook her head and grinned as though everything was fine. "First time for everything."

The start-work horn blared, and hundreds of pairs of eyes fixated on the spot on the conveyor belt immediately before them. Small screens built into the side of the belt lit up with the day's instructions for each station. Deedra gnawed her bottom lip and selected a powerdriver from the tool holster. She'd be attaching a fan blade to a motor assembly.

"What am I building today?" Lissa asked in an overserious tone.

"'We're building safety, security, and the future,'" Deedra deadpanned, quoting the standard answer to that very question.

Another horn blared, followed by Jaron's voice over the speakers. Deedra mouthed, *Told you*, to Lissa, who grinned.

"Begin the Patriot Oath," Jaron ordered, and hundreds of voices spoke the familiar words as one:

"I am a good citizen. I follow the rules. I do as I'm told. I swear loyalty to the City and my Magistrate, for which he stands, one Territory, under his protection, without question, with food and safety for all."

The conveyor belt coughed, belched, and then lurched into action. Within minutes the parts were cruising by too quickly for any talk between Deedra and Lissa.

Deedra had performed this part of the assembly many times. She'd done almost every job a worker could do on the factory floor. Four years times fifty-two weeks a year times six days a week meant a lot of opportunities to sample different stations on the assembly line. She quickly fell into a rhythm, plucking the fan blades from an automated cart that brought them to her, screwing them into place with the power-driver, then letting them go on to Lissa, who wrenched a housing cover into place on each one. She found it easy to turn off her brain and let her hands do the thinking for her. Usually, she just blanked out, but today she found herself thinking of Rose. Again. It was as if he'd vanished into thin air, then reappeared in her head. A neat trick, but an aggravating one. No point thinking about what was gone.

About a half hour into the day, Lissa waved quickly for Deedra's attention. *The preacher's coming*, she mouthed, rolling her eyes.

"Don't be so mean," Deedra upbraided her. "He's harmless."

"Whatever."

Moments later she heard the booming, deep bass voice of Dr. Dimbali as he strode the path along the conveyor belt. Dr. Dimbali was L-Twelve's head of engineering. Technically, he and Jaron were equals, but Jaron's last name gave him the edge.

As did his youth. Dimbali was old—at least forty, maybe older—and insisted on wearing a threadbare suit and tie every day. He also wore an old pair of SmartSpex, the lights flickering across his eyes. A webby fissure fanned out from one corner of the SmartSpex, but Dimbali treated them like fine jewelry. He claimed to have worked for the government at one point in his life—not the local Magistrate, but the Mayor-Governor or even higher—which never failed to induce laughter behind his back. Sure he had, everyone thought. Sure he had.

He also had an annoying habit of walking the factory floor, lecturing the workers, who were the very definition of a captive audience. It was harmless, but annoying. Lissa hated it; Deedra found something soothing in his voice on bad days, but today she found it oddly cruel for Dimbali's voice to yank her from her memories of Rose.

"*E* equals *mc* squared!" he thundered. "That is, energy is equivalent to mass times the speed of light times itself! This is fundamental! This is truth!"

"This is useless," Lissa muttered. "This is garbage."

Deedra shrugged. Dr. Dimbali could be pushy and annoying, yes, but he helped keep a workday from devolving into complete boredom. She had even occasionally logged on to his vid feed, though she would never, ever admit that to anyone, not even her best friend.

"Humanity descended from the baser life-forms!" he continued, now standing directly behind Deedra and Lissa. "From mighty apes, came we! Millions of years of evolutionary progress, stepping from single-celled organisms to the vast, infinite complexity of the human brain and body! This is fundamental! This is truth!"

Mighty apes? What was he was talking about? Then again, did anyone ever really know what Dr. Dimbali was talking about? If he wasn't so talented at programming L-Twelve's systems and designing the widgets they assembled, she suspected the Magistrate would have gotten rid of him long ago.

"Remember," he intoned with fervor, "my vid feed is available every Thursday night! Don't waste your bandwidth on wikinet nonsense! Plug in and expand your mind! Hearken to my lectures! They are fundamental! They are truth!"

Following this pronouncement, he came up on her left side. She flinched, too close. Her scar. The ponytail couldn't entirely cover it; she could feel part of it exposed as her shirt had shifted while she worked. And she could feel his eyes on it.

"Child," he asked in a slow, calm tone so unlike his usual bombast, "do you know the first element of the periodic table?"

Deedra's mind slipped a gear. From somewhere in the well of her memory, another one of Dr. Dimbali's lectures bubbled up to the surface, and she found herself blurting out, "Hydrogen!" without even really thinking about it.

Dr. Dimbali paused, and she detected a smile out of the corner of her eye. "Well, well," he said softly.

Deedra glanced over at him. He wasn't standing over the belt all day, so he didn't wear a mask. His expression was one of delight, of joy, and for a moment Deedra felt that same joy in herself.

"Dee!" Lissa cried, and Deedra realized that she'd missed an assembly while she'd been looking over at Dr. Dimbali. She swore and tried to snatch it back. If she could get it back onto the belt quickly enough, no one would—

The belt ground to a halt. *Oh, great.* An annoyed groan ascended from the workers on the line. Their ration count depended on productivity, and while an unscheduled break wasn't the worst thing, it meant less ration with each passing moment.

Deedra's cheeks flamed. She'd never, not even once, been responsible for the line stopping. The anger and frustration she'd felt at others in the past now doubled back on her as shame. She couldn't even look up. Dr. Dimbali edged away from her.

And then she heard it.

A great, banging *Clong!* reverberated throughout the entire factory.

Her spine stiffened. No. This couldn't be happening. It was her first time stopping the line! No one was punished for a first infraction!

Beside her, Lissa drew in a deep, sharp breath.

Clong! It resounded again, ringing out loud and clear over the background noise of hundreds of feet shuffling, of the sound of tools shifting from hand to hand to holster. She turned—everyone else did, too—to see four figures striding across the factory floor, each carrying a long, heavy metal pipe. As she watched, the smallest of the four reared back and smote the concrete floor with his pipe. *Clong!*

"Listen up!" he shouted into the clanging echo. "Listen the hell up!"

The Bang Boys were on the floor.

Jaron Ludo's four lieutenants. Enforcers, more like. They projected his will from above. Deedra froze in place. She'd seen the Bang Boys "explain" a finer point of L-Twelve protocol to a recalcitrant worker before. They weren't just called the Bang Boys because of their penchant for banging their pipes against the floor to announce their arrival. They banged on flesh, too, when needed.

First infraction. How could they punish her for her first infraction?

The smallest one—Lio Delfour—stood a couple of paces before the others, grinning. Lio was always grinning. She'd heard that one time Lio had accidentally caught his thumb in a door and had kept grinning the whole time, despite the pain. Today he wore an old army throwaway camo jacket patterned in white and gray, a relic of some relative who'd fought in Antarctica.

"Hustle up and form up!" Lio shouted, then banged again for good measure.

Everyone on the floor rushed to fall into line, arranging themselves into rank and file on the factory floor. Deedra and Lissa ended up at the front of the pack, right where Deedra didn't want to be.

But Lio wasn't looking at her. He didn't even seem to be looking *for* her. He kept up his insane grin as he watched the workers form ranks, turning at one point to say something to Hart Graenger, who stood just behind him. Hart chuckled and passed it along to Rik Aarin, who shook his head and laughed, then passed it along to Kent Massgrove. Kent stood behind them all, arms crossed over his chest, glaring down at everyone and everything from his towering six-foot-five-inch vantage point.

Kent's expression didn't change a whit when Rik whispered to him.

L-Twelve fell silent, save for the background hiss of the air scrubbers. Deedra waited to be called out of line and reprimanded.

Instead, Lio pointed up with his pipe. Along with the others,

Deedra craned her neck to look up, where Jaron Ludo stood on one of the catwalks.

"Thanks for your attention, everyone," he called, his voice echoing. "We have an announcement. We need to go on a materials run."

A muted groan rippled through the crowd, hushing almost as soon as it began. A materials run was basically scavenging for the factory instead of for yourself. *So that's why they'd stopped the belt.* Deedra couldn't believe her luck. Most people didn't want to bother with a run—factory work was easier and safer, after all.

"We're looking for forty volunteers," Jaron called. "Volunteers will ration out at a hundred and fifty percent."

Lio banged the pipe for attention and pointed to Dr. Dimbali. "You've got the floor, Dr. Dimbulb." The other Bang Boys tittered.

"It's, ah, Dimbali," said Dr. Dimbali, as though believing Lio had genuinely misspoken.

"Thanks, Doc."

Dimbali stood before the group and mumbled something that Deedra had trouble understanding. He gestured a bit wildly and smiled.

"Louder," Lio said.

"Oh, yes, right," Dr. Dimbali exclaimed. Then he cupped his hands around his mouth. "We are looking for very specific materials today!" he shouted, much more loudly than was necessary. The acoustics in L-Twelve were earsplittingly good. "Today I need nonrusted metals, preferably unpainted. Also, glass. You will run in pairs. Volunteers, please step forward."

No one moved.

"Quickly, now!" Dr. Dimbali clapped his hands twice. "We need to get the belt going again."

A few volunteers stepped forward. Deedra shrugged at Lissa.

"Don't do it, Dee. The air's getting worse out there. You'll burn through your mask cartridge in no time."

"At a hundred and fifty percent, I can afford to burn one. I need to ration up."

Lissa shook her head. "Not me. Not today."

"I'll see you later, then."

She stepped out of line into the group of volunteers. A moment later the belt started up again, and Dr. Dimbali began dividing the volunteers into pairs. He came to Deedra last and frowned; they both realized at the same time that she was the only one left. An odd number had volunteered.

"I can go alone," she offered. "I go all the time. It's okay."

Dr. Dimbali looked her up and down. She had the oddest feeling that his SmartSpex gazed right through her. "No, no. That won't do. Too dangerous. And you'd miss the opportunity to bring back larger or heavier pieces." He *hmm*ed and tapped the side of his SmartSpex.

"Dr. Dimbali!" The voice came from above. When she craned her neck she saw that Jaron was still on the catwalk, now standing right above them. "What seems to be the problem? Get the materials teams out there."

Dr. Dimbali grumbled under his breath and adjusted his SmartSpex. "Yes, Mr. Ludo. We seem to have a, well, a mismatch, as it were. An odd woman out. Never fear, though—I will find a—"

"Don't waste your time," Jaron called down. "I'll go with her."

CHAPTER 3

*R*ose watches the building labeled LUDO TERRITORY PRIDE FACILITY NO. 12 *from a nearby rooftop. A cluster of people emerge, then break up into pairs and split away in different directions. He has seen facilities like this in the past, during his travels. The word* pride *seems odd to him, though. Do they actually manufacture pride within those walls? The idea seems absurd, but he can think of no other reason for the word to exist on the sign. He purses his lips and whistles soft and low so that only he can hear.*

The last pair exits the building. Rose recognizes the girl—Deedra— and for a moment loses his tune. It has taken days, but he's finally found her again, followed her to this building. He settled in on the rooftop, ready to wait a long time for her to come out. And here she is.

With someone else, though. Not the other girl he'd seen her with by the river. Together, they head off to the west.

Rose begins to whistle again, a song no one has heard in years.

CHAPTER 4

Normally while scavenging, you kept whatever you found. That was what made it worth doing. But on a factory-materials run, there was no putting something aside for yourself, and no snatching up anything not on the list. People had tried, but the Bang Boys paid attention to what you carried or had in your pockets when you left L-Twelve, as well as what you had when you came back. Stuffing a chunk of some unwanted material into your pocket could lead to a ration demerit and a reminder that the pocket space could have—and *should have*—been used for that tiny bit more of the needed materials.

Deedra couldn't have tried to sneak something even if she'd wanted to. Not with Jaron Ludo as her partner. She was partly horrified to be teamed with him, partly intrigued. She'd seen him before, of course, at L-Twelve. Heard him speak to the assembled workers. But she knew nothing about him, other than he was in charge. What was he like? Did he deserve the scorn heaped upon him by those who called him "the Little Magistrate"? Or was he just like everyone else, trying to get by?

She figured Jaron might be soft and unused to scrambling over the heaps of busted concrete, fallen steel, and general detritus left throughout the Territory. At first, she went slow—for his sake—but soon realized he was having no problem keeping up with her. He had an excellent eye for scavenge, too, it turned out, spotting bits of glass and metal that she missed on her first scan of an area. They each carried a sling-bag and soon they were half full.

They pressed out farther from the center of the Territory. The inside of Deedra's mask had become humid and stale. She glanced over at Jaron, who had paused to stretch his back and arms. With an unconscious shrug, he pulled off his mask and tested the air.

"Not too bad," he told her. "Try it."

She didn't want to, but he was Jaron Ludo, so she slipped off her mask. To her surprise, the air's ever-present metallic tang was softer than she'd expected.

"Here's a secret," Jaron told her, his eyes sparkling. "Air-quality ranges shift during the day. But we only test in the morning."

Deedra nodded slowly. *Right.* That made sense. They couldn't just keep testing all day long. So if the air was bad in the morning, everyone wore a mask, just to be safe.

"Take a break, maybe?" Jaron said. He gestured ahead of them, down a slight, rolling grade. The buildings pressed tightly together here, with only the narrowest of alleys between some of them. Down the hill, an old vehicle had rusted into near nonexistence, but its seats somehow survived.

"I don't need a break," she assured him. She was exhausted, actually, but she didn't want to admit it.

Jaron chuckled and held up both hands in surrender. "I believe you! But *I* need a break. You're killing me. You're like a machine. In the best possible way, of course," he added hastily.

Deedra returned the chuckle and watched Jaron as he picked his way carefully down the incline to the seats. At L-Twelve, he seemed like such a harsh taskmaster, but out here, alone... he was just like anyone else. He wore skintight blue jeans, black boots, and a gray long-sleeve

41

shirt. No poncho, but it wasn't raining, so it didn't matter. His clothing was clean and unpatched, one of the many perks of being a Ludo. His sandy hair was long, straight until the very ends, when it curled ever so slightly at the nape of his neck. Like many, he'd enhanced his Ludo brand by tattooing around it: A large starburst exploded in yellows and reds and oranges along the left side of his neck.

Maybe, she thought as she joined him, the Bang Boys were projecting a false front. Everyone thought they'd inherited their bad attitude from Jaron, but from what she could tell, the Bang Boys were taking liberties.

She stood before him, hesitating; he patted the seat next to him. When she sat, he sighed expansively and leaned back, staring up at the sky. Deedra didn't know what to do. She was technically shirking her duty, but Jaron had essentially told her to. So that made it all right.

Didn't it?

She sat as stiffly and as uncomfortably as she could. Ready to jump up and scavenge at a moment's notice. She had no fear of him, though. Not like the fear she had for the Bang Boys. Someone should tell him. Someone should tell him how they acted, in his name. Someone...

Maybe her...

"Do you ever think of the people who built this stuff?" he asked.

"Which stuff?"

He gestured to encompass the crumbling buildings and leftover junk all around them. "All of it. Everything."

She shrugged. "Why would I do that? They're not around anymore."

Jaron nodded thoughtfully and sat up, regarding her coolly. His eyes were pale gray, a liquid metal melding almost to silver at the edges. "But do you ever think about what it was like when it was new?"

Deedra didn't understand the question. Not really. She supposed that everything around them had once been new, but so far as she knew, that time was so long in the past that no one alive remembered it. So who cared? It didn't matter what this building or that building had been like—they were the way they were *now*, and that was what mattered. And how different could anything have been, anyway? A building with a hole in its wall wouldn't have the hole. Big deal.

"Pretty close to the way it is now," she told him.

He nodded. "Yeah, maybe." He tilted his head back again and closed his eyes. "Sometimes, if you try real hard," he said quietly, "you can feel the sun on your face. Even through the clouds." He paused. "Try it."

Deedra leaned back, imitating him. She closed her eyes and tried to picture the sun. It was somewhere past the clouds, of course; just because she couldn't see it didn't mean it had gone away.

Like Rose. Just because she couldn't see him didn't mean...

What was she thinking? *Why* was she even thinking about him? Ridiculous.

"In the morning, there's usually a little bit of sunshine," she heard herself say. "I try to catch it. It's my favorite time of the day."

"Mine, too," Jaron said, and Deedra couldn't help but grin. He was right—she could have sworn her face felt a little warmer.

"It's just that..." Jaron shifted next to her and she opened her eyes. He'd sat up and now stared off into the distance, his chin propped up on a fist. "Sometimes, I try to imagine the world as a better place, you know?"

"Like how?"

"I'm not sure," he admitted.

"Well, I don't know that you can look to the past for that," she said with a confidence that surprised her. "It was *worse* back then, not better. Twice as many people in the world. Even *more* crowded."

"That's true. But maybe we can build a better world."

"Is that what we're doing in L-Twelve?" She bit her lip even as she said it. You weren't supposed to ask.

43

But Jaron merely grunted. "L-Twelve. You know ours is only one of dozens, right? They're all throughout the Territory."

"I knew that."

"But my dad watches mine especially close. Because of me."

Deedra nodded in sympathy. Due to their swagger and their quick punishments, she'd always held the Bang Boys—and Jaron himself, truthfully—in a web of interlinked strands of fear and contempt. They were the ones who watched over her and ordered her around. She'd never thought about how they, too, were bossed around by someone higher up than them.

"'Meet your quotas, meet your quotas,'" Jaron said suddenly in a dead-on impersonation of his father's gravelly voice. "That's all I ever hear. Not 'How'd it go today?' Not 'I hear you figured out some new methods to get more work done.' Nope. Just 'Did you meet your quotas? Meet your quotas, Jaron. Meet your goddamn quotas.'"

He stood up and kicked at a rock, sending it clattering off into the distance, a smallish cloud of dust in its wake. "If *I* were in charge..."

Deedra held her breath. Jaron was treading close to treason. Magistrates were appointed for life and were granted almost total control within their Territories. She glanced around, making sure no drones were nearby. Of course, one could be just above the cloud cover, recording.

"If you were in charge, what?" she heard herself say.

Jaron took in a deep breath. He turned to her and flashed a wide grin. "Maybe we'll find out someday," he told her, and held out a hand. "Come on. Rest time's over, right? Let's get scavenging."

■ ■ ■

Jaron stopped them by a relatively intact building in the midst of a crumble of brick, mortar, and steel. It stood like the last living person in a field of the dead. The sky was still cloud gray but getting a bit

44

darker. Somewhere out there, the sun was heading west. Night would come. Curfew would come sooner, though.

"Here?" he asked, jerking a thumb toward a yawning entrance.

Deedra shook her head. "I've been in there."

Jaron raised an eyebrow. "Really? All the way out here?" He clapped.

Blushing at the applause, she found she could hardly speak. "I roam a lot. It's not a big deal."

"And you've already picked over this place?"

"Well..." She considered. "I've never actually been all the way to the top."

He flashed the grin again. "Let's make it a day of firsts, then!"

"Do we have time before curfew?" she asked.

Jaron tugged up his sleeve. She was stunned to find he wore a watch. She'd heard of them and even found some when scavenging, but never a working one. "We're good," he said. He hefted his sling-bag. "We're pretty heavy, but if we can find a few more bits and pieces, so much the better, right? You up for it?" he teased.

"Watch me," she said, and stomped into the building.

Her eyes adjusted quickly. Jaron's footsteps echoed behind her as he joined her. The entire first floor of the building was one big, open space, filled with dust and broken chunks of brick and shattered glass. None of the glass was large enough to make it worth collecting. Heavy, thick weeds curled up from the ground and wound around slanting posts and half-rotted planks and beams.

"You've been in here?" Jaron asked.

"A few times. There's an old staircase this way." She pointed and then strode off in that direction.

"Hang on!" Jaron shouted. "Wait up!" He was picking his way around a mound of debris, moving slowly. His eyes hadn't adjusted to the darkness as quickly. She paused to let him catch up, half-turned back to him, and something wrapped around her ankle.

Deedra yelped and tried to step away, but she was held fast. She tugged—hard—and couldn't move, her leg pulled in the wrong direction. She could barely make out a strand of weed tangled around her leg.

It was moving. Slithering up her calf. She heard a snapping sound.

Oh, God. It was tooth-weed.

"Jaron!" she shouted. "Be care—"

Before she could finish the word, the tooth-weed tugged harder and she lost her balance, falling over. Her breath whooshed out of her in a rush, and she struggled to regain it. Somewhere in the near distance, teeth snapped over and over. She couldn't see them, but she could picture them: rows of needle-thin, fang-sharp teeth growing out of the sides of the weeds, ready to sink into her flesh once she was dragged closer. Once hauled to the densest part of the tooth-weed cluster, the vines would wrap themselves around her and eat her alive from every direction.

Stupid! So stupid! There'd been no tooth-weed the last time she'd been here, but it could grow almost anywhere. Still gasping for breath, she flailed around for her makeshift knife. But just then, Jaron darted past her, a shadow melting into shadows. He cried out and brought both hands down. Something flashed in the meager light, and she felt the weed loosen its grip.

"Haaaa!" Jaron breathed again, chopping once more. She saw now that he had a piece of sharp, heavy metal from his sling-bag and was using it like an ax, hacking away at the center of the weed mass. The extended weeds retreated under his onslaught, shriveling back to their nucleus. The weed around her leg gave up, slackening enough that she could pull away.

Panting with exertion, Jaron staggered over to her and dropped to his knees. "You all right?" he gasped.

Her breath returning, she nodded. "Yeah. Yeah. Thanks."

"Stupid of me," Jaron said, shaking his head in self-recrimination. "Should have brought some killspray. Stupid."

Killspray. A toxic mist that could choke tooth-weed in a matter of minutes. Deedra would . . . well, she would *kill* for a supply of the stuff. The DeeCees—the Territory's complement of troops from the Department of Citizen Services—carried it, but regular citizens weren't allowed.

Jaron looked back at the tooth-weed's nucleus. It was wounded but not dead. Most of its vitals were in the root system, beneath the surface. Killspray could soak in, get to the roots, kill it for good. With Jaron's help, she moved farther back, out of range.

"Did you bring any?" Jaron asked.

"Any what? Killspray?" When he nodded, she couldn't help laughing. "Not allowed."

Jaron stared at her, his face slowly crumbling into an expression of sheer outrage. "Are you kidding me?" he said after a moment, his voice low and barely controlled. "We send you out on these runs without any killspray?"

"You didn't know?"

Jaron ground his teeth together. "No, I didn't." He helped her stand. "Are you okay?"

"I'm fine."

Clearly, he didn't believe her; he crouched down to examine her leg, insisting on rolling up her pant leg to make sure her skin hadn't been damaged. "Sometimes they have little vestigial mouths on the ends of the vines," he told her. "You might have gotten nipped."

"I'm really fine," she assured him. And she was. She'd gotten a scare and had the breath knocked out of her. Nothing that hadn't happened to her a hundred times before.

Satisfied that she hadn't been bitten, Jaron rolled her pant leg back into place and stood. "Well, we're out of here, then," he said.

"No way! We came in here to scavenge. First rule of scavenging: You have to actually scavenge something."

He shook his head and said firmly, "The stairs are past that thing and it's too risky."

"There are other ways," she informed him. She showed him a hole in the ceiling above them. "We don't have to use the stairs."

"But you—"

"Do you really want to go back to L-Twelve with your bag only half full?" she asked him.

Jaron opened his mouth to protest, then stopped. He blew out a breath and smiled. "'Half full is half empty.' That's what my dad says."

"Your dad is right."

"I guess anything's possible, then. Okay, lead the way, Expert Scavenger."

They picked their way across a floor littered with broken chunks of mortar and glass, then climbed up an incline of planks and beams that took them through the ceiling. The second floor was picked over, so they kept going, using collapsed floors from above to make their way higher.

"Do you do this all the time?" he asked as they passed the third floor.

"Scavenge?" she asked. "As much as I can. Climb?" She considered. "Whenever I get the chance." She risked a self-satisfied grin, and Jaron chuckled.

She hoisted herself through a hole in the ceiling and onto the fourth floor. "Lower floors get picked over fast. Second rule of scavenging: Start at the top and work your way down."

"Makes sense," Jaron agreed. He kept up with her easily.

Six floors now. She could tell Jaron was having a little trouble breathing, but he wasn't about to let on. Floor seven loomed. She pretended she needed a break so that he could catch his breath. Maybe he'd scavenged in the open air, but that was a lot different from crawling and climbing through the wreck of an old building.

She frowned as she made her way up a rickety set of old stairs to the eighth floor, steadying herself with her palms planted on opposing walls. She had to focus. One wrong step and the stairs would collapse.

Finally, ten stories up and one floor below the top, Deedra spied the clouds through gaps in the ceiling and the roof.

"This is it," Jaron said from behind her, clapping the dust and dirt from his hands. "Might as well see what's available up here and work our way down."

Deedra peered up through one of the holes in the ceiling. "Don't you want to see from up there?"

"There's no way up."

Deedra shrugged and then, without a word, wrested an old door off its weak and rusted hinges and leaned it against the remains of a table to create a stable-enough platform. Balancing atop it, she managed to grab a ceiling beam and clambered up to the very top floor.

She stuck her head down into the building and smiled at Jaron. "Come on! Do you want to miss this?"

With a shake of his head, he climbed onto the platform, took a moment to steady himself, and then heaved himself up through the hole. Deedra reached down and helped him up, taking his hands in hers. His skin was smooth, scarless. Her knuckles were scabbed over, her palms lined with healed-over cuts and gashes. She wondered—not for the first time—what it was like to live without needing to scavenge.

Silently, they paced the length of the rooftop, stopping at a parapet. The top of the building had been sheared almost completely off at some point in the past, the walls crumbling around them in a jagged, craggy rampart, so they had a mostly unobstructed view of the entire Territory. The buildings thrust up from the ground in ragged ranks, most of them banged and dented by some long-ago war or tragedy. Something that had happened during the Red Rain, maybe, or even before then. Back in the centuries of lost history that didn't matter anymore because the world was as the world was, and nothing could change that.

She wanted to weep, seeing it all arrayed around her. All the wrack and ruin, the blunt grays and browns, the shattered facades and broken spires. This was her Territory, her home, and it was destroyed. She'd always known it, but now she could see it.

"This is my father's world," Jaron said tightly. She felt him tense up beside her, noticed his fists clenching. A part of her wanted to take his hand—again—but she held back. He was in the throes of something she didn't understand.

"Stupid old man," he whispered. "Stupid, foolish old man."

"It's not his fault," she ventured. "There are too many people to keep track of, too many mouths to feed. It's—"

"Don't defend him!" Jaron turned away from her and stomped off to another edge of the building. She wanted to tell him to be careful—the old roof could collapse easily—but he was beyond listening.

Instead, she joined him and stood quietly as they gazed out on the skyline together. The clouds darkened to a steely gray. Curfew would come eventually. She would have to tell him.

"I can make it better," he said at last, and then, as if defeated by the very idea, he sank down to sit. "I really could."

She crouched down next to him. A lock of his hair was in his eyes, and she swept it out of the way. He didn't flinch. Didn't recoil. Sweat from her exertions rolled down the back of her neck, and, without thinking, she lifted her hair to cool off. Jaron stared at her scar. Deedra quickly rearranged her hair to cover it.

But Jaron, with the same casual intimacy, brushed her hair back, exposing the scar again. Betraying its hideousness to the open air.

"Where did that come from?"

She shrugged and tugged her hair back into the concealment position once more. "I don't know. It's always been there."

"Your parents don't know?"

"I don't have parents. I grew up at the orphanage. Before it shut down."

At the age of twelve, Deedra had been released, along with the other kids. She'd slaved at the orphanage, so switching to L-Twelve meant the only real change in her life was that she now had her own little apartment, not a wide-open room that she shared with ten other girls.

She touched her chest briefly, feeling the shape of her pendant through the poncho. That was the only other remnant of whatever her past happened to be. The pendant and the scar were reminders of what she could not remember, of the mystery of her life before the orphanage. For a moment, she considered showing it to Jaron. He'd seen the scar; why not?

Jaron leaned against the crumbling parapet in a way that alarmed her. "I've been watching you," he confided. "I know you all on the floor think I'm hardly ever up there. And that when I am, I'm not doing anything."

"We don't think that." The lie came out so quickly and so smoothly that for an instant, she was convinced it was the truth.

He laughed. "You do. It's okay. I get it. Magistrate's son, must be lazy, right? I understand. Honest. But here's the thing, Deedra: I have to work twice as hard as any of my father's other supervisors. Twice as hard, and I get half as much credit, half as much respect."

"I'm sorry," she said.

"Don't be. I signed up for it. I asked for it. I know you all think being the Magistrate's son is easy, that I have all the rations I could ever want, but it's not like that. It's tough for me, too. Not as tough as for you, but still plenty tough."

She was surprised to find that she believed him. She and Lissa had often fantasized about what it would be like to be a supervisor or even on the level of a Bang Boy. She imagined unrestricted rations, maybe no curfew. But Jaron, she realized now, was just as entangled in the system as she was. The Territory and the government were like tooth-weed: They tangled up and ate whatever came their way, without prejudice.

Even the Magistrate's son.

"Do you want to know why I came with you today, Deedra? Why I volunteered?"

His eyes held hers, and she forgot to worry about the parapet, the roof, everything. She suddenly *did* want to know. Why *had* he come with her today?

"Like I said, I've been watching you. All of you down there, but you specifically. You, more than most."

"I don't know what to say to that."

"You don't have to say anything. You work hard. You don't screw up. If I had ten more like you, I could turn out more product than any two factories in the Territory. In the *City*. Hell, maybe the Collective!"

Deedra rarely if ever thought of the Collective. The Territory was huge, the City bigger still, stretching for hundreds of miles in every direction. The Collective was epic atop epic, a confederation of Cities. A part of her didn't even believe there was such a thing. But Jaron would know better, wouldn't he?

He reached out and took her hands in his own, staring at her. Staring *into* her. She couldn't believe he was touching her like this. Her hands felt hot and cold at the same time. "I'm trying to do my best. But I don't want to just do what my father tells me, how he tells me. I want to do more. I want to do better. You know?"

"I do. I think I do."

"Why don't people get it, Deedra?" His voice took on an anguished tone, and his grip tightened on her hands. "It's so simple. You get it. I know you get it. I've watched you. You keep your head down and you work hard and you don't mess around. It's so simple, but so many people just don't understand. It makes my job harder. And when my job is harder, their lives get harder. I don't like that. I don't like doing that to them. But they make me. Do you see? They make me."

"I understand."

"I knew you would." He pursed his lips, blew out a frustrated sigh, and then twisted his lips into a lopsided grin. A moment of silence vibrated between them like a wire pulled taut, and then Jaron leaned toward her.

Was he going to kiss her? Was that actually happening?

More important: Did she want that to happen? And she decided that, yes, she did, and she hoped he was, and then he was, he was kissing her right at the moment she decided she wanted that, and how perfect was that?

His lips on hers, parting hers. She leaned up, into the kiss, surprised to hear and feel a small, low mewl deep in her throat as she did so.

Jaron broke the kiss, pulled back a bit. "Did you like that?" he asked, his voice a whisper.

Had she liked it? Her rib cage felt two sizes too small. Her cheeks flushed.

"Yes."

"Okay, great." He leaned in again, nuzzled her cheek, and whispered in her ear, "Take off your pants. Now."

CHAPTER 5

Deedra blinked. She'd been so entranced by Jaron's lips at her ear as he spoke that her own lips parted in midgasp. Now the gasp froze. Then began to melt.

"What did you say?" she asked.

He kissed the shell of her ear. "Get undressed. We're going to have sex now. You and me."

She pulled back. "Look, maybe we're not understanding each other." Her heart pounded in her too-small rib cage, tightening now in fear, not lust. "I mean, I like you a lot, but I'm not ready for that."

He tilted his head and smiled. It was a beautiful smile, and it made her question whether she'd heard what she thought she'd heard.

"Don't make a big deal out of this," he said. "You want this as much as I do."

"I don't." She realized she was still holding his hands. It took a small effort, but she pulled her hands back from him.

Jaron's smile collapsed on one side of his face, turning into a confused smirk. "I don't understand."

"I . . . I don't want to have sex," she said, as though to a very, very stupid person. But Jaron wasn't stupid, and she didn't understand why this was happening.

Jaron nodded thoughtfully. "Right. I see." He began to peel up his shirt from his torso. "The thing is, I *do* want to have sex. So…"

He paused with his shirt midway up his chest, regarding her with a baffled expression. He gestured for her to take off her clothes, and Deedra stood up, backing away. As she did so, it was as though a lever had been thrown somewhere deep inside the machinery that made Jaron run. His expression contorted into an agonized confusion, and a sick sort of light flickered in his eyes. Standing, he squared his shoulders and cocked his head as though seeing her for the first time.

"Jaron," she began, "it's not about you personally or anything. I just—"

He moved toward her, getting close. Deedra took a step back, keenly aware that she was near the edge of the building. There was a foot-high crumbling jut of bricks behind her and then nothing for ten stories down.

"Are you *rejecting* me?" he barked, and stepped closer. "Are *you* rejecting *me*?"

"No! Look, I just—I know that you—I know you're the son of the Magistrate, but—"

"You have no idea what it's like being the son of the Magistrate," he told her. "I'll run this whole Territory someday. It's a done deal." He reached out and grabbed her wrist, pulling her toward him. "So why won't you be *nice* to me?"

Reflexively, she recoiled at his touch, pulling back, colliding with the tooth of brick. The top layer crumbled on contact, spilling over the precipice, and Deedra staggered there, bent backward, ready to tumble, but Jaron jerked her arm, hard, and she fell forward against him.

"That's more like it!" he said, wrapping an arm around her. She thought of her knife, sending up a silent prayer that he wouldn't feel it back there.

"Please let me go." She struggled against him, and he clenched her poncho in his grasping hand. When she tried to pull away, he wrenched her right back to him.

Her knife was the only way out. But to cut him, to cut Jaron Ludo...to hurt the son of the Magistrate would save her now but plunge her into a world of even greater pain, one she could scarcely imagine.

Hurting him would not be enough. She would have to kill him. That would be the only way out. She couldn't believe she was even contemplating it, but as his hand brushed the underside of her breast, she realized this was the choice: Kill him or let him have his fun and know that he would ever after feel entitled to it.

Her right arm was pinned to her side. Inching her arm backward, she stretched out her fingers toward the knife....

"What are you doing?" a voice asked from nowhere.

Jaron sighed heavily in her ear; his breath was hot and loud. When he craned his neck to look behind him, his grip loosened just enough that Deedra could wrap her fingers around the knife handle. She could also see over his shoulder now.

There stood Rose, in his long green coat, hands thrust into his pockets.

"This is none of your business," Jaron snapped.

"I believe you," Rose said equably, so equably that Deedra realized he would leave in a moment and she would be alone again. Her grip tightened on the blade. *Slash across his throat.... Turn quickly and push him over the edge.... The only way...*

"But," Rose went on, just as calmly, "it's probably none of *their* business, either."

He pointed up and slightly to the left. Deedra and Jaron looked in

56

that direction and beheld a drone, hovering about ten feet above them, silent. Drones usually didn't hover, so it was easy to forget they could. Until one was *right there*.

Jaron released Deedra and jumped back as if she'd caught fire.

"Nothing is going on here," Jaron said slowly. Maybe speaking for whoever could lip-read the drone video. Being the son of the Magistrate was one thing; being caught on drone video committing a crime was another. The local DeeCee contingent reported to the Magistrate, but they technically worked for the City. There was no guarantee Jaron could weasel his way out of a charge laid upon him by the DeeCees. Especially if his father was as unsympathetic as Jaron made him sound.

Deedra exhaled and then inhaled a great gulp.

Rose said nothing. His jaw locked, jutting out. He was immobile, a statue.

"We were just messing around." Jaron flashed his smile again, his beautiful smile. And what kind of horrible irony was it that he possessed such a beautiful smile.

Deedra said nothing. What *could* she say?

"I don't know what you *think* you saw," Jaron said, turning to Rose, "but you didn't see it. Understand?"

Rose simply stared straight ahead at Jaron, who fidgeted and shuffled his feet back and forth, back and forth. Finally, he threw his hands up in the air.

"This whole thing is ridiculous!" he exclaimed. "Why am I even wasting my time here? I tried to be a nice guy, tried to help her out with her run. Tried to get to know her. And this crap happens. Whatever. If you two want this rooftop, it's yours."

He stalked over to the hole that led down to the lower stories, shoving Rose out of the way as he did so. Only then did Deedra finally release her knife.

The drone twisted, then glided away.

∎ ∎ ∎

Alone on the rooftop with Rose, Deedra found herself unable to speak. For long moments they simply stood and gazed at each other. She kept expecting him to speak, but he said nothing. He didn't even move.

He had two cuts, she realized, along his left cheek and another one just above his ear, but he didn't seem to notice or care. The one on his cheek was insignificant, but the other one was still bleeding. She'd suffered enough cuts to recognize a wound that kept pulling open.

Finally, she broke the silence: "What are you doing here?"

He took a moment to consider before answering. "I was looking for you. And I found you."

His position didn't change. He stood between her and the only way off the rooftop. Had she traded Jaron for someone just as bad?

She didn't think so, but she couldn't be sure. She let her hand drift back to her knife again. Just in case.

"Well, yes. Is this the part where you disappear again?"

He shrugged, still not taking his hands out of his pockets. "The noise startled me."

"You vanished. Like, into thin air."

"I'm good at hiding, when I need to."

She pondered that for a moment. He hadn't threatened her at all. Hadn't moved, really. And he had managed to save her from Jaron without making the situation worse. Almost without meaning to, she released her grip on her knife.

"Why were you looking for me?"

For the first time, he seemed worried. No, not worried—shaken. As though that question had struck him, while all the others had been deflected by some kind of invisible armor. He hung his head, as though ashamed, and took a step away from her.

"I'm sorry. I shouldn't have come here. It was stupid."

He turned to leave. Stopped. Looked back at her. Then he took one long step in her direction. His right hand came out of his pocket, and he put something on the ground between them.

"Just wanted to give you…" He trailed off, and once again turned to leave.

She stared at what he'd left. It was a mangled tin can, its colors faded blues and reds. The VITABEV! logo was still visible.

"Wait!" she called, stopping him before he could drop down to the floor beneath them. She rushed forward and picked up the can, holding it out to him. "This? You came back for this? To show me an old can?"

Rose shrugged, hands jammed in his pockets again. "Look at it." He leaned in a bit. "Closely."

She stared at it, but it was just a crushed and shredded can.

With an almost physical reluctance, he came closer to her, a war etched into his expression and his stride. He obviously wanted to leave but felt compelled to explain.

He carefully—as though her skin were poisonous—plucked the can from her hand without touching her. They were as close now as they'd been at the river, and the delicate angles of his face seemed even more refined than before. The cuts on his face threw his beauty into starker relief.

Beauty. Was she crazy? He wasn't beautiful. He was just…

She suddenly smelled something sweet on the breeze. It made her dizzy for a moment, and when she came out of it, he was still standing there, turning the can over and over in his hands before her eyes.

"See?" he asked with a strange urgency. "See?"

"It's just…a can." Helpless, she added, "I'm sorry," even though it wasn't her fault. "How did you get cut? What happened to you?"

He blinked at her. "Cut? Oh, when I went for this." Again with the can. He was obsessed. "It caught the sunlight this morning out by the river. It was under two cars that had tumbled and turned on top of each other. I had to crawl under. It was a tight fit."

"You could have gotten really hurt," she said. "They could have collapsed on you."

"I guess so."

"You guess so? You risked your life for a *can*?"

"Not just a can." He thrust it toward her, insistent. "Look again. Here," he said, and tilted it just so. "It looks like a flower, doesn't it?"

A flower? She searched her memory. She'd seen images. And, yes, when you looked at it just right, the old can did sort of look like a flower, its petals made of peeled-back aluminum. It even sparkled a bit when rotated.

"It's..." She couldn't believe it. "It's sort of pretty."

His eyes lit up. "Yes! At first, it wasn't totally like a flower. I had to bend some parts of it. But now it's nice, right? Here, take it." He pressed it gently into her hands. "I thought of you when I saw it. That's why I went to get it."

She nodded slowly, still captivated by the grungy, old, beautiful can in her hands. "I'm glad you came back," she said at last.

He nodded to her and once again retreated toward the exit.

"Wait," she said. "Stay."

■ ■ ■

From the top of the building, Deedra could barely make out the outline of the Broken Bubble.

"The 'Broken Bubble'?" Rose asked, sitting next to her.

He had stayed. And even though he kept his arms close by his side, as though fearing her touch, he sat beside her, watching the sun muddle behind the clouds.

"There," she said, pointing to a large structure off in the distance. She didn't know what it actually was, but it looked like a decapitated bubble. It was roughly circular, rising against the horizon, its top hacked off. It stood amid old cars and rusted-out buses, fallen steel beams, and massive slabs of concrete and pavement that seemed frozen in orbit, blocking the approach to the Broken Bubble. It loomed at the very edge of the Territory, close to the southern border where Dalcord and Sendar both abutted Ludo. Too dangerous to approach. She'd never seen it from this angle before.

"Oh." Rose grinned. "That. Yes. Very interesting."

"I sort of want to go there someday. Just because it's impossible."

"Nothing's impossible."

"You can say that, but it doesn't make it true."

Rose considered this for a moment. "I suppose that's right. Saying something does not make it true." He craned his neck to peer out along the skyline. "Isn't it beautiful?"

Again with the beauty. She boggled. Was he seeing the same thing? The devastation?

"Look," he told her, pointing. "If you look over there, that cluster of buildings almost looks like a hand with its fingers like this." He gestured *come here*. "Like it's inviting you over."

"I...guess..." She squinted, doubtful. But what he'd said was true, and now that she'd seen it, she couldn't unsee it.

"And over there. Right down by the horizon. You can almost see the sun through the clouds. It's sort of purple and red, almost like the sky's blushing."

That, too, was true.

"It's all in how you look at it," he said.

She closed her eyes, took a deep breath, and thought of the metal flower, of how it had looked like junk to her until she'd really paid attention to it. Then she opened her eyes and tried to see the world his way.

The sky blushed in that spot, the pale shadows of the clouds cast along the upper reaches of the buildings like intricate tattoos on the concrete and brick. The entire panoply of the Territory sprawled before her.

She realized, with a tiny thrill, that she was seeing something most people from Ludo Territory would never see in their lives: the entire skyline of the Territory, the river as a grayish worm inching along the ground, the Broken Bubble, the far-off towers of the Mad Magistrate's Territory looming. From up here, she felt as though she could see the entire City. Maybe... maybe she could even see to *another* City. There were rumors that they had real names, like ChiPitt and SanAngeles. What were *those* Territories like? The wikinets said all Cities were the same, but maybe, just maybe...

She picked up the metal "flower," turning it over and over in her hands. It seemed new every time she changed its angle. "Was it worth it?" she asked. "Getting all cut up?"

His lips quirked into a smile as he remembered. "Completely worth it!"

She handed it to him, but he refused. "No, I got it for you. Keep it."

Tucking it into her poncho pocket, Deedra pulled her knees up to her chest and rested her chin on them. She didn't know what to say next. No one had ever made her feel remotely like this. No one had ever given her a gift. The last time anyone had given her something...

She couldn't remember. Maybe it had been the pendant she wore around her neck. She didn't know where it was from, but she liked to imagine it came from her long-lost family.

She'd been orphaned as a baby, had grown up surrounded by people who, if she was lucky, merely disregarded her or, if she wasn't, outright assailed her. Sometimes verbally, sometimes not. Nothing in her experience prepared her for this.

Maybe this was what family felt like. Rose, too, had no family, so maybe they could be each other's.

No, that was crazy. She blushed at the mere thought. She couldn't say something like that out loud.

So she said nothing. Rose gazed out at the Broken Bubble, as if yearning for something. In the diminishing light of day, his appearance was even more delicate, more refined, the glow highlighting his cheekbones and the fine hollows of his eyes, the thin line of his mouth. She was possessed by the sudden urge to kiss him, but she couldn't tell if that was real or just delayed gratitude for his rescue earlier.

He turned and looked at her, almost as if he'd read her mind. A breeze blew her hair across her face, and he swept it aside for her.

"Where did this come from?" he asked, and she knew what he was talking about. His gaze on her scar burned; she turned away and rearranged her hair to cover it again.

"I didn't mean to—"

"I don't know where it came from," she said. "It's always been there. It's just part of me, is all."

"You shouldn't hide it. There's nothing wrong with—"

"I have to hide it. I hate it. Other people hate it. Why should they have to look at it?"

"They shouldn't treat you like that," Rose said. "And you shouldn't believe them."

She realized she was touching the scar through the shield of her hair and jerked her hand away as if she'd infected herself. She didn't want to think about her deformity. Not now.

"I have to get back to L-Twelve," she said, not wanting to. "I have to deliver my sling-bag. And it's close to curfew." Off in the distance, the sky lit up in alternating bursts of orange as the drones flashed the thirty-minute curfew warning. She would have just enough time to get back.

She stood to leave, and he got up as well, but otherwise did not move, staring out at the skyline.

"Are you coming?" she asked.

"Not yet," he said.

"Curfew." No other words were needed. Curfew was an inviolable fact of life.

Rose tilted his head to one side. It was as though she'd fed him the idea of curfew and he was trying to decide if he liked the taste. Standing by the edge of the rooftop, his form outlined by the gray light of twilight, he smiled at her confidently. "I'll be all right," he said.

Just before she climbed back down, she looked over at him, a bundle of green against the skyline.

"Will I see you again?" she called.

He waited so long to answer that she thought he either hadn't heard or was ignoring her. But at last he answered, with great difficulty, "I don't know."

That made her sadder than she expected. It was a longer walk back to L-Twelve than it would have otherwise been. She let Rik scan her bag at the door and left quickly, not wanting to see or speak to Jaron.

Still, as Deedra fell asleep that night on her government-issued mattress, safe under the webbing of government-issued roach netting, she did so with a smile on her face. And with the metal flower perched on the edge of her bed, close at hand.

CHAPTER 6

*N*ight falls, and the City stretches for hundreds of miles in every direction. Rose feels it around him. Even with his eyes closed, he is acutely aware of the dark buildings and the lassitude of the masses within, sitting or lying down, lit only by the strobing lights of cracked, ancient thumb-flicked touch screens. The City itself is a dead body—mute concrete, dumb steel, insensate alloys. Scurrying on it and in it and through it are the people.

Fog has rolled in, gray and stinking. He stands in it, arms outstretched, taking in what the sky has to give.

Above hover the drones, insect-silent and flat black to blend into the cloudy night sky. Rose senses them, too, unnatural eddies in the damp night air, crisscrossing the sky endlessly, seeking, searching, seeing, reporting.

A drone glides overhead, far beyond rock-throwing range, scanning the ground for curfew violators. Rose stands directly in its sweep and does not fear.

It is long past curfew.

The drones cannot see Rose. He cannot see them, either, but he knows of their presence.

The air smells of old copper and rust and ozone and feces. Rose imagines *he can peer through the cloud cover and see the stars. They are still out there, after all. The stars, the moon, the endless horizon of the universe.*

He breathes in deeply. Any breath is good, no matter the foul taste that lingers. Breath means life. Life is good, for no other reason than it is life.

With another deep breath, Rose walks down an alley and disappears into a darkness penetrated by neither human nor drone.

CHAPTER 7

There was a little patch of dirt just outside the door to Deedra's building. It was the only spot for blocks around that wasn't covered by pavement or concrete, and Deedra couldn't figure out why the Magistrate hadn't paved it.

Or why, the morning after she'd scavenged with Jaron, Rose stood right at that spot, waiting for her. Whistling. Softly.

The clouds had not yet gathered to obscure the sun, so Rose stood still and calm on that spot of dirt, his face tilted skyward, eyes closed. It reminded her of how she'd sat with Jaron the day before, and yet it was different. Jaron, she realized now, had craved the sun as though it belonged to him. As though it were meant for him, and it would never, ever be enough. Rose's expression was one of mingled delight and concentration.

She approached him, meaning to ask exactly what he was doing here, but something about his stance, his focus, made her stop. It was as though she'd be intruding on something private and holy, even though it was outside, where anyone could see. She stared at him, captivated by him, even as a clock ticked in the back of her mind, warning her that she would be late to L-Twelve.

And then someone from a passing crowd plowed right into him. She stiffened, expecting Rose to collapse, but instead he remained standing, oblivious. The person who'd collided with him staggered back several steps and almost fell down, saved only by the press of other people.

Then, as if awoken from a deep, deep trance, Rose suddenly flinched and opened his eyes. He seemed relaxed and pleased to see her.

"This is a surprise," she said. Air quality was "middling" that day, according to her vid. She didn't wear her mask. So she couldn't hide the grin that spread across her face.

He thrust his hands into his coat pockets, like always. During a food riot a couple of years ago, she'd watched the DeeCees quell unrest from her window. They had holstered their weapons the same way. But Rose's hands weren't weapons.

"Good morning," Rose said.

"Right," she said. "Good morning. What, uh, what are you doing here?"

It was a simple enough question, but he took a while to think it over. "I really enjoyed our talk yesterday," he said. "I thought maybe we could—"

"I have to go to work," she interrupted, too quickly. Immediately she felt cruel for doing it, expecting him to be upset.

But, instead, he simply shrugged. "I'll go with you, then."

There was no talking him out of it. And she realized she didn't want to. Jaron could be at L-Twelve, of course, and she had no desire to see him. To speak to him. The day before had been a fluke, she told herself—there was no reason for Jaron to come down to the factory floor, no reason for them to see each other at all. She would just pretend nothing had happened. But in the meantime, it would be good to have Rose by her side.

Soon they were at the factory gate together. The Bang Boys were monitoring intake today, flanking the brand scanner, their pipes at the ready. Deedra thought back to the moments by the river, to Rose's perfectly unblemished body.

"Look, you can't go in," she said. "You're not branded. You're not from around here."

"Don't worry about me," he said with utterly misplaced confidence.

And then it was her turn to go through the scanner, backward, as usual. One of the Bang Boys—Hart, she thought—muttered something about "looking good either way" and she wished her poncho covered all the way down to her ankles.

Then it was Rose's turn. Already through security, she paused to see what would happen and was shocked to find him tilting his head to reveal a Ludo brand, right where it was supposed to be.

But how—

Lissa nudged her from behind. "Hey. You all right?"

"I'm fine," Deedra said absently, still watching Rose.

"Everything was all right yesterday? With Jaron?"

Deedra glanced at Lissa, who was gnawing at her lower lip, watching with concern. "Everything was fine," she lied. She didn't want to tell Lissa what had happened on the rooftop. There was no point. What would or could Lissa do about it?

"You sure?"

"Yes, of course!" She turned back to the entrance, but Lissa plucked at her sleeve.

"Then come on, Dee. Let's grab our stations."

"Wait. I want to see what happens."

Lissa squinted at Rose. "Who's that? Never seen him before."

"That's him. The guy by the river."

Lissa goggled. "I thought you were hallucinating or something! You mean he's real?"

"Seems like it, huh?"

At the scanner, Lio was arguing with Rose, trying to show him how to expose his brand to the device. Rose balked.

"Look, jackhole," Lio said with heat, "are you some kind of idiot? If you want to work, you get scanned."

"Why?" Rose asked mildly.

Lio threw his hands up in the air. "So you can get your ration, dumbass! If we don't know how long you worked, how the hell do we keep track?"

"Don't worry about me," Rose said. "I'll be here every day."

"Great. Good to know. Who the hell are you, anyway?"

"My name is Rose."

A chorus of titters rippled through the Bang Boys. Except for Kent, who openly guffawed.

"Are you kidding me?"

"I'm pretty sure I'm not."

"That's a girl's name," Lio said, still chuckling.

"Which girl?" Rose asked.

Lio did a double take. "What?"

"You said it's a girl's name. Which one? I'm curious. I've never met someone with my name before."

"That's not what I..." Lio fumed. "Are you a smart-ass?" he demanded, and banged his pipe against a nearby fence post. *Clong!*

Rose didn't flinch, didn't so much as twitch a muscle. "Am I supposed to be afraid of you?" he asked.

No one had ever asked that before. The answer had always been so obvious. So the question threw Lio off, and he gabbled for a few seconds, searching for the best response.

"Shut your hole," Kent advised, picking up the slack. He *thwack*ed his pipe into his palm for emphasis. "You don't scan, you ain't comin' in here. Now buzz away; you're holding up the line."

"But I want to work. I want to contribute."

"Then scan your brand."

"No."

"Look, you've *got* the brand. Just scan it! Scan it and work."

"What does one thing have to do with the other? Why do you care if I get my ration or not?"

Kent grunted something unintelligible. Rose didn't move, and for a second Deedra thought the Bang Boys would—all of them at once, maybe—take a swing at him. But a voice sounded out from a speaker mounted on a nearby pole, a speaker adjacent to one of the security cameras.

"Let him in," said Jaron Ludo's disembodied voice. "And bring him up to the office."

Inside, she strained to listen through the air duct. But as usual, she could pick up only the sense of voices, nothing specific. Down on the floor, they ran through the Patriot Oath, swore fealty to the Magistrate, then got to work.

Deedra had trouble focusing. The conveyor belt zipped by her station, and she worked as quickly as she could, but she couldn't help tossing furtive, useless glances upward, toward the office into which Rose had disappeared, escorted by Lio and Hart. Kent and Rik stayed on the floor, occasionally living up to their group name and startling anyone within hearing distance. Which, given the loudness of the pipes, was everyone.

After a little while, Rose exited the office with Lio, strode from the catwalk to the stairs, and came down to the factory floor. Lio banged his pipe three times in rapid succession, setting up a tooth-jarring chain of echoing clangs that stopped everyone at their stations.

"Listen up!" he shouted. "I need a volunteer to show Rose"—he couldn't say the name without a chuckling sneer—"the ropes."

Deedra's hand was in the air before the sentence finished, and soon Rose was deposited with her.

"I don't get you," Lio snarled before leaving them. "We got a system, you understand? You work, you eat. Simple. It's worked for a long time. I don't see why you have to go mucking with it."

Lio stalked off, and Deedra found she'd been holding her breath the whole time. She let it out in a silent whoosh.

"So here we are," she said.

"Indeed."

She'd never taught anyone how to work before. She wasn't sure where to start. "Have you ever done this before?"

He looked at the conveyor belt as it chugged by. Paying only half-attention, Deedra was bolting a housing onto a cylinder. "No. Nothing like this. What are you building?"

"An air scrubber," she said. "See the fan blades?" She pointed to the cracked, dusty screen mounted at her workstation, which displayed a graphic of the various components coming together, a visual cheat sheet if any of the workers lost their place. Air scrubbers were probably the most important pieces of machinery in the world. Without them, even staying inside would provide no respite from the oft-poisonous air.

"I see," Rose said. He picked up a screwdriver. "So each piece comes down the line...."

"And you do whatever the schematic says needs to be done." She installed another housing. "Today I'm doing this, for example."

He nodded. "All day?"

"Pretty much."

They fell silent for a while as she guided him through the steps. He learned quickly, and soon she was able to take a step back and watch him do her job as efficiently as she could, with much less time to learn. A vague and indistinct part of her thought she should be aggravated or maybe even jealous, but she couldn't muster either emotion. Rose was *whistling* as he worked.

She was pretty sure he didn't even realize he was doing it. It wasn't a loud, piercing, attention-getting whistle. Or tuneless and random. There was purpose and pattern to it. Low and rhythmic, it was just loud enough for her to hear, and it lulled her into a sense of safety and security.

He interrupted her almost trancelike state to ask, "What does 'Waiting for the Rain' mean?"

It took her a moment to realize what he was talking about. WAIT-ING FOR THE RAIN was graffitied all over the Territory. The Magistrate kept ordering it scrubbed clean, but it was everywhere, to the point that Deedra hardly noticed it anymore.

"The Red Rain," she said. "Some people think it will come back."

He frowned. "I see."

"I don't know why people worry about it," Lissa said. She'd over-heard them. "That was a while ago. What are the odds?"

"Don't sound so sure." It was a new voice—a man across the belt from them, slight and pockmarked. His name, Deedra remembered, was Lanz. That was all she knew. He could have been fifteen or thirty-five. "It happened once," Lanz said, "it can happen again. And the last time, fifty billion people died."

Deedra shook her head. So he was one of *those*. The Red Rainers. The Doomsdayers. Lanz was one of those people who believed in God. They went around exchanging bizarre, meaningless quotations with one another, bits of nonsensical stories they'd memorized and passed down from generation to generation.

"No," she told him, "that's not what happened. Fifty billion people died, and *then* the Red Rain came."

"No, no," Lanz chided. "The Red Rain killed those people. And it could come back for us. It's the power of God."

"That's not what I was told," Lissa said, jumping in. "It wasn't *God*." She snorted at the word. "And the rain wasn't even red. That's just what they call it."

73

"It was red," Lanz insisted. "My parents were alive at the end of it. They saw it. And it was the wrath of God. Matthew 24:30 to 36—'At that time the sign of the Son of Man will appear in the sky, and all the nations of the earth will mourn. They will see the Son of Man coming on the clouds of the sky, with power and great glory. And he will send his angels with a loud trumpet call, and they will gather his elect from the four winds, from one end of the heavens to the other.'" Lanz nodded smugly.

"Oh, please," Lissa said, rolling her eyes. "Spare me that crap. It was *aliens*."

Deedra blinked. This was the first time she'd ever discussed this with Lissa. *Aliens?*

Lanz smirked in disbelief, so Lissa went on: "There's all kinds of evidence for it. My dad told me about it. Everyone knows. There were these big ships. People saw them. They flew below the clouds. And they were shaped like cigars, with lights along the sides, and moved with a low-pitched humming sound."

"Where do you get this nonsense?" Lanz asked snidely.

"My *dad*," Lissa shot back. "I said that already. And it's true."

"It's not. Acts 1:9—'After he said this, he was taken up before their very eyes, and a cloud hid him from their sight.' That's—"

"That's just religious garbage you found on the wikinets. I'm talking about the truth. Aliens came and took people away and used the Red Rain as a distraction. Tell him, Dee."

Deedra held her hands up. "Don't get me involved."

"What do you think?" Rose asked her.

She was keenly aware of his eyes on her. Lissa and Lanz had already become exasperated with each other and with the conversation—they were focusing on the belt again. Deedra shrugged and watched Rose as he did her job. "It doesn't matter."

"It does."

"Not really. There's nothing I can do about it."

"What if it happens again? Wouldn't you want to know what's coming?"

"Really, there's nothing I can do about it. So what's the point?"

"Tell me what you think."

She blew out an exasperated breath. "I don't know, okay? You hear all kinds of things. People say stuff. I've heard it all. Like, some people say it was just nature. Just part of the environment dying. And that all the people who disappeared had nothing to do with it—they just went away in the confusion. Or maybe Lissa's right—maybe it was aliens."

"It was," Lissa chimed in. "And when they come back, this time the rain will be *black*. And they have stretched-out bodies, but without noses, and they don't have the black part of the eyes—it's just all one color."

Sounded convincing to Deedra.

"How do you know that?" Rose asked quietly.

"Everyone knows that."

"So maybe that's it," Deedra said. "And then, yeah, there's nothing we can do about it, so why worry about it?"

"What if it's not aliens, though?" Rose asked.

"You mean what if it's God?" Deedra barked a laugh. "Well, we can't do anything about that, either. And what if it's just the world? That's another one I've heard. That it was the world itself, scrubbing people off the planet the way you would sweep away roaches. There were too many people, so the planet itself just wiped away half of them."

"Do you believe that?"

"Why do you care what I believe?"

"Don't *you* care what you believe?"

"No, because it doesn't matter what I believe!" she exploded at him. Why was he goading her like this? "It happened. And now it's over. And it'll either happen again or it won't, but either way, there's nothing

I can do about it. I try to focus on things I can do something about."
A thought occurred to her. "If you're so interested, what do *you* think
it was?"

Rose took a half second to abandon his work, gazing at her. Then,
without even looking back down at the belt, he nimbly assembled the
fan housing.

"I don't know what it was," he admitted, "but I know what it *wasn't*.
It wasn't aliens. Or God. Or the planet itself. It was something else.
I've seen a lot in this world, and I'm sure of this: It was something else
entirely. There's no shame in admitting we don't know—it's the only
way to learn."

You have to decide which one you believe.

How? How was she supposed to do that?

"And let me tell you something else," Rose said. "I don't think we're
building air scrubbers."

Clong!

Hart was right behind her; she not only heard the bang of his pipe
but also felt it vibrate her entire body, starting with the soles of her feet.

"Does Rose have the hang of it? Good. Then get him over to the
other end of the line and get back to work. You don't get rations for
standing around."

Rose went where he was directed to go, and Deedra took up her
spot on the line again just as Dr. Dimbali's perambulations brought
him close to her station, shouting about valences and electron shells
and the weak nuclear force.

"And Jaron has a message for you," Hart continued.

"For me?" Deedra asked.

"Yeah. He said to tell you that when nothing happens, nothing *will*
happen. Got it?"

"What does that mean?"

"He just told me to tell you. Now get back on the line."

Next to her, Lissa whispered, "What's going on?"

Deedra knew, though she couldn't tell Lissa. It was about the rooftop. What had happened and almost happened and not happened. Jaron must have been worried about the drone. If its video feed came to light, he would probably get some very uncomfortable questions, questions he wouldn't want to answer. Questions that would make him look bad. The video itself would be inconclusive, but if they asked *her* what had happened... A factory supervisor accused of forcing himself on a subordinate would be one thing. Add in that it's the son of the Magistrate...

And so, a threat. So that she would keep her mouth shut. Well, fine. She'd half-expected some kind of punishment from Jaron today, but he'd done nothing. She could say nothing for a very, very long time if it meant keeping the peace.

She fumbled through the rest of the day, constantly looking up at Rose. As if he could tell when she was looking, he glanced up at her each time. And smiled.

A part of her was angry. So angry. Why had he pushed her about the Red Rain? Why did it matter anymore? Who cared?

But she had to admit: A part of her had been glad he'd done it. He'd made her think. In fact, she spent the rest of the day thinking about everything she'd heard about the Red Rain, the theories, the notions, the people who were so certain they were right.

Rose was right: There was no shame in saying, "I don't know." At least she was thinking about it.

But there was one thing she had to know. And only Rose could tell her.

■ ■ ■

When the second shift came in, Deedra caught up to Rose as they left L-Twelve. "What are you doing here?" she asked, keeping her voice low.

"Working," he said plainly.

"No kidding. You're not from around here, right? So you don't have to work. Especially for nothing."

"Nothing?" He took a step away from her as they walked, keeping a bit of distance between them. She closed the distance again so that no one could overhear.

"Yeah, nothing. You didn't let them scan you, so you don't get a ration for what you did today. It's free labor for them. That's not how it's supposed to work."

"I don't mind. I don't want anything from them."

"Then why are you here? And what happened up in Jaron's office?"

"Not much," he said in a tone that revealed that quite a bit had happened. "He wanted to know why I was here. He'd never seen me around the factory before."

"Did you tell him you're not from around here?"

Rose hesitated. "I may have neglected to mention that. There are so many people in the Territory, he can't know all of them. It seemed wise."

"Good call."

"So then he told me I was the worst kind of citizen, one who didn't contribute."

Deedra winced.

"He said, 'We all contribute. What are you contributing, you freak?'" Even though it had happened hours ago, the insult still stung, Deedra could tell. Rose's whole demeanor changed when he said the word *freak*. He stiffened and squared his shoulders and crammed his fists into his pockets. "I told him I wanted to work. I said I could contribute twice as much as anyone else."

"And what did he say to that?"

Rose's lips quirked into a smile. "'We'll see.'"

He stopped and she wondered why, then she realized they had reached her building. "Good night," he said, and walked off before she could respond.

She was already inside and nuking a block of turkey steak when she realized that she had originally asked him two questions. And one of them—"Why are you here?"—he had never answered.

CHAPTER 8

Sunday.

That was the name given to this day of the week. Sunday.

Rose peers up at the sky and tries to imagine why the day has been named so. There is no sun on this day. Nor did the sun shine for more than five minutes at a time on any other day, but the name Sunday *seems to demand sunshine, and it inevitably disappoints.*

Still, he convinces himself that if he only waits long enough, the sun will break through the clouds. And so he stands. And waits.

Rain showers greet him instead. Gray, not red. Dirty rain from a dirty sky the color of old bruises.

When the rain ends, he sighs and thinks for a moment of the girl—Deeee-draaa—and then he continues in his labors, in his secret work, the task he has set for himself.

The task of changing everything.

CHAPTER 9

The arrival of Rose, the mystery of him, should have marked something of a change, she thought. After a lifetime under an oppressive cloak of sameness, something had changed, radically. But all too quickly that same cloak was dragged over her days again.

Days became weeks, a month, then more. She kept her mouth shut, and there were no more threats from Jaron. No communication from him at all, actually. In some part of her mind, she began the process of erasing the memory of that day on the rooftop.

Rose was just a part of her life now. On the days when they shared a shift, he met her to walk to work together, waiting on that patch of denuded dirt outside her building. She came to realize that his expertise at dodging questions trumped her obstinacy in repeating them. So often he whistled as they walked, and she discovered that the walk to work seemed shorter and more pleasant when he did so.

He tried to teach her how to whistle, puckering his lips to lead by example. She couldn't make her mouth contort like his, so he reluctantly took her face in his hands, pinching her mouth into an unfamiliar oval.

"Now blow."

She blew, spraying him with spittle. Far from being annoyed or angry or offended, he burst into laughter, high and uncontrollable. And that just set her off, and soon the two of them were convulsed with laughter as Territory citizens jostled past them on the way to L-Twelve, staring at them with confusion or muttering about their lunacy. She didn't care.

"I think I'm probably hopeless when it comes to whistling," she confided in him when the giggles subsided.

But he didn't give up. Their walks to work—sometimes with Lissa, sometimes without—became tutorials on whistling, even though Deedra was certain she would never figure it out.

Jaron kept Rose moving. He changed his shifts at the last minute, moved him from station to station with a frequency that would have made anyone else's productivity suffer. But Rose just took it, bore down, and soon had mastered every aspect of the production line. Routinely, the Bang Boys would hassle him about his coat, insisting he remove it, pointing out that it was a "safety hazard," that it could get caught in the belt. Rose nodded and agreed with them, but every day he came to work with the coat on. And left it on.

Life at L-Twelve otherwise had returned to something like normal. Jaron never came down from his perch, so Deedra had to see him only on vid, and even that was rare. The Bang Boys were his influence on the floor, his appendages. For a time she feared their dragging her up to the office and to Jaron, but as the days passed, she came to fear them only as much as she always had.

Dr. Dimbali began hovering around Rose early on. Unlike every other person at L-Twelve—or in the Territory, for that matter—Rose did not ignore Dr. Dimbali. In fact, he almost seemed to enjoy the crazy old coot's rants and raves. One day, when Rose had been stationed next to her, she suffered three solid hours of the two of them discussing something to do with blood flow and veins and heart muscle. She couldn't imagine anything more boring than that; just being in proximity of the talk made her want her ears to explode so she wouldn't have to listen any longer. But Rose seemed to enjoy it, even thanking Dr. Dimbali enthusiastically when the man moved on to harass someone else, shouting, "Hearken! Hearken! Mankind descended from the now-extinct apes! Will we follow in their path? This is fundamental! This is truth!"

That was one weird thing about Rose. There were others.

Like this: Every day, she noticed, his lips would not move when they all recited the Patriot Oath.

No one had noticed except her. She knew this because if anyone else had noticed, the Bang Boys would have "persuaded" Rose in their own inimitable way to recite the oath.

She asked him about it one day, quietly, not wanting anyone to overhear. And he said the strangest thing she'd ever heard:

"I work hard. Why does it matter what I say?"

She'd never thought of it that way before. Ever. And now, every day...

Every day, she still recited the oath. But every day, she thought about what he'd said while she did so.

Every day, she wondered.

■ ■ ■

And every night, she looked at the "flower" Rose had given her on the rooftop and wondered anew. Why was he here?

She could think of only one reason. It was as plain as her vid, which brought her news every morning and every night.

ANTARCTIC WAR: NORTHERN FORCES ON THE MOVE!

And the next day: NORTHERN FORCES ROUTED IN ANTARCTICA!

And the next: MAGISTRATE LUDO WARNS OF POSSIBLE TERRITO-
RIAL WAR!

And the same, over and over. War was the constant on her vid.

The war in Antarctica, which had always been going on. And the war between Territories, which had been threatened as long as she could remember. Territories served the Cities, of course, but as long as there was some kind of order, the City didn't care who was keeping it.

I can make it better, Jaron had said to her that day.

Meet your quotas, meet your quotas.

Was there going to be a war? Dalcord Territory had been threatening to encroach on Ludo for years and years now. That was one reason for the curfews, for the occasional shelter-in-place orders. Dalcord was responsible for the gridhacks.

Was Ludo preparing for war?

Was Rose a spy?

Had he come here to learn about Ludo's manufacturing? To sabotage it?

What better way to figure out Magistrate Ludo's plans than by infiltrating his son's operations?

And I brought him here. I rescued him from the river.

No. It couldn't be. Rose was kind and sweet. He was teaching her how to *whistle*! What kind of spy did that?

Was he fearless? Yes. Resolute? Yes. But dangerous? No. Not at all.

She tossed and turned. After a certain hour, lights were disconnected to conserve power, so she had no choice but to lie in bed, sleepless and confused, questioning herself, Rose, Jaron, everything she knew.

She risked a hand out under the netting. A roach scrambled over it, then climbed up the outside of the netting. She was used to it. During the day the roaches were quiet, hibernating, perhaps. But at night they scurried forth from their hidden nests and commandeered the dark Territory.

Finding by touch what she'd been seeking, she pulled her hand back into the netting. A single roach managed to sneak in before she could affix the edge of the net, so she crushed it and brushed its remains onto the floor. She sat up, holding the metal flower Rose had given her on the rooftop.

He'd saved her from Jaron. Or from the need to kill Jaron, if she could have gone through with it.

He'd risked himself to bring her this bizarre and disquietingly beautiful gift.

He'd come *back*.

She didn't know why.

The not knowing kept her from sleep for a long, long time as she turned the flower over and over in her hands, memorizing the touch and the curve and the shape of it in the dark.

After a while, she realized—much to her surprise—that she was whistling.

CHAPTER 10

*R*ose roams the empty streets. Curfew has fallen along with the sun, and no one dares go outside. Not that many went outside before the setting of the sun, either. The air is too poisonous, they claimed. It is safer inside, they claimed. There is no reason to be outside, they claimed.

Who needs a reason? Rose wonders.

It has been the same everywhere he's been, in every Territory he crossed on his way here. The City is a fractal, the same in every direction, identical in every cut.

Except for one thing.

Deedra.

By paths and byways unavailable to most, Rose makes his silent and swift way to a specific housing unit. He does not ring the buzzer; that would automatically alert the DeeCees to the presence of someone outside after curfew. Instead, he climbs in the manner that is uniquely his, scaling the side of the building until he reaches the right window. It has been left open for him.

He slips inside. A cockroach skitters by and Rose picks it up, studying it. He marvels at the twitch of its antennae, tasting the world for food, for pathways, for danger. So efficient.

After a few moments of examining the cockroach—which sits patiently in his hand, jittering only a millimeter to and fro—Rose places it on the windowsill and goes into another room, where the occupant sits under roach netting.

"Well, good evening, Rose," he says, looking up. "Something wrong?"

"Why do you ask that?"

With anyone else, the return question would be a delaying tactic, a way to avoid answering the question. But the man under the netting knows better, knows that Rose genuinely wants to know.

"Your expression," he says. "The look on your face. You look troubled."

"I see."

"Are you troubled?"

"I'm not sure," Rose admits.

"Well, tell me what's wrong."

"I think I've made a connection."

"I see."

"To a person."

"A . . . girl? A boy?"

Rose cocks his head. "Is that relevant?"

"I suppose not. So you've made a connection."

"Yes. And I'm not sure if that's good or bad."

The man shrugs and gives it a moment's thought. Then he smiles broadly. "Well, we'll just have to figure that out, won't we?"

CHAPTER 11

On Deedra's vid the morning of her weekly optional workday, there were competing headlines. One said POPULATION RISING FOR FIRST TIME SINCE RED RAIN. The other said SCIENTISTS AGREE: POPULATION CONTROL WORKING.

She didn't know which one to believe, and she wasn't sure it mattered.

She had a little bandwidth, so she linked into the wikinets and looked up *rose*.

ROSES are mythical flowers described in literature. While old photographs purport to show them, these are conclusively determined to be falsified, since roses never existed. They were, instead, theoretical plants (see: plants) used in fiction. Roses "smelled good" and were "beautiful" to behold. Symbolically, the attractiveness of the rose was offset by the presence of its "thorns" (more accurately known as prickles), which were sharp enough to draw blood.

There was also an image. *Artist's rendition* was written under it.

She stared at the picture. It was beautiful. Beautiful—maybe appropriately—as Rose himself was beautiful. He'd been named well.

Mythical flowers, the wiki said.

Mythical.

Roses, the wiki went on, *predate the Red Rain as a mythological construct.*

She frowned.

Any of them could be true. You have to decide which one you believe. That's what Caretaker Hullay had said to her.

And she had said that she didn't want to *decide* what she believed; she wanted to *know* what was true.

And, she realized suddenly, she still did.

There was nothing she could do, though. Nowhere to turn. The wikinets were useless: She would accomplish nothing other than a massive headache and eyestrain from flicking through them. None of them jibed with any other one, and some of them—she knew from experience—would change in an instant, having been reedited or modified from what she'd seen just minutes earlier.

She sighed and gave up. It was nearing the end of the month, and her rations were running low again. Always. Every month, no matter how much she starved herself and no matter how parsimoniously she doled out her bandwidth, she hit the end of the month with two or three foodless days and little to no bandwidth.

Time to scavenge. She'd been lax all month and was now paying the price. Maybe she could find something to trade for someone's excess ration. Maybe she could find a nonblue rat out there. Maybe...

She thought of those eggs from so long ago. Her mouth watered at the cruel perfection of her memory. She would never get *that* lucky again.

She slipped on her poncho and her mask, as well as her threadbare, old backpack, and headed out. Between factory shifts, the streets were nearly empty. She marveled at how the Territory could be so congested, so packed with people, yet appear desolate. Staying inside was the safer course, the easier course.

Making her way toward the Wreck, she was determined to climb the bridge today. This time nothing would stop her. And even if she found it to be picked over and barren, at least she could say she'd accomplished something.

But by the time she made it to the Wreck, she was surprised to find Rose there, as if waiting for her. He leaned against the turned-over hulk of an old car, the hem of his long green coat nearly touching the cracked, dusty asphalt. Maskless.

"What are you doing here?" she asked him.

"Just waiting."

"No. I mean..." She broke off. She meant why was he here, waiting for her, but in that instant, she realized what she really wanted to know was something else, something more important. "Why are you *here*?" she asked. "In Ludo Territory. Why did you cross the river?"

He shrugged. "Should we talk while we walk?"

They began to thread their way through the Wreck. After many minutes of silence, she came to understand that he was not going to volunteer anything.

"Why did you come here?"

"It's not why I came that matters," he told her. "It's why I stayed."

She considered that. "So... are you a spy, then?"

"No."

She laughed. "You would be a pretty bad spy if you answered *yes* to that."

He paused and barked out a surprised laugh. "That's true!" he said, as though he'd never considered it before. And something in the innocence of his answer made her believe him.

"How come you hardly ever touch people?" she asked. "Why do you always stand away from me, like now?"

At that, he nodded slowly, climbing atop the shell of a dead truck.

He towered over her, set off in relief from the backdrop of clouds above and behind him. "I'm afraid I'll hurt people," he said.

She offered him a hand. "Help me up."

Hesitating at first, he reached down and took her hand. She didn't need the hand up to climb something as prosaic as a truck, but she was making a point.

"Here I am," she said, now standing next to him. "Not hurt."

"Yes, well..." Suddenly self-conscious, he withdrew his hands and stuck them back in his pockets. The truck underfoot became fascinating, and he stared down at it.

There was something wounded and pained beneath him. "Have you done that?" she asked gently. His self-recrimination was etched in every angle of his face. "Have you hurt..." She thought. Yes, she had to ask. "Have you hurt someone?"

"I try not to."

Which wasn't a *no*. And still, the pain etched so clearly on his face.

"What about something more than hurting? Have you..." She stumbled over the word for an instant. "Have you killed?"

Rose became even more serious. "Many, many times. So have you. So have all of us. Every day, every single thing we do kills. There are bacteria on your skin that die when you wash. There are insects in the ground that die when you scavenge."

"I don't mean *things*. I mean have you killed *people*."

For the first time with him, she felt like a child being scolded. "I don't make that distinction," he told her. "Everything that lives matters."

She thought of the bird eggs she'd scavenged long ago from the nest out by the river. Those had been living things she'd eaten. Living things she'd *gobbled down* was more accurate. She gripped her pendant between her thumb and forefinger and raced it back and forth along its chain. She'd never considered that the eggs were alive. That she was killing them by eating them. She'd just been...

So hungry...

Always hungry, it seemed.

"The world isn't that simple," she told him, unable to meet his eyes.

"The world is very simple." His voice was gentle, but firm. "People make it complicated because it's too difficult for them to live with simplicity."

"So we're all murderers? You? Me?"

"You're doing what you have to do to survive. Just like me. Just like everyone. I'm not judging you. I just want you to think about it."

■ ■ ■

Rose whistled as they walked, and partway into their journey, Deedra surprised them both by whistling along with him. Tentatively at first, fearing reproach for her poor skills, but then with more confidence. He smiled and nodded in time with her, pleased at her progress. Under her mask, the whistling echoed weirdly, so she risked taking it off. The air tasted acrid and smoky.

They managed to harmonize a little as they trekked out to the river. By the time they got there, she'd almost forgotten her desire to climb the bridge. The proximity of the river reminded her of that day she'd first met Rose, of what had happened since then. And it made her worry for him.

"You should just go back across the river," she said. "You did it once. No one ever really crosses Territories, but you're not from here originally anyway."

"Why?" he asked, blinking in innocent confusion.

She blew out a breath in frustration. "Look, you've been lucky around here so far. But I've been selfish to want you to stay."

"How so?"

"I felt safer with you around. Which is crazy, because I've never needed anyone to make me feel safe before. But Jaron's not going to forget what happened on that rooftop."

And as she said it, she realized that she wouldn't forget, either. Couldn't forget. She'd tricked herself into thinking she could just delete the memory, but it was impossible. She hadn't thought of that day for a long time, but here it was now, as bright and as real as when it happened.

"It's been a while. If he was going to do something, he would have by now."

"Maybe. But..." She told him about the threat Hart had delivered on Rose's first day at L-Twelve. "If he's worried about what I might say, then he must be keeping an eye on you, too."

"That's fine. I don't care."

"I don't think you understand what he's capable of. He can seem nice, but—"

"I never thought he was nice," he said, biting out the words.

She felt queasy all of a sudden, right there by the river, and the idea of climbing the bridge or doing anything else bled out of her along with her words.

"He's up to something," she said. "I don't know what. I was an idiot to think he would just let it all go. He's going to do something. To you. Or me. Or both of us."

Rose's expression did not change. "That won't happen," he said.

"How can you be so sure?"

"Because I won't let it happen."

CHAPTER 12

*L*ater, Rose lies perfectly still on the table as the man inserts a needle into his lower arm with cool, methodical precision.

"Something's on your mind again. You have that troubled look."

"Do I?" Rose asks.

"Is it your 'connection' still?"

"No. It's something else. I've been thinking about it."

"We have time. Tell me."

Rose stares at the ceiling as he speaks. The rough-hewn concrete sweats, and the pipes suspended in a crisscross pattern occasionally groan and gurgle. "I don't fit in. As much as I try. I still stand out. I'm a freak."

A derisive bark of laughter. "Oh, if only the world had more freaks like you! Trust me, Rose—humankind is not some sort of apotheosis to which to aspire. We are not to be admired. We are poor, hairless apes who've lost all our bananas. If there were any apes left after what happened in Africa, I could extract their DNA and show you how similar humans and apes are. Well, were, I suppose."

"I understand," says Rose. He continues staring at the ceiling. Water drips steadily for three seconds, then stops, the pattern broken. Chaos *theory, Rose knows. Or thinks he knows. There is so much information in the world and so little knowledge.*

"You still seem disturbed."

"I don't think of you as apes," Rose says. "More like worker bees, serving the queen."

At the flick of a switch, the tube in Rose's arm begins nursing. The man chuckles. "An apt description, I fear."

"And I just wonder, I suppose... if you all are workers and your Magistrate is the queen... what does that make me? What am I?"

"That is what we are going to find out."

CHAPTER 13

She wanted to be nowhere near Jaron and whatever his schemes might be, but Rose refused to back off. And she wasn't about to let him go to L-Twelve alone the next day.

Not that she had much of a choice. If she missed work without some kind of proof of illness, she would either lose her job or be physically moved to the factory by the DeeCees.

"Last chance," she whispered to Rose just before they passed through the scanner. "Go back to where you came from." Wherever *that* was.

"I'm not going anywhere."

"If you keep going in there, he has you right where he wants you."

"I'm sure he thinks that."

Inside, she stowed her poncho and took up her position. Rose made sure to get the station next to hers. She tried to focus on her tools. Couldn't. Stared at the vid mounted before her.

I don't think we're making air scrubbers, Rose had said.

What else, then? What else could it be?

It didn't make any sense. She blinked to clear her vision, forced herself to concentrate.

"Hey, Lissa."

From her left, Lissa said, "Yeah?"

"What happens to drone video? Do you know?" Lissa's father had once spent a six-month shift in the DCS Monitoring Division. He'd been a low-level tech, but maybe he'd learned something. And maybe he'd told Lissa.

"What do you mean?"

"I mean, when do they arrest people for the crimes the drones spot?"

Lissa cocked her head. "What crime did you commit now?" she joked.

She couldn't tell Lissa that she was wondering why no one had at least come to her to ask about the video from the rooftop. For example, if you were out after curfew and a drone videoed you, you were given demerits at the very least. So shouldn't someone have started an inquiry into the day on the rooftop by now?

"Just wondering why it would take more than a month. Did your dad ever—"

Lissa chuckled. "If it's been more than a month, then you got away with it, Dee. I hear they wipe the vids after a month."

Deedra forced herself to smile at Lissa's joke, but fear froze her innards. If the video was gone, then there was no evidence that Jaron had ever done anything or tried to do anything. No evidence at all except for her word. And Rose's, too, if anyone would listen to him. Two freaks against the word of the Magistrate's son.

"What? Really?"

"I guess, unless it's flagged for some reason."

"But what if it wasn't flagged?"

"Then no one'll ever see it."

Suddenly the belt stopped. Deedra looked over at Lissa, who shrugged. Next to her, Rose nodded patiently, as if he'd been expecting this.

Clong!

Clong! Clong! Clong!

97

Her teeth rattled at the ringing that presaged the arrival of the Bang Boys. When she turned around, all four of them stood with their pipes at the ready, Jaron at their center.

"Dr. Dimbali!" Jaron called out.

The doctor scrambled over. "Mr. Ludo," he began, "the protocols currently in place require an adjust—"

Standing with his hands clasped behind his back, Jaron didn't even look in Dimbali's direction as he spoke. Deedra felt as though he was staring right at her instead. "You assured me that we could increase our productivity, Dr. Dimbali."

"Yes, well, the human reflex and muscle memory—"

"You assured me," Jaron cut him off, "and I assured my father. Do you understand?"

Dr. Dimbali smiled nervously and adjusted his SmartSpex. "Mr. Ludo, one cannot make assurances with regard to unknowns. Improvement requires time."

"We don't have time, Doctor."

Dimbali opened his mouth to speak, but Jaron held up his hand, silencing him. He stared out onto the workforce and suddenly pointed across the belt to Lissa.

"You! In the back! How many units have you completed today?" Jaron demanded.

"I...I don't know," Lissa stammered. It was impossible to keep track of how many units slid by on the belt.

"Unacceptable!" Jaron pronounced, and Hart banged his pipe on the floor to punctuate the disapproval. "Two ration demerits," Jaron ordered.

"From now on," he shouted, "your quotas are doubled. The belt will be sped up." A ripple of concerned whispers bubbled up, and the Bang Boys each slammed their pipes against the floor to silence the babble.

"This is how it is!" Jaron cried. "You want to eat, you contribute!

You know that! This is how it's always been! And this is what contributing means! Now, does anyone have a problem with that?"

Silence.

"I do."

Of course it was Rose, Deedra thought. Of course. Maybe he wanted to die. Maybe that was his big secret.

Don't do this, she thought fiercely. *Don't goad him.*

"You have a problem?" Jaron stalked over to Rose's station, brushing past Deedra as he did so. "You know, the last time I checked, you don't even officially work here. You're here on my sufferance. So if you have a problem, maybe you should just leave."

"I don't think you want that. I'm twice as efficient as anyone else here."

Jaron snorted. "The door's that way, Rosie. You know how to use it."

"Maybe if we knew what we were really building and why, it would be easier to—"

"No one asked you."

"I'm just saying. It's easier to do work like this when you can see the whole picture. Why are the fan blades arrayed this way? Why are the power couplings so large? An air scrubber with that much power would be counterproductive. Shouldn't—"

"Shut up." Jaron looked around a bit nervously. The longer Rose spoke, the more people were beginning to murmur among themselves. Deedra had never noticed that. Rose was right—what was going on here?

Clearly sensing that he was about to have more questions from more directions than he wanted, Jaron took a step back from Rose. "You put your piece in the right place, and you keep your mouth shut. And then you get fed. You don't get rations for questions!" he announced. "You get them for *work*!"

Ignoring Jaron, Rose turned and spread his arms wide. "Wouldn't you like to know?" he asked everyone, his voice echoing. "Wouldn't you like to know exactly what you're building? And why? Wouldn't—"

"Shut up!" Jaron yelled, but Rose kept talking.

Jaron gestured to the Bang Boys, who stepped forward. As Deedra watched, frozen in shock, Hart and Kent each grabbed one of Rose's arms. "C'mon."

Rose planted his feet and refused to budge. "For talking? You're taking me away for *talking*?"

"You've been warned about your coat," Jaron said. "Too dangerous on the line. So we're removing you. For safety reasons."

It was too convenient by half, and everyone knew it. But still, no one said anything. Lio and Rik joined in, tugging at Rose, who struggled to maintain his position.

"Just go along," Jaron said. "It's not so bad."

And then, as Deedra watched in horror, Lio took a swing at Rose with his pipe.

Now Rose moved, ducking out of the way at the last possible instant, shoving Kent and Hart aside. The pipe missed Rose by less than an inch and smashed into the vid at his station. Sparks flew and shards of glass and metal exploded outward. If that blow had made contact, Rose's head would have been smashed wide open.

"Hey!" Deedra heard herself yell. "Hey!" And she ran toward Jaron, who stood off to one side, watching. "He could have been killed! Stop messing around!"

The Bang Boys encircled Rose, who stood amid them with no more armor than his green coat, which seemed as pathetic as a baby's security blanket.

"Make them leave him alone!" Deedra insisted. "He didn't do anything."

Jaron favored her with a quick look over his shoulder. "Back off, citizen. This has nothing to do with you."

Rose checked around himself, confirming that he was surrounded. His expression didn't change in the slightest. He didn't adjust his stance. He didn't even raise his hands from his sides.

The poor kid was going to get creamed. He didn't stand a chance.

Deedra grabbed Jaron's shoulder and spun him around, too gratified by the look on his face to be shocked at her own boldness.

"If you hurt him," she whispered in a voice only Jaron could hear, "I'll tell the DeeCees what you tried to do on the rooftop."

For a moment she enjoyed the panic dancing in Jaron's eyes. But only for a moment. The panic was replaced quickly enough with a self-confident sneer. "You think anyone will believe you? Tell anyone you think will take your word over mine. And if you do, just remember that I can hurt you more than you could ever hurt me."

It was the only stone in her sling, and it was gone. Either Jaron didn't care or the video was gone or both.

She tightened her jaw. Nearby workers had gathered, in amusement or in horror, she couldn't tell. Two rings formed around Rose—the inner circle of the Bang Boys and an outer rim of fellow workers. Deedra didn't even consider asking them for help; she knew they would never risk angering Jaron Ludo and, by extension, his father.

"Get her out of here," Jaron told Hart, and Hart peeled away to snatch Deedra by the elbow.

"Let go of me!" Deedra shouted as Hart dragged her away. "Let me go! Rose!" she screamed as she realized she couldn't break away. "Run! Get away!"

"Aw, don't run away, Rosie," Jaron said, grinning. "What would we do for fun?"

"Are you planning to hurt me?" Rose asked mildly.

Jaron gaped for a moment, then guffawed. The others joined in. "Hurt you? Not too bad." He thought about it for a second. "Or maybe pretty bad. We'll see. I'm improvising."

"I understand," Rose said. "Are you sure this is something you want to do?"

Jaron answered with a haymaker from the right, smashing his fist into Rose's face, just above the jawline. Even as she was hauled off by Hart, Deedra caught sight of that blow and gasped as if punched herself.

Rose's head snapped to the left with such precise violence that no one would have been surprised if it popped off and rolled along the floor. Then he shook his head, his arms still down, hands relaxed, and gazed levelly at Jaron.

"Okay," he said, even-tempered still. "Now that you've hurt me, are you happy?" His tone and his searching eyes were unironic.

Jaron blinked rapidly, as if unable to process what Rose had said. "Can you believe this guy?" he asked Lio, who was closest to him.

"Totally not," Lio said.

"Hold him still for me," Jaron ordered, and Rik and Kent stepped forward, reaching for Rose's arms. "This will be an instructive example, won't it, Dr. Dimbali?"

Dr. Dimbali adjusted his SmartSpex and cleared his throat. "Well, uh…" He stumbled over his words. For a man who always seemed to have something to blurt out to anyone who would listen, he seemed suddenly and uncharacteristically dumbstruck. "Look, Mr. Ludo, perhaps… that is to say, maybe…"

Rose took a step forward, then seemed to duck somehow, but without ever bending. He didn't hurry; he didn't jerk or jump. He was just suddenly, barely out of range of Rik's and Kent's hands.

"Stop messing around," Jaron growled. "Hold him still."

"We're trying!" Rik said.

Meanwhile, Hart shoved Deedra as hard as he could, sending her colliding with a clutch of workers. With yelps and cries, they all collapsed on one another, a tangle of arms and legs, and Hart rejoined the Bang Boys.

Rik and Kent made another grab at Rose, who seemed to shrug them off like dust, his movements fluid and nimble. Lio and Hart jumped in, but Rose avoided them, too.

"Maybe we could talk about what's really bothering you?" Rose asked with infuriating, impossible calm.

Enraged, Jaron lunged toward Rose, jostling Lio out of the way. In close quarters, he threw a punch at Rose, ready to bash that serenity right through his face.

Rose slid to one side gracefully, his movement precise and economical. Hart and Rik tried to grapple with Rose, but he ducked down, then scooted forward, and they found themselves crashing into each other instead. Lio tripped over them as he sprang at Rose, blocking the way for Kent, who tried stepping around them, but by then Rose had made it halfway toward the door.

At the same time, Deedra had managed to get to her feet in the crowd. She got close enough to hear Rik tell Jaron, "Let's just call the DeeCees on him."

"Are you crazy?" Jaron asked, rounding on Rik. "You want my dad to know we can't handle this? Don't let him go! Get that freak!"

Deedra realized Rose had paused at the door, his hands still not clenched, his arms still not raised in defense. He'd been lucky so far, but he would be ground into paste by the combined fury of the humiliated Bang Boys.

"Run!" she shouted to him.

Jaron charged. Behind him by only a few paces were the Bang Boys.

Rose hesitated just a second, then turned and ran.

Deedra never made a conscious decision—she ran, too, chasing them all as they raced out of L-Twelve.

• • •

Outside, Rose ran with a fleetness she could barely perceive. He ran with long, effortless strides, seeming to float above the ground for the space of each step.

Jaron and the Bang Boys were not half as elegant. Deedra followed them, pumping her arms and churning her legs.

Rose was still far in the lead, his arms wide and swinging as he ran, the coat flapping in his wake. But Jaron was closing in, and it would take only one Bang Boy to bring Rose down. Then the others would pile on. And it would be over.

"Don't stop!" Deedra tried to shout, but she had no breath to spare. She was dead last in this particular race. She had to catch up so that she could...

So that she could...

What? What was she going to do? *Talk* Jaron and the Bang Boys out of their bloodlust? Maybe offer up a second target for them? What would she get out of that?

And she realized without even taking the time to think it that it didn't matter. Rose was her friend. She would do whatever she had to in order to help him.

Keep running, Rose, she thought. *Don't stop until you find somewhere safe.*

She didn't know where "safe" might lurk. They were on a main thoroughfare now. Buildings loomed on either side, but most of them were government housing—Rose would need to buzz in with his fingerprint or brand scan, and only residents could do that. Her lungs were burning by now; how much longer could he run?

Maybe he could turn down a side street...lose them in the maze of alleyways that sprawled throughout the Territory. That was possible.

Maybe then the Bang Boys would split up, and he might have a chance against them one-on-one.

Almost as soon as she thought it, Rose darted to the right with a new burst of speed, putting some more distance between himself and Jaron as he launched himself into an alleyway.

No! Deedra thought furiously. *Not there!*

That way, she knew from long experience and exploration, led to a blind wall, thirty feet or more of bricks and mortar blockading the end of the alley.

Rose had just trapped himself.

The Bang Boys knew it, too. She heard one of them shout in triumph, and they slowed down a bit, now able to take their time. Save their energy for the beating.

Deedra ran all out. She had no plan, but that didn't matter. She couldn't get the image of Rose hitting that brick wall out of her mind. *He runs and runs; he thinks he's safe.... He sees the wall. Maybe he stops. Looks around. But there's nowhere to go. Nowhere but back. And when he turns...*

The Bang Boys fill the opening of the alleyway.

They were there now, she realized, massed together, the five of them nearly shoulder to shoulder, stalking into the alley.

She wished for a drone, but the sky was maddeningly empty of them. Had Jaron arranged this? Was his influence that great?

She paused to catch her breath. She would be no good to Rose or herself if she couldn't breathe.

From the alleyway, she heard a clang. A pipe against a trash can, maybe. Then a crash. Steel against brick.

A shout.

How did you get into this, Deedra? Why couldn't you just keep your nose out of it? You're going to end up in SecFac.

"You let him get by!" Jaron screamed from within the alley.

Deedra crept over to the entrance to the alley. She could make out the brick wall, still as stout and implacable as she remembered.

Where she'd expected to see Rose curled up on the ground while Jaron kicked his head in, the Bang Boys were milling about.

They were alone.

"I did not let him go!" Kent retorted, with heat.

"Well, *someone* let him slip through!"

Deedra crouched low against the wall. What was...?

"Look everywhere!" Jaron ordered. "He has to be hiding. Somewhere."

The alley was strewn with trash and rubble. Garbage drums and an enormous trash bin stood against one wall. Deedra watched the Bang Boys knock over the drums, sending a resounding series of gongs and clangs into the air. Jaron stood off to one side, fuming, pointing, commanding. Deedra could have burst into flame, and they still wouldn't have noticed her, so focused were they on tearing apart the alley and scrutinizing every inch of it.

When the drums proved Rose-less, Jaron browbeat Rik and Lio into climbing into the bin. Deedra's breath lodged in her throat like gristle. The bin was the only place big enough for Rose to hide.

But a minute passed. Then five. Then ten.

The Bang Boys had scoured every conceivable inch of space in the alleyway.

Rose had disappeared. Again.

■ ■ ■

She should have run, should have vacated the area before Jaron and the Bang Boys saw her. But the impossibility of Rose's disappearance froze her muscles and locked her into place, staring. She was still standing there, paralyzed, when Jaron emerged from the alley with Rik, Lio, Hart, and Kent following him sheepishly.

Run, Deedra, she urged herself as Jaron caught sight of her. *Run, now.*

But running would be pointless. She had no head start. They would catch up to her easily. She eyed the pipes the Bang Boys carried and winced at the thought of them on her flesh.

"What are you doing here?" Jaron demanded, getting close. "This is all *your* fault."

"No, I—"

"Shut up." He grabbed her by the arm, just above her elbow, and squeezed. Hard. "You were warned, remember? You were told to keep your mouth shut, and you better *keep* keeping it shut. I've been patient and I've been good to you, but that won't last forever. So just shut your mouth. I'm in no mood, understand?"

Wrenching herself free, she took a step back. Jaron's eyes blazed, and she found herself speaking soft and low, trying to calm him just long enough for her to get away. "Look, I'm just going to leave, okay?" She swallowed with great difficulty. "You're in no mood, like you said. I'll just go."

Jaron said nothing. He was staring at her. More precisely, he was staring at her chest. She backed away some more. This? Again?

She swallowed hard and got ready to run.

"Where did you get that?" he demanded and, closing the distance between them, reached out.

She bit back a useless scream and almost turned to run, but then Jaron yanked hard, and she felt the chain of her necklace break against the back of her neck as he snatched away her pendant. It must have flopped out from under her shirt as she'd been running.

"Where did you get this?" he shouted, holding it up in a fist. His face flushed, and behind him the Bang Boys came closer, fanning out behind their leader, pipes at the ready.

Why did Jaron even care? Rooted to the spot, she opened her mouth, but nothing came out.

With a snort and a dismissive jerk of his shoulders, Jaron said, "Doesn't matter. What matters is that I have it now. Get out of here. You're useless to me. You and your boyfriend."

Her legs came unstuck and she began to walk away.

And then she ran.

CHAPTER 14

When the time came for him to rule the Territory, Jaron realized, he was going to need a higher caliber of flunky. The Bang Boys had failed him in the most humiliating fashion possible.

As he stomped into the factory, the belts were running, but everyone was moving slowly. Hundreds of faces gawked at him as he entered. Jaron clenched his jaw. This was his life: He couldn't leave the factory for even a few minutes without things slowing down. He looked around for Dimbali, that useless piece of trash.

But the longer he stayed on the factory floor, the more uncomfortable he became with the eyes on him. "Get these people working," he snarled under his breath to the Bang Boys. "See if you can get *that* right today."

Orders issued to his lieutenants, he stomped up the stairs to the catwalk and into his office. Alone, he gave full vent to his outrage, screaming to the ceiling, then picking up the tab he used to log on to the wikinets. It was only a year old, but that didn't stop him from hurling it at the wall. Its face shattered with a satisfying crackle, and the wall dented, plaster raining down.

The satisfaction didn't last long.

Rose was gone. Rose was gone, and who knew how many hours of productivity had been wasted at L-Twelve in the meantime....

He paced the length and width of his office. This would not do. The video of that day on the rooftop was gone now, but there were still witnesses. Deedra. Rose. He'd thought that they were going to play along, keep their mouths shut. That he had them under his eye, under his power, anyway.

But now Rose was proving that he liked to talk. Questioning what the factory was building. Maybe he would decide to blather about other things, too.

Maybe? More like *definitely. Maybe we could talk about what's really bothering you?* Rose had said.

That would be bad. Depending on what mood Jaron's father was in, a charge of attempted assault could go either way. If he woke up on one side of the bed, Max Ludo would laugh and shrug it off and toss the charge into the trash. But if he woke up on the other side...

Jaron could find himself tried. Maybe even conscripted as punishment, sent off to hump a chain gun up a hill in Antarctica.

His vid bleated from the wall. "Please hold for the Magistrate," said one of his father's secretaries. Jaron grimaced as the screen went staticky. How long would his father make him wait this time? It had gone as long as an hour in the past. He was never sure if he was being taught a lesson about power or if his father just couldn't be bothered to talk to him.

After a few minutes of frustrated pacing, Jared paused as the vid lit up again, this time with Max Ludo's annoyed face.

"I hear you got yourself into some trouble today," his father grumbled.

Great. So someone had already passed word up the chain to the Magistrate. Looking for a handout, no doubt.

"Nothing I can't handle."

"Not what I've heard," his father said with a mean little chuckle. "You know what's worse than being weak?"

"No, Pop. Tell me. What's worse than being weak?"

"Being strong, but stupid."

Jaron bristled but held his tongue.

"If you're weak," his father went on, "then people have no expectations. You don't matter. And you can fly under the radar and maybe eke out one of the pathetic lives you see around you all day. Purposeless and dull and pointless, but safe.

"But if you're strong," he continued, "and stupid . . . well, then that's a problem. You make yourself a target. Because weak people and strong people alike see what you have, and they realize you don't have the smarts to back it up, to keep it for yourself. And even the weak can be strong in numbers."

Jaron nodded, mute. *We'll see who's strong. And who's smart. And who's figured out when to watch his own back.*

Max Ludo leaned in close to his own vid, his face filling the screen on Jaron's end. "So stop thinking about how tough you are and start thinking, period. If you're an idiot, you're an embarrassment to me. A liability. Don't be a liability, Jaron. I have a whole damn Territory full of them."

"Right, Pop."

But Max Ludo had already broken the connection.

Jaron gritted his teeth and jammed his hands into his pockets. His fingers brushed against something there: Deedra's pendant.

He produced it, stared at it as it dangled before him. Then he tucked it away again and pulled up some schematics on his vid.

Yes. Yes, there it was. Just as he remembered it.

Stupid, huh? Well, you'll see. You'll see who's smart, Pop.

He thumbed his comm and barked, "Dr. Dimbali, report to the overseer's office. Now."

An instant later his door opened, and Dr. Dimbali stepped inside.

"Where the hell have you been?" Jaron demanded.

"I was—"

"Never mind. I don't care. When I came back here, Doctor, this factory was in pathetic shape. If I have to leave, it's your job to keep things on an even keel in my absence. No excuses."

"Mr. Ludo, the workers were rattled by the—"

"I just said no excuses!" Jaron said in disbelief. Was this guy for real? "I literally *just* said no excuses, and now you're giving me an excuse!"

Dimbali paused, blinking rapidly. "Well, less an *excuse*, and more of an *explanation*, really—"

"Just shut up. Okay? Shut up and listen to me." Jaron stood and clasped his hands behind his back. "We need to step things up around here. Increase productivity."

"Mr. Ludo, we're already operating at near-peak performance."

"Then get us *to* peak performance. We're doing important work here."

An uncomfortable silence filled the office. Dr. Dimbali programmed the machinery and the vids—Jaron had a feeling that he knew exactly what was being built at Ludo Territory Pride Facility No. 12. No one was supposed to know. Different factories across the Territory—hell, across the City—were building pieces of a larger whole, and no one knew what that whole was.

But Jaron did. His father's belief to the contrary, Jaron wasn't stupid. He'd been able to extrapolate from his own schematics and arrive at the right conclusions.

"Yes, Mr. Ludo," Dr. Dimbali said hesitantly. "We're doing...very important work."

Jaron grinned. "You know, don't you?" He turned to face his second-in-command. "It's okay. It's just you and me. You know what we're building."

Dr. Dimbali fidgeted. "I spend a lot of time with the schematics," he said defensively. "And I get adjustments from the other factories. It's difficult not to speculate...."

With a shrug, Jaron waved off Dimbali's nervousness. "Breaking it up, giving each factory a piece of the puzzle... No one ever thought it would be possible to solve the puzzle anyway. But let me tell you this: I've seen the other schematics. I know that L-One is building a control pod. I know that L-Six is working on—"

"Mr. Ludo, please." Dimbali winced as though in actual pain. "Such things shouldn't be discussed."

"Really? Well, what would you say if I told you that I could get ahold of those other components. That I could have a complete unit of my own?"

Dimbali held his breath for a moment, as though not sure whether he believed it. Then he shook his head, pursing his lips. "It wouldn't matter. If you've seen the same schematics I've seen, then you know that there's a component so rare and so guarded, one that no factory is manufacturing. Not here, at least. And without that..."

As Dimbali drifted off, Jaron laughed. He dove into his pocket and produced the necklace, holding it high. "Sometimes, Doctor," he said as Dimbali gazed, astonished, "if you're a good person and smart and strong, the world delivers exactly what you need."

CHAPTER 15

Her poncho was balled up outside her building when she got home. Unfurling it, she beheld a day's worth of rations. Lissa. Lissa was taking care of her.

She should have vidded her friend, but she was still too stunned by what she'd witnessed.

Hours later the question still echoed: How had Rose escaped the Bang Boys?

It baffled her as she ran home. It confounded her as she prepared dinner: a glistening cube of compressed, lab-grown turkey steak studded with genetically modified vitamin pockets. The steak wobbled gently on the plate when she took it out of the microwave, steaming and giving off a smell like mold. Its surface was slick, its center dry and crumbly.

She ate without tasting, which was the only way to eat any of this stuff. It was called turkey steak, but she had no idea what was actually in it. She'd never seen an actual turkey, but the Magistrate's Office assured everyone that the materials in the turkey steaks were genetically modified from the finest extant turkey DNA. That was some comfort, she guessed.

All the while, the question of Rose's disappearance plagued her.

Evening came and she perched on the sill of her sole window, gazing out at the light gray smoggy band beyond which lay the setting sun.

Out of dumb reflex, she reached for her pendant, to race it along its chain, and her fingers discovered nothing. They never learned, her fingers. She knew the necklace was gone. But her fingers kept seeking it out, only to find nothing, and then to tremble at the empty space they knew should be occupied.

She closed her eyes. A vague, half-formed image of an old man floated there. She'd seen him in dreams, imagined him even while awake at odd intervals for no apparent reason. Had he been a worker at the orphanage? Had he been her father? Had he given her the necklace?

It didn't matter. It was gone now, for good. There was no way to get it back from Jaron. He would keep it or he would throw it in the river, according his whim.

A part of her wanted to vid Lissa, but the greater, ashamed part of her resisted. What would she say to Lissa tomorrow? Should she even go to work? How could she go there and encounter Jaron after this latest affront?

Then again, she wondered, pondering her miserable stock of rations, how could she not?

Just as the day deepened to full dark, the sound of her door buzzer shook her from her reverie. It was almost curfew—who could be buzzing her?

The DeeCees. This is it. Jaron sent them for me.

She contemplated not answering the buzz, but the DeeCees had the authority to march right in if they wanted. They could track her anywhere in the Territory, anywhere in the City. If the DeeCees wanted to talk to her, she couldn't stop them.

But she *could* tell the truth about Jaron Ludo, she decided, even as she thumbed the button that opened the door to the building. She would tell them everything: how he had provoked Rose, how he

115

had tried to molest her on the rooftop. The DeeCees worked for the Department of Citizen Services. They reported to the Magistrate, true, but they ultimately worked for the City. Maybe they would take action against Jaron.

It was her best option, she decided. She defiantly pulled her hair back, exposing her scar to the world, then crossed her arms over her chest and faced the front door.

"Come in," she said when the knock came.

And all her defiance melted into astonishment when the door opened to the slender figure of Rose.

CHAPTER 16

Deedra grabbed Rose and hustled him inside, slamming her door.

"How did you get away?" she demanded. "What are you doing here—it's almost curfew."

He stared all around her before his eyes finally locked onto her, his expression exhausted and confused. It took him a long moment to recognize her, and when he did, he took a step away from her, turning aside, hands jammed into his pockets. With considerable effort, his words slurring at first, he said, "I can go. If you want. I understand if that's what you want."

Was that what she wanted?

"What's wrong with you?" she asked.

"Just tired," he said, leaning against the wall. "But I'll go. If that's what you want."

She'd never seen him like this before. He was always so self-assured, so self-possessed, so capable. He never seemed...

Needy.

In that moment, yes, Rose needed her. He needed anyone, really, but he'd come here, to her, and so he needed her. Right now.

And she could do as he needed. She could take care of him.

She thought of their time on that rooftop. The moment when she'd thought that maybe they could be each other's family. But that wasn't what she really wanted, she realized.

"You can stay," she whispered. "Of course."

Rose exhaled a relieved breath and slid down the wall to sit on the floor. "Thank you," he said. "Very much. Not just for now. For earlier. You were the only one who tried to help."

Her cheeks went hot with shame. She hadn't helped. She hadn't done anything. She'd just told him to run. Big deal.

"I should have done more." Without realizing, she once again reached for her pendant. Once again tapped her fingers together in the empty space where it belonged. "I wish I had. It was the right thing to do."

"Your pendant," he said. "Where is it?"

"What do you mean?" She'd never mentioned it to him. Never showed it to him.

"I've noticed it. You play with it all the time. But it's not around your neck, and I don't see it anywhere."

She considered lying but found she couldn't bring herself to lie to him. Not to those limpid green eyes. She told him how Jaron had taken it, trying to downplay the anger and sadness, but her voice cracked as she spoke, thinking of all the years she'd had it—her entire life as far as she knew—and Rose could tell.

"How long have you had it?"

Rose's voice snapped her back to the present. Just as well; the first thing they taught orphans was not to dwell on the past. "I don't know. I've always had it," she whispered. "*Always*. At the orphanage, they told me I had it when I came to them. Sometimes I had to fight off other girls when I was there. They wanted to steal it. There was even a . . ." She shuddered with memory. "One of the workers there always wanted it. Stared at it. Tried to take it off me one night while I was asleep." The pendant was the mystery of her life, the secret of her history. It was the one thing in the world that told her that maybe—just maybe—she hadn't been discarded as a baby. Maybe someone had actually cared about her. Maybe even loved her.

She drew in a deep breath and blew it out. Rose stared violence into the empty space off her right shoulder, as if imagining Jaron there. She'd never seen him so furious.

"My fault," Rose said. "This is all my fault." He gnashed his teeth in anger. "I should have—"

"Stop it. You couldn't have done anything. I chose to run after them; you didn't make me."

Rose considered this and seemed to relax a bit. "I'll get it back for you." There was a resolve in Rose's voice that startled her. "Don't worry. I'll get it back. Somehow."

She took a deep breath. Sure he would. What were the odds of *that* happening? "You have more to worry about than my pendant. The Bang Boys are one thing—they're just thugs. But what if Jaron got his father to sic the DeeCees on you? They could already be at your—"

And she stopped.

She realized she had no idea where Rose had been living all this time.

"Where have you been staying?"

"I've been all right. Don't worry about me."

"Don't answer me like that," she snapped. "What aren't you telling me?"

Rose looked down at his hands, as if only now noticing them. "It's difficult to explain."

She uttered a short, sharp laugh. "It's not like I can go anywhere. I have time."

He nodded slowly, then folded his hands before him, as though he'd been trying to figure out what to do with them. "I didn't apply for housing because they would have to register me with my brand."

"So?" She remembered seeing him by the river that first day. She'd thought he had no brand, but she'd been mistaken somehow—it was obvious and black against his skin right now, in the same place as everyone else's. Except for hers. He wouldn't let them scan him at L-Twelve, but that was just to annoy Jaron, right? He *had* to have been scanned for housing. There was no other way...

He shook his head. "It's complicated—"

She cut him off. "So you didn't get ID scanned at *all*?" Deedra's thoughts whirled. No ID scan...that meant he wasn't on any of the rosters. Not in Ludo Territory at least. How was he surviving?

He wasn't registered. It was impossible. Everyone was registered. That's how the system worked. That was how everything functioned, here in Ludo Territory. Maybe in other Territories they had a different system, but that didn't matter. People rarely crossed Territories, and, in any event, Rose was here, in Ludo, and he was flouting the rules in a way so illegal that Deedra couldn't even imagine the penalty. She'd never, ever heard of anyone going unregistered. At all. Not even for a day, much less the time Rose had been in Ludo.

"What have you done?" she whispered, covering her eyes with her hand. She would be an accomplice, most likely. That's how it would work, right? She had pulled him from the river. She had brought him into Ludo. And she was harboring him right now.

"Should I go?" he asked without recrimination.

Hell, yes! she longed to say. It was the only sensible thing to do, her only option. But he would be stuck outside after curfew, and his luck at avoiding being caught couldn't last forever. Kicking him out would be like delivering him right into the hands of the DeeCees. She couldn't do that. Not to Rose.

"No," she said quietly. "Don't go."

He favored her with a smile that she tried to ignore. It almost made her forget the danger they were both in. She had to stay focused. "Look, you're not from here. Maybe you should…" She didn't want to say the next bit, but it was for the best. "Maybe you should go back to where you came from. First thing tomorrow. It's dangerous for you here. Jaron—"

"I'm sorry to interrupt you," he said, "but I'm too tired to think straight. I need to sleep."

Deedra suddenly had trouble swallowing. *Sleep?* She knew what that meant. Sleep meant the bed. The bed meant…

He wanted to stay. Here. With her. All night. Of course. She wasn't thinking straight. Staying here after curfew meant he would *have* to be here all night.

And, yes, that was exactly what she wanted, too. If she was being honest with herself, she'd wanted it since she'd met him. *Family. Ha!* She wanted more than that.

Her eyes flicked to the metal flower he'd given her.

This. This moment, and all the others leading up to it. And the heat she'd craved, with no way to quench it. Now. Here. With Rose. Who could be so gentle. How could this be happening?

But he's a criminal.

Technically.

Technically *means he is a criminal.*

And I want him anyway. What is wrong *with me?*

"Of course," she heard herself say. "Yes, of course."

And Rose nodded gratefully, crawled onto her mattress, and, to her stunned disappointment, dropped immediately into a hard, oblivious slumber.

Deedra couldn't move. She couldn't believe it. He had actually gone to sleep!

Well, *of course* he had. She touched her scar. Who was she kidding?

Rose could be kind and Rose could be a friend, but the only person who might want her in that other way would be a molesting jerk like Jaron Ludo.

As the night darkened further, she wanted to scurry under the netting with him, lest the roaches begin to crawl all over her, but she settled for sitting on the floor near the bed, where she could watch him sleep, her knees drawn up to her chest. A strange smell filled the unit—something almost sweet. She thought maybe she had smelled it before, but she couldn't be sure.

Until she was.

On the rooftop. I smelled it there, with him.

Even stranger, where were the cockroaches? One or two huddled in the corner, nowhere near the usual numbers.

Is it Rose? Is he keeping them away somehow?

She chuckled under her breath. That was ridiculous.

Inside L-Twelve, the recycled air, the smell of the machines, and the face masks obscured the perfume. So did the mask she usually wore outside. But here, in her house...on the rooftop, maskless...

Rose's scent. *Smelled good*, the wiki had said.

Ha! She *was* losing her mind. Rose was Rose. He had nothing to do with some old flower that had never even actually existed.

Time passed. She sat in the dark. A bit of light seeped through the window, enough to cast the sleeping nook in a veil of gray gloom. She could make out Rose's form as he slept, the steady and unchanging rise-fall of his breath. Still, the roaches stayed away. Deedra's eyes grew heavy. Rose's breathing was like a mantra, lulling her.

And then she was running again. Running harder and faster than she'd run earlier in the day. Until black-armored soldiers with sheerglass helmet faces that shone like beetles in the lingering sun captured her and dragged her away with others. Lissa. Lissa's family. Dr. Dimbali and the Bang Boys. Even Jaron—even his father, Max—was not immune. They were all gathered into a tight knot of burbling panic and marched through a smog-filled valley to a building with a sign that read **PRIDE EXECUTION CAMP NO. 12**. Above, cigar-shaped vessels hovered in the sky. And aliens who looked like stretched-out people without noses or the black part of their eyes watched from balustraded balconies as the soldiers brought rifles to bear and with an air of bored contempt casually shot them all to pieces, one at a time, picking off fingers with precision, shooting off ears. It took long minutes for each person to die, and everyone was forced to watch in paralyzed horror.

"Just too many," someone said.

Occasionally, one of the aliens would applaud from the balcony.

Red Rain began to fall.

"Not air scrubbers!" Max Ludo shrieked. "Not air scrubbers!"

Even though she knew it was a dream, as she sometimes did when dreaming, Deedra was powerless to do anything to stop it. Try as she might, she could not bend the unreality of it to her will. She was stuck with no choice but to watch as those around her jerked and spasmed in bullet dances. She even felt a swell of pity for Jaron as slugs tore chunks from him.

No one should die like this.

That's what she thought—more accurately, that's what she *knew*—as the Red Rain spilled all around her, drenching her until the blood spatter from those around her was indistinguishable from the water. She thought maybe she saw God up there on the balcony, too, standing behind and slightly above the aliens. But she couldn't be sure because she didn't know what God looked like.

No one should die like this.

No one should *live* like this.

The yawning tunnel of a rifle barrel swung toward her, and she thought, *This is where I'll wake up*, but she didn't. The first bullet creased her scalp.

The second ripped through her scar, right where her neck and shoulder met.

She lost count, but she was pretty sure she didn't wake up until the fifth or sixth.

■ ■ ■

She was in her apartment, on the floor. Rose in her bed. She wanted to crawl under the netting and curl up next to him.

She was terrified to crawl under the netting and curl up next to him.

It would be safe there. For her. For him. For now. And maybe that was enough.

Sucking in a deep, heartening breath, she lifted the corner of the netting and slipped under. Normally, the bed would sleep only one; there was barely enough room for the two of them.

As long as they lay close.

She stared at him through the murk, focusing to pick out his features. His high cheekbones. His soft red lips. His wispy eyelashes, trembling slightly in her breath.

She flashed back to the moment across the river, the startling moment of understanding. Of yearning. It was natural, wasn't it?

It was wrong and wrong and wrong, but it was *right*.

She leaned toward him, his face becoming more and more distinct, then blurring at the closeness. Unwilling to close her eyes, she pressed her lips to his.

The perfume in the air intensified. She was awash in it, drunk with it.

Rose was the sweet smell of anything that wasn't garbage and steel. He was whatever lay beyond the sun and the clouds.

She pressed more firmly, closing her eyes, dissolving into the moment. It was so different from Jaron's kiss. She chased the comparison away, not wanting anything of Jaron to intrude on this moment. She let herself melt against him, into him.

When had it happened? When had she realized how intense her feelings for him were? Not by the river that first day, though it had surely started then. On the rooftop? Or maybe at L-Twelve, when he'd pushed her to think about the Red Rain, to question what she knew and what she thought she knew.

It didn't matter, she realized. Time was a fleeting thing, and it just didn't matter.

And Rose awoke, pulling back just enough to break the kiss, to break the moment.

Deedra's eyes snapped open. Rose stared at her with wonderment and intensity.

"Why did you do that?" he asked, his fascination terrified and childlike at the same time.

Deedra blushed and pulled away, scooting to the farthest reach of the mattress. She self-consciously ran her fingers along her scar. "I'm sorry," she said. "I didn't mean to...I don't want to make you uncomfortable."

"You didn't," he told her. "I just wasn't expecting it." He touched his fingers to his lips, gently, as though he expected them to be different. Fragile.

"I've never...Everywhere I've been, everywhere I've seen, no one has ever..." He was, for the first time, at a loss for words, his surprise and confusion and delight warring to express themselves on his face all at once. "I've never been, well, touched. Like that. Never felt such a..." He drifted off.

"Me, too," she said. Her body ached. It had a mind of its own; it surged toward him, and he backed away from her, curling into a tight ball in the corner.

Face flaming hot with rejection, she pulled away from him. "Fine," she said, more coldly than she'd meant. "I thought you wanted—"

"It's complicated," he said.

"No, it isn't. It's easy. You think I'm hideous. Join the club."

"No. No." He thumped the wall with his fist in frustration. "I can't explain it. It's not about you. It's about me. I'm worried for you. It may not be safe to be with me. Near me."

"Because of Jaron and the Bang Boys?"

"Not them," he said. "There's more."

"What are you talking about? Whatever it is, we can figure it out. Figure out a way around it."

He shook his head. "No. I don't even know where to begin."

"Are you…" She didn't want to think it, but it was the only thing that made any sort of sense. "You *are* a spy, aren't you? From Dalcord Territory."

"No."

"They sent you through Sendar to throw off suspicion. They removed your brand so that you could give yourself a Ludo brand and see what happens in our factories." *Stupid!* She was consorting with an enemy of the Territory. Worse than that, she *liked* it. He was dangerous and a criminal, and she barely even cared.

"No. Not at all. I'm not from Dalcord or Sendar. I don't belong to any Territory."

"That's impossible. Everyone—"

"Do you have a glass of water?" He rolled up his sleeves, revealing bare, slender, almost muscleless arms.

"Water," she said, disbelieving. "You want a glass of water."

"Please."

"Now? Right now? While we're talking about…" She sighed. "Fine."

She crawled out from under the netting to fetch him a glass of water. The meter warned her that she was near the end of her allotment for the month. She couldn't help noticing that the entire unit was suffused with the scent of the perfume now. The cockroaches in the corner had scurried off somewhere else.

She scooted under the netting and handed him the water. He hesitated.

"It's okay to drink," she assured him. "The filter is pretty new."

He ignored her, staring at the water, as if this glass of water represented the biggest decision of his life. Then, resigned, he brought it closer.

Deedra coughed a spasm of laughter when he didn't raise it to his lips but, rather, dipped his fingers into it.

"What are you—?"

"Wait for it," he told her. His voice was as quiet and gentle as ever, but there was a new firmness to it. A resolve. It was decisive.

She watched. In the murky gray, she saw something and realized it was a trick of the light. For a moment it had seemed that—

Her eyes bugged out as she saw it again. She leaned in close. Close enough to know that it wasn't a trick of the light.

The water level in the glass had dropped. And as she watched, it dropped farther.

"What in the world...?" Even as she said the words, the water dipped below half its volume.

"How...how are you doing that?" she asked. She stared as the water continued to drop. "It's some kind of trick, right?" Her eyes were at war with her brain; they insisted that what they were seeing was real, but her brain wasn't buying it. The back-and-forth paralyzed her.

The water. Was going. Away.

Where? Where was it going? How could he be doing this? A tube? But no—his sleeves were rolled up. Nothing there but skin.

The paralysis broke. Her eyes and her brain were still fighting, but now something more primitive had crashed through and galvanized her to action. She backpedaled away from Rose, her body moving without conscious direction until she collided with a wall.

Nowhere to go.

"What. Is going. On. Here?" she asked, pressed against the wall.

The glass was empty now. Rose's eyes shone as he handed it back to her. With trembling fingers, she accepted it. Stared into it. A few beads of water clung to the sides, but it was otherwise dry.

"I realize that what I'm about to tell you may be difficult for you to believe," he said. "Or even to understand, but..."

She held up the glass, incredulous. Her heart trip-hammered. Her brain said, *This is absolutely impossible,* and she wanted to believe that so badly, but she couldn't. She just couldn't. Because here it was, *right in front of her.*

"Here's the thing." He spoke with a quiet confidence made all the more frightening for its lack of bombast. "I'm pretty sure I'm not human."

PART 3

BY ANY OTHER NAME

CHAPTER 17

Without thinking about it, without actively making the decision, she grabbed his hand and pulled his arm to her, running her fingers from palm to elbow.

Dry.

Cool, dry, slightly rough. Nothing hidden. No moisture from decanting the glass drop-by-drop down his arm.

He had somehow—

(She couldn't think it. Couldn't let herself think it.)

—somehow—

(It was insane. It was too crazy even to think, much less say.)

—drunk the water with his fingers.

There.

"What *are* you?" she asked, and immediately regretted it when his face became crestfallen and abashed. Still, her sympathy did not keep her from backing away from him again. There wasn't much room and nowhere to go, but she at least could remove herself from his reach. All her internal alarms were screaming at her, but they had to struggle to be heard over the voice in her mind repeating, *This is* Rose. *This is* Rose. Over and over.

Rose was a friend.

Rose was a criminal.

Rose was a *friend*.

Rose was a...freak.

So are you, Deedra.

"What am I?" he asked quietly, then nodded as if to say, *That's exactly what I should have expected from you.* She half-anticipated his snorting and asking, "What are *you*?" in a snotty, almost-Jaron voice.

Instead, he folded his arms over his chest and leaned back, putting a few more inches between them. Deedra pressed herself against the wall. The corner was just inches away. Could she round the bend and get to the door before he leapt on her? Unlock the door and get out into the hall and...

And what?

Scream for help? Her neighbors would ignore it. No one would be foolish enough to open a door after curfew. Anyone out after curfew was, by definition, undesirable, if not outright dangerous. No help would come for her.

"I don't know *what* I am."

There was no recrimination or reproach in his voice. Just regret.

"I'm a freak," he went on, morose. "Like a blue rat. Like tooth-weed."

"No." She found herself probing at her scar without intending to. "You're a person."

"Am I?" he asked. "I knew early on that I was different. And that being different was dangerous. So I don't let people know." He hesitated just a bit. "Until I came here. And I learned I would need to have a brand to stay, so I..." He gestured to his neck. "But then I learned that *real* brands have circuits embedded in them. For scanning. So mine doesn't work. But I had to try because I had to come back. I had to stay."

"Why?"

"You."

Deedra softened, some of the tension bleeding from her. She didn't think someone planning to hurt her would sound so sad. Rose shrank against his wall, tucking in on himself as though he wanted to vanish into the corner, melt away.

"I didn't mean to scare you," he said. "I just wanted..." A shrug. "Never mind. I'm sorry. You should stay away from me. I'm not safe."

He said nothing more, simply leaned against the wall, ashamedly not looking up. She studied him, the angles of him. He took no glee in her fear. No sign of joy at her discomfort. There was only his own discomfort and maybe—beneath it—fear.

This isn't Jaron Ludo. It's Rose. Get past it, Deedra.

She understood now why he hadn't registered for housing or rations. Why he kept to himself, by and large. He was afraid. For all his strength and all his smarts, he was afraid. Of his difference. Of being targeted for something other than just his appearance and his mannerisms.

He can drink water with his fingers. That's weird, sure, but...

"Did it hurt when you branded yourself, or..."

"It's just...something I can do."

"Like sucking up water through your skin?"

"Like...like a bunch of things."

She thought of the alley he'd run down. The brick wall at the end. "What kinds of things?"

"No." He shook his head violently. "Too dangerous. I won't risk hurting you."

She counted off on her fingers. "You can...absorb water. Somehow. You can make your own brand. Again, somehow. You can jump over a thirty-foot wall—"

"I didn't jump the wall."

"Then what *did* you do?"

133

He shook his head again.

"Come on! Tell me! I want to know what else you can do. No one else is like you. You're amazing."

"I'm just doing what I'm able to do. There's nothing amazing about it. *Amazing* is when someone... when someone does something contrary to themselves. When they take a risk. Like... like you. That day," he said, "by the river? When we met?"

Her cheeks flamed. Now he was condescending. "If you could get out of the alley, you never needed my help that day. I risked myself for nothing."

"No, no!" he cried. "Don't be... don't be embarrassed. Did I do that to you? I'm so sorry. Deedra. Deedra, please look at me." He leaned in and cupped her chin, tilting her head. She locked with his green eyes and did not look away.

"What you did that day *was* amazing." He spoke with an earnestness she'd never heard before; its magnetism held her in place. "You don't understand—I thought I could get across just fine. But the river was more toxic than I realized. By the time I knew how dangerous it was, I was already halfway across and weakening quickly. You saved me.

"But even if I had been fine, you couldn't have known about my... abilities. You thought I would drown. And even though it was dangerous for you, and even though there was no obvious reward in it, you took a chance. To save me. To save someone you'd never met before. That's why I stayed. Why I went to L-Twelve. For you." He smiled and stroked her cheek. "I've walked this world for so long. I've seen the very worst of it. I've seen families kill one another. I've seen friends turn on each other. But I've never seen someone take a chance like you did. Selflessly. Just because."

They stared at each other. He moved closer, then pulled away.

Do it, she thought. *Kiss me. I made the move before; now it's your turn.*

She didn't know if her scar was covered or not, and for the first time in her life, it didn't matter.

She tilted her head up, parting her lips, and he sucked in a breath and then leaned away.

"We can't. I don't...I don't know everything I can do. By myself, it's one thing. But around someone else, I have to be careful. On alert. All the time. I might be dangerous."

Anything could be dangerous. The whole world was dangerous. But danger came from somewhere or from something. It was a part of the nature of a thing. Jaron was spoiled and corrupt, and that made him dangerous. Rats carried disease, and that made them dangerous. The water in the river was unfiltered and toxic. Tooth-weed could lie in wait, silent and still, then strike. So what could make Rose dangerous? What was in him that could threaten her?

"Everything can be dangerous. The question is how? So, how are you doing these things?" she asked. "Because maybe that will tell us how to avoid the danger."

"I don't know."

She goggled at him, not sure whether she was more astonished by his answer or by the infuriating, almost apathetic calm with which he delivered it.

"You *have* to know," she told him. "No one else can do what you do. There has to be some kind of an explanation—"

"Do you know how you walk?" he asked. Before she could respond, he went on: "Do you know how you breathe? How you listen? How you *think*? No. You just do these things. They happen when you need them to. And you don't question them." He shrugged. "It takes some concentration on my part, but it's still the same. I don't question what I do, either."

"Have you met others like you?" The thought was out of her mouth before she fully processed it. The very *idea* of more people like him, all with strange powers and abilities... It made her woozy again.

"No. Just me, as far as I know."

"How—"

"I really don't know." He didn't seem impatient or fed up with her questions. But he also, clearly, had nothing new to contribute.

She sat up, legs folded under her, and tried another tack. "Where do you come from? Before you were here, you had to live somewhere."

Again, he beheld her with that mix of eagerness, calm, and curiosity. "I don't know what it was called. My earliest memory is of rain."

"The Red Rain?" It spilled out before she could stop herself. That was ridiculous. He was too young to remember the Red Rain.

He considered it, though. "I don't know. I don't know how long ago it was. I was lying on the ground, and the rain was coming down. Hard, at first, then gentle. And I opened my eyes as it tapered off to nothing. There were stones around me. Tombstones."

Deedra shivered. A graveyard. In Ludo Territory, the dead were processed. The bodies were desiccated with a special dehydrating chemical, and then the dust was studied in labs as a source of DNA that scientists could learn from in order to figure out better ways to clone body parts and food. *From dust and death, food and life*, went the saying. Modern. Rational. Civilized.

But she'd heard of graveyards. In other Territories, human bodies were taken—whole and reeking—and buried deep underground. It was a waste of space, but it didn't stop there. Because after storing the corpses underground, they would then place stone markers over them, so that no one could doubt what lay beneath the surface. The idea of walking over dead bodies sent shivers from her neck down her back and arms. She was glad she didn't live in such a barbaric Territory.

"I woke up," Rose recounted, "and I began walking. Out of

the graveyard. Into the world." He paused. "And I suppose I'm still walking."

"Where was that?" She didn't know of any graveyards in any of the adjacent Territories. She tried to calculate how far he must have walked. . . .

"I don't know." Rose moved next to her and took her hand, squeezing gently. His cool touch comforted her, and she squeezed back. "I woke up and I walked. There was nothing else to do. It's not easy," he confessed. "Along the way, I learned to do many things to survive.

"There were flowers—roses—when I woke up," he said. "In the graveyard. A cluster of them, in mottled reds, oranges, and whites. They were beautiful. I didn't know what they were, then, of course. What they were called. I left them behind, but I have thought of them often. As I walked the world, I regretted not taking them with me. Eventually I learned what they were and took that name for myself."

"Because you're beautiful, too?" she blurted out, and immediately regretted it.

But if he was startled or put off by her blatancy, her forwardness, he didn't show it. Instead, he cast his eyes at the floor and blushed fiercely. "No. Because I didn't understand them, and I don't understand me, either. I saw them that one time and then never again. They seem unique."

Like me, he did not need to add.

He went to the window and looked out over the miserable, never-changing skyline.

"I've seen a lot." His voice fell into quiet sadness, as though sodden with memories. "So much. One time . . . one time, I spent a week walking through a city and never saw a single living thing. No people. No animals. No plants. Nothing. Concrete and steel and pavement and glass and metal. I walked seven full days, the empty buildings looming over me, the empty streets and sidewalks fanned out around me in every direction. And I saw no one."

Some impulse drove Deedra to approach him. She stood behind him, a hand raised, vibrating, desperate to touch, to soothe. Petrified.

"There was a space of ten miles or more that just burned," he went on. "I watched char and dust dance on the winds. Endless vistas of burning trash heaps, the sky blackened for days in every direction.

"I've seen people dying of starvation," he whispered. "I watched them collapse in the streets, heard the final hiss of breath. I've seen gang wars, rockets launched from window to window across the empty boulevards. So much empty space for such a crowded world, Deedra. People stay inside unless they have to be outside. They built this world for a hundred billion people, and now there are just half that. Have you ever thought of what might be under all that concrete and glass and steel?"

She hadn't. The concrete, glass, and steel had been there long before she'd been born, and there was no way of removing it. So what mattered whatever lay beneath?

While distracted with those thoughts, her hand, disconnected from her consciousness, came down on his shoulder. He didn't flinch. If anything, he seemed to relax into it, to lean toward her.

His reflection in the window was haunted.

"I've seen everything you can imagine and more, Deedra. But until recently, I'd never seen anything beautiful in the world, other than those roses. They were out of place. Like I am."

She waited a moment. Rested her other hand on his right shoulder. When he didn't move or speak, she came closer, pressing herself against his back. Gently. Not seeking him. Not looking for a return touch. Just letting him know: *I am here. You are not alone.*

"You're not out of place anymore," she said. "You have a place now. You can trust me."

We *are not alone.*

"I hope that's true." He nodded slowly, then sighed heavily. "Okay, you're right. I need to trust you. Are you ready?"

"What are you going to do?"

He inhaled deeply and turned to face her. "Stand back. I'm going to show you my biggest secret."

■ ■ ■

Before she could say anything, he held out his arms and grunted in pain and exertion.

Something shot from them.

Some*things*, really. Long, thin tendrils snaked out, jolting an involuntary yelp of shock and fright from her. She covered her face for protection, but the tendrils whipped around her, smacking into the wall.

Her eyes tightly shut, her heart pounding in her ears, she kept her hands over her face. When nothing happened, she splayed her fingers so that she could see. Rose stood against the other wall, the tendrils connected to him at his forearms, a mingled crestfallen and exhausted expression on his face.

"So now you know," he said, sadly. "I'm a complete freak. A monster."

She looked right. Left. A tendril was pressed to the wall on either side. Without thinking, she poked one with a finger. It was firm, smooth, and green in color. Like Rose's coat.

"What is it?"

"It's me, I guess. A part of me." He gestured and groaned with effort; the tendrils retracted into his arms and vanished. He turned to one side, not able to look at her. He was breathing hard, as if he'd run far.

Deedra blinked. *This is insane. People can't do things like that. It just doesn't happen. It just isn't possible.*

"Do it again," she heard herself say.

"What?"

"Yeah, you're a freak, all right. So am I. We'll be freaks together."

Rose's face erupted into the widest, most joyous grin she'd ever seen. He steeled himself, braced himself, and an instant later, the tendrils fired out again, but this time there were more of them, each one rooted at a different spot along his arms. Four struck out in her direction, each one deftly avoiding her as they surrounded her.

"Be careful of the sharp parts," he warned her through gritted teeth. She saw that studded along the lengths of the tendrils were conical protrusions, tough and pointy.

"How strong are they?" she asked.

"Hard to say," he said, fighting for breath. "Not easy to use, always. Takes it out of me. Have to work to keep them under control." Beads of sweat had collected along his hairline, wending slowly down his forehead and cheeks. "Especially around other people."

"Can you pick me up?"

"Too danger—"

"Stop saying that and just do it."

Then she felt them tighten gently around her, wrapping around her waist and upper arms.

She shrieked in terror, then dissolved into a choking fit of laughter. He would not hurt her, maybe *could* not hurt her.

His tendrils contracted and pulled her close to him.

Then Rose said, "Hang on..." and he strained, his expression mightily focused.

And Deedra caught her breath as she felt herself lift off the floor, her feet no longer solidly planted, her arms reflexively pinwheeling for balance.

"Stay still," Rose grunted. "I've never lifted someone before."

Stay still? Stay still? How could he ask that? She was *flying*!

She hovered near the ceiling. In disbelief, she stretched out a hand and touched it. Rose's tendrils wrapped delicately around her waist, her calves, her shoulders. Below, he gazed up at her. She grinned down at him. She felt weightless and free.

"This is amaz—" she began, but then Rose dipped her low and darted her back up to the ceiling with a mien of concentration. She whooped involuntarily, then shrieked with joy at the sudden rush.

"Again! Do it again!" Would her neighbors hear her cries? She didn't care.

Rose twisted his body. The tendrils shifted, and Deedra spun around the close confines of the room, the walls whipping by.

Outside. What would this be like outside?

Sky above. Ground below. So free. She promised herself she would find out.

There wasn't much room in her tiny apartment, but the ceilings were high. Rose used the vertical space as much as he could, running her through plunges and arcs and circles and spirals, adjusting the tendrils to turn her body this way and that. She supposed it should have been frightening, the lack of control she had. But her whole life had been about control. About the Magistrate controlling her with laws, Jaron controlling her with fear.

Controlling her*self* with fear.

And here, now, she had nothing to control. Rose flipped her upside down and spun her at the same time, and she laughed in pure, undiluted delight as her grimy, tiny room transformed into a wondrous silo of surprise and motion.

With another dip, something sharp stabbed her side. She tried to cry out, but her breath had fled with the bouncing in the air. Rose swept her in an arc around the room, and this time something gouged her leg.

Now she found her voice, screaming out in pain. Rose staggered, stumbled, and his tendril loosened. Before she could react, before she could even think, she was suddenly loose in the open air, captive of gravity once more. Her momentum flung her across the unit at dizzying speed.

Fortunately, she landed on the bed, crashing into it so forcefully that she ripped down the roach netting.

She lay on the bed for long moments, catching her breath, collecting herself. Her right shoulder, which she'd landed on, throbbed painfully, and her back felt wrenched out of place. She'd been cut up further by the sharp protrusions when she'd been flung across the room. Her pants were slashed, trails of blood leaking there. Not bad—shallow cuts, she could tell.

Rose stood by the window. His tendrils were gone, and he was pale, leaning against the wall for support. He looked horrified and exhausted and drained. And guilty.

"I'm so sorry," he said. "I knew this would happen. I knew it. I shouldn't have risked—"

"It was an accident, Rose. It's okay. I understand."

"No. No, I hurt you. I knew this would happen. I have to go."

She managed to haul herself off the bed, her back protesting. She interposed herself between him and the door. "You can't go. It's past curfew."

To her surprise, he didn't move toward the door. He opened the window instead. "Good-bye, Deedra."

Before she could move or speak or even think, he leapt out the fourth-floor window and was gone.

CHAPTER 18

Jaron sprawled on the massive bed in his personal suite. He was glad to be alone. Sometimes being a leader was nothing more than a headache. In fact, most times it was nothing more than a headache. He figured it was good to learn this now, before he took over the entire Territory.

And he *would* take over the Territory. His father would either give it to him, voluntarily, or Jaron would take it from him. With a threat no one could withstand, built under his father's own nose, in his father's own factory.

Spread-eagled on his back, one arm held up, he dangled the necklace he'd taken from Deedra. It quivered back and forth in time with his breath, sparkling in the dim light.

Staring at the pendant until it doubled his vision, he thought back to the moment he'd taken it. No, "thought back" wasn't strong enough. He relived that moment. He sank into, wallowed in it. The thrill he'd experienced when his hand closed around it, the charge that shocked his heart when he felt the necklace snap and come free to him, the look in Deedra's eyes—anger and helplessness and resignation.

Oh, that moment! That moment when he'd seen it, when he'd

realized what it was! The pattern, the size...a perfect match to something he'd seen before.

What were the odds?

He decided he didn't care. He'd spent his whole life trying to prove himself to his father, his whole life under that man's thumb. And now the universe was rewarding his patience.

He grinned.

Rose was still out there, of course. Rose, who was a witness to the incident on the rooftop. Rose, who seemed to think something was amiss at L-Twelve. And Deedra, too.

But she could be dealt with easily. And if Rose showed up again, well...this time, Jaron wouldn't give him the chance to run. This time, Jaron would overwhelm him with swift, unrelenting force.

Despite Max Ludo's fears, Jaron knew that he was strong *and* smart. He'd misplayed his last encounter with Rose, but he learned from it. Next time would be different.

A bleating chime interrupted his reverie. Someone was at the door. It was after curfew. Who could be out?

He knew the answer already: One of his idiot Bang Boys. Probably mistimed curfew and couldn't make it home. This happened at least once a month, one of those morons at his door, begging for a waiver or at least to crash at his place for the night.

Probably Kent, Jaron thought. Kent had rat turds for a brain.

Jaron hauled himself out of bed. Still, he would let Kent in. Because that's what leaders did—they protected the people who were loyal to them. Right?

Right.

He threw on a robe, tossed the pendant on a shelf, and went out into the main room. Mounted to the wall was a screen connected to the building's security grid. Jaron checked the cam feed. Most people didn't have security like this, but most people weren't the only son of the Magistrate.

Vaguely visible on the screen was a figure outside his door. The picture was fuzzy and pixelated, as always. He kept telling his father that everything needed to be upgraded. His father—when he bothered to respond at all—usually said, "The whole world needs to be upgraded, Jaron. Get in line."

Nice. Nice way to talk to his only son. When Jaron was Magistrate, he would run things differently. He would give people everything it was in his power to give. He would march on the Dalcord Territory and more than double the size of Ludo. His people would happily go to war for him; he would be beloved. With the resources of Dalcord and none of the people, he could make the new Ludo Territory a paradise for those who obeyed him.

He tapped the cam-feed screen, trying to zoom. Sometimes that straightened out the pixels. Not this time, though.

It wasn't Kent, that much was for sure. Kent's gigantic frame would have been instantly recognizable even through static and digital fuzz. Maybe it was Lio. Lio thought he was something special, a breed apart from the other Bang Boys. Always trying to curry favor with Jaron, always laughing too loud and too soon at Jaron's jokes. Jaron appreciated the attempt, but it had lost its luster a long time ago. Once, Lio would have been his second-in-command, his Vice-Magistrate, but the idea of hearing that hideous chuckle all day long…

The chime sounded again.

Screw it.

He thumbed open the door.

Oh.

"What are you doing here?" Jaron demanded. "And what the hell do you want?"

Other than some screams and the occasional whimper, it was the last sound he ever made.

CHAPTER 19

*W*hat are you? *Deedra asked, and a part of Rose winced and retreated at the impersonality of the question, at the stone-dead thud of the word* what.

But another, larger part of him admitted: *He had asked himself the same question over and over in the years of his wandering.*

What am I?

And it is this question, with its ineffable, undiscovered answer, and the horror of harming the one person who has accepted him that chase him through the night. Clouded, blank sky above and cooling ground below, he races to a familiar building.

Alone, there is no fear of hurting someone else, and he allows his tendrils to lash out. With light, elegant movements more akin to dance than to climbing, he rises higher until attaining the sole open window, his tendrils snapping silently into the dark, finding crevices and holds.

Inside, the man waits for him, lurking in darkness. Together, they slip into a hidden staircase, then down, down, down, into the basement, the way lit by handheld fluoro-tubes.

Soon Rose lies on the table again as his companion fusses with tools and wires and needles and scalpels.

"You're late tonight," the man says, annoyed.

"I spoke to her again," Rose says, staring up at the ceiling. He has become inordinately familiar with the intricacies of this ceiling over the past month. He knows every bend of every pipe, knows the shadowy junctures. A spiderweb glistens in one corner, a little larger each time he visits. He has never seen the spider that weaves this web, and he longs to do so.

"I see." The voice is a study in neutrality, but Rose is aware of the discontent beneath it. He does not want to fight—not now, not tonight, not with the scent and the heat of her still lingering—so he says nothing.

"What did you speak about? With the girl?" The tone has changed, just slightly. The discontent bleeds into resignation. There will be no fight.

"Me."

A pause, a surgical knife held just so. "Did you speak to her of the... work we perform together?"

Rose shakes his head. "I don't even know how to describe..."

"Best that you don't. People... need the familiar. They crave normalcy. If we were to tell people what we're trying to do, it could be disastrous. Do you understand?"

Rose understands, but he does not understand. More precisely, he understands the desire for secrecy, but not the need for it.

Still, he has traveled long and hard. He has suffered pain and longing and isolation for longer than he cares to remember. And though he does not care to remember, he has no choice but to remember, for memory is a tide, relentless and constant, its every ebb presaging a surge. He can forget his past for stretches of time, but always, always, it returns, washing against him.

"I just need someone to talk to sometimes," he says, knowing—even as he does so—that the response will be...

"You have me."

And then the scalpel comes down.

CHAPTER 20

In a filthy nighttime fog, Rose stands atop a building that overlooks Deedra's. He keeps watch there, gaze fixed on the black rectangle of her window.

He is troubled. By what he's done.

Good and evil, right and wrong, were easier concepts to grapple with when there was so little at stake. Alone on his trek through the world, he could decide what mattered and what did not with no fear of anger or reprisals or disapproval. The world had been so simple.

Simple. He'd told Deedra that the world was simple, and now he knows it is not. She brought warmth and compassion into his life, but she also brought complexity.

The line between right and wrong no longer seems as easy to discern. The world has gone as gray as the mist.

He's been trying to protect Deedra all along. From himself. From what he knew to be true. But Deedra doesn't need his protection. She survived this world for many years before he came along. She risked herself to pull him from the river.

She deserves the truth. All of it.

A wind buffets him; Rose anchors himself to the rooftop by wrapping a tendril around an old ventilation pipe. He perches there and settles his gaze on what he holds in his hand.

Deedra's pendant.

He whistles, but the sound does nothing to cheer him.

CHAPTER 21

She tended to her cuts—they were minor, not worthy of the guilt he'd felt and expressed—and managed to sleep. When she awoke, he was still gone. In those first muzzy moments of waking, she thought maybe he might have returned, entering through the window. But she was alone in a bed that, for the first time, seemed too big. She could have been disappointed or agitated.

But, instead, she found herself thrilled. She'd kissed him.

That kiss...it had been too short, and afterward they'd both been flustered and in shock, but it had been perfect nonetheless. The memory of it made her woozy, a pleasant and unpleasant feeling at the same time. She could replay the kiss too easily. She could feel his lips lingering on hers, long after the kiss had been broken. She wanted another. But who knew if Rose would even come back?

Optimism was hard to come by in Ludo Territory.

Until recently, he'd said. *Until recently, I'd never seen anything beautiful in the world.*

Did he mean...

He couldn't mean.

No, he didn't mean.

She touched her scar, wishing—as she often did—that she could sink her fingers into it, prize up an edge, then peel it all off. But she knew what lay beneath—blood and bone, not fresh, new skin.

If only it were that easy. If only you could tear away the old and the ugly and reveal something new and beautiful and perfect.

Like the City itself, maybe, and its broken, crumbling facade.

What lay beneath the buildings and roads of the City? If she could peel them back the way she wished she could husk her own skin, would the building equivalent of arteries and bones be revealed to her? Or was there something else under there? Something horrifying and deadly?

Something mysterious and grand?

Something beautiful?

It could be anything, she realized.

She'd spent her life in these buildings, on these roads, so certain that the Territory and the wider City and the Cities beyond were the same in every direction.

Never thinking to look *down*.

CHAPTER 22

She threw on her poncho, as always, and grabbed a sleeve of fruit discs to eat on the way. They were old, but fruit discs were genetically modified to last just short of forever. They'd be stiff but edible.

Air quality was mixed. She slipped on her mask, just to be safe.

She stood stock-still in the doorway. With reflexes born of thousands of repetitive days, she'd prepared for work....

But she wasn't *really* going to work today, was she?

It would be crazy to go to L-Twelve. She couldn't imagine what Jaron had in store for her, but it couldn't be good. He couldn't let her mingle with everyone else. Not now. She wasn't entirely certain he would kill her to eliminate one of the witnesses from the rooftop...but what else might he do? He could have the Bang Boys throw her out of the Territory, sure. He could trump up some kind of charge and have her arrested, even.

But she kept coming back to the easiest, most obvious solution. He and the Bang Boys had chased Rose down, and she didn't think they were just going to drag him out of Ludo if they'd caught him. It was wholly possible that Jaron had decided that the best, safest course of action was to kill Rose and her, after all. And Jaron, she knew, would do whatever was best for Jaron.

Meaning she should stay home, where it was—

Where it was no safer than L-Twelve. He could send the Bang Boys there just as easily as he could send them to the factory floor.

She was shaking. She took deep breaths and leaned against the doorjamb. What was the best move? She couldn't stay home. She couldn't go to L-Twelve.

Hide. She had to hide. But where? The Territory was empty and crowded at the same time. The empty places were just as dangerous as the full ones, maybe more so. She could stumble into a nest of tooth-weed and a death that would make her long for the Bang Boys and their pipes.

I have to leave, she realized. *I have to leave the Territory.*

It was a thought so huge and impossible that there seemed not to be room in her head for it. She couldn't just leave. It didn't work that way. She would have to cross the river into Sendar. No way she would go to Dalcord. And what would the people in Sendar think when she showed up with her Ludo brand? How would they treat her?

And what about Rose? She couldn't just disappear on him. . . . But hadn't he done precisely that to her? Was she supposed to stay in Ludo and hope he would come back? Or should she vanish into safety?

You have to figure this out, Dee. It's up to you. What are you going to do?

Maybe Jaron *wasn't* going to kill her. He could have done so yesterday, easily. Just as easily as taking her pendant. Maybe he would let her live.

For now. But once he became Magistrate, his power in the Territory would be complete. What then?

She would spend the rest of her life in Ludo wondering.

Self-exile? A life on the run in some other Territory? Or life here in Ludo, terrified and wondering? Both solutions sucked. There was no other way to put it. No matter what she did, she would be in danger.

But the danger in another Territory was hypothetical. The danger here was real.

She took off at a run toward L-Twelve. If nothing else, she had to intercept Lissa before she got there. So she could tell her best friend she was leaving, and why. She owed Lissa much, much more than a quick good-bye, but it was all she had to offer.

Deedra was halfway to L-Twelve when Rose appeared from nowhere, hustling up to her, grabbing her by the arm. It took her a moment to process him, to realize that it really was him, out on the street as though nothing had happened, as though nothing had changed.

"Act normal," he told her, and she laughed because she had no idea what the word meant anymore.

She slowed down, but only to about half speed, not a normal walking pace. "Normal? Are you kidding me?"

"No need to draw attention or act suspicious." As he said it, though, he darted his gaze around. It made him look completely suspicious.

"*You* act normal," she chided him. She dug out a fruit disc and handed it to him. Distracted, he stopped peering around like a fugitive and took it with one hand. At the same moment, he brought up his other hand, opening it.

On his palm lay her pendant.

Deedra gasped. Where the chain had broken when Jaron yanked it from around her neck, a little bead of resin—probably from a discarded ration pack—healed the breach. "Where did you—"

"Don't ask." He shook his head. "You don't want to know. Like I said, act normal."

"But—"

"I have something else for you, too." He looked around. "Not here, though. At work."

"Work? I'm not going to L-Twelve."

"Why not?"

She gaped. "We can't go there. Neither of us, but especially you. You humiliated him. He'll kill you."

"I'm not worried about Jaron," Rose said with brute confidence.

"He's the boss. And he's the Magistrate's son. He can do anything."

He cocked his head, a small smile playing at his lips. "Do you really think he can hurt me?"

"If you can do the...things you do, why didn't you stop Jaron and the Bang Boys yesterday? Why did you just let them chase you and hit you?" A bruise had formed overnight along his jaw, flaring tender and purple against his fair skin. "Was it worth it?" she asked.

He shrugged, scrutinizing the fruit disc, then gingerly tapped at the bruise. "It didn't really hurt me. And I guess it made them happy."

She wrinkled her nose. "Who cares about making them happy? They're *wrong.*"

"True. And they need to realize they're wrong. But if I overpower them and force them to stop, all they learn is to hate and be afraid of something stronger than them."

"If I were stronger than them, I would *love* for them to be afraid of me."

"And they would just exorcise that fear by bullying the people under them even more. And you would be no better than them."

As she considered that, they kept walking. It wasn't raining, but the humidity was high, sweltering. "It doesn't matter anymore. We can't go to L-Twelve. And you might not be in the system, but I am—I have to run. I don't have a choice."

"You don't need to run anywhere," he told her. "I'll protect you."

"I don't need your protection."

"You might be right. But you're getting it anyway." He raised the fruit disc to his nose and sniffed. His expression said it all.

Deedra chewed her way through a plum-melon disc. "They taste better than they smell," she confided.

"They would have to."

"Try it."

He sniffed it again, this time even more gingerly. The downturn of his lips was sad and hilarious at the same time. How could he have gone all this time without eating a *fruit disc*? They were one of the few food items the government had figured out how to mass-produce at the necessary scale. One of Deedra's first memories was tasting a fruit disc at the orphanage. (One of her *other* first memories was of spitting it out, but still.)

"I really can't," he said at last.

"It won't hurt you. Everyone eats them."

"No, I mean I can't. I'm sure it's... good." The disbelief written blatantly on his face made his lie funny, and they both laughed at it. The laughter was a relief and a danger at the same time, given the circumstances. "No, really! I'm sure it is! But I don't need this." He handed it back to her. "I take nutrients from the soil."

"You do *what*? From that little patch? You, what, absorb it through your feet or something?" She looked down, but Rose's feet were unremarkable.

He smiled. "There are some other spots, too. Not many." His expression, so mournful, made her think someone had died. Or, worse, had been hauled away by the DeeCees. "Everywhere I go, I find more and more of the world is dead."

"There are still people—"

"I'm not talking about people. I'm talking about the *world*. The earth. Things are bad."

"They used to be worse," she countered. "It's actually better since the Red Rain. There aren't as many people, so there's more room. More food. I read somewhere that it used to be so crowded that you couldn't even go outside without getting crushed or having someone try to steal from you."

"Where did you hear that?"

She shrugged. "Everyone knows."

"It used to be like that, true. Before the Red Rain. There were so many people on the planet that they had to cover the entire planet in buildings."

Deedra frowned. The entire planet *was* covered in buildings. That was just the way it was. There were once a hundred billion people living on earth, and the world was barely able to sustain that many. After the Red Rain, the population was cut in half, and there was more room. So much room that some days—like today—you could walk the street without being jostled or molested by a hundred other people along the way. On days when the Magistrate called for Territory-wide searches of apartments, though, the Territory overflowed with citizens camped out on sidewalks and streets, waiting for the DeeCees to finish conducting their investigations.

"Well," she said diplomatically, "it doesn't matter one way or the other. Things are the way they are. The Magistrate runs the Territory, Jaron and the Bang Boys do whatever they want...." She realized she'd clenched her fists in anger; her palms hurt and her fingers had gone numb. "And that's why we have to go away." It had been a pleasant distraction, talking to Rose, but it didn't change the concrete facts of her situation. She would run. She would forever surrender her rations.

"I'll end up scavenging all the time," she said. "It probably won't be so bad, I guess. Maybe it'll be better than the junk the government gives us." Even as she said it, the pasty aftertaste of the fruit disc seemed to linger overlong in her mouth.

"Once upon a time," Rose said slowly, "that's how it was. People didn't eat...this." He gestured to the fruit disc in her hand. "Genetically modified synthetics grown in a lab."

"What do you expect us to eat? Where else are we supposed to get food?"

"From the ground."

Deedra laughed. "You want us to eat concrete and pavement? Or that little bit of dirt?"

"That's not what…" He sighed. "Once, you didn't have to filter the water to drink it. People decided where they wanted to live and what they wanted to eat. And when."

"When was that?"

"Before the Red Rain. A long, long time ago."

Despite herself, she chuckled. "That's totally not true, Rose. It's always been like this, except for when it was worse. There's no point in fighting it."

"We're here," Rose said.

She gazed past him. Yes, they'd arrived. Lissa was nowhere in sight. Was she inside already?

If so, that was too bad. Because Deedra was *not* going in there.

"We have to go," she told Rose, backing away from the building. "I'm going. I'm leaving the Territory. I've decided. Are you coming with me?" *Please say yes. Please, please, please. I can do this alone if I have to, but I don't want to.*

Rose said nothing. He was staring up, not moving, a slip of green against the grayed white and beige backdrop of the Territory's buildings. The sun struggled through the clouds, and bands of dust-filled light strobed around him.

"Rose. Come on. Let's go."

He pointed above them. What seemed like an entire fleet of drones soared over L-Twelve. Deedra barely had time to take in their presence when they all screamed through their speakers with one voice:

"Lockdown!"

CHAPTER 23

"L ockdown!" the programmed voice commanded again, also blaring from speakers mounted high on poles along the street. The
sound was so huge and thick that it pressed against Deedra and nearly
knocked her over. She stumbled against Rose, who steadied her.

"Lockdown!" it blared again. "This is a lockdown!"

Lockdowns happened all the time, especially more and more lately,
as war with Dalcord seemed inevitable. There were lockdowns when a
group of scavengers from another Territory dared to cross the border.
When a lunatic with a homemade bomb threatened to blow up the factory. When a derecho blasted through the Territory, or when the rain
was too toxic to risk going out into it.

"This is a Territory-wide lockdown! All citizens remain in place
until released by the Department of Citizen Services or representatives
of the Office of the Magistrate!"

A Territory-wide lockdown was the most serious of all. Maybe the
Dalcord people had finally gone over the line, as everyone in Ludo
feared they would. Or maybe it was just the weather. At least once a
month, everything shut down because of drastic weather or dangerous
air quality.

"Get inside!" a voice shouted above the alert. "Now!"

It was Dr. Dimbali, standing in the door of L-Twelve, waving people in as they rushed past the scanner without pausing. He looked up to the sky, then back to the crowd gathered outside, hustling them inside.

"We have to go inside," Rose said. "It's safer there."

"No way. Not a chance."

"Deedra, don't be ridiculous. We have to get inside."

"But Jaron—"

"It'll be fine," he promised, and grabbed her by the arm, pulling her toward the factory.

Deedra wanted them anywhere *but* inside L-Twelve. Trapped in there for who knew how long, they'd be penned in with Jaron and the Bang Boys. Her stomach tightened as they got closer, and, without even trying, she began dragging her feet on the ground, resisting. Rose was right: Whatever was happening, they needed shelter and L-Twelve was the closest, but she still couldn't bring herself to go inside.

Ultimately, she had no choice. Between Rose's pulling and a press of bodies, she was unwillingly thrust through the door, tripping past Dr. Dimbali, who waited until everyone was inside before going in himself. He slammed the door shut and locked it.

"This is bad," she muttered to Rose. "This is not good at all." They were locked down with Jaron, with the man who had proved he would beat Rose with pipes, would chase him down in the streets. She wanted to shrink into invisibility, crushing herself down to vanish between the bodies around her.

Dr. Dimbali cupped his hands around his mouth and shouted, "Everyone please remain calm!" The buzz and burble of frightened voices did not abate. He shouted some more, but the overlapping echoes of frightened voices in the relatively confined space overwhelmed him.

As Deedra watched, he strode over to Lio and grabbed his pipe.

Then he slammed it against the floor twice, three times: *Clong! Clong! Clong!*

Now everyone paid attention. Breathing heavily from his exertions, Dr. Dimbali called out, "Please remain calm! We are well fortified here! Stay calm!"

Deedra wasn't sure of that. A lockdown was different from the shelter-in-place order that day by the river.

"Are you all right?" Rose asked.

"It'll be okay," she said with a confidence she did not entirely feel. "This happens sometimes. We just have to sit tight for a while. They'll update us. If it's weather, we're stuck here until the weather's over. If it's something else…" She drifted off. Was she trying to calm him or herself? If Dalcord had attacked, they could be stuck there for days.

Or they might not get out alive.

Or Jaron might…

She clutched her pendant, twice as glad that she had it back. One day of reaching for its ghost was more than enough. She raced it back and forth along its chain and stared up at Jaron's office.

As the alarms tapered off, L-Twelve grew quiet and still. Tension hung in the air like tattered cloth. Everyone was listening for whatever would happen next.

Nonchalantly, Deedra sidled into place at her favorite workstation and focused her attention on Jaron's office: He wasn't in it.

Relief flooded her. Jaron wasn't here. Good. And maybe that meant the lockdown was a drill. If Jaron had known about it in advance, he might have stayed home, rather than be stuck all day at the factory. Jaron's air scrubbers had to be top-notch; he would be much more comfortable at home than at L-Twelve.

She murmured, "Jaron's not here," to Rose, then sought out Lissa in the crowd, finally spotting her in the back of the building, pressed into a corner. They signaled to each other that they were each all right. Lissa shrugged as if to say, *Sorry I'm all the way back here.*

Rose nudged Deedra and pointed out Kent Massgrove, who was glaring in their direction. "I think we should get out of his line of sight."

She agreed. The Bang Boys would be distracted by the lockdown for a little while, but then who knew if they would take advantage of it to mete out what they perceived as justice for the previous day's humiliation. Without Jaron, it could go either way.

Taking Rose's hand, she dragged him back toward the relief room, where people took their ten-minute break each shift. Together, they huddled in a corner.

"Look, there's something I need you to have," Rose told her, speaking very quietly, making certain no one else could hear.

"What?"

"It's a long story," he told her. He reached under his coat and—after glancing around to make certain no one was watching—pulled out a flat, somewhat thick rectangle. He handed it to her, sure to keep it between them so that no one else could see it. "I want you to know everything I know, Deedra. I want you to learn what I've learned."

The object felt old and fragile but still substantial. It had the surface area of a tab but was much thicker and heavier.

"It opens," he said, and she realized it did. It was somehow hinged on one edge, then open on the other three. She peeled back the stiff outer covering to discover words: *This Side of Paradise*. Reflexively, she tapped the words, but nothing happened.

"It doesn't work like that," Rose said, chuckling kindly. "It's not electronic. It's a book."

"What am I supposed to do with it?"

"Keep it hidden."

"Why? Is it illegal?"

"I don't think so. But it's different. I don't want someone to take it from you."

"Would that be bad?"

"Well, it's for you. Not for someone else."

A book. She'd heard of books, of course—the wikinets were full of them, diatribes about politics and the war and DNA recombination and the Red Rain. This didn't look anything like a book, but she took Rose's word for it.

The lockdown siren blasted again. She winced into its intensity.

"The Territory-wide lockdown is over," said a different voice. She recognized this one as the voice of L-Twelve's systems. "Lockdown is now isolated to this building. Please turn your attention to the nearest screen."

"Something's happening here," she told him. "Probably a bomb threat. That happens sometimes."

Out on the factory floor there was a large screen mounted up near the catwalk, for instruction and directions. The relief room had a smaller one, and they turned to it as it flickered on.

Deedra was shocked to see Max Ludo's face appear. It was cracked and offset from the broken display, but it couldn't have been anyone but Max. Father and son shared the same gray eyes and the same cruel twist of a mouth. Max was Jaron in fast-forward, with the dew of success and power clinging to every wrinkle and the hollows of his cheeks.

"I am speaking to you personally," the Magistrate said, his measured voice rebounding and echoing from the display and the speakers on the factory floor, "because of a great personal tragedy. . . ." He paused and growled at someone off-camera. "No. Not like this. Go to hell."

He leaned forward, his lips trembling and his eyes flaring with rage. When he spoke this time, his voice was laden with grief and injustice. "Listen to me, you little puke-ants, you ungrateful dung-dwellers.

One of you murdered Jaron. We believe it's someone in this building. Troops will interrogate everyone within, and believe me, whoever is responsible *will* be found." Max ground his teeth together with an animal ferocity. "If I have to haul each and every one of you into SecFac and cut your fingers off one at a time, I will! I will!" He was ranting now, pounding a fist on the desk before him. "My advisers tell me I should offer you little rat-chasers a *reward* for information about the killer. A *reward*!" His voice—usually deep and commanding—pitched high and quivering with uncontrollable rage. "I'll give you a reward! If you didn't kill him, you *get to live another day*! And if you killed him, I will personally rip your heart out and shove it right! Up! Your! Ass! Your family will eat *cement* for a month!" Spittle flew from his lips and spattered on the camera as he ranted.

"Show them!" he bellowed. "Put the picture up! Show these animals what one of them did to *my* boy!"

Heaving his breath, he waited a moment, then screamed to someone off-camera, "Don't give me that crap! Put it up! Now!"

The screen shifted to a static image. A bed. A body lay on it. Deedra recognized Jaron immediately. He was naked from the waist up, and she couldn't not recognize that tattoo—the starburst. Until she saw the picture, she hadn't believed he was actually dead. Even Max Ludo's outburst hadn't convinced her. But the picture left no doubt. What would be the point of faking this?

Jaron's body was twisted out of proportion, limbs turned in ways limbs had never been designed to turn. He looked *squeezed*, as though a giant had picked him up in its massive hand and crushed him to death as he struggled.

Lacerations raced up and down his flesh, strips of skin hanging, a map of blood chiseled into him. Somehow, the worst part was that Jaron's eyes (well, the one eye visible in the picture at least) were still open, staring emptily.

It was bloody. It was terrible. Yes. But her tormentor was dead. She felt guilt and relief at the same time.

Next to her, Rose drew in a startled breath, and his grip tightened.

And she really *looked* at the image. Looked beyond the body, which had so commanded her attention.

Something green and sinuous and studded with wicked projections lay entwined around Jaron's lower leg, as though it had slipped down. In the upper left corner of the image, another, similar length of *something* lurked there.

Something? Who was she kidding? It wasn't *something*.

It was a tendril.

■ ■ ■

The feed cut away to a black screen with the logo of the DCS and the words:

YOUR ASSISTANCE IS MANDATORY. THANK YOU.

"Put that away," Rose murmured. The book. He was talking about the book. She slipped it under her poncho, into her waistband, not even feeling it go. Her muscles had gone slack, her fingers numb. "No one can change what's in there," he whispered. "It's permanent. It's not like online, where people just say whatever they want and it gets all mashed up. This is the truth. This is real history."

What was he *talking* about? Who cared about his stupid *book* right now? Jaron was dead, and it was obvious who had killed him. "I can't believe you did it," Deedra said, her voice pitched low. "You killed him!" The idea thrilled and terrified her. Jaron's death was a gift and a horror at the same time.

"I didn't."

165

She didn't believe him. It was almost impossible that he hadn't. *He had the pendant.* Where else would it have come from, if not from Jaron?

Oh, God, she thought. And she remembered what he'd said to her the other night.

Have you killed?

Many, many times.

And then he'd talked about bacteria and insects, but when she'd asked if he'd killed a person, he hadn't said *no*, she realized.

I don't make that distinction, he'd said.

"Did. You. Do. It?" she asked. Along her leg and side, the places where he'd cut her the night before itched and throbbed. Moments earlier she hadn't felt them at all. Now it was as though the rest of her body had gone numb and she could feel only those cuts.

"I swear, no."

"You saw the picture. Those tendril things looked like, like…like *you*. He was cut. That's like—"

Voice urgent and huskier than normal, Rose grabbed her by the shoulders and locked eyes with her. "I *swear*, I didn't do it. I could have, but I didn't. I don't want to *hurt* people, Deedra. I want to *learn* about them. Learn *from* them. And maybe fix things for them, if I can."

"You can't fix the world. I told you—it's always been this way." She shook him off. "And stop trying to change the subject!"

She glanced over to the others in the relief room. No one had taken notice of them yet, but that wouldn't last. She imagined the misery headed toward them right at that moment. It would take hours to interrogate everyone, and in that time, no one could so much as open a—

The door opened. Two beetle-helmeted DeeCees stood there. It was Deedra's dream come to life, and she realized she was crushing Rose's hand. His expression remained blank, impassive.

"You." One of the DeeCees pointed to Rose. "With us."

Rose gently extricated his hand from Deedra's. "Don't worry," he told her, and she suppressed a horrified burst of laughter. *Don't worry.* He was telling *her* not to worry? He was being hauled off by the Dee-Cees! *She* should be telling—

He disappeared out the door, flanked by the DeeCees.

But there were two more standing there, as if one of the L-Twelve machines mass-produced them and conveyored them in.

"You."

The DeeCee was pointing at Deedra.

"With us."

CHAPTER 24

They took her to a small office off the catwalk, not to Pride Execution Camp No. 12. But they both had sidearms at their hips and rifles slung over their shoulders, and she would be just as dead no matter the location. It had taken half a dozen bullets to shock her from dream to waking; how many would it take to shuffle her off from life to death? On the way, her body had begun tingling all over, that strange pins-and-needles sensation she sometimes got when a limb fell asleep, but this time it was over every inch of her. Her ears filled with static, and her vision flashed orange, pixelated.

Somehow she managed to keep walking, managed to keep time with the DeeCees on either side of her. She'd never been so close to them before, having seen them only from a distance. They usually stayed out of sight, patrolling remotely via the drone army. Their body armor clicked as they walked, and she thought that if she had to listen to that clicking all day, she would go mad. She'd watched them quell the food riots two years ago from her window, occasionally catching a burning, throat-charring whiff of suppression gas. They'd used plastic bullets to stun, not kill, but the bullets sounded just as loud when fired and made a peculiar, thwacking sound when slamming into human flesh.

The room was nearly lightless. It had no windows, only dirty, cracked glass panels to view the factory floor. One of the DeeCees lowered the blinds to close off the room. The other guided her into a chair on one side of a table pitted and scarred from years of abuse. An old-fashioned electric light flickered from a table lamp. The DeeCees said nothing; they took up positions flanking the door.

Gradually, her body came back online, sensation returning first to her toes and fingers and the tips of her ears, then to her limbs and, finally, her chest and core. Her hearing fuzzed and sparked until she took deep breaths. When the rushing in her ears subsided, the silence in the room was *loud*.

Her vision came back last, resolving from pixels and bumps to the real world just as the door opened and a man in a suit walked in.

Other than Dr. Dimbali, Deedra had never been this close to someone wearing a suit in her life. The elbows shone with age, and the cuffs were frayed, but it was higher quality than anything she owned. The tie knotted around his neck looked extremely uncomfortable; she thought of Rose's vine things encircling Jaron's neck. And crushing.

She thought of the vine things around *her*. Thought of being slashed and thrown across the room. Had he? Had Rose killed Jaron?

"You okay?" the newcomer asked as he sat across from her.

Did he actually care? It seemed like a trick question: How would a guilty person answer? How would an innocent person answer? More important: Which was she?

She didn't know.

"I'm scared," she said quietly. There seemed to be no shame in admitting it and no point in denying it.

"I'm Top Inspector Jona Markard," the man in the suit said, studying his tab and ignoring her answer. The back of the tab was scratched and dented. There were worn-in smudges where he held it. It was probably only ten years old. He pointed its camera at her, and she automatically turned and bared her shoulder to give it a shot at her brand. "Ah. And you are…" *Flick. Flick.* The tab snapped away, and Markard studied it for a moment.

He looked up at her. "Deedra, right?" He smiled, but there was no mirth there, no warmth. It was purely exercise for his facial muscles.

"Yes." She didn't intend to whisper, but that was how it came out.

"Deedra…Ward?" The smile went away. "Orphan, then?"

"Yes." A little stronger this time. What did they do to conspirators? She usually didn't pay attention to Territory crime reports. Too depressing. Didn't matter in this case—this was the murder of the Magistrate's only child. The usual laws and rules didn't apply.

TI Markard nodded and put down his tab, then he leaned forward on his elbows. He had one blue eye and one green eye, and his hair was cut short, cropped almost to the scalp. So short that it could have been black or brown or gray, but it was impossible to tell. He had a tattoo of a complicated knot of arrows arrayed around his brand, picked out in shades of green and blue.

He had very long fingers, which he steepled as if building a tunnel between them, a tube to gaze through. Into her eyes. Through them, maybe, to her brain, to her mind, to her secrets. Once upon a time, she'd had no secrets. Now she did. Rose, out after curfew. Rose, who could do impossible things.

Rose, who had brought back her pendant from a corpse.

"You're not under arrest, but I'm going to read you your rights anyway. Just so you know them." He recited them from memory. Deedra barely heard. Right to speak in her own defense. Right to say what she wished and have it recorded. And so on.

"This is going to be very simple, Deedra." Markard had a marvelously deep voice, unnaturally so. It was distracting. "Very simple. Do you know anything about the murder of Jaron Ludo?"

She tried to swallow, but her throat locked up; and even though her lips moved, nothing came out.

"There's no reason to be anxious." He said it without grace or charm. Just plain fact. "Let me explain the situation: If you know nothing, then that's that. You know nothing. And you go home."

Now he flattened his hands on the table. Nothing obstructing her view of him. Those mismatched eyes consumed her, threw her off balance.

"But if you do know something, well...we'll figure it out. Even if you lie to us. Because that's what we do. We learn things. So it's better not to lie in the first place. Understand?"

He smiled again. It was the same smile. As though he had a pile of them and plucked one out and slapped it on when he needed it, then threw it away when he was done with it.

"I understand."

"So I'll ask you again: Do you know anything about the murder of Jaron Ludo?"

Did she? She couldn't be sure. Was a bad image on a broken screen evidence? Had she really seen the tendrils?

And did she *know* Rose was involved? It made sense that he was, but he said he wasn't. So it could go either way.

Any of them could be true, Caretaker Hullay had said. *You have to decide which one you believe.*

She straightened in her chair and looked Markard squarely in the blue eye. "I don't believe so," she said.

He nodded and consulted the tab again. It had shut down while they spoke, and he fiddled with it for a few moments, rebooting it and finding his documents again.

"Tell me, Ms. Ward: Where were you last night after curfew?"

Despite herself, she choked out a laugh. Where *was* she? Where was she? At that time? Where was *everyone*?

"Home. At home."

He nodded, pleased. "Yes, you were. Your building system logged you in and you never left, obviously. Heat sig shows you at home all night." He turned the tab's screen to her. It took her a moment to realize what she was looking at: a 3-D infrared heat map of her apartment, mostly bluish-cold, with a curled bundle of yellows, oranges, and reds off to one side.

Her. Sleeping.

She'd always known that the Magistrate had this capability, but seeing its fruits made her shiver, raised goose bumps along her arms. The heat pattern was blurry and indistinct, but it still felt like seeing herself naked in public.

"What I'm trying to say, Ms. Ward, is that we know you were not directly involved in the death of Mr. Ludo. No one is saying that."

Heat map of her apartment...Did they have a similar map from earlier? When Rose was there? How much did they know?

"What we're trying to determine is this: Do you know anything about it?"

"I don't believe so," she repeated.

He smiled his fungible smile. "Of course. We've established that. But you may know things that are relevant that you don't realize are relevant. So." He flicked and thumbed the tab a bit, then showed her the screen. It was a picture of Rose. The effect it had on her was instantaneous and shocking; she fought gamely to suppress the gasp that wanted to claw out of her throat, to resist the tears. Desperate, she faked a coughing fit.

"Could I get some water?" she asked.

"Do you know this boy?"

It was pointless to deny it. Half of L-Twelve had seen them together. "Yes."

"How well do you know him?"

Bravery was a funny thing. Bravery and foolishness might not have been twins, but they were certainly siblings, siblings alike enough that oftentimes it was difficult to tell one from the other, even when viewing them up close, as now. Was it brave or foolish to say that Rose was one of her only friends, that he understood her, that they'd spent that day atop the abandoned building talking? That he'd been to her apartment and had been infuriatingly gentlemanly enough not to take advantage, even though she wanted him to? That he'd defended her from Jaron and that she'd done the same for him?

Jaron. That brought her back to the moment.

"He's a friend of mine," she said, "but you know that already."

"We do, indeed. What do you know about him?"

I know he can scale walls with his tendrils and lift me up and spin me around, that he doesn't eat food and he's named for something beautiful, and he is beautiful, but you don't care about any of that.

"Not much," she said. She wondered if she should explain how Rose had come to Ludo, but she figured that story should go untold. "He works hard. Learns quickly. He's still settling in."

"Do you know where he's from?"

"Sorry?" She could muster only the single word. Most of her energy went into trying to keep her face placid and unrevealing.

"We suspect he's from another Territory. Now, it isn't illegal to move among Territories, but most people don't bother. Unless they have a compelling reason. Like, say, being wanted for a crime in their home Territory. Do you know where he's from, perhaps?"

She resisted giggling. What would Markard say if she told him, *Well, he's from a graveyard nowhere near here.*

"He never said." She shrugged. "He's quiet. He doesn't talk a lot."

"I understand that yesterday Mr. Ludo and his floor supervisors got into a fight with this Rose boy. Over an issue of clothing and line safety. Everyone saw."

"Well, yes. Jaron started it."

"Are you sure about that?"

She thought back. Yes, of course she was sure about that. Rose had even taken a punch to stop the fight. "Yes. Jaron started it. Him and the Bang—him and his friends." She didn't know if Markard would know that everyone called Jaron's lieutenants the Bang Boys. Probably. He seemed to know everything. "They would have really beat him up if Rose hadn't run away."

"Sounds pretty bad."

"It was. He had a bruise and everything." Let Jaron's brutality take a little of the heat off Rose.

"So the kind of thing someone might seek revenge for, then." It wasn't a question. Questions weren't offered up with a tone of triumph and another interchangeable smile.

"No! That's not what I—"

But Markard just stood up. "Please wait here."

He left her there alone. Except for the DeeCees.

Which was really the same thing.

■ ■ ■

There was no clock in the small room, so Deedra had no idea how long Markard was gone. When he returned, there was something energized and excited about him, as though he'd learned a secret he just *had* to tell, damn the consequences.

"Well," he said gleefully. Still, his smile didn't change at all. Deedra wondered if there was something wrong with his face. "Well, well, well." He sat down across from her again. "Given that you call him a friend, Deedra"—she was no longer Ms. Ward—"you don't seem to know much about this Rose person. So let me tell you a little bit about him. A little information we've just picked up."

What was he getting at?

"We scanned his brand. Brands are unique, Deedra. They look the same to you and me, but they have microscopic circuitry embedded in them."

She knew that already. That was one reason why her brand couldn't be overlaid on her scar—the scar tissue resisted the implantation.

"When we scanned Rose's brand, guess what came up?"

She had an idea, but she couldn't let on. "What?" she whispered, mouth dry, voice trembling slightly.

"Nothing." He put a hand palm-down on the table between them. The motion was somehow threatening. "Nothing at all. Not *nothing* as in *no data*. *Nothing* as in *no circuitry at all*. It was like scanning a wall. His brand is fake, Deedra. Burned it into his own flesh himself. He duplicated a legitimate Ludo brand. That's not just a crime, it's supposed to be impossible."

She said nothing. Markard nodded and went on.

"The branding equipment is kept under careful guard. There are technicians trained to use it. It produces a brand that is precise down to the micron. Do you know how Rose could have duplicated that?"

She didn't. Or maybe she did. She imagined the water leaving the glass, the tendrils lifting her into the air. Who knew what else Rose could do?

"We suspect he's working with Dalcord forces. That he was branded using stolen equipment and sent here as a spy. To observe our manufacturing capacity. To learn our strengths and weaknesses."

No. Not true. She'd asked him, and he'd said it wasn't true, and she believed Rose more than she believed TI Markard.

"This is what they do, Deedra," he said gently. "They infiltrate. They're trained for emotional warfare. I've seen it before. You know how they do it? They pretend to be weak."

Deedra tried not to listen to him, turning away from him, but his words scored. She thought of the day by the river. Of Rose flailing.

Needing help. But…but he'd never *really* needed her help, had he? Even with the river being toxic, with what *he* could do…

"They play on your compassion," Markard went on. "On your insecurity. They find your weakness, and they tell you it doesn't matter to them."

Involuntarily, her hand crept to her scar.

They shouldn't treat you like that, Rose said that time on the rooftop. *And you shouldn't believe them.*

She closed her eyes. Gently. Too tight and tears would leak out, and she couldn't let him see them. She breathed in deep, settling herself. She couldn't show weakness. Not now.

"They become your friend. They tell you secrets, Deedra. You know why? Because then it seems like they trust you. And the way people think, the way we are, if someone trusts *us*, then we tend to trust *them*."

"Some of these spies," Markard went on, "may even have been genetically manipulated. It's illegal to do that, but do you think the Mad Magistrate cares about Citywide law? There have been rumors that he's using DNA recombination on his soldiers, prepping them for war."

And she thought of the tendrils, of Rose's strength, of the way he feared his own body. The air fled Deedra's lungs in a whoosh as physical as it was audible. She tried to inhale, tried to reclaim the air, but none would come. Gripping the edge of the table with both hands, she stared down at her knuckles as they gradually whitened. The tingling was coming back, the roar in her ears, the narrowing and pixelation of her vision.

He'd lied.

No. No, it couldn't be.

But her body believed it. Her body rebelled against her mind. Shutting down.

A spy. He'd denied it to her, but then Jaron had been killed. He'd murdered Jaron. . . . Too much of a coincidence to believe otherwise.

The proof lay against her chest, under her shirt, nestled in the crook of her breasts, where it had been her whole life except for one night, except for the night it had been in Jaron's possession until Rose brought it back to her, until Rose reclaimed it, and how did he do that? He never told her. How did he bring it back to her? How did he get it back if not by going to Jaron and shooting out his tendrils, the ones granted to him by Dalcord's scientists, and folding them around Jaron the way he'd folded them around Deedra; but this time, this time he hadn't even tried to be gentle. No, this time he'd been brutal, and he'd squeezed and squeezed and squeezed. . . .

No. Don't believe it. If you don't believe it, it's not true. That's what Caretaker Hullay said, right? Many truths. Decide which one you believe. Decide.

She couldn't. She knew she didn't *want* to believe Rose had killed Jaron, but there could be no other explanation. It was time to open her eyes to the truth.

Rose was the only person she knew who could do the things he did. Maybe somewhere out there, there was another Rose, but the odds of *both* of them being in Ludo Territory? That was too absurd even to dignify with a thought.

"It seems as though your *friend*"—he came down hard on the word—"was involved in some sort of skullduggery. We think his identity was uncovered by Jaron. Or maybe he was blackmailing or extorting from Jaron to some effect. That's damn close to an act of war—" Markard broke off, as if woken from an embarrassing daydream. "Never mind. Look, we know that Rose never applied for housing, so that means he would have been out after curfew last night. The only one in the Territory capable of killing Jaron Ludo. It's cut and dried."

Then why did you have to interrogate me? she thought, and then realized: *Oh. Because they wanted to see if I was involved. If he had an accomplice.*

"I think you can go now, Ms. Ward." She had come to hate that smile. She wanted to put her fist through it. "You're not planning on leaving the Territory anytime soon, are you?" He chuckled at the impossibility of it.

"No."

"Very well, then. Please be careful on your way home."

■ ■ ■

Deedra's legs barely worked as she shuffled out of the room, past the DeeCees, and down the stairs to the factory floor. Dr. Dimbali was announcing that everyone who had not yet been interrogated should remain on the main floor. Everyone who had been interrogated should leave. L-Twelve would reopen in the morning.

She stumbled on the last step. It wasn't numbness this time; it was weakness. She felt drained and picked over. Scavenged of all her vitality, as though a tiny Deedra had scrambled in and around the muscles of her body, stealing them and stashing them away for later. She felt a kinship with tiny Deedra; *we do what we do to survive.*

Bracing against the wall, she paused for a moment, gathering her wits and her strength. Literally and figuratively, she did not know her next step. Was it safe for her in Ludo now that Jaron was dead? Now that Rose was exposed? Would Rose tell the DeeCees that she'd helped him? Should she still run? Forget about Rose and run?

She touched her pendant. *Ha. Forget him? Right.* Every time she touched the pendant now, she would think of him.

But what do I do right now?

A babble of overlapping voices assaulted her.

"—*killed* him!"

"They told me that—"

"I always knew that there was something—"

"—earlier curfew from now—"

She closed her eyes against it, but she couldn't close her ears.

"Just gross. *Squeezed.*"

"—did you see—"

"There was blood on the sheets—"

"—bet he was *shredded*—"

"Brutal, man."

"—slaughter."

Her pendant offered no respite, no refuge. She dug the nails of one hand into the tender flesh of her other lower arm. The shock of pain snapped her eyes open, and Lissa stood before her, as though conjured.

"Lissa," she whispered, and without thinking she hugged her tightly. "Lissa..."

So many things she wanted to say. The moment cramped with them; they collided against each other and caromed off to places where she could not follow before ricocheting back too quickly to be spoken. Instead, they just clutched each other, submerged in the thrum of bloody talk on the factory floor, keeping each other's chins above the waterline.

"He's really gone, isn't he?" Lissa said.

"Yes."

A pause. A strain.

Lissa put her lips directly on Deedra's ear and whispered so softly that Deedra could barely hear her:

"*Good.*"

Deedra scanned the area around her. She half-expected TI Markard to show up and arrest Lissa for sedition and Deedra for conspiring.

How could Lissa actually be *happy* that Jaron was dead? Sure, he was the boss and the son of the Magistrate. And he threw his weight around with or without the Bang Boys, but to wish him dead...Deedra had her own reasons for being relieved, but Lissa was just being cruel for no reason.

"Be careful what you—" Deedra started and never finished because just then a door up above exploded open with such force that those nearby screamed, a wave of terrified falsettos rippling out from the epicenter. The door hung off its jamb, held by a single hinge, and before Deedra could process what was happening, Rose flung himself through, his green coat flapping behind him, his body a blur of motion.

He moved like a darting insect, his lithe form skipping around stunned, frozen workers. He was airborne, almost dancing along the crowd, touching down lightly and just long enough to push himself up again, racing along the open air above the throng. So swift was he that no one had time to react until he had already pushed off and moved on, scrambling down the stairs to the main floor with such speed that the space in his wake became a bustle of too-late pushes. Deedra and Lissa jumped out of the way as he blew past them.

"How is he *doing* that?" Lissa's voice was still at a whisper, but a louder one. She disentangled herself from Deedra and stared, agog, at Rose.

Before Deedra could answer—and what would she say, anyway?—a cluster of DeeCees trampled after him, with TI Markard at its center. "Stop him!" Markard screamed over the noise. "Bring him down!"

Rose scampered over the tops of the workers, now grabbing a light fixture overhead and swinging himself farther along. He had only a few more feet to go, and then he'd have clear floor and—Deedra checked behind herself—one more door to get through before he could make it outside.

Once he was outside, she knew, nothing could hold him.

But the door behind her opened, and more DeeCees were there. More DeeCees than she'd ever seen in her life, even during the riots.

Rose didn't stop. He hurled himself to one side and bounced off a wall, sending himself hurtling in the opposite direction so quickly that by the time the DeeCees lunged at his old position, he was already on the other side of the room.

"Stop that kid!" Markard yelled from halfway down the staircase. "Permission to open fire!"

Deedra locked eyes with Lissa. Her friend was trembling in fear. They couldn't have possibly heard him say that. Not inside. With everyone here—

The first burst of gunfire cut the chatter to nil, and there was a moment of perfect silence before the guns spoke again and the screams started. The open factory floor became too crowded with panic and the *brrt-brrt* of machine guns as Rose somersaulted in midair and landed on the floor three feet from Deedra. For an instant, their eyes met, and then Rose leaped straight up. Bullets pocked the floor where he'd been less than a second earlier, kicking up dust and fragments of concrete.

Deedra realized she was screaming. But everyone was screaming. Bullets whined and kicked and sizzled in the air. Rose was a greenish blur, launching himself from floor to ceiling, zipping back and forth in a zigzag, headed for the door.

Deedra grabbed Lissa's arm; her friend wasn't screaming, she was standing frozen. The crowd had split, half running away from them, half toward them, everyone in a panic. Lissa would be trampled. A forceful tug did nothing; Lissa was rooted to the spot. A hard slap to the face snapped her out of it, and the two of them ducked to the side and behind a section of conveyor belt just as several DeeCees opened fire.

From her vantage point, Deedra could barely make out Rose as he raced from side to side, trying to reach the door. But there were always more DeeCees coming through, fighting against the wave of workers trying to push out, and he was soon in the middle of the factory, dodging as bullets spun and whirled around him.

Even though it was impossible, Deedra imagined she could see it in him: the moment of decision. The DeeCees were firing indiscriminately, not caring that innocents were stampeding into the line of fire. Rose had been able to keep the bullets concentrated on him at first, but now the usually open space in the factory was too crowded and chaotic—there was nowhere to run, jump, or dodge that wouldn't put someone else in harm's way. Nowhere for him to step out of the path of a bullet without that bullet hitting someone else.

He stopped. Stopped dead. He was panting. She could only imagine what this was doing to him.

"Stop shooting!" he shouted, raising his hands above his head. "You're going to hurt someone!"

In that instant, she knew: Rose had not killed Jaron Ludo.

With the cessation of the gunfire, the screams and footfalls of panicked workers resonated louder. They pushed and shoved at one another and at the DeeCees, trying to run away, anywhere. The DeeCees, with methodical precision, pressed through the crowd, tightening the circle around Rose, who knew that if he moved, they would open fire again.

Finally, they surrounded him, rifles mere inches from his body. The slightest move...

Even Rose wasn't that fast.

"Deedra?" Lissa said. Deedra ignored her, sickly fascinated by what was happening. Some part of her longed for Rose to whip his tendrils around, to knock the guns from their hands, to escape....

But the expression on his face said it all. He wouldn't risk it.

Her cheeks went hot with shame. She'd believed the worst about him. But she knew now that he hadn't killed Jaron, wouldn't have killed Jaron, even though he easily could have.

Have you killed?

Many, many times.

Yes, he'd said that.

I don't make that distinction.

He'd said that, too.

But she had forgotten until that moment his very next words:

Everything that lives matters.

And that, too, was what he'd said.

Everything that lives matters.

She watched with tears in her eyes as they shoved him down to his knees, more roughly than was necessary, then pushed him even more harshly onto his stomach. Shackled his wrists behind him.

"His ankles, too," Markard said, pushing through to the center. "No chances."

With his arms and legs bound, he was helpless.

Markard nodded to one of the DeeCees. The man raised his rifle, and Deedra bit a knuckle to keep from crying out as he brought the butt down on Rose's head—hard enough to hear even where she crouched.

Rose lay there, completely still.

"Nice," said Markard.

"Hey, Deedra?"

From behind her, Lissa's voice had taken on a high, dreamlike quality, wavering and indistinct. Deedra turned around, and Lissa said, "I don't think this is good," in that same queer tone.

This was the swath of blood spilled like a lake along her left flank.

"Told you you'd get me killed some...day..."

Before Deedra could react—before she could even blink—Lissa's eyes rolled up in her head and she collapsed.

CHAPTER 25

*H*ERO COPS NAB LUDO MURDERER! read the headlink. The story itself was more of the same, with no mention whatsoever of the local police and the DeeCees opening fire in the confines of L-Twelve. No mention of the paramedics who'd rushed to Lissa's side—eventually—and then carted her off to MedFac without so much as a word to Deedra, who'd kept her alive until they'd arrived by pressing her rolled-up poncho against the wound.

She was tempted to edit at least one of the wikis to include this information, but she'd forgotten how. Editing the wikis seemed like a waste of time, so she hadn't done it in forever. As kids, they'd all done it, logging in to change some important news story to include a definition of flatulence or a link to the entry for *penis*. It had been giggle-inducing funny back then, but the skill set just never seemed important enough to maintain.

It wouldn't matter anyway. Others would reedit it however they wanted. In fact, maybe someone already had. Maybe the wikis originally got it right, and someone had changed it. And maybe the person who'd done so thought the adjustments made the story more true.

With so many truths flying around, who could tell what was *actually* true?

A boy named "Rose," the news feed went on, *is being held in Ludo SecFac until he can be transferred to City SecFac for processing and trial. He is accused of top murder and spying.*

She did not remember going home; she could only remember leaving L-Twelve and then a blank of time and then her home.

Still in shock, she was in no condition to flee the Territory now. Especially since TI Markard had warned her against doing so. She paced her apartment. After the gunfire and Rose's arrest and Lissa's being hauled away on a stretcher, an early curfew had been imposed. Lissa might not live and Rose...

Rose was an accused murderer.

She weighed the idea, hefting it, testing its contours and density. Two questions—and only two—mattered at this point. One: Had Rose done it? And two: Did she care?

The answer to the first question was no. She knew it. Could she prove it? Not a chance. The vine-like tendrils at the murder scene. Plus, Rose had recovered the pendant, which Jaron had stolen. Too many coincidences piled one atop the other. At some point, all those coincidences got tamped down and fused by the pressure of logic into a nugget of pure evidence. Who else could have committed the crime?

Although, given Jaron's belligerence and hatred of Rose, it was entirely possible—likely, even—that Rose had gone to Jaron's apartment to ask for the pendant back, been attacked, and defended himself so effectively that Jaron ended up dead.

Leaning back to think, Deedra swept her hair over her shoulder, touching her scar as she did so. Its pebbly, rough texture felt unfamiliar. She realized she hadn't been touching it as often as usual. Whole days sometimes went by now when she didn't think about it or probe its hard, nigh-insensate topography.

The second question: Did she care?

It was just Jaron, after all. Jaron, who'd been a distant threat at

L-Twelve, then pretended to be a friend before showing his true colors. Who cared if he was dead?

So now you *get to decide who lives and dies, Deedra? Is that it?*

Everything that lives matters.

Rose was right: It was simple. And it was also so, so complicated.

She groaned and rubbed her hands down her face. She didn't want to have these questions taking up space in her mind. When she'd met Rose, her world had changed in many ways, some small and subtle, some large. For the first time in her life, she'd felt wanted and needed, content. Nothing had changed in the world—the food was still too little and barely edible, the air still thick with alternating days of humidity and smog, the clouds still ever present, and the Territory still ugly. But for days and weeks, something had grown in her and near her, and for one magical night, she'd felt as though she'd brushed up against something pure and beautiful and true.

Now it was gone.

It was gone, and all that replaced it was an inchoate, unformed anger. She imagined Rose confined to a tiny cell in SecFac. That wouldn't do. She pictured herself attacking SecFac, guns blazing, mowing down row after row of DeeCees....

Instead of making her feel better, the image only made her feel worse. It was an impossibility atop an absurdity. She didn't even know where to get a gun. She didn't even know how to *fire* a gun.

She snarled and kicked out at her backpack, lying on the floor. It thunked too heavily.

Oh, wait...

The thing. The thing that Rose had given her. The book.

She rummaged under her poncho until she had it in her hands. It was heavy and solid and so old. Where had he found such a thing? And what was the point? Opening it, she was confronted with its running stream of text, broken up by the necessity of turning over each sheet of paper to find more. It was crazy. The book looked to contain maybe a few hundred sheets of paper, each with a limited amount of text. So thick and heavy for so little information.

There was no way to jump from one bit of text to another. No way to check the meaning of a word. No way to change the size of the text.

Really: What was the point?

Still, Rose had had it. And he'd given it to her. And he was gone.

He must have had some *reason for giving it to me. Right? He said he needed me to have it. Why?*

She settled into bed with the book. One way or another, she would figure this out.

CHAPTER 26

Top Inspector Markard waited patiently in the Magistrate's outer office. His career was about to skyrocket. Apprehending the murderer of the Magistrate's only son? Doing so after a dramatic firefight? Markard would be promoted to superior inspector in no time, he knew.

He glanced around the outer office. Yes. Superior Inspector Markard. With all the perks that came with such a position. Bigger monthly rations. Maybe nothing as swank as the Magistrate's digs, with its wall coverings and carpet. Carpet! Every place Markard had ever lived either had rough concrete floors or old, broken wood. Without shoes, you'd either tear up your feet or end up pincushioned by splinters. The idea of being able to take off his shoes in his own home seemed divine.

"Send him in!" a voice bellowed from within.

An assistant flicked a hand at the door without so much as a glance at Markard.

Markard wiped his palms on his pants and stood up. He'd never met the Magistrate before. He wondered if his tie was straight.

Cool air blasted him as he entered the inner office, and he shivered. Air-conditioning. It tasted chemical, but the coolness was welcome.

And—he realized—the aridity. The air did not hold the ever-present sag of moisture he'd become so used to.

"Close the damn door!" the Magistrate barked. He stood behind his desk, fidgeting with a stylus, tapping it without rhythm.

Markard shut the door. The inner office was carpeted, too, of course, with only three or four threadbare spots he could see. It must have cost a fortune. Tapestries hung from the walls, their ends only a little bit frayed. Only one of them was stained that Markard could notice.

A sofa sat against one wall, and a desk was at the far wall, positioned under the seal of Ludo Territory, a bas-relief of a dolphin in midleap. The same creature as in the brand on his neck. Markard couldn't remember if dolphins were made up or if they were extinct, but either way, there weren't any around, so it didn't matter. The motto of the Territory—*Quis custodiet ipsos custodes?*—encircled the dolphin. Markard stood stock-still at the door, taking it all in. The desk was the size of the bed he shared with his wife. He'd heard of the splendor of the Magistrate, but never thought he'd witness it.

Hands clasped before him, he stood before the Magistrate's desk as the man himself eased into his chair. Markard tried not to goggle as the chair actually *moved*, tilting slightly backward on its own. Amazing.

"You're the one who caught the killer?"

It had been a group effort, really. Entire platoons of local peace militia and DeeCees had swarmed the Territory and quickly narrowed the possibilities to the facility in question. Ten teams of inspectors and DeeCees had worked in a blitz of interrogations, getting to the workers before they could collude and change stories. It had been pure dumb luck that Markard had been the one to get Rose.

But dumb luck didn't get promotions. "Yes, Magistrate."

"This goddamn place!" Ludo slapped a hand on his desk. "You have any idea what I do for you people, Markard? Any idea the crap I have to put up with from the nationals, from the DeeCee bureaucracy? And someone murders *my* kid? That's the thanks I get?"

"If it's any consolation, Magistrate, the killer isn't a local or a native. We believe he came in from Sendar. We're still investigating."

Ludo's eyes narrowed until they were tiny gray-black beads set far back in his face. "Not Dalcord? Are you sure?"

"Anything's possible, I suppose. But all our information indicates—"

"Well, damn. If it was Dalcord, this wouldn't have been a complete waste. Would have given us pretext to go after them. Dalcord's been agitating for years."

"The boy wasn't registered, so we can't be sure exactly where he's from. It could very well be Dalcord." No harm in giving the Magistrate what he wanted.

Ludo smirked. "You want to—" He broke off and leaned forward, squinting. "What the hell is wrong with your eyes?"

"It's a birth condition called hetero—"

The Magistrate waved as though fanning himself. "That's all, Inspector. Good job catching this piece of puke."

"Thank you, Magistrate."

Markard stood still and silent as the Magistrate collected his tab—it had a perfectly shiny screen and only a couple of minor dings on the casing—and began flicking through it. After a moment, Ludo looked up.

"I said that's all, Inspector. Can't you see I'm busy?"

Markard hesitated. "Yes, Magistrate. I apologize, Magistrate. I just...wanted to be sure...there was nothing else...?" He drifted off, hoping.

Max Ludo ground his teeth together and snorted. "If there was something else, I would have *said* something else and not...Oh, wait." A sly expression came over his face, settling into the creases. "You *want* something, don't you? I've been running this Territory for thirty years.

I've seen every hand stuck out in every way you can imagine. 'Magistrate, I need this.' 'Magistrate, I need that.'" His voice paradoxically deepened as its agitation and volume rose. "'Magistrate, button my shirt, tie my shoes, hold my dick while I piss.' No one in this goddamn Territory can do anything for themselves. And they don't *have* to do anything for themselves because I do it all for them, and all I ask in return is a little gratitude and a little loyalty. All I ask is that people do the little I ask of them. Why in the world should I reward you for doing your job?"

Markard's face flamed.

"I apologize for any misunderstanding, Magistrate. I..."

"See that motto?" Ludo jabbed a finger at the crest behind him. "It's Roman for 'Who looks out for me?' I do! I look out for all of you! But who looks out for *me*, Inspector?"

Max Ludo snorted blasts of air through his nose, his expression that of a man who believed himself capable of breathing fire, should he so wish. After several rough exhalations, he began strumming his strong fingers on the desk. "But maybe..." *Thrud-duh-dum*, went the fingers. *Thrud-duh-dum*. "Maybe *you* can look out for me."

"Me?" Markard wanted nothing more than to get the hell out of there.

"Yes. You. You're the arresting officer, right? You have the datawork?"

Markard nodded. A few details to take care of and the DCS Citywide reps would come take Rose away. Crimes like murder were always tried at the City level, not the Territory.

"Maybe," Ludo mused, still thrumming away, "maybe you don't have a chance to get to that right away. Maybe you're busy, and you take some time to process that information before the City boys can snap him up. Let him rot for a little while here. In my SecFac. I think that's right. I think you were busy celebrating, weren't you?"

"Celebrating?" Markard said.

"Your promotion, of course."

"Yes. That could put off my finishing the processing by a couple of days."

Max Ludo raised an eyebrow.

"Did I say *days*?" Markard shrugged. "I misspoke. I meant to say weeks. My apologies, Magistrate."

Max Ludo's smile widened into something that Markard would be able to accomplish only with a knife. "All is forgiven, Superior Inspector."

CHAPTER 27

It was a story.

It took Deedra a while to realize it, but the book Rose had given her was one long story. A made-up story. She hadn't realized it at first because she wasn't familiar with them. There were made-up stories on the wikinets, of course, but they dealt mostly with scavenging, figuring out ways to stretch rations one more day, that sort of thing. Some were stories of the Red Rain and what had caused it.

But she understood now that this book was no more real than half of what she saw on the wikinets. It was no more real than Lanz's God or Lissa's aliens.

This story puzzled her at first, but she found herself absorbed into it nonetheless. The rigid structure of it baffled her, the nearly obsessive use of punctuation and capitalization, the unbending grammar. But the words, the language, pulled her in, and she sat up the whole night reading. The unfamiliar sensation of turning the pages quickly became second nature.

It was a story about a world she could scarcely imagine, and yet here it was, laid out for her. There was an obsession with clothing and with putting a certain face forward to the world. And no one ever seemed to work. Still, beyond that—through it and beneath it—ran a sense of yearning she understood. A need for more.

A boy named Amory, who had everything Deedra could imagine and more, seemed to be constantly seeking something else, something elusive. At first, she had nothing but contempt for him. There was no scavenging, and the constant pursuit of resources had been reduced to simple transactions that—in his world—were so routine as to hardly merit mention. And, yet, he wasn't satisfied. What a selfish, horrible person.

Despite herself, though, she found herself drawn in. Amory had *penetrating green eyes*, like Rose. Maybe that helped a little. She couldn't help but imagine Rose when she read about Amory, and that softened him for her.

Amory also reminded her of Jaron, though. At least a little. Early on, *Amory wondered how people could fail to notice that he was a boy marked for glory*, which seemed to be Jaron precisely. She didn't know how to feel about Amory. He was desperate and sad, so she wanted to like him and help him. But he was also arrogant and baffling and selfish. In fact, he seemed to enjoy being selfish. She couldn't reconcile the two sides of him.

And every time someone in the book *bought* clothing or coffee or food, Deedra chewed her lip a bit and gripped the book a little tighter. The people in the book thought nothing of food or clothes or shelter. They had no Magistrate, no DeeCees, to fear. They drove in cars—which in the real world were strictly limited to government use. They rode in buses and on trains—which in the real world no longer functioned.

She remembered one time she'd argued with Rose. He had been trying to convince her that the world had been better in the past, not worse. He'd pointed out the bridges in the distance, the train tracks underfoot.

"Why would these things be here if people didn't use them at one time?" he asked. "People *had* to travel. To go places. To go from Territory to Territory in vehicles, not on foot. The evidence is literally under your feet."

And she had laughed indulgently and told him not to be ridiculous. "Those were for government use," she'd told him. "Not for citizens. I bet they used to transport goods that way, before the Territories became self-sufficient with the factory system. And anyway, the environmental hazards were too risky, so they had to shut them down no matter what."

He'd given up the argument, but she knew she hadn't convinced him. And now, reading the book, she wondered.

In the world of the book, people—normal, average, everyday people, it seemed—went where they pleased, when they pleased. No need for passage papers to move from one Territory to another.

It was an absurd world, an impossible world. There was sunshine and no need for air masks, and Amory actually owned a house that had once belonged to his father, and...

She ran out of exceptions, stopped counting the ways in which this place could never truly exist, immersing herself in it, embracing the futility of it.

By the end, she was near tears. Not from Amory's travails and triumphs—he was too privileged to garner her empathy—but rather from the unattainability of the world in which he lived. It thrilled her and crushed her in the same instant, this vision of a world that could not be.

She never knew she could want something so badly.

She couldn't bear to part with the book, even though it was over. Craved contact with it, even though it saddened her. Clutching it to her chest, she lay back in bed, staring up at the ceiling through the weave of the roach netting.

Why had Rose given her this book? What had he wanted her to glean from it? Maybe Rose *was* cruel and crazed, a soulless murderer. Maybe he took pleasure in introducing Deedra to a life she could never have, forcing her to live it through the power of the book's words.

Or maybe it had to do with the very end, when Amory cried, "I know myself, but that is all." She wondered if maybe that was the point. If maybe that was why Rose had given her this book. To expose her to a world that she couldn't imagine, and at the same time to show her what he undoubtedly already knew: That figuring out herself mattered more than anything else.

It's a long story, Rose had said, speaking of how he'd recovered her pendant.

He'd recovered the pendant, but more than that, he'd told her to hide the book. The book was somehow more important than the pendant. More important than Rose's own freedom.

Still holding the book to her chest, she drifted off to sleep. She dreamed that night not of the DeeCees nor of Pride Execution Camp No. 12, but rather of Rose. He stood before her, dappled in sunshine, and the air was redolent not of metals, but of something akin to the perfume she'd smelled the night Rose had stayed with her.

He was the source of that perfume, she realized in the dream, and upon realizing it, she perceived it rolling off him in subtle, pink-tinged clouds.

"Take my hand," he said, holding it out to her. When she touched him, his hand transformed, becoming a collection of sinuous tendrils plated in green. She should have recoiled, but instead, she gripped the "hand" tighter.

Then vines shot out all along Rose's body, wrapping themselves around her, just as they must have wrapped around Jaron. She caught her breath (in the awake world, her body twitched once, twice, then lay still again) and stiffened but soon enough sank into them as Rose's green coat billowed out and caught a wind. They were airborne, drifting up and out, gently aloft on the breeze.

The Territory peeled away beneath them, and a rolling field of tall golden grass wavered into view, dotted here and there with the bushy green explosion of a tree. The buildings of the Territory were long behind them, and she spied other buildings far off to the west, but they were a forever away. In the meantime, below them scrolled endless fields, broken occasionally by blue rippling brooks and downy, soft carpets of fescue.

"It's almost too beautiful," she said.

"The world was like this," he told her. "Once upon a time. Long ago."

"Before the Red Rain?" she asked.

"Before even the thought of the Red Rain."

They drifted farther. The golden grass gave way to fertile browns and greens, grayish rills threading the land. The sun beat down on them, and they raced their shadows along the ground.

"What happens now?" she asked.

And Rose's arms and tendrils slackened. The air above them grew rocky and forced them down, hard. Still airborne, Deedra realized that Rose would lose his grip and she would plunge to her death on the rocky ground below.

She did not panic. A part of her knew it was a dream, but even the part unaware did not sound the alarm.

To die in a world like this, her dream-self thought, *would be fine.*

■ ■ ■

In the morning, she realized it: The book was real.

It lay heavy on her chest, so, yes, obviously it was real. The revelation was more along the lines that the story *within* was real. Or at least described a version of reality. It wasn't entirely made up.

It's always been this way. She had said that to Rose once, and she'd believed it. Nothing she had ever seen, read, or experienced had even hinted at a better world. To the contrary: Everything she knew told her that the world had been *worse*, that the Red Rain and the time before it had been even more crowded, more brutal, more desperate.

But what about *long* ago? So long ago that no one alive today could know someone who knew someone who knew someone who lived then?

Decades, even centuries, before the Red Rain.

What had the world been like *then*?

There was nothing on the wikis, but she thought it might be like the world described in the book. Otherwise, what was the point of the book? It was an ancient thing, to be sure. No one possessed such things now, though now that she knew its contours so intimately, she thought that perhaps she'd seen the burnt, charred remnants of books during her scavenging. Were they all like this one? Or were they like the wiki-nets cast in physical form, each one a different universe, united only by language and shape?

Maybe Rose was right. Maybe the world used to be a better place. After all, if someone wanted to tell a story about a better world, wouldn't they pretend it was the future? Or even the present? Why pretend it was in the past? What would be the point?

She flipped through the book to a passage that had captivated her, a simple description that she had read over and over, trying to envision it, suspecting she was failing: *As they neared the shore and the salt breezes scurried by, he began to picture the ocean and long, level stretches of sand and red roofs over blue sea.*

She closed her eyes and tried to picture it. With no frame of reference, she couldn't be sure she was getting it right, but she hoped so.

The book, she realized, described the world that had been. Because who could otherwise imagine something like *long, level stretches of sand*? Just as people writing a wiki today would reflect the world around them, so, too, had the person who'd written this book reflected the world at the time of the writing.

And such a world!

* * *

Lissa was still in MedFac; the rumor mill said that she was "expected to make a full recovery" after being injured "by the murderer of Jaron Ludo."

It was already spreading—Rose had shot Lissa during his escape attempt. Even though he'd never had a gun.

And people—even the ones who'd seen it happen—believed it.

In the absence of truth, everything was true. And so, nothing was true. Deedra had lived her whole life this way, and it had gnawed at her, had itched. But she'd never understood until now, until she saw people blithely ignoring the evidence of their own eyes.

People believed what they were told. And if they were told too much, or if accounts conflicted, they just believed whatever was easiest.

But not her. Not anymore.

The world has always been ruined.

Be a good citizen.

I deserve what I am given and am grateful for it.

The Patriot Oath.

These were the slogans and dogmas bashed into her head all day, every day. Rose had given her the first inklings of it, but his presence had proved so distracting that she'd never made the connection until he was gone.

And until the book.

She listlessly made her way through work each day, robotically assembling, missing Rose, missing Lissa beside her. The book was with her, in her backpack. It would always be in her backpack, she thought. She wanted it near her all the time, readily accessible. More important

199

than her knife, even. It lay hidden there like a secret made solid. Even when not touching it, she could feel the too-dry roughness of the paper pages, of their ineffable tactility. Running her fingers over the paper, she'd felt a direct connection to the text, as though it transferred to her through osmosis.

After a shift, she headed for the abandoned building where she and Rose had encountered Jaron and, luckily, a passing drone. She heaved herself up the makeshift ramp to the very top again. The ugly sprawl of the Territory lay splayed out all around her. In the distance was the Broken Bubble, which somehow seemed sadder and more neglected than ever, even though it had not changed at all.

The clouds gathered. The clouds always gathered. A little sunlight in the morning, then tufts and gatherings of slate gray until nightfall, when the sun filtered through at the horizon line long enough to dapple the bellies of the clouds before sinking behind the western skyline.

But there was enough light to read, and so Deedra curled up against a section of wall that still retained enough integrity to support her weight. She'd packed up some rations—fruit discs and some leftover scraps of dried synthetic turkey and a small bottle of water. It was three days until Ration Day, and she could ill-afford such a snack, but she munched mindlessly as she delved back into the book. Far from being bored reading it a second time, she found a new urgency, a special kind of kinship with the story. This time, she saw layers she'd missed before, and the characters' struggles took on new dimensions. She knew what would happen already but found herself just as invested, as if the story could change, like a wiki, at any moment.

But it couldn't. It was already set. And that thrilled her. She was powerless in the hands of the person who'd written the story.

Snack finished, she shifted position and kept reading.

I've found that I can always do the things that people do in books, Amory said.

Deedra couldn't. But, she realized, now she *wanted* to.

She fished her pendant out from under her poncho and ran it back and forth along its chain as she read. The touch of it made her think of Rose, and the only antidote was to submerge herself back in the story. She could do nothing for Rose but miss him. And remember him. The penalty for murder was often death itself, but for the killer of Jaron Ludo, she imagined the Magistrate wouldn't wait for a trial. There were dozens of ways to eliminate Rose before he ever had his day in court, and no one would dare speak up.

Not even me.

The thought made her sad. It was cowardly, but realistic. What could she do? What was within her power?

Nothing. She had no power.

As the sky darkened to night, she tucked her pendant under her poncho again, put the book in her backpack, and scrambled down to street level. She had just enough time to get home before curfew. She was depressed and exhausted, even though she'd done nothing.

Nothing but read. And maybe that was something. Maybe tomorrow she could figure out what to do next. Figure out what her next step could be. She couldn't just slip back into her old life. Not after Rose. Not after his arrest. Not after reading the book. There had to be *something* she could do. And she would figure it out. No matter how long it took.

"Ms. Ward?" The voice came from behind her as she darted out into the street, meaning it came from someone who had been lurking in the building.

Waiting for her.

She froze.

"Ms. Ward, we need to talk."

CHAPTER 28

It was, she saw with relief, Dr. Dimbali. He stepped out of the shadows of the building and kept his distance, standing a nonthreatening ten feet from her. He was old and out of shape. If she had to, she could outrun him.

Something about his bearing now seemed almost powerful. He seemed regal, haughty as he stood ramrod straight, his hands clasped behind his back. Even the cracked-lens SmartSpex perched atop his nose was glaringly cyclopean, the unblemished lens wide and all-seeing, the other dark and glowering.

"What do we have to talk about?" she asked. Maybe he knew about the book. Maybe she wasn't supposed to have it. Why else would he have followed her here?

And...ugh! He *must* have followed her. It would be too much of a coincidence otherwise. There were damn few good reasons for men to follow women, and all too many bad ones. This place still bore the memories of Jaron's hands on her, under her poncho. She put one hand behind her back to touch her knife. For reassurance.

"I'm not here to hurt you," he said, and held out both hands, palms facing her. She wondered what the SmartSpex were doing. Was he recording her? Analyzing her somehow? "I just want to talk."

"Well, it's almost curfew. Maybe tomorrow."

"I think it's best we speak now. In private." He smiled. She'd seen that smile any number of times, and now it suddenly seemed dangerous.

"I really don't want to be out after curfew." Would he suggest he follow her back home? There was no way in the world she would let Dr. Dimbali into her apartment.

Clasping his hands at his waist, he chewed on the corner of his mouth. "I'm not going to hurt you. The very notion is anathema to me. I want to talk about Rose."

Overhead, a drone silently glided by, its underside pulsating a gentle blue. Ten minutes to curfew. Just enough time to get home. She turned to go.

"Please come with me," he said. "I think we can help each other, and maybe help Rose. You do know his secret, don't you?"

That made her pause. Rose's secret. Which secret did he mean?

"He can do things," Dr. Dimbali said, glancing around to make sure no one was in earshot. Even so, he lowered his voice and leaned significantly toward her. "He can do things no one else can do. Am I right?"

"You want to help him?" she asked.

"Ms. Ward, if my suppositions are correct, I can help *everyone*."

■ ■ ■

Dr. Dimbali's apartment was just far enough that curfew fell as they entered the building—the sky lit flashing red with crisscrossing drones as he thumbed open the door. Deedra's stomach lurched and clenched with curfew panic, but also with the knowledge that she had committed herself to spending the night there. Dr. Dimbali had assured her that he had room for her, but she had already decided that—if she had to—she would break curfew and take the ration hit. Her record was relatively clean, and if it meant more scavenging, so be it. She had just escaped forever the clutches of one molester—she wouldn't willingly give herself to another.

Dr. Dimbali's apartment was massive—at least four separate rooms, each beyond a rough-hewn archway. He had several tabs of different sizes scattered around, as well as something she recognized as a near-ancient portable computer. It seemed massive and clumsy, its lid hinged like the book in her backpack, its keyboard chunky and too textured. The lighting in each room was dim, weak, naked bulbs strung along the ceiling. Dr. Dimbali went straight to a room that looked as though it was exclusively used to cook in.

"How did you get such a—" Was it rude to ask? But she couldn't help it.

He chuckled. "Do you merely accept what you're given, Ms. Ward?" He puttered at the stove. "Tea?"

She didn't know what the stove had to do with tea, but she accepted his offer. While she waited, she paced the length of the apartment, in awe of its size.

"I knocked down the walls myself," he told her. "And made what poor improvements my skills allowed."

He definitely had enough room for her to stay the night. He had a bed, of course, but in another room she saw a spare. It boggled the mind. He'd taken over other apartments.

"You can *do* that? What about the people who lived there?"

Another chuckle. She looked back to see him sprinkling something into mugs, then pouring boiling water over it. This was how he made tea? Where were his TeaPaks?

"What makes you think there was anyone *in* those apartments? This Territory once held in excess of two million people. It now has a population of slightly under one million. There are huge amounts of wasted space to be taken advantage of."

"But you just *did* it? You didn't have to ask someone—"

"Ask whom?" He stirred the contents of the mugs. "Did you ask permission before you went into that building I found you at earlier? No. It was abandoned and so you went there as you pleased."

Dizzy with sudden possibility, Deedra felt around herself, found a chair, and sank into it. How many people lived in her building? She didn't even know. She'd been assigned her unit when the orphanage had surrendered her. She knew none of her neighbors, and she had never even considered the idea that the spaces surrounding her own might be empty. That she could capture them for herself.

"It never occurred to me."

"Of course not." Dr. Dimbali approached her with both mugs, one of them held out to her. She accepted it. It smelled wonderful. Better than the perfume Rose had brought to her apartment. "It's hot—don't drink it right away."

He pulled a chair over and sat across from her. He blew gently on his tea. She inspected the mug. She'd had tea before but not like this. "Why are there things floating in it?" she asked.

"Those are . . . well, tea leaves."

"I don't understand. Like from a tree?" She'd seen trees before. Even grass. They were rare, but they did exist. She wasn't sure what their purpose was, but there they were anyway.

Dr. Dimbali sighed and shook his head sadly. "And this brings us back to the earlier topic: You've never contemplated, well, *modifying* your circumstances because nothing in your world, nothing in your experience, tells you that you *could* do so. From the moment you were born, you've known only one world, one system, one way of life. And as far as you can tell from what little history bleeds through the wikinets, the world has *always* been thus. So why would you try to change or improve things? There's no evidence anyone ever has."

It was the very conversation she'd had with herself since talking to Rose—was the world in decline or getting better? According to the Magistrate and the rest of the government, things were improving all the time. No more riots. No more mass starvations. Fewer wars over the Territories. But if things continued on this path, would the world ever resemble the one in the book she'd read? She didn't think so.

"Now," Dr. Dimbali said, leaning forward, "I understand that you and Rose have become close since he joined us here in the beautiful, Edenic Ludo Territory."

"We're friends." Something about the way he said *close* jabbed at her and made her heart jerk at the same time.

"Yes. Friends." He grinned and sipped at his tea. "Fine. Whatever. I need to know: Did he leave you anything before he . . . left?"

The book. The book that even now was in her backpack, resting on the floor near her feet.

What could he possibly want with the book?

"I don't know what you mean," she said.

"Let us not be coy, Ms. Ward. I know Rose's secret. I know of his . . ." He gestured with a finger in the air, as though fishing for a word.

"Powers," she supplied.

He laughed. "Yes. Let's call them *powers*. That will do nicely. I know of his *powers*. His abilities."

She gazed down into the murky water of the tea. Such a lovely scent from such a bland-looking liquid. "I don't know if we should be talking about this," she said quietly. "Inside. Or anywhere, really."

"Are you worried about surveillance?" He waved it away. "We're quite safe here. There are vulnerabilities to every system, Ms. Ward. Every system has security flaws. Don't believe everything you're told. The drones are not infallible. Your apartment's security is not undefeatable."

She thought back to the heat map TI Markard had shown her. Maybe Dr. Dimbali was right, but "not undefeatable" was a long way from useless.

"They watch me—"

"Don't be absurd. Of course they're not watching you."

"But they showed me a heat map of my apartment. And—"

He sniffed as though offended by the mere mention. "There are in excess of fifty billion people on this planet. To watch everyone, fully half of those people would have to work for the government, watching the other half. And then someone would have to watch the ones doing the watching to make sure no one falls down on the job. You see how ridiculous this is?"

"They had a heat map. They knew exactly what I was—"

"Oh, don't get me wrong—they have…systems that monitor everything we do, everywhere we go. But no one is watching those systems. Unless you give them a reason to. And then they can go back and check and see where you were and what you were doing. So they wondered what you were doing the night of Mr. Ludo's murder and they checked. But if they'd never suspected you, nothing would have alerted them to your activities. And if they'd waited two or three more days, the files would have been gone, automatically purged to make room for new ones." He grinned at her with what she supposed was intended to be a reassuring expression, but she didn't quite believe him, so the assurance went unappreciated. "It's valuable to know how things work. There are a million people living in Ludo Territory alone. Do you really think Max Ludo and his contingent stay up nights watching you sleep?"

He was right. She'd always known it, she supposed. After all, a drone had witnessed Jaron threatening her on the rooftop, but no one had ever done anything about it. No one had ever seen that video, and now it was gone.

She sipped at the tea, which had cooled by now. It was delicious, possibly the most delicious thing she'd ever tasted in her life. Sweet and pungent and so very strong, its flavor smooth on her tongue. With great restraint, she resisted the overwhelming urge to gulp it down at one go. Better to make it last. She sipped again, savoring it.

"In fact," Dr. Dimbali went on, "I could take you home right now. Despite curfew. There are ways. And if you wish, I'll do so. But first: Rose."

"He didn't leave me anything," she said, and then immediately regretted the lie. "Except for a book."

Dr. Dimbali's eyes lit up at that. "A book! Wonderful. For you. I hope someday, perhaps, you will allow me to see it. But I didn't mean something like a book. I meant..." He trailed off. "Something more personal."

She sipped again, thinking of the metal flower he'd brought to her. "I don't know what you're getting at, Dr. Dimbali. Maybe if you just told me what you want..."

He leaned back and drank his tea and stared at her uncomfortably long. "Did he leave anything *of himself*?"

That was unexpected. When he said *personal*, she thought he meant a note or a picture. "Like what?"

"Like what you're drinking, for example."

The mug was already at her lips for another lingering, savoring sip. She froze and stared into the liquid's depths, at the swimming leaves.

She swallowed hard and put the mug aside.

"Do you understand?" Dr. Dimbali asked quietly.

On her leg, an itch. From the healing scab where Rose had inadvertently cut her the night he'd spun her around her apartment. She'd known then. She'd known and she'd denied it. But she remembered what she'd read about roses.

About their thorns.

That's what had been on Rose's tendrils: Thorns. And roses *smelled good*. And so did Rose.

It was insane, but now she would say it anyway.

"I was thinking about his name," she said slowly, staring at the floor. "And what he can do. I went on the wikis and I looked up *rose*. They said they were mythical flowers, but Rose saw them, he said." She looked up at him. "He said he saw them, and I believe him."

Dr. Dimbali nodded approvingly over his mug. "Go on."

"And, well…" She shook her head. It was foolish. And stupid. She couldn't say it out loud. And yet, she would. She knew it. Because she'd been thinking it for a while now, and to say it to someone else— someone who would laugh and mock her and make her feel foolish— was the best possible idea. The humiliation would flush this absurd notion from her head for good.

"I was thinking…what if Rose, well, what if he *was* a rose?"

The humiliation she so craved did not come. Instead, Dr. Dimbali drank his tea down to the dregs and then stood, hands clasped with no-nonsense intent. "Come with me, Ms. Ward. I have something to show you."

■ ■ ■

In his kitchen, Dr. Dimbali moved aside a large wooden plank to reveal a door. Another room? How much space did one man need?

But the door led not to a room but, rather, to a stairwell, its concrete walls stained and rancid with mold. Dr. Dimbali offered her a face mask and apologized for the smell. "I am used to it by now, but I understand it may bother you. No matter what I do, it just grows and grows and grows. In a way, it's comforting to see something of nature so resilient, our best efforts to the contrary. Too bad it's useless."

Still clutching her mug of now-cool tea, her face mask secure, she followed Dr. Dimbali into the stairwell and down several flights and landings and turns. "This was once the southern fire stair," he explained as they descended, echoing slightly in their confines. It made him sound even more serious and somehow alien. "I suppose the old fire codes just didn't apply anymore once they were desperate to house people, so it was boarded over. I discovered it quite by accident."

Dr. Dimbali had a fluoro-tube; but for its shivering, bouncing beam just ahead, she was steeped in darkness.

They arrived at the last stair, with no further descent possible. Dr. Dimbali opened a door and flicked a switch—a series of lights sputtered to life overhead, varying in colors and intensities, bathing them in a vibrating, warm, flickering glow. Overhead, pipes sweated condensation—indoor drizzle. This space was huge, as big as Dr. Dimbali's apartment, but not chopped into separate rooms; it sprawled the length and breadth of the building, it seemed, its area broken by tables, chairs, desks, some of them intact, others cobbled together from cinder blocks and boards and cushions. Large containers were scattered here and there, most of them with small, spindly green shoots of some sort poking up from them.

"My babies," Dr. Dimbali said with a gentle smile. He leaned over to one. "How are you this fine day?" he asked it, then put his finger into the pot. "Your soil is a little dry. I'll water you soon enough."

Deedra turned away as he chatted briefly with the pots; she scanned the rest of the space. A variety of touch screens and older computers cluttered the desks, and a scratched and dusty SmartBoard flickered quietly to itself in one corner.

She recognized the image on it instantly.

Rose.

She lowered her face mask. The air here was musty but breathable.

"What is this place?"

"This is the old basement. No one was using it, so I appropriated it

210

for my needs." He strode to the SmartBoard and tapped it. The image of Rose rotated and magnified. "At first, I worked alone. But for the past little while, Rose and I have been . . . collaborating." He clucked his tongue absently. "Most of my collaborations have not gone so well, but this one has been rewarding."

"This is where he stays?" she whispered, taking in the dank, dark basement. "He lives here?" She couldn't imagine bright and enthusiastic Rose squatting here, but . . .

Dr. Dimbali blinked at her as though waking. "What's that? Oh, no. Not here. He has a project of his own out there somewhere." He gestured to encompass the Territory. Maybe the world. "I've offered a bit of assistance, but he spends most of his time without—" He seemed to catch himself, as though disgusted with his own rambling. "No matter. If he wishes to dillydally with his own ideas, that's fine. As long as he comes back here to do the important work."

"What's the important work?" She held out the mug. "And what did you mean when you asked if he left me something like this tea?"

Dr. Dimbali rolled an old chair over to her, its wheels shrieking in complaint against the rough concrete floor. She sank into it, realizing that this was what he'd always wanted: an audience.

"You hypothesized before that Rose, perhaps, might actually *be* a rose. Reduced to its simplest terms, this was precisely *my* hypothesis, early on. He approached me one day, you see. He was endlessly curious. About *everything*." Dr. Dimbali sighed and stared off into the middle distance. "After years and years of trying to get through to the incurious and the clueless, you cannot imagine what it was like to encounter someone who genuinely wanted to learn.

"Eventually he came to trust me with the mystery of his past and with the even more intriguing mystery of his present. Of his biology. We began conducting tests, right here in this facility I've cobbled together."

"Why?"

A grunt. "My dear Ms. Ward, the pursuit of knowledge is its own reward."

She wasn't buying it. No one did anything just to do it. There had to be a reason. Though cold, the tea weighed heavy in her hands. She knew what Dr. Dimbali was going to tell her, but she didn't want to hear it, didn't want to know it. Even though she already did.

"When he first demonstrated his *powers*, as you called them," Dr. Dimbali went on, "I was, perforce, stunned. But I quickly recovered and began to develop a series of theories."

"That Rose really is a...rose." It still sounded worse than absurd, when spoken aloud. She blushed.

"Simplistically put." He swiped at the SmartBoard, and the image of Rose shrank and moved to one side. An image of an actual rose filled the remainder of the screen. "The two have nothing in common, phenotypically. Rose—our Rose—presents traits of an adolescent human male, androgynous in appearance, but possessed of all human exterior attributes, including fully developed primary sexual characteristics."

Deedra thought of the day by the river and blushed deeper red. In the sallow light of the basement, she hoped Dr. Dimbali wouldn't notice.

"Externally, he is insignificant. So I had to delve deeper."

And then the SmartBoard image rotated, and as she watched, Rose's skin peeled back to reveal strips of corded muscle and the tracery outlines of blood vessels. She recoiled; the tea sloshed over the brim of the cup and spattered onto the floor.

"I assure you I was quite humane," Dr. Dimbali said with a mild note of rebuke. "He volunteered for the experiments, in the name of science. I am no butcher." He considered. "Then again, Rose is no slab of beef."

The reference flew past her. She didn't know what a *slab of beef* could possibly be.

"Rose himself is unaware of his true nature. He's been...struggling with his sense of identity. He feels he isn't human, and that makes him wonder what his place in this world is."

"And now he knows?" It made a crude sort of sense to her and opened up a new possibility: Maybe Rose *had* killed Jaron. He'd always been so worried about his own humanity—if he discovered that he *wasn't* human, wouldn't that make it easier to commit murder?

"He still knows nothing. I finished my analysis only last night. Ironic timing on my part, perhaps, to arrive at the answer at precisely the moment when I cannot explain it to Rose himself."

The SmartBoard zoomed in, past the tissues and the vessels. The new image was an interlinked series of balls, connected by pulsating beams of light. Letters ghosted the space near the balls: OH, NH, H, CH, MG...

"I've lectured on plant anatomy and biology at L-Twelve in the past. If you remember any of it, then you no doubt recognize the basic structure of the chlorophyll molecule and its distinctive porphyrin ring."

She was surprised to find that she did have some dim memory of it, from one of Dr. Dimbali's factory-floor pronouncements long ago. Chlorophyll. The molecule central to plant life. It was what made weeds grow.

"Is this in Rose's blood?"

"If only it were that simple." The molecule doubled and the new copy shifted. They were almost identical, but some of the letters had changed. "*This* is the heme molecule, building block of hemoglobin. Hemoglobin is the molecule in our blood that allows us to transmit oxygen through the bloodstream."

She squinted at the SmartBoard. The heme and the chlorophyll could have practically been overlaid atop each other and fit precisely. "They look the same."

He chuckled. "Indeed. The primary difference is that chlorophyll contains a molecule of magnesium, whereas hemoglobin contains iron."

"Which one is Rose's?"

Dr. Dimbali grinned—a truly joyous expression that caught her off guard. "My dear, *he has both.* That's the whole reason I brought you down here. To explain. He has both."

"So he *is* a rose?"

"No!" The joy vanished, replaced with the dour expression of resigned frustration she was so used to. "He's not a rose. He has *both* types of molecules in his system. And through some process I have yet to discern, they shift from one to the other seemingly at random. His body is a playground between flora and fauna, an impossible blend of two incompatible life-forms, somehow coexisting. Rose is not a rose. Rose is not a human being. He's *both*, Ms. Ward. He is, quite literally, a hybrid rose—as far as I know, the first and only specimen in a new breed. He would be...let's see..." Dr. Dimbali stroked his chin and gazed at the ceiling. "Perhaps take genus from the plant kingdom..." he muttered under his breath, then snapped his fingers and grinned at her. "*Rosa sapiens* is probably as close as our taxonomy can get. No doubt we'll need to invent a new one at some point. In any event, he is a bizarre and quite unforeseen combination of human and rose."

She sat perfectly still for a long, long time, staring at the images on the SmartBoard until they bled together, as she imagined them blurring in Rose's body.

Not human. Not entirely, at least. It was impossible. She closed her eyes as a long, high-pitched whine echoed and pierced her. She was going numb again, as when TI Markard had interrogated her. She was leaving the world.

Don't. Don't do this. Stay here. Stay strong.

"How can this be possible?" she whispered, and barely heard his response.

Dr. Dimbali snorted. "I'm sure I have absolutely no idea, young lady. But he is most assuredly a hybrid of the two species. You've no doubt witnessed strange mutations yourself: Tooth-weed. The hybrid rats with blue fur. Science tells us this is impossible, but science has told us many things were impossible in the past. In fact, there is even the chance that this is no natural phenomenon, that Rose was actually genetically engineered or modified in some way. We've made tremendous strides in such things, as you know every time you eat rations." He chuckled. "I'll say this: If he *is* a genetic recombinant, whoever built him did truly excellent work.

"Ultimately," he went on, waving a hand, "there will be an explanation, but for now I care less for the hows and whys and more for the simple whats. What can he do? What can we do with him? You and I excrete nitrogen and phosphorous—he devours them. Needs them, in fact, to live. He can breathe oxygen, as we do, but most often he inhales our carbon dioxide, as though he's evolved to breathe the toxic brew we call an atmosphere. And he exhales pure oxygen, in such low supply these days. In short: He is the most splendid, absurd thing I have ever witnessed in my life."

The whine died away, and her hearing returned to normal.

"Person, you mean."

"I beg your pardon?"

"You called him a thing. He's a person."

Dr. Dimbali smiled indulgently. "But of course he is, my dear. I was speaking metaphorically."

She looked down at the tea. At the leaves floating in it. "These are from him, aren't they? They came off him. Like a plant."

"Rose hips. Not really tea leaves," Dr. Dimbali admitted. "Harvested from one of his outgrowth appendages. A delicious tea, you'll agree."

No. Not a chance. He's joking.

The thought of *drinking* part of Rose should have seemed grotesque, but she raised the mug to her lips and drank off half its contents. And she knew. Without the slightest room for doubt. She'd held Rose and been held by him. Touched him. Kissed him. This tea was *of* him.

215

Though cold, it was still delicious. Rose's last gift to her, perhaps. Who was she to forsake it?

"Loaded with vitamin C," Dr. Dimbali prattled on. "Much better for absorption than the supplements they hand out or the artificial levels of C impregnated in our usual rations."

Could he just shut up for a minute? Or even just a few seconds? Just give her time to absorb not the vitamin C but, rather, the insanity of it all? Because, she realized, the most insane part wasn't even that Rose was part-boy, part-flower. The most insane part was that it made perfect sense, that as soon as Dr. Dimbali had explained it, she'd felt as though she had remembered it, not learned it, as though Rose's true nature had been a fact uncovered long ago and then lost in the jumble and fog of memory. It was the only explanation for...for *everything*. His loitering in the sunlight every morning. His absorbing the water through his fingers. All of it. She'd been drawn to him not because he was a boy and not because he did not recoil from her scar, but because he was different. *Different* was actually too small a word for it; there was no word in language for what Rose was. *Hybrid*, Dr. Dimbali had said. Even that word couldn't capture it.

Rose was Rose. Singular and exceptional. In ways Deedra knew she never could be.

The tea soothed her. It brought her closer to Rose, brought him closer to her. And she didn't care that everyone thought he'd killed Jaron. She only wanted him back. She wanted to tell him that she understood, at least part of it, and that she didn't care about the parts she didn't understand.

Dr. Dimbali was rambling about hemoglobin and iron and magnesium and photosynthesis, swiping and gesturing at the SmartBoard, causing molecules and atoms to dance. She broke in. "What now?"

Flustered and more than a bit annoyed at being interrupted, he turned away from the SmartBoard. "Whatever do you mean?"

"You asked if he'd left me anything. You mentioned the tea. You wanted to know if he left...a piece of himself. Right?"

With a sigh that seemed to well up from a place deeper even than this basement, Dr. Dimbali nodded sadly and removed his SmartSpex, rubbing his eyes. Without the SmartSpex, he was just a sad, old man, sunken-chested and weathered and conquered. She could not forget the image, even when he replaced the SmartSpex and fixed her with a gaze.

"Yes. I was hoping he'd left a...clipping."

"A clipping?"

"Perhaps the wrong word. Some part of himself. Hair. Blood. Skin. Anything at all."

"You have the..." *What was the word? Oh, right.* "Rose hips."

"They were dried. And they contain only plant matter, without any of the hybrid tissues. All the samples I've taken from him are the same—animal or plant, not both. I had samples that contain animal and vegetable tissues working in concert. Blood samples. But they've been destroyed in the testing and analysis. I need more of them. As much as possible."

"Why?"

Dr. Dimbali clasped his hands behind his back and stood fully erect, his bearing proud. "Why? Because once upon a time, we lived like human beings, not slaves. Because once upon a time, the world gave forth bounty, not poison."

She thought of *This Side of Paradise*.

"I've seen things. Vids. Some documents. Evidence of a world that existed long, long before the Red Rain. We killed the world, Ms. Ward. We people, with our machines and our technology and our breeding like damn-fool rabbits. We ate everything that grew until nothing more could grow. We vomited toxins into the air and the water until the air and the water became toxins themselves. We spread out across the planet and paved and covered every last bit of ground to house an

217

exploding population. And when the world died, we began feasting on its corpse.

"But with what exists in Rose's DNA...with the commingling of molecules in his veins...I believe I can resuscitate our dead planet." His eyes gleamed behind the SmartSpex, and his posture straightened even more, which she'd thought impossible. "Ms. Ward, *I can fix the world.*"

Just as quickly as he'd puffed up, he deflated, crumpling in on himself, hands feeling for the SmartBoard to brace himself. "Or, rather, *could*. Could have. If they hadn't taken Rose away."

Deedra stared down into her mug again. Little bits floated there. All she had left of him. She thought of the blue rat. Of the poisonous river that divided this Territory from Sendar. She felt Rose's tendrils wrap around her and lift her into the air, the sudden rush in her chest.

And she thought of another meal of lab-grown turkey and fruit discs. Thought of days trapped inside when the rain was too toxic to go outside, so acidic it could eat through a poncho or umbrella. Thought of wikis that knew everything but nothing at the same time.

"There's only one thing to do," she said.

Dr. Dimbali tut-tutted. "There's nothing to do. There are no options. You were my last hope."

Deedra drank the rest of the tea in one shot. It warmed and cooled at the same time. She fixed Dr. Dimbali with a hard look as she stood.

She said, "We're going to break Rose out of jail."

CHAPTER 29

They'd taken his coat.

Rose didn't have the word for it, but Dr. Dimbali would have known: The coat was made up of his sepals. They grew from the back of his neck, and he naturally shed them as time went on. He had taken them from himself and fashioned them into a coat. The coat was more than a garment—though no longer connected, it was a part of him, and its loss shocked him.

"You think this is bad?" a guard said. "Just you wait. It gets worse than stripping down."

They passed the coat among themselves, curious as to its texture and color. He watched them cut and slash at it with knives and then toss it, ragged, into a corner.

They crowded around him. Five of them, then six, then ten. Then more. Their mocking voices overlapped in the confines of the jail's intake room. Combined with the ever-present buzz of the artificial lights and the stale, metallic tang of the processed air, he could barely focus enough to keep his balance.

In his years-long wander, he'd remained outdoors as much as possible. The excess carbon dioxide in the atmosphere made others flee indoors, where old air scrubbers did their best to "purify" the air, but the CO_2 didn't bother Rose. And even the tiniest bit of natural sunlight—a rare commodity—did more for him than all the light-bulbs in an entire Territory.

Now he was penned up inside. Surrounded by DeeCees and local cops, all of whom wanted to be able to say they'd taken a shot at the kid who killed Jaron Ludo. He was shoved from one to the other, hustled back and forth, stumbling from one set of clutching, angry hands to another. Spat on. Tripped to the ground. Hauled back to his feet and hurtled across the room again. They stripped the rest of his clothing from him.

Would he die there?

A part of him hoped it would happen soon, if it was to happen. They threw him into a small concrete room, no more than seven feet to a side. There was a single barred window near the ceiling, coated with grime and dust, a metal toilet pocked with blossoms of rust, and an equally run-down metal sink. On a miserable cot, they tossed a messily folded square of cloth. His inmate clothing. Piss yellow and stained with blackish smudges.

If I die now, he thought, sprawled on the rough, cold floor, *it may be for the best.*

He thought of the coat. Thought of new sepals growing from his neck. It would happen soon. What would his captors think of that?

The mental image of their disbelieving, gasping faces as they espied him in his cell, sepals folding down from the back of his neck, coaxed a weary smile out of him. He struggled to all fours and crawled to the cot. It was only marginally more comfortable than the floor.

If I die now, I'll never know. I'll never know what I am. Who I am. I'll never know my place in this world.

He lay naked on the cot and stared at the ceiling. He thought not of the nights he'd lain thus, gazing up at the sweating pipes in Dr.

Dimbali's basement lab, but rather of the single night he'd lain in Deedra's bed. The netting overhead. The soft weight of her against him.

Cold and shivering, he groaned as he rolled over. It took him long minutes to creep along the floor to the sink. Thrusting his hand into the running tap, he drank, absorbing the water through his flesh. It was polluted and treated with chemicals, but better than nothing.

If I die now, I'll never see her again.

"So I suppose I'd better not die," he said aloud.

■ ■ ■

He suspected a day had passed.

The tiny window had darkened, though not completely, never to full dark. It had dimmed, then—after interminable hours—burnished and glowed for what seemed seconds. He'd managed to rouse himself from the cot and scrabble over to the minuscule patch of sunlight that dribbled into his cell. He lay there, absorbing what he could, trying not to think of the mornings waiting for Deedra, sucking up the sunlight as his roots descended into the mineral-poor earth, deeper each time, seeking the refugee nutrients buried so far down. Farther down each day.

The sun was his first clue. The arrival of meals was the other. He'd been thrown into the cell in the early evening, and he counted three meals, confirming his suspicion that a day had passed. The meals were indistinguishable from one another, united in their sludgy color and consistency. The food—like all food—had been conceived in a laboratory somewhere in the Territory, grown under the watchful eye of scientists attempting to mimic dead Nature's absent bounty.

It reeked of chemicals, true, but more than that—deeper than that—it reeked of *wrong*. It reeked of *untrue*. There were no compatible words to describe fully the assault on his senses, the way the food repulsed him. He couldn't have eaten the food if he'd wanted to, and he worried that before long he *would* want to. Instead, he drank the water they gave him. It was no better than what came from the tap, and he feared the toxins within, but he had no choice. If he was going to stay alive, he had to at least have water.

He spent that first day scrutinizing every last inch of his cell, running his fingers over the rough concrete, stroking the welds on the pipes under the sink and toilet. He tested the heat of the water, its velocity as it spurted or dripped or gushed from the spigot, depending on how he turned the handle. He crawled under the cot, inspecting the bolts that held it in place, the near-rotted straps that held the mattress down, the lumpy, slender insult of padding. The blanket he'd been given was worn almost transparent in places, its ends frayed and gossamer.

The cell measured ten of his footsteps long by nine deep. There was a discreet plastic bubble high in one dark corner. A camera. They were watching him. The bubble was just out of reach, but he knew he could reach it if he had to.

For now, though, he had to be careful. Not let them know what he was capable of.

The door was steel. Its touch sent cold shivers from the pads of his fingers up to his shoulders and around to his spine. It was implacable. A slit at roughly eye level was shut tight from the other side, and another one—where his food had come through—was at waist height. He probed at both and found no way to open them.

He pushed the tray of food into the farthest corner of the cell and curled up on the cot. He closed his eyes.

They wanted to break him.

He would bend, instead.

CHAPTER 30

On the second day, he had a visitor.

He paid careful attention to the procedure. First, they ordered him to stand in the center of the room, facing away from the door, his fingers laced together behind his head. He heard the click and rumble of the door unlocking and opening, and then hands harshly shackled his wrists behind his back. A moment later, the door clanged shut.

"You can turn around," said a voice.

He turned slowly. Before him stood a tall man, his shoulders broad. His ropy arms terminated in long fingers that flexed constantly. He wore a purple robe over a charcoal-gray suit with a pale yellow shirt. With cold gray eyes sunk deep in his face, he glared at Rose, alternately pursing and sucking in his lips. He was the man from the vid. Jaron's father.

"You're the dung-drop who killed my boy," he said, his voice inflectionless.

"Mr. Ludo, I didn't—"

Max Ludo said nothing. With a surprising swiftness, he crossed the few feet between them and belted Rose with the back of one heavy fist.

The blow rocked Rose and sent him reeling back until he collided with the sink. His vision blurred for a moment.

"First of all," Ludo said, "it's *Magistrate* Ludo. *Mister* is for ditch-diggers and dung-pilers."

Was that a trickle of blood running down Rose's jawline? Or sweat?

"Second of all, I didn't tell you to talk. When I want you to talk, I'll tell you. Got it?"

Rose nodded. He suddenly suffered a dramatic and unexpected surge of empathy for poor dead Jaron Ludo. And for the first time in his life, he was actively afraid. He'd seen fear before; he'd had it explained to him. But he'd never felt it himself. He'd always been aware of his own skills, his unique talents. Few and rare were the threats he could not evade.

But right now, he was shackled and pinned down in a concrete box.

He planted his feet and braced himself against the sink to stay upright.

"Look at you." Ludo took Rose's jaw in his hand and twisted his head this way and that. "So goddamn *pretty*. What the hell Territory spawned you? You look like a girl, but my cops tell me you have a dick, so you're a boy." He clutched Rose's jaw harder and pulled, dragging Rose away from the sink, then shoved him full in his face, driving him backward. The backs of Rose's knees collided with the cot, spilling him onto it; he narrowly avoided cracking his head on the wall.

Ludo towered over him, teetering on the brink of collapse. Rose yearned to lash out, to batter Ludo away from him, to shove back the threat. But he was so weak. And giving away his abilities would only summon the guards. Too many for even him to overcome.

He was keenly aware of the camera in the corner, bulbously concealed, watching everything.

"Is that what happened?" Ludo went on, his cheeks and jowls suffused with crimson outrage. Droplets of sweat fell off him and splashed onto Rose's chest. "Did my boy think you were a girl? Make a move you didn't appreciate? So what? Big deal. You couldn't just *take it*? You couldn't just *live with it*?"

Rose still said nothing. He could shift the shape of his hands if he had to. If Ludo commenced a beating, he could slip the shackles and...

And what? Kill Ludo? Invite a swarm of guards to descend on him and beat him to death? Or worse, ship him off to a Territory lab somewhere, to dissect him in ways Dr. Dimbali never would?

"Did you trick him?" Max asked. "How did a pissant like you overpower Jaron?"

Ludo grabbed the front of Rose's prison-issue shirt, hoisting him out of the bed. Their faces came even—the stench of bad food washed over Rose, along with stray spittle.

"Who sent you? I want to know! I want to know now. It was Dalcord, wasn't it? He's been spoiling for war for years. Wanting to expand his territory. Capture my food tech. It was him, wasn't it?" He shook Rose. "Answer me!"

"I wasn't sent by anyone." Rose measured his voice carefully, avoiding stresses and deep inflections. He didn't want to present even the slightest threat to Max Ludo. "I've been roaming for—"

Max Ludo howled, a single note of incoherent rage. He spun around, shoving Rose, who stumbled, fell, and sprawled on the floor. Rose's vision swam for a moment, and when he recovered, Max Ludo stood over him, fists planted on his hips.

"You know things, pissant. And you'll tell me. You'll tell me *everything*. About my boy. About the tech you used to mimic our brand." He crouched down with great effort and poked Rose in the gut. "I'll know it all, you hear me? I want to know where those vine things came from. It's not tooth-weed or any other kind of weed. What has Dalcord been up to? What are his scientists making? What's going *on* over there?"

There was nothing to say. Rose could keep telling the truth, but to

Max Ludo, the truth was a lie. And there was no lie Rose could conjure that would satisfy a man who was so patently insatiable.

It was not Rose's first encounter with the irrationality of humanity. Nor was it his inaugural introduction to outright evil. Over the years he'd come across any number of rapacious, greedy, destructive people. Those he could not assuage with words, he'd always been able to escape before violence became inevitable. As with Jaron Ludo, running away was always the most expedient course. Better than hurting someone.

But now there were no words to mollify Max Ludo. And no way to escape.

Huffing and panting, Ludo jabbed an irate and accusatory finger at Rose.

"You'll tell me. You'll tell me *all* of it. Trust me on that. I control this Territory and everyone in it. That means you, little spy, little murderer. If I have to reach inside you and pull out the secrets with my own hands, I will."

"When do I get my day in court?"

"We'll get around to that. You'll have a lawyer. That's the law, even though it's stupid. But I get to appoint your lawyer. Isn't that a kick? Isn't that great? I get to pick your lawyer. Trust me, little girl-boy— you're not getting the finest legal mind the Territory has to offer."

He kicked Rose in the side just above the hip, right where it hurt the most. With a shout of "Guard!" he was out the door, still wheezing as he went.

■ ■ ■

Rose must have passed out, because when he opened his eyes, he was on the cot and his hands were no longer bound.

They're going to kill me. They're going to torture me for information, and I don't have any. Or they'll learn that I'm not human. Either way, they're going to take me apart, piece by piece.

He thought about his experiment. The secret one, the one only Dr. Dimbali knew about. He intended to carry that secret with him beyond death, but would they eventually make him tell? What would they do if they saw what he'd done out at the place Deedra called the Broken Bubble? Would they even understand it?

He imagined not. And the thought of how they might react, their violent, fiery instincts...

So much work. So much time. And they'll destroy it all in moments.

He probed his jaw, his side. The injuries were tender and painful, but not debilitating.

If they're going to kill me, I won't make it easy for them.

CHAPTER 31

He promised himself again: He would bend. Not break.

With his days and nights equally blank, with nothing to do or hear or read, he could have lost his mind. It would have been easy. Time passed, marked only by the meals and the dimming of the light through the window. He counted mornings, but lost count. He knew only that he'd been in prison for at least a week.

They couldn't know about his secret weapon.

Not his abilities. Those had weakened, flagged with his energy as he subsisted on water and what little sunlight he could glean. Just enough to stay alive.

No, his secret weapon was his memories.

He'd spent years traveling. He had seen things unimagined by Max Ludo and his jailers. And now he spent each day-merged-with-night recalling every footstep, every blink.

Beginning with the first.

The roses. He does not know their name yet. He does not know his own name yet. That hovers in the time to come, glistens in his future like dew on rocks. But the roses are there, in the now of memory, the first thing he sees when he opens his eyes, their semidouble petals in crisp yellow, architected around the stamens and pistils, the sepals folded like bowing servants. How many people witness such beauty in their first eye-opening? He knows beauty in that instant, and he knows luck as well.

He is lucky.

"I'm lucky," he murmured from his cot.

He stands on legs disused to supporting weight. His own sepals have curled down from his neck and begun to close around him, forming a safe, temperature-regulated cocoon. When they shed, he will keep them with him, safe in the form of a long coat.

The sepals were beginning to regrow. He felt them unfurling from the back of his neck. For now he could conceal them under his clothes, but eventually they would become too large to hide, and his captors...

Memories. He tried to recollect every detail of his trek across the continent, but his remembrances were always interrupted....

Her touch.

Interrupted by more recent memories...

Her eyes.

Deedra.

Fear and curiosity in her eyes, intermingled, combined. She touches him. In the dead and dark of night, she kisses him.

He walks a blasted wasteland, ten years ago, buildings burned out and collapsed all around him. Someone has spray-painted on a trestle YOU ARE ENTERING HELL!!! *and Deedra is suddenly there, reaching out for him, and her eyes consume him, and he wants to be consumed, devoured, by her.*

YOU ARE ENTERING HELL!!!

∎ ∎ ∎

A fine silvery fuzz began to appear on his skin. This had happened once before. Five years ago. Up north, where the nights were humid and cool, like now. Each morning, he scraped at the fuzz as best he could, sloughing it off into the toilet. It would devour him, he knew. If he couldn't get rid of it, it would eat him alive.

At least something will get to eat in here.

Each morning he scraped it off and returned, exhausted by the effort, to his cot.

"Can you hear me?"

He craned his neck so that he could see the door. A man stood there, half in shadow. "I said, can you hear me?"

"Yes." Rose's voice sounded rough and guttural. He hadn't spoken in several days. The word stabbed his throat.

"Good. I thought maybe you were unconscious. If you keep up this hunger strike, they'll force-feed you. You should know that."

"Force-feed?"

"It's . . . unpleasant."

Eating the gross swill they called food was a nauseating enough prospect. Having it shoved down his gullet against his will was enough to make Rose's insides clamor to escape his body. He propped himself up on an elbow. Cleared his throat.

"I can't eat. I want to. But I can't eat what they're giving me." A thought occurred to him. "Are you my lawyer?"

The man snorted. "Your lawyer will get here when she gets here. They're in no hurry to have you prosecuted. Once you get sent to the Citywide facility, you're out of the Magistrate's hands. And he likes you where you are. No, I'm here to talk. Can we talk a little?"

Rose considered. He had no other options, after all. He nodded.

The man came out of the shadow. His eyes were mismatched, one blue, one green, and Rose couldn't help staring. "You can change your eyes!" he exclaimed.

"What?" The man shook his head. "I was born like this."

"Oh." Rose deflated. He could, with concentration, alter the pigments in his skin and other exterior surfaces. That was how he'd created the fake brand that allowed him to remain—for a time—in Ludo Territory. For a brief, shining moment, he'd fantasized that he'd discovered someone like him.

"I'm Superior Inspector Jona Markard. I'm the one who arrested you."

Ah. Yes. Rose remembered now.

"You shot at me. With people around." He mustered enough accusation that SI Markard flinched.

"I was chasing a murderer."

"I haven't killed anyone."

Markard folded his arms over his chest. "Listen, Rose. They sent me in here because they figure you're pretty close to breaking by now. I don't want to hurt you. I'm authorized to do it, but I don't want to. Do you believe me?"

Rose wasn't sure he did, but there was no harm in saying yes.

"You're never leaving a cell. As long as you live, for the rest of your life, you'll be in a cell. Do you understand?"

Unfortunately, Rose did. *The rest of his life*, though, was a vastly shorter amount of time than they could imagine. There'd been a fine coating of more silvery fuzz along his legs when he'd awoken before. And while he couldn't see his back, he could *feel* it there, growing, sinking its excruciatingly small talons into his skin. Blooming into him. Becoming him. Or he was becoming it.

Either way, it meant the end.

Would he surrender? he wondered. Would he eventually confess to something he hadn't done? Would he show them what he could do and let them dissect him, all to end the agony?

"You need to come clean," Markard said. "Tell them what you know. Look, the Magistrate's not an unreasonable man. He's very concerned about the plans your territory has. If you give him the information he needs, he—"

"He'll overlook the murder of his son?" Rose sat up, back to the wall, and mimicked Markard's arms-across-the-chest pose. Even dying, he wasn't stupid enough—or desperate enough—to believe that Max Ludo would forgive Jaron's death.

Markard's mouth moved without sound and then he recovered. "You'll always be on the hook for Jaron. But if you give up your people, tell us what we need to know, the other charges could go away. The spying—"

"I didn't spy."

Markard sighed. "I'm trying to help you, Rose," he said softly, gazing at him with those beautiful, mismatched eyes.

"You're not doing it very well," Rose replied. He was exhausted. Without even being aware of it, he drifted off to sleep.

■ ■ ■

The meals began to blur, and his vision began to blur, so he was no longer certain how much time had passed.

He began to wonder if perhaps he *had* killed Jaron Ludo. He *had* been there, in Jaron's apartment. He had gone there to recover Deedra's pendant. Slipped in through a window, as he'd become accustomed to doing. Jaron lived so high up that he never would have imagined someone entering through the window.

The pendant had been on a shelf in the bedroom. Rose had taken it and only then had he noticed the humped figure in the dark. The body. The blood.

He'd fled. Safer. Always the safe route. And yet...

There was a tendril, so like his own. Jaron had been crushed and slashed in a way Rose knew he could crush and slash.

What if there was someone else like him? What if some other Rose had...

There was no other Rose, though. None that he knew of. But who else could...

I wouldn't do that. I wouldn't.

232

But what if he had? What if he had done it and simply...didn't know?

He could not recall doing so, but was that definitive? Could he have murdered Jaron and *forgotten* doing so? The human mind, Rose knew, was capable of truly astonishing feats. And his mind was probably not even human.

Maybe I did it. Maybe they're right about everything. Maybe I'm a spy. Maybe I was built in a lab in some other Territory, created in a test tube and sent out to wreak havoc on my Magistrate's enemies.

And what of his other memories? The ones of his long trek across the Cities? They'd never existed. He'd conjured them in prison, as a way of pushing back against the solitary confinement. Inventing a history to ruminate on, something to think about beyond the four concrete walls.

What about Deedra, though? She was real, right? She exists, doesn't she?

Yes. Yes, she did. He had touched her. She had kissed him. Those things were real. He clung to them.

His arms had become spindly and twig-like, with a gray cast to them. When he lifted his shirt, his rib cage stood out against his thin flesh in stark relief, like ripples frozen on the surface of a pond.

The sepals growing from the back of his neck were a day, maybe two, from being unconcealable under his shirt. He contemplated ripping them off himself. Aware of the camera, he decided he would have to do so under the blanket. They would probably think he was having a seizure, so he would have to move quickly.

It turned out to be a moot plan. When he awoke the next morning, ready to do it, he felt the sepals shifting under him. They had curdled and fallen off in his sleep.

Dead.

Staring at the gray-green fold of his own body, now separate from him, he thought, *So am I. Not long now.*

CHAPTER 32

Tired of waiting for him to come to them, they came for him.

It was—as best he could tell—the middle of the night. His cell suddenly exploded with bright artificial light as the door clanged open, shocking him from a stupor.

No shackles this time. That, more than anything else—more than the silvery mildew on his body, the dead sepals, the ribs—convinced him that he was near death.

Once, they'd respected his power. Now he was nothing to fear.

They dragged him down a hallway. It blurred, a gray-white smear lit by the hellish artificial lights overhead. Something deep within him yearned and strained for the lights, mistaking them for true light. But they held nothing for him. No nutrition. No life.

A new room. This one dark, with a chair and a single penetrating light glaring at the seat. They put him in the seat and shackled him to it.

Not, he soon realized, because they thought he was dangerous.

"Your hunger strike is a failed gambit," Max Ludo said.

Rose raised his head, desperate to peer beyond the brightness stabbing his eyes. When had Max Ludo gotten there? Had he been there all along?

A hand grabbed his hair and jerked his head back. Another grasped his lower jaw, squeezing and prying it down, his mouth agape.

"Our chow not good enough for you?" a voice asked, and the next thing he knew, something slimy and rancid and gritty all at once was shoved between his teeth. It tasted like death and loss and chemicals.

Rose hissed and shook his head, but he was held fast. The hands jammed his teeth shut. Pinched his nostrils closed.

"Eat it, you bastard!" Ludo cried. "It took years to come up with just the right combination of spliced genes to make something like that. Eat it!"

Rose couldn't breathe…which normally wasn't a problem. He'd learned early on that when he couldn't breathe, his body had ways of absorbing the air around him. But the air here was stale, and he was too weak. They wouldn't let him breathe until he swallowed. He struggled against it, his body clamoring to swallow, his mind crying out against it.

He started choking and gagging and seizing, his body a jerking, uncontrollable thing that moved of its own volition.

The hands came away from his head, and he vomited the sludge they'd forced into him. It spattered the floor in front of him and ran down his chin in rivulets.

Even with his eyes closed, the bright light stabbed him. Gasping, he said, "I can't. You have to understand. It isn't natural." He had to make them understand. If they wanted him alive at all, they had to understand. He didn't know what words to use. He barely understood himself; how could he expect them to?

"Not *natural*?" someone spluttered. "That's cloned from original stem cells, spliced with the DNA of the extinct turkey. It's the most natural thing in the world!"

"Wait." Ludo's voice. "If he wants natural, maybe we should give him natural."

There was near-silence, filled with a low murmuring among voices out in the darkness that lurked beyond the harsh lighting. And then chuckling, which grew into laughter, and he was hauled to his feet and dragged again, into a corridor, past several doors. They flung open a door before he could read the word stenciled on it. They dragged him in.

His vision blurred, then sharpened for an instant. Cold tile under his feet, cracked with age. Ahead of him, an ancient-looking metal box, weeping trails of rust. A guard went to the side of it and cranked open a small hatch.

"Most natural thing in the world," Max Ludo chortled, "is being in the womb, eh? Am I right?"

A chorus of obsequious yeses.

"This is as close as it gets," Ludo went on. "Old-style sensory-deprivation tank. Almost forgot we had this damn thing down here." He poked his nose toward the open hatch, then recoiled, exclaiming. "Whew! Okay, so maybe not *all* your senses will be deprived. Four out of five isn't bad, though. Right?" Before Rose could respond, Max gestured. "Dump him in."

The smell hit him before they got him through the hatch, a rancid miasma, thick and noxious. He could taste as well as smell it. He struggled, but was too weak—they shoved him through the hatch, and he fell into a too-thick pool of water. The smell was all around him.

"You'll float in there for a good long while," Max promised him, his face filling the hatch. "No sound. No light. We'll see how long you last before you beg us to pull you out. How long before you're willing to spill all your secrets in return for something, *anything* but your own thoughts and that smell."

"I don't have anything to tell—"

Max slammed the hatch shut, leaving Rose in darkness and in silence.

He inhaled the stench.

Eyes wide, he could see nothing. Ears on alert, he heard nothing, the tank designed in such a way that its walls and water absorbed even the sound of his own breathing.

He reached out a hand, stretching his fingers to their fullest extent, brushing against the side of the tank. At least he had smell and touch going for him. There was something out there in the great blackness, he reminded himself. He was not floating in a void; he was floating in a metal tank filled with old, stale water in the middle of a building in the middle of a Territory, in the middle of a City, on the face of the planet.

He reminded himself of this over and over.

Metal under his fingertips. Then a patch of something fuzzy. Mold, he thought.

Hello there, living thing, he thought.

He smiled.

And closed his eyes.

Nothing changed.

. . .

Later—how long, he could not tell—they hauled him, reeking and soaking wet, out of the sensory-deprivation tank. The first sound to his ears was the tired, fading laughs of the men around him.

And Rose felt disoriented. Vulnerable. The light was too bright, the room too loud. Huddled on the floor, he could not find his bearings, could hardly move on his own.

But...

"Go hose him off and throw him back in his cell," Ludo said.

Hands under his arms lifted him.

But as he adjusted to the light and the sound, Rose realized something.

He felt better than he had in *days*.

They threw him into a tiny stall clad in cracked tiles.

Why did he feel better? Something they'd done. The moss in the tank. Paramecia in the stagnant water.

And now...now water! Cleaner this time, and more water than he'd encountered since his imprisonment began. He lay on the floor and spread his arms and legs wide, letting the water touch every inch of him. Cleansing him, yes, but more important than that...

Hydrating him.

Fortifying him.

It was over soon enough, over sooner than he would have hoped. But as they hauled him back to his cell and hurled him in—"Take some time to think, pissant. You'll talk soon enough."—Rose realized two things in the damp, cooling clarity of his postshower euphoria.

First, that he would die in prison.

Second, that this meant he had to escape.

CHAPTER 33

Cognizant of the camera monitoring his every move, Rose feigned continued weakness and depression. In truth, he felt stronger than he had in days. His color had improved, and the mildew along his skin was retreating. He felt the press and burst of new sepals beginning to grow.

This wouldn't last forever. Soon enough, he would weaken again. He had to act now, while he had any strength at all.

So he planned his escape. He was certain it was the smartest move he could possibly make.

It turned out to be the worst.

CHAPTER 34

"You see, Ms. Ward, they move in patterns."

Deedra still couldn't believe that she was out after curfew, brazenly flouting all the curfew laws and all but daring the drones to detect her. The Territory—so bereft by daylight—became something of a magical wonderland by night. In the weeks since she'd first been approached by Dr. Dimbali—since she'd learned the truth about Rose and decided to liberate him—she'd spent more and more nights outside, roaming the streets with Dr. Dimbali. She heard no "This is fundamental! This is truth!" from him when they were alone. That bombastic, preaching part of his persona was a put-on for L-Twelve. When it was just the two of them, he spoke quietly but confidently, his tone utterly self-assured, even when outside after curfew.

By night, the Territory was a haze of shadows and murky light scudding along the undersides of clouds. The cracks on the facades of buildings became art. The scorch marks from some long-ago riots became mere shadows. It was quiet and still and almost something beautiful.

"Once you understand something's pattern," Dr. Dimbali went on, "you can exploit it."

He was droning on—appropriately enough—about the drones.

Once, she had feared them, but now she understood that they were just machines. Highly intelligent machines, yes, but still yoked to their patterns. Dr. Dimbali had pointed out certain dead zones in their coverage, spots on the streets where—at the right moment—no camera spied.

She'd been fearful at first, but he had gone out that first night and returned an hour later, no worse for wear. He walked the streets with impunity. It was easier for him because he'd uploaded the drone patterns to his SmartSpex. But with each day that passed, she became more and more confident, especially once he showed her the new poncho he made for her.

"The drones detect you at night through active infrared," he lectured, "which looks for differences in temperature and zeros in on your ambient body heat. But what many people don't realize is that you can disguise your body's heat signature. This poncho is made of a stretched polyethylene terephthalate—a polyester film, if you will—married to a thin sheet of reflective foil. Made it myself, and don't think it was easy. It will reflect back on you your own body heat. Somewhat warm in the short term, but it will prevent the drones from seeing you."

Weeks later, she still wore the poncho, its hood up. As long as she kept it on, she was invisible to the drones.

Invisible. To the drones.

Words she never could have imagined thinking, not in a million years.

She had more to fear than just the drones, though. The systems that monitored her apartment door, for example...

Dr. Dimbali had an answer for that, too.

"Well, yes, of course the doors log your comings and goings, but so what? There are other ways in and out, if you're clever." She'd witnessed this firsthand—Dr. Dimbali's basement lab sprouted a rough-hewn tunnel that led to some sort of old delivery ramp that extended into an alleyway.

"I don't have a secret door," she told him.

"No, but you have a window. And no one ever thinks to go out the window because they assume the drones would see them anyway. And since no one goes out, there's no reason to go out. And so the windows aren't wired. It really is an amazing ouroboros of cluelessness and fear."

The next night, she'd opened her window, slipped on her antidrone poncho with the hood up, and scaled the wall down four stories. It had been both more terrifying and easier than she could have imagined. The building had protrusions and ledges, old water pipes, and pocks where riot shells had dented its walls years before her birth. Perfect handholds and footholds.

She was no longer bound by the restrictions of curfew and the confines of her apartment. That first night, she lingered on her way to Dr. Dimbali's, not caring that he would lecture her on tardiness.

The Territory was hers. Its empty streets, its hollow-eyed facades, its blind drones. She spread her arms and danced down a boulevard, forcing herself not to shout and whoop for joy.

"Why doesn't everyone do this?" she asked now. They huddled in a building within sight of the Secure Territorial Prison & Justice Facility—SecFac. "Why doesn't everyone figure out the patterns and come outside at night?"

Dr. Dimbali grunted in something like disgust and annoyance. "Because most people don't bother looking up. And those who do don't pay attention to what they see."

"Is there a way to avoid them during the day, too?"

"My dear Ms. Ward, as the very nature of our mutual friend Rose should make abundantly clear, *anything* is possible."

Even, perhaps, breaking Rose out of prison.

Weeks ago, she'd been a normal girl. There'd been nothing exceptional about her. Now she was violating curfew regularly and planning to help free an alleged murderer and spy from prison.

From their vantage point on one of the upper floors of the abandoned building, they could make out the entire sprawl of the Magistrate's Complex, which consisted of three edifices joined together by rough concrete passageways. One building housed the Magistrate's Office and administrative functions. Another contained offices for the local police and the DCS officers. The last building was the squattest, the ugliest, in a Territory filled with ugly buildings. This was the prison section of the Complex, SecFac, its gray exterior interrupted sporadically by slitted, barred windows. Rose lay beyond one of those windows, and every time they came to "reconnoiter the prison" (that's how Dr. Dimbali put it), Deedra had to tamp down the urge to run screaming to that building and cry up and out to each window in turn until she found Rose.

The drones were thickest over the Complex, swarming the air like cockroaches on scrap food. "This is new," Dr. Dimbali told her gravely. "They stepped up the Complex's surveillance patterns." He grimaced. "They're more worried about Rose than they're letting on in the wikis."

Since Rose's arrest, the wikis had maintained a steady stream of reports from deep within the guts of the Complex, averring that Rose had already confessed to the murder of Jaron Ludo, as well as to being a spy from Dalcord Territory. Magistrate Dalcord screamed treachery and massed troops along his border; Ludo responded in kind. The proof seemed unassailable:

OPERATIVES OF DCS, WORKING UNDER THE SUPERVISION AND PERSONAL GUIDANCE OF MAGISTRATE MAXIMILIAN LUDO, ARE MAKING PROGRESS IN EXTRACTING FURTHER INFORMATION FROM THE PRISONER. "WE'VE FOUND," MAGISTRATE LUDO

STATED IN A WIKIPOST, "THAT HUMANE
TREATMENT OF EVEN THE VILEST
VILLAINS PRODUCES THE BEST
RESULTS. SO WE ARE TREATING THIS
'ROSE' AS CIVILLY AS POSSIBLE,
AND HE IS REWARDING US WITH
INFORMATION."

Deedra didn't believe any of it.

"Why so many drones?" she asked.

Dr. Dimbali didn't turn to look at her; he was busy scanning the sky with his SmartSpex, recording the movements of the drones. "Rampant paranoia, the currency of our realm. They think his confederates will come to break him out."

"But...we *are* planning on breaking him out."

With a harrumph, he said, "Well, yes. But they don't *know* that."

Curfew had been cut back even further—usually it lasted from sunset to sunrise, but now it preceded the former and extended past the latter. The original reports had focused mostly on Rose murdering Jaron. That was bad enough. But as time went by and the shock of the Magistrate's son being murdered faded, the accusations of espionage took center stage. What had begun as a killing had morphed into a conspiracy that sprawled from Territory to Territory, sinking its tendrils into every heart and mind.

"If they change the narrative," Dr. Dimbali pointed out, staring out the window, "they can change your behavior. They can alter our society—such as it is—to meet the new, paranoid reality they are constructing—have *been* constructing—before our very eyes. We live in a world without history. That's exactly how the powers that be want it. When you cannot imagine a better world, you cannot demand it.

Or fight for it. So they drown you in half-truths and speculation and ignorance."

Deedra raced her pendant back and forth along its chain. "It can't be that simple. They can't just do that."

He chuckled, still watching the scene outside. "I wish such naïveté weren't a liability. In another world, in another time, perhaps. It not only is that simple, it *has been* that simple in the past."

She tucked her pendant away; he turned his attention away from the window and the drones, and she sighed, leaning against a wall. Sometimes, the idea of defying the Magistrate and his government seemed inevitable and righteous. Other times, it seemed foolish and suicidal. Most frustrating of all? There were times when it was all those things at once.

Dr. Dimbali stooped so that their eyes were level and grasped her urgently by the shoulders.

"I want you to understand something. Listen to me carefully and believe me. I do not dissemble easily, and I won't do it now. What I am about to tell you is the unvarnished truth. To wit: all these people you're so afraid of, Ms. Ward, these police and the Magistrate and the DeeCees. All of them. They're much less clever than you are."

"And you."

He permitted himself a small smile. "Well, that goes without saying. But all they have on their side is machines and guns. Yes, and numbers. A good brain can think around those things. I've been watching you—I know you have such a brain."

Deedra flushed with the unanticipated praise.

"I'm just not sure.... I know it was my idea, but there's so *many* of them...."

"Think of what's at stake, Deedra." It was the first time he'd used her first name, and that—even more than the desperate urgency in his voice—compelled her total focus on him. "The world before—the world from that book Rose left, the one you let me read. That world was real. The book was fiction, but I've seen the facts."

"You lived it?" she asked.

He favored her with an indulgent smile, his thin lips quirking upward for a rare instant. "I'm not quite *that* old. The world we're discussing existed a long, long time ago. Centuries before the Red Rain."

"What caused the Red Rain?" she asked. "What was it?"

He stiffened in discomfort. "The fact is: No one knows. It began over a hundred years ago, ended probably before you were born. The world was already in dire straits, of course. The Red Rain was one more insult, one more injury. But the documents I had access to when I worked for the government...they proved what I'd always known. That once, the air was fresh, the world unpaved, the trees abundant, the food not from labs. That is the world we deserve. It's our birthright. We need to get it back, and Rose is the key!"

She wrenched away from him; his grip had tightened painfully, crushing her shoulders.

He stared at her, as though uncertain as to why she'd pulled back. Then he returned to the window, hands clasped behind his back.

"I went to my superiors. I showed them what I'd learned. 'We need to go back to this,' I told them. 'We need to find a way to restore the world.' 'It's too late,' they told me. And when I pushed and pushed and pushed, they fired me. Blackballed me. Exiled me here.

"We've been plotting and planning and observing for weeks now." He came back to her, tears in his eyes behind the SmartSpex, his expression forlorn. "And we're so close."

"There's one thing we haven't talked about," Deedra reminded him. "One last thing to consider."

"What's that?"

She took a deep breath. Reluctant to speak the words, but someone had to. "What if he did it? What if it's all true? If he killed Jaron and is spying on us so that Magistrate Dalcord can take over the Territory?"

"You don't really believe any of that."

"No. But you told me that a good scientist never discards a possibility based on belief, not facts."

Dr. Dimbali straightened, pleased. "Yes, well, I did, didn't I. Still, I can tell you with complete honesty that I don't *care* if Rose killed Jaron Ludo or not. In fact, Rose could murder half of Ludo Territory, and I still would not care. Because what that boy is—the very biology of him—is so important that it removes him from the petty concerns of individual morality."

"What are you saying?"

"I'm saying that..." He paused and adjusted his SmartSpex. "I'm saying that if my hypothesis is correct, I can change the world. But I need Rose to do it, and that necessity trumps anything as petty as murder. The needs and concerns of fifty billion people far outweigh the death of even the scion of our Magistrate."

She pondered this for a moment. "You didn't really answer my question."

"My dear, your question is irrelevant."

Maybe it was. She put it out of her mind.

■ ■ ■

Deedra hadn't bothered going to work very much in the weeks since Rose had been arrested and Lissa had been shot, but with Dr. Dimbali covering her absences via a little opportune hacking, she feared no loss of rations. Her nights became about reconnaissance and planning, while her days were devoted to catching up on the sleep she missed.

Lissa had been released from MedFac. A stray round had perforated her left side during the shoot-out, and she lost a kidney. Too busy plotting and planning with Dr. Dimbali, Deedra didn't have a chance to visit her friend until Lissa had been home for a week. She buzzed at the building and was let in, then knocked at the apartment door. There was such a protracted period of silence that she wondered if Lissa was even home, but then she heard a thump, a click, and the door creaked open. There, in the sliver of space between the door and the frame, was Lissa.

Deep black bags sank her eyes far into her face. They were moist, glittering gems at the bottom of twin wells. Her skin was the color of old cement, her hair lank and knotted. But she perked up at the sight of Deedra, just as Deedra had hoped she would. There was something to be said for surprising a sick friend.

Not sick, she reminded herself. *Shot*.

"Deedra." Lissa's voice croaked at first, but perked up. "Deedra!"

She opened the door the rest of the way. She was using a walker to get around, and Deedra immediately felt guilty for making her come to the door. "Are you alone?" she asked as she slipped inside.

Clumping over to a chair, Lissa nodded. "Everyone else is out. Work or scavenge. I mean, we're glad for the sympathy ration and the compassion bonus, but no one knows if I'll be able to go out on my own or not. Not yet." She settled into the chair, which groaned and creaked. Deedra sat across from her on the old sofa she knew Lissa slept on. There was a single door to another room, and a kitchen nook. The main room was crammed with mattresses for Lissa's siblings, boxes of clothes and other personal belongings. Deedra couldn't help thinking of Dr. Dimbali's enormous, sprawling quarters. Was there more room just for the taking? Could Lissa have her own room, her own apartment?

"How do you feel?" she asked Lissa.

Lissa smiled wanly. "Everything hurts. I can't even eat crispies. They're feeding me sludge."

Sludge. It had some kind of official name, but everyone called it sludge because, well, if it looks like sludge, feels like sludge, and tastes like sludge, why not call it sludge? It was a thick, viscous "nutritionally dense food-supplement product" usually given to those who couldn't get by on standard rations. And apparently, to people shot through the kidney who were having trouble eating after surgery. Everyone had slurped it (*eaten* was the wrong word) at some point. Never voluntarily.

"Gross." Deedra didn't know what else to say and was horrified to feel a smile creeping along her face.

But Lissa smiled back, her face lighting up just a bit. "It *is* gross. Remember a couple of years ago when we had that fever...?"

Ugh. Yeah, she remembered. A week of sludge, mostly because it was "genetically modified to promote health and regular bowels." At one point, Deedra had vomited her "dinner" of sludge, and Lissa had collapsed into hysterical laughter, pointing. "It looks exactly the same! *Exactly the same!*"

"That was gross," Deedra said, grinning. "And you were no help."

"After you puked, it was all I could do to hold it down myself. I *had* to laugh. Otherwise, I'd spew, too."

They chuckled themselves out of memory, then into silence. Deedra leaned in and put a hand on Lissa's knee. "Other than that. How are you? Your parents being cool?"

A shrug, followed by a wince. "They're dealing. I don't know. They were looking forward to having *one* of us out of here, and now..."

Deedra had lived on her own since the orphanage had closed down. She'd been happy to get out of there and imagined Lissa was similarly looking forward to some privacy. Sharing one big room with your brother and sister couldn't be much fun for anyone involved.

"Maybe you could move in with me," she said brightly before even considering how complicated that could be. Or how impossible. She would probably be dead or in prison soon enough for her part in Rose's rescue.

"You don't want to have to take care of me." Lissa wiped a tear away. "But thanks for the offer. Honestly, Deedra...honestly...I'm just..." She glanced around—unconsciously, almost instinctively—at the corners of the room where the safety monitors nestled in shadow, then dropped her voice so low that she was almost only mouthing the words:

"I'm just so glad he's dead."

Deedra's hand tightened on Lissa's knee.

"Him and his Bang Boys, all those years...Being afraid at L-Twelve, under his command. You know what I mean, Deedra."

Something in the way she said it made Deedra think that maybe she *did* know.

She shivered at a recollection of Jaron's hard, seeking hands on her.

"Lissa...did Jaron ever...were you ever..." She tried to think of the best way to put it, the right words to use. She'd been able to lock away that day on the rooftop in a steel box in her mind, to decorate it with memories of Rose, to make it disappear. And now Lissa's hatred of Jaron threatened to make perfect sense, and she was afraid knowing the truth would open the box of memories.

"Were you ever alone with him?" she settled on.

Lissa stared at her for too long. "There's no point talking about it anymore," she said at last. "It doesn't matter anymore."

"Oh, Lissa..."

Lissa shook it off, raised her voice. "So what are the rest of the Bang Boys up to? Now that their leader is dead." Lissa was going to keep saying the word *dead* as many times as she could, apparently.

"Not much." And that was true. Deedra had witnessed the Bang Boys in a scuffle with some workers. Kent Massgrove had seemed to be in charge, and things weren't going well. Halfway through the melee, Lio declared the whole thing "stupid" and backed away. When Kent ordered him back into the fight, Lio had said, "If you want to kick their asses so bad, do it yourself."

Rik had joined Lio's mutiny, leaving just Kent and Hart. The next day the two groups ended up pummeling each other almost into MedFac.

"Good," Lissa said, leaning back and sighing. A small, satisfied smile played at the edges of her mouth, flickering back and forth with a grimace. "Good. I'm glad. I hope they all end up off-ration."

Off-ration was the nightmare scenario in Ludo Territory. It wasn't official or sanctioned, but everyone knew it could happen: You could be cut off entirely from the government ration program, set adrift, and forced to survive on whatever scavenge you could dig up, whatever charity you could beg. Fleeing to another Territory was a possibility, maybe. But she'd never heard of anyone managing to do that, and arriving in another Territory with nothing to offer would make it hard to persuade that Territory to share its rations. She supposed between scavenge and outright thievery, it might be possible to survive...but in the end, she couldn't find it in herself to wish it on anyone. Death seemed far kinder. Off-ration was death with slow torture preceding it.

"They're not all idiots," she told Lissa. "They'll straighten out, now that they don't have Jaron around to protect them."

Lissa shook her head fiercely. "You think you know them. You don't. It's not about being an idiot. They think the world owes them something. They think they should be able to take whatever they want. Believe me, Deedra, they're going to keep taking what they see in front of them. They're not going to stop."

Deedra nodded soberly, but deep down she couldn't muster the emotion to care overmuch about the disposition or ultimate fate of the Bang Boys. Rose was still in prison, and she was going to be the one to rescue him.

"Do you want a blanket?" She noticed Lissa beginning to drift off, as if her rant and her fantasy of the Bang Boys starving in the streets had lullabied her. Her head dipped low, her chin against her chest.

"It's the meds," Lissa said, slurring slightly. "They make me tired. Help me up? I've been sleeping in my parents' room. Can you help me get there?"

Deedra helped Lissa up and walked her to the other room. She'd always been in awe of people who had more than one room. After seeing Dr. Dimbali's on-the-sly suite of rooms and massive basement laboratory, though, she was a little more difficult to impress. Lissa's parents' room was cramped and tiny, barely bigger than Deedra's own sleeping nook, with a grimy slit of a window set at floor level. She felt for the light control, couldn't find it, and decided not to bother.

She let Lissa lean against her as she lowered herself into bed. To be alone all day, in such pain, so helpless...

Then again, at least Lissa had a family. At least at night, there would be someone. If Deedra had been shot...

There would be no one. Once, she might have imagined Rose being there for her. But now...

What would it be like when he was rescued?

Lissa cried out, and Deedra snapped back into the moment, helping her settle onto the bed. "Can I get you anything?"

"Sure. A turkey steak with tomato pellets."

"And a side order of sludge?"

"Yum!"

She sat with Lissa for a few moments as her friend began to drift off, then picked her way carefully through the dark room. But she'd only taken a couple of steps when her foot collided with something that almost tripped her. She stooped down to push it out of the way so that it wouldn't trip Lissa later. When her fingers touched it, they recognized it immediately. It took her brain a moment to catch up.

It was a tendril. A vine. Whatever you wanted to call it.

One of Rose's *extensions*.

In the murky light, she could barely make it out. It was mottled green and brown, clearly old and decomposing. But unmistakable. Similar tendrils had wrapped around her and borne her aloft; she knew them instantly.

"Lissa!"

Sleep-clogged: "Hmm?"

"Where did you get this?"

"Hmm?"

She hauled it up off the floor. It was at least five feet long. "This."

Lissa's eyes fluttered open and took a few seconds to focus. "Found it. Before I got shot. On the way to work. Thought it might be edible."

"Are you sure?"

But Lissa had drifted into sleep. Deedra coiled up the vine as best she could, then tucked it under the bed.

First, though, she drew her knife from the small of her back and cut off a two-inch-long section.

■ ■ ■

When she got to Dr. Dimbali's basement lab, the place resounded with a harsh, unrelenting mechanical buzz. Deedra clapped her hands over her ears and pressed forward until she spied Dimbali himself, leaning bodily against some kind of machine that looked like the offspring of a drill and a jackhammer. He was hollowing out a hole in the concrete wall, and from the amount of dust in the air and the evidence of other, similar, breaches of the wall, this wasn't the first. His belly jiggled amusingly with the vibration of the machine, and she couldn't repress a giggle. Some of the potted plants strewn around the lab shivered with the tremors caused by the machine.

After a few minutes, he thumbed off the machine and leaned back, gasping for breath, sweat streaming down his face and neck. He pushed his safety goggles up onto his forehead, and once again, she saw him without the SmartSpex. Humbler, maybe? More normal, maybe?

He startled when he noticed her watching him. "Ms. Ward! You gave me a fright!"

So much for *normal*.

"Sorry. What are you up to?" She gestured to the four, five, *six* holes in the walls. Seven, if you counted the new one.

He shrugged. "An experiment. That's all. Testing a hypothesis. Nothing for you to concern yourself with."

And so much for *humbler*.

"I have something to show you." She dug into her pocket for the chunk of vine she'd taken from Lissa's place. He managed to tuck the machine under one arm and reached for the chunk. Closer, the reek of his strong sweat, mingled with concrete dust and an undertone of something rich and dark and alien, made her nose wrinkle. If Dr. Dimbali noticed, he didn't show it. Or care.

"Fascinating," he murmured, turning the chunk over before his eyes. "Where—"

"My friend had it. Lissa Stanhope. She said she found it. I'm thinking it comes from Rose, doesn't it? That's the only explanation."

"I won't know until I run some tests to compare with specimens already in my possession. An mRNA comparison should be dispositive. Sadly, I'm sure it won't contain the necessary human/rose tissues that I require."

Deedra blew out an exasperated breath. "Come on! It's his. You know it and I know it."

"I am unwilling to commit to a specific—"

"Dr. Dimbali!"

He sighed with a peculiarly adult annoyance. "I do believe he mentioned once that he sometimes . . . *sheds* such things when he's done with them. So, yes, anecdotally we could assume—"

"What if someone found a bunch of them while scavenging? What if *that* person killed Jaron, using these?"

Dimbali said nothing.

"We could prove Rose is innocent!" She almost shouted it, infuriated at his calm, at his reticence. "We could take the evidence to the Magistrate and prove Rose didn't kill Jaron. We wouldn't have to break him out of jail—we could just get him out that way."

Dr. Dimbali considered this for a moment, then chuckled and shook his head. "You had me actually contemplating it for a moment! But it's useless. To begin with, the powers that be don't need evidence. They don't even understand Rose's true nature; they have no connection between him and the vines left at the scene, and they don't care. They don't *need* a connection. Not when they have suspicion and a stranger."

"But that's not fair. And besides, they *do* know that Jaron was killed by the vines, so if we can show someone else had access to them..."

"You are behaving as though some sort of conventional explanation is needed, some kind of rationale for what has happened. I'm telling you—I've told you—that all that matters is rescuing Rose. We don't need to prove his innocence or someone else's guilt because those matters are irrelevant."

"But if we can prove he didn't kill Jaron—"

"Trust me—it would take longer, *vastly* longer, to do that than to rescue him from prison. And in any event, as we've discussed in the past, we can't be sure that he *didn't* kill Jaron. Not that—"

"Not that it matters," she interrupted. She'd heard it before.

"Something else to consider. Let us assume—simply for the sake of our current discussion—that this is, in fact, an...artifact of Rose's presence. Let us further assume that this artifact presents compelling and true evidence pointing to the actual killer of Jaron Ludo. What would be the logical conclusion in such an instance?"

She didn't understand what he—Oh. "Lissa."

"Precisely. If you present your evidence to the DeeCees or even to the police, the most likely scenario is that they will simply ignore it. They have their orders from Max Ludo, and they won't deviate from them. But let's say they decide to pay attention. First, they would put you under twenty-four-hour surveillance. Then they would interrogate you until you crack as to where you found it—"

"And go straight to Lissa."

"Exactly."

Was she willing to trade Lissa for Rose? Those were the kinds of questions she never wanted to hear, much less answer.

"I just feel like it's safer. Maybe there's a way to try. To send it in anonymously and then..."

Dimbali clucked his tongue and shook his head sadly. "There is one path ahead of us. It goes in one direction. I wish I could tell you exactly what will happen. Some consequences are more likely than others. All I know for certain is this: Once he is free, I will be able to use what I know of him to change the world for the better. How long that will take, I cannot say. People's reactions, especially those in power? Again, I cannot say. The world is the way it is because someone somewhere has a vested interest in it being so. Entrenched powers are difficult to..." He paused and looked down at the machine in his hands. "Difficult to drill through, if you will."

It was his idea of a joke. Deedra forced herself to smile. To encourage him.

"I might remind you as well," he went on, "that rescuing Rose from prison was *your* idea." He tapped at the SmartBoard, and Deedra was shocked to see herself appear on-screen.

"—were my last hope," the voice of Dr. Dimbali said from the screen.

Deedra watched herself drink the Rose-tea from her mug, then stare at the video version of Dr. Dimbali, stand up, and say: "We're going to break Rose out of jail."

"You've been recording me?" she asked.

He waved away her concern. "Of course not. Why would I do that? I record *myself.* You were simply here at the time. My presence activates the recording."

"That's...weird." Who would want a video record of everything they did?

"This is a place of science, Ms. Ward. Everything that happens here matters. Everything I do must be recorded for examination and posterity. Who knows when I might do or say something that will prove crucially important to my research later?"

She sighed. *Whatever.*

"I promise you," he told her, "we will do all we can in this situation. But our lives after the rescue will not, I fear, resemble their current states. In all likelihood, we will be on the run, hunted."

Some part of her had assumed this from the beginning. But that part had a quiet voice and never spoke much anyway. Had she ever imagined that she could break the law, retrieve Rose from prison, and then go back to her oh-so-ordinary life?

Then again...what was so great about that oh-so-ordinary life anyway?

"Are you all right?" Dr. Dimbali asked. He asked it with the clinical air of a man wondering if a wall's structural integrity is still viable, not a man genuinely concerned with her.

She was used to it. *This is my life*, she thought. *A scientific genius with all the warmth of a dead rat, and a beautiful, imprisoned boy who is also a plant.*

The laughter burbled out of her involuntarily. Before she realized

257

what was happening, she convulsed with it, doubling over and howling, gasping for breath at the same time.

I'm in love with a plant, and the only person I can trust is probably more than a little bit crazy and thinks he can save the world.

The laughter came harder, and she leaned against the wall for support, heaving out guffaws. Tears streamed down her face. As she caught her breath, she looked up to see Dr. Dimbali gazing at her, his goggles still pushing his hair up in a spray, his face gritty and gray with a fine coating of concrete dust, his expression one of such earnest befuddlement that she started laughing all over again.

Her oh-so-ordinary life? Ha! That life had ended—if it had ever really existed in the first place—that day by the river, the day she'd seen the blue rat.

She palmed the tears away, choking down air, forcing herself to breathe. She was never supposed to have to make these decisions. No one was ever supposed to have to make these decisions. How was any one person supposed to decide the fate of another person, much less the fate of the world?

Why her?

But hell—why *not* her?

"Let's do it," she said.

CHAPTER 35

T he plan had to be simple, as all good plans must be, according to Dr. Dimbali.

As an enemy combatant, Rose would not be permitted visitors, except for his attorney. Dr. Dimbali was known at the Complex, having visited there on L-Twelve business with Jaron. But Deedra was unknown to them. She would have to be the one to perform reconnaissance within the facility itself. To capture the floor-plan information they would need to execute the rescue.

"If my calculations are correct," Dr. Dimbali said with a tone of voice that left no doubt that they were, "then Rose is no doubt extraordinarily weak right now. We need him strong, but the conditions inside his cell would prevent him from recouping his strength."

She thought of him on the patch of dirt outside her apartment, absorbing his food through the soil and from the sun. Precious little of either in SecFac, if any.

"My research indicates that roses need nitrogen and phosphorous in particular to thrive. Fortunately, these are easily distilled from waste matter. We will develop *concentrates* of these nutrients, delivered in a solution no larger than a standard hypodermic needle. This will give

Rose the nutritional jolt he needs to escape. It is imperative that he conserve his strength, that he not act until the precise moment *we* are ready for him to act. With his biomorphic capabilities, he should be able to escape through the window."

"Biomorphic?"

"Shape-shifting."

She thought of the tendrils Rose had extruded from his body. Of course. If he could do that, what other ways could he change his form? She suffered a sudden jab of jealousy that Dr. Dimbali knew more about Rose than she did, then quelled it. Rescuing Rose was what mattered.

"Then what?"

"Then he and I can complete my work and begin reviving the world."

"No, no, I mean . . . I mean, I go in and reconnoiter, and we make a solution out of our . . . you know. But how do we get it to him?"

Dr. Dimbali's face lit up. "That is where you are fortunate to be working with me on this endeavor. There are a few possibilities. Still, let us not get ahead of ourselves. One step at a time. Your reconnoiter comes first."

"What if it doesn't go well? What if I don't learn anything useful?"

"You must. Once they learn *what* Rose is, I'm afraid he will be nothing more than a lab specimen to them. One that talks. Until he no longer can."

Deedra shuddered. Dr. Dimbali had a way of delivering the most unpleasant news possible in a flat, apathetic tone that made it even worse.

"Then let's not waste any more time," she told him, and held out a demanding hand. Dr. Dimbali—with a moment's hesitation and more genuine regret than she'd ever witnessed in him—slowly removed his SmartSpex and placed them in her hand.

CHAPTER 36

Under cover of night, Rose had tested himself. The camera was infrared-equipped, he was certain, like the drones he evaded so easily. His body temperature fluctuated, sometimes involuntarily, depending on the ambient climate, but the conditions in the cell never changed. He could change his core temperature at will, making himself cool enough to blend into the background at night when the drones were looking for him, but while in the cell, he had to maintain a human range of body temperature so that he wouldn't vanish on the camera and cause suspicion.

Now that he felt stronger, he began plotting his escape. No one would be coming to rescue him—how could they?—so he would have to be his own savior. Which was fine. He'd survived so long on his own, after all. For years, he'd needed no one but himself.

And then Deedra.

Why had she extended a helping hand to him that day by the river? And why had he accepted it? In all his travels, she was the first person who ever tried to help him for no other reason than to help. She wanted and took nothing from him in return for her aid; she baffled and charmed him at the same time. Not that he couldn't or didn't understand the impulse; he understood it intimately.

He'd just never witnessed it outside of himself before.

In all the places he'd visited since that first day in the graveyard, since that sighting of what may have been the last rose in the world, he'd encountered hundreds if not thousands of people on his path. Some, he'd helped. Some had helped him. Some had shunned him, avoided him, tried to kill him, or persecuted him. Of those who had helped, though, none had done it without cost. None had offered one hand without the other open and waiting for repayment.

Until Deedra.

I was fine. I was fine until you. And then I had to stay, I had to stay here, and look what's happened to me.

Now he would leave. He would leave this prison, and he would leave Ludo Territory. A fugitive. A year ago, it would not have bothered him, having to flee.

Now, though, he was leaving someone behind.

He forced himself not to think of her, focused on practicing in the dark. The camera could read his heat signature, but not the fine details of his shape.

Or his color.

He practiced. He was almost ready.

In the morning, then.

CHAPTER 37

The Complex loomed ahead of her that morning. From ground level, it was much more imposing than it had been from an angle above, and its formidable gray walls and electrified fencing nearly weakened her knees and made her reconsider.

But that time was past.

She slipped on the SmartSpex. They smelled faintly of some kind of piquant spice and the peculiarly male odor of sweat. They were a bit too large for her, and she had to keep poking at them to push them up on her nose.

The world was fractured through the broken lens on her left. Clouds gathered overhead. Rain? She couldn't tell. The day was humid and hot, the only alternative to freezing cold.

At the gate to the Complex, two DeeCees stood in full riot armor, with weapons at the ready. One of them glanced at her. "Move along, citizen."

"I have business here," she said, drawing herself erect.

Nothing to fear, Deedra. Not right now. This is just part one. Recon. Nothing to fear.

"No, you don't," the DeeCee barked. "Move along." As if she didn't get the point—and the threat—he gestured up the road with the barrel of his gun.

"The Territorial Code states that citizens may visit the Magistrate's Office to register official complaints or to request commendations for Territory personnel."

The DeeCees exchanged an amused glance. "Which are you here for?"

"I want to commend my supervisor, Suresh Dimbali." She fixed the obstinate DeeCee with a glare. "But maybe I'll file something else while I'm here."

Weak threat, maybe, but it showed her spine. The DeeCee relented. He produced a handheld scanner and ran it over her body. It bleeped as he passed it over her breasts and he tilted his head. Without a moment's thought, Deedra lifted her poncho so that he could see her pendant dangling there against her shirt. The DeeCee scanned the pendant, shrugged with satisfaction, and then continued.

"No goggs in the Complex," the DeeCee said when he'd scanned her and found nothing. He held out a hand, palm up, and wiggled his fingers, demanding the SmartSpex.

"They don't actually *work*," Deedra said with careful, measured sarcasm. *How* stupid *are you?* her tone asked. "I just like wearing them. They look cool." She removed the SmartSpex and held them out to him, twisting them around so he could peer through them and see nothing but glass.

Abashed, the guard shrugged. Of course they wouldn't work. How many people had functional tech like that? He waved her in.

As soon as she was within the bounds of the gate, Deedra fiddled with her pendant, removing the tiny battery attached there. Pretending to clean the lens of the SmartSpex, she loaded the battery into its compartment, then slipped the goggs on.

There was a disorienting moment of flashing colors as the SmartSpex rebooted, but then the heads-up overlay settled into place. Deedra pretended to cough into her hand, but instead whispered, "Let's go, Spex."

A hovering light blinked at the periphery of her vision. The SmartSpex were listening.

"Start capture," she said, and the SmartSpex began recording everything she saw. There would be a complete layout of everywhere she went in the Complex, a record of things she didn't even remember seeing. Guard numbers and patterns. Security measures. Everything.

Hold tight, Rose. We're coming.

■ ■ ■

Dr. Dimbali had taught her a whole range of commands—he called them "murms," short for "murmurs"—that controlled the various aspects of the SmartSpex. As she made her way to the first building—the Magistrate's Office—she tested the murms, switching from normal light to infrared to ultraviolet to gamma scatter and back again. The SmartSpex worked without complaint, and she saw through walls, through skin. She was beginning to think that Dr. Dimbali had intentionally broken one of the lenses. As camouflage. If people knew what he was capable of doing and seeing, they would never trust him.

The Magistrate's Complex was three buildings arranged around a central concrete courtyard, the whole thing hemmed in by ramparts topped with razor wire. To her left, going through the gate, was the Magistrate's Office building. To her right lay the headquarters for the local police and the Territory's DeeCee contingent, including the Emergency Stocks—the Magistrate's arsenal and supply of emergency rations in case of attack.

And straight ahead, at the other end of the flat, dead courtyard, the squat, square tumor that was SecFac.

That was her goal. But she couldn't just wander in there. She veered left.

The inside of the Magistrate's Office wasn't nearly as cramped as the other buildings she'd been in, but it was almost as dusty and dirty. The floors were carpeted, true, but the carpets were ragged and pockmarked with spots worn see-through thin, even without SmartSpex. Armed guards stood everywhere at attention, watching her as she walked the halls. She tried not to gape at them, as the SmartSpex spat out information on them, revealing their model of body armor and weapon complement.

We're in deep.

She found a desk with a sign that said TERRITORIAL CITIZEN ASSISTANCE and stood patiently until someone showed up.

"Can I help you?" the woman said, clearly interested in anything but. "The Magistrate isn't in today, so don't even bother asking."

"I was actually wondering," Deedra said, speaking the line exactly as she'd rehearsed it with Dr. Dimbali, "how I apply for a permission visa to visit someone in the prison."

The woman arched an eyebrow. Deedra tried not to show how nervous she was. There was nothing criminal about visiting a criminal. It just felt that way.

"I have a friend who did something stupid," she went on. If the woman demanded details, she had a whole story invented about her "friend," including a name and details of crimes, culled from reports on the wikis. She would never admit to knowing Rose. Not here. Not for this purpose. But if she could get into SecFac, she could record more information that would help them spring Rose. If not, she would at least walk by the building. But getting in would be better.

"Permission visas take ten days to process," the woman snapped, and slid a tab to Deedra.

Ten days? She hadn't known that. Dr. Dimbali hadn't mentioned it.

"Is there any way to get in sooner?" she asked.

The woman simply glared at her until Deedra took the tab and went to stand in a corner. There were no chairs or sofas.

The tab flickered on, the image wobbling, displaying a Permission Visa Request Form. Deedra grimaced. She didn't want to waste time filling this out, but if she didn't, it would look suspicious.

She sighed and started tapping the screen.

CHAPTER 38

Rose stayed under the blanket as long as possible, even though he longed to uncover himself and enter the sunbeam falling into his cell. The clouds were thin today, the sun a little stronger than usual, and its light sang to him, tempting him out of bed. He resisted. He'd spent the night preparing, and if the camera saw his preparation, his escape would be over before it began. Now he only needed to wait for—

There it was. The telltale tread of a boot just outside his door. Bringing what passed for breakfast for the prisoners of Max Ludo.

The food slot slid open from the outside and the tray prodded into the cell, waiting for him to take it.

He slid off the cot, still wrapped in his blanket. Overnight, he had coaxed his skin color to change, deepening and darkening it to a mottled black, like the body armor worn by the guards. As his strength had returned, his sepals had regrown as well, and he'd focused his concentration, shaping them around him. He knew the camouflage wasn't perfect, but he hoped it would be close enough to fool people at a distance, and maybe those not paying rapt attention to security cameras.

It had been hard, exhausting work, and it had taken a night of rigorous single-mindedness. But it was nothing compared with what he had to do now.

He had to perform violence.

He did not want to do this. In the past, he'd often been able to reason his way out of situations that called for violence, or used his powers to evade those who would not be rational. But there was no way to reason with Max Ludo or his underlings, and no way to run away. Not without hurting someone.

Holding the blanket around himself with one hand, he took the tray with the other, slowly pulling it into the cell.

The hand on the other side of the door let go. The slot was open and unblocked for just this moment. He dropped the tray and thrust his hand into the slot.

And fired out tendrils from his arm.

On the other side of the door, he heard a gasp of shock. Lashing out with the tendrils, he flailed until they wrapped around something. A leg.

Unlike the time he'd wrapped up Deedra and lifted her into the air, this time he was glad for the thorns.

A yelp from the other side of the door. He tightened his grip. The thorns ripped at the bulky body armor.

He thickened the vines. Going by feel, he extended them up the guard's body, encircling the throat and cutting off his voice before he could call for help. Through the tendrils, he could feel the rapid, panicked pulse in the man's neck. He tightened his noose of vines, and thorns bit into the man's flesh.

How much time had passed? Seconds. Maybe. He hoped. If someone was watching him on the camera, they would just be wondering why he was still crouched down at the door. Maybe they wouldn't react yet. Maybe curiosity would keep them watching.

Throwing away that worry, he focused on the man outside. He needed the guard helpless and terrified, not injured or dead.

"If you want to live," he said into the slot, hoping his voice would carry, "then open the door."

There was a gurgle of speech, unintelligible.

"You have no idea what I can do to you," Rose said. He tried to make his voice threatening, but it came out more informative than anything else. Oh, well. The thorns biting the man's neck should be threat enough.

Another gurgle. The man moved against the vines. Rose closed his eyes, visualizing the other side of the door. He had the guard's holster securely closed with a vine, and one hand bound to his waist. The other hand was free, tugging at the vines choking him.

"You only have a few seconds before you pass out from lack of oxygen," Rose told him. "Open the door and you'll live."

Still dry, academic. Maybe that was actually more frightening than doing a Jaron Ludo impression.

More gurgling. Was the man struggling against the vines, or struggling to reach the controls to the door? Rose retracted his vines a tiny bit, pulling the guard closer to the door.

Would he kill this man, if he had to? Would he carry through on the threat? He didn't think so. His mind was sharper now than it had been in weeks, but still fuzzy. Fuzzy enough to kill? No. Certainly not.

And yet...if this gambit failed, they would know what he was capable of. He had no choice but to get out of his cell *now*. It would be his only opportunity.

"I can constrict these even tighter." He forced himself to growl a bit, turning his voice deep and husky and alien. "I can crush you like cheap glass. *Open the door!* Do it now if you want to live!"

More flailing beyond the door.

And then the click of the lock.

Rose sighed in what he knew to be premature relief. This, as hard as it had been, was the easy part.

He retracted his vines and yanked open the door. The guard—purplish, gasping, bleeding—staggered there. Rose shed his blanket and pushed the guard aside, darting into the hallway.

Alarms rang out.

CHAPTER 39

Deedra finished filling out the useless form and made her way back outside via a different route, recording. Just in case it could help.

The form had asked for the name and Citizen ID of the inmate she wished to visit. She'd used one of the names she'd found while on the wikinets, hoping no one would actually check into it. She didn't think anyone would, especially since she had no intention of coming back. The few people she saw milling about the Magistrate's Office were listless and slow, in no hurry to accomplish anything. She didn't think they were particularly detail-oriented.

Outside, the sun broke through the clouds just long enough to remind her it was still there. Maybe this was a good omen. In *This Side of Paradise*, sunlight always seemed to mean something beautiful and delightful. She turned her face to the sky and luxuriated in the warmth on her skin. Was this what Rose felt when he photosynthesized? She liked to imagine that was the case, that they could share this sensation, but she knew the truth was more likely that he experienced the sun on a deeper, truer level than she ever could, that he had a connection to the sky and the rain and the soil and the air that she could never understand. Maybe she could come to appreciate it, but she would never *know* it.

Then again, she reminded herself, *he'll never fully know what it's like to be human, either.*

The thought saddened and gladdened her at the same time. She and Rose would never truly understand each other...but they would always surprise each other.

That's assuming you can get him out of here. And you're not doing a very good job so far.

SecFac loomed ahead of her, a blunt chunk of squared-off concrete three stories high. Squat, gray, and mottled, it made her think of a bad tooth in a near-empty mouth. She wondered how close she could get. There were guards stationed nearby, ten or twelve of them—TWELVE LIFE-FORMS LOCKED, the SmartSpex reported an instant later—and they seemed pretty attentive. The opposite of the lassitude in the Magistrate's Office.

She wandered a little closer. "Magnify," she mumbled, and the SmartSpex zoomed in on SecFac. Text and numbers scrolled by; she ignored them. All this information would be preserved for her—well, Dr. Dimbali, really—to examine later. Right now, she just had to see how close she could get. There had to be *some* way to figure out which window led into Rose's cell.

Give me a sign, she thought fiercely. *Shoot a vine out the window. Do something!*

"Ms. Ward?"

Deedra startled and turned to her left, staggering for a moment as the SmartSpex had to catch up, zooming back out so that she could see the man who'd come up right next to her.

"I thought it was you," said TI Markard. His lips quirked into a half smile, unsteady and wavering, as though he were trying it out. He glanced at SecFac, then back at her. "Here to see Rose?"

"What? No! No, not at all. Of course not!" It didn't sound persuasive, even to her. She was too adamant, her voice high and guilty, and she knew it, but she couldn't stop herself. "Why would I be here to see him? That's crazy, Top Inspector."

"It's actually Superior Inspector now," he said, almost absently, and the casualness of it infuriated her. He'd been promoted. For letting someone shoot her friend. For beating and arresting Rose.

"Goggs aren't allowed in the Complex," he said, pointing. "The guards should have told you."

"They don't work." At that moment, the SmartSpex were recording every word and motion from SI Markard, including a slightly elevated heart rate. SUBJECT STATE: AGITATED (98.43% ACCURATE), the readout claimed. Deedra thought it was more like 100 percent. SI Markard wasn't very good at hiding the annoyance on his face; SmartSpex could read his body's functions but not his expression.

"Let me see them," he said, holding out his hand.

"Why?" She'd never in her life refused a direct command from a DeeCee or a cop. And here she was, in the very center of DeeCee and police authority, resisting. *You're either brave or completely crazy, Deedra.*

Or desperate. She didn't know what to do, so she had to stall. She could speak the murm that would shut down the SmartSpex, but with the battery still in, he could just turn them on. And he would probably notice the murm anyway. No matter what she did, she was in serious trouble.

Which meant Rose would be in serious trouble. Well, even more serious trouble. Was there a penalty for having friends try to break you out of prison? If there wasn't, she was sure Max Ludo would come up with one.

"Don't BS me, Ms. Ward," said Markard. He was still smiling, but his words were cold. Did he even realize? Was it on purpose? The combination was unnerving as hell. "Your name popped on CentServ when you signed in at the Magistrate's Office."

"You have an alert on me?" Still stalling.

"For all persons of interest in something as important as the murder of Jaron Ludo."

"I told you I wasn't involved—"

"Give me those goggs, Deedra," Markard said in a voice that was undoubtedly intended to be kind. "Give them to me now, or I'll take them from you."

She cleared her throat, murmuring "Die, Spex," hoping the goggs heard her and Markard didn't. His expression changed just slightly as she did so, and she figured she was screwed. She slipped the SmartSpex down the bridge of her nose. Was that graphic in the corner of her eye part of the shutdown process? She hoped so. Just another second or two...

Markard grumbled and reached out to snatch them away.

And the air erupted with a loud, piercing siren that seemed to emanate from heaven itself.

CHAPTER 40

As soon as he was in the corridor, Rose realized his error. He also realized it didn't matter. Not really. He'd had no choice—he had to be out of the cell.

The camera in his cell had, of course, noted his escape. He'd hoped for just long enough to shuck the blanket and appear as another guard when he emerged into the hallway. Sure, an alarm would go off, but with the right timing and the right luck, he could blend in with the guards responding to the alarm.

But he hadn't counted on cameras in the hall. Stupid.

And he'd forgotten about the helmets. He couldn't mimic those—too bulbous and plasticky and unfamiliar. Even more stupid.

But most stupid of all: His disguise just wasn't that good.

Viewed through a lens of desperation, alone in his cell, his disguise had seemed spot on, but the instant he climbed over the body of the struggling guard outside his door, he could tell—with depressing certainty—that his faulty memory and his drive to escape had conspired to convince him his fidelity to reality was greater than it actually was.

He looked nothing like the guards. His coloring was too mottled, compared with their flat black. He wasn't bulky enough, his "body armor" thin and lumpy, where it should have been heavy, planar, regular.

Still, there was nothing for it. He couldn't very well shrug his shoulders, chuckle, and say, "Can't blame me for trying, guys!" and go back to his cell. Only death lay in that direction.

Crouched on the floor of the corridor, wincing at the screaming alarm, he sensed the guard in his cell scrambling to his feet. Rose sent out a vine to trip him and was rewarded with a muted thud.

He normally didn't like hurting people, but after weeks of captivity, he admitted to feeling a certain amount of satisfaction.

Footsteps. The sound of harsh breathing. He looked up and down the corridor.

In both directions, the hallway was clogged with a rush of black-armored DeeCees.

Rose took a deep breath.

All right, then. So we'll have to fight.

CHAPTER 41

W hat's that?" Deedra shouted over the piercing sound.

SI Markard had spun around at the noise. His right hand went under his jacket. While he was turned, Deedra slipped the SmartSpex off. She slid out the battery and slipped it into her pants pocket, while also tucking the goggs themselves into her poncho pocket.

"Lockdown alarm," Markard said. "Someone's . . ." He turned back to her. "What did you do?"

"Nothing!"

He grabbed her by the elbow and with his other hand drew his firearm. "You did *something*. Too much of a coincidence. He's escaping, isn't he?"

Deedra had no idea. All she knew was that her head was about to split wide open from the endlessly shrieking alarm and that a small army of DeeCees was charging toward SecFac. And Markard's grip on her arm was too tight.

Markard seemed caught between two desires—to run toward Sec-Fac, or to drag Deedra off somewhere, lock her up. He vacillated for a moment, then split the difference, hauling her with him toward the action.

■ ■ ■

First, they tried gas.

Of course. They wanted him alive, if possible. They all wore gas masks, and after a series of soft, blunt *puft* sounds, the corridor filled with a hazy green fog.

They thought it would knock him out. They thought it would blind him.

Rose stopped breathing. He adjusted his internal body temperature.

"Where the hell did he go?" a voice complained.

They were trying to track him on infrared. *Good luck with that.*

He dropped to the ground, where the good air was, and scuttled along the floor. Using a series of thorns and vines for grip and pull, he moved quickly, flat on the floor and smoothly gliding. Ahead were the boots of the DeeCees. As he came to them, he bounced upright in their faces, flinging vines in every direction. The men screamed in shock as a flurry of green, sinuous tentacles burst at them from out of the gas haze. Rose attached to a light fixture in the ceiling and pulled himself up and over them. In panic, someone opened fire—a voice screamed, "*Cease fire! Cease fire!*"—and he heard the flat impact of bullets down the corridor, causing the DeeCees on the opposite end to open fire, too, thinking they were under attack.

Rose knocked two DeeCees down just before they could fall to friendly fire. There was no reason for anyone—*anyone*—to die. He did his best to push them out of the paths of their own bullets, but he couldn't stop them from exercising their own worst instincts. Driven by fear and an ignorance they themselves had generated, they reaped what they'd sown. He spared an instant to mourn them, then hurtled himself forward, releasing his vines as he did so, bulleting into the cleaner air of the corridor beyond the DeeCees.

■ ■ ■

"*Lockdown!*" a voice blared. It was disturbingly dissimilar to the one from L-Twelve, from home, the one she'd heard warning of lockdowns her whole life. This one was deeper, meaner. More serious. She hadn't thought that was possible. "*Lockdown! This facility is in lockdown! Visitors and unauthorized personnel, report to the Central Office.*"

The voice repeated on a loop. Deedra didn't know which building housed the Central Office, but it didn't matter—SI Markard swore and kept a tight grip on her elbow. He drew her close to him and shouted over the blaring alarms. "Tell me what you did! Right now!"

"I didn't do anything!" she bleated. It had the benefit of being absolutely true. She had no idea what was going on.

"You can't—"

He was interrupted by an explosion from the prison building. His mismatched eyes widened, and he looked in that direction, swearing. His grip on her tightened, and she struggled to pull away from him. Without even looking back, he cuffed her across the face with the back of his hand, releasing her so that she fell to the ground.

He loomed over her. "What have you *done?*"

■ ■ ■

Rose had no idea where he was going, only that he was going *away*. He ran, moving ever forward. The walls around him were all disturbingly the same, the doors all identical to his own cell door.

There was nowhere to hide. Nowhere to go, but forward.

He rounded a corner and collided with a brace of armed guards, who shouted in surprise. He was too slender and light to knock them down, and they immediately brought up their rifles.

Instinctively, Rose reached out with vines and stripped the guns from their hands. The guards, shocked, froze in place.

"Holy—" one of them said, and Rose didn't stick around to hear the rest. He threw himself against a wall, ricocheted, and somersaulted over their heads, then kept running, checking over his shoulder to make sure they hadn't recovered their weapons too quickly.

They hadn't. They were just standing there, stock-still, goggling at one another in disbelief at what they'd just witnessed.

He felt a change in the air currents. Looked ahead. The good news: There was a large entrance, which clearly led to another part of the building. No more cells. More room to maneuver. Closer to freedom.

The bad news: A squadron of DeeCees was barreling through, and a massive blast door was sliding down behind the troops to seal them all in.

He grimaced. He didn't slow down. He couldn't afford to.

"Target!" someone shouted. "Target in range! Target in range!" A dozen or more rifle barrels swung at him.

As the bullets fired, Rose flared his sepals further to catch air currents and leapt. He caught the edge of the thin air current and drifted there in the air, close to the ceiling, the hail of bullets passing beneath him. With a vicious kick against a wall, he launched himself toward the squadron from above.

The troops scarcely had time to react, and even if they had, they wouldn't have known what to do. Nothing in their training had prepared them for the sight before them—a slight, humanoid form bristling with black faux armor, winglike protrusions extended, flailing tendrils—as it hurtled at them from above. Trained soldiers all, they broke discipline. Someone shouted, "Kill it! Kill the goddamn thing!" at the top of his lungs, his voice high and quavering with utter panic.

A shuffling chaos followed, as guns clattered against one another, jostling and throwing off targeting. Bullets whipped and whined and chipped the walls and ceiling, but Rose was already on them, crashing into the thick of the squadron.

"Kill that thing! Extreme measures! Extreme measures!"

So great was their panic that they fired away, directly into the thick of their comrades. Rose twisted and turned. They had body armor to—hopefully—protect them from their own friendly fire. He had nothing. He dodged behind one, then another, then ducked and spun and doubled back where they didn't expect him to go, his slightness and lightness allowing him greater freedom of movement than they had with their bulky armor and unwieldy weapons.

"Retreat!" someone yelled, and Rose couldn't imagine why—he was surrounded.

And then he realized why. The man who'd called the retreat was holding a grenade in one hand.

"Fall back! Fall back!"

What he'd thought to be panic and chaos a moment ago was really nothing more than disorganization. *This* was chaos. The squadron completely fell apart, soldiers running in every direction, tripping over each other.

"Don't!" Rose screamed. Was the man insane? He would kill himself and his comrades if he loosed that grenade. "Don't do it!"

But he'd sent them—all of them—past rational thought. When he'd revealed the truth of his abilities, the truth of his very biology, to Deedra, she'd been shocked, but she'd come to embrace it. She'd had the chance to adapt, to think it through, to adjust.

These men had no such opportunity. Confronted with something alien and—to them—monstrous, something beyond their ken, beyond their imaginations, they were panicking, and they were willing to die to kill the threat.

Rose reached out with a tendril, grabbing the grenade.

Too late. The man's finger was in the pin. If Rose pulled, it would—

The choice was made for him. The DeeCee yanked the pin.

"No!" Rose shouted, but his voice was lost in the explosion.

CHAPTER 42

Markard took a step toward SecFac, then stopped. He turned, looked at Deedra. Stepped toward her. Stopped again. Toward the building again. Couldn't decide what to do.

Finally, he turned to her and leveled his gun, sighting down the barrel at the center of her forehead.

"Tell me. What the hell. Is going on. Here." Biting out the words like chewing on steel.

"I don't know," Deedra said. She propped herself up on the ground on her elbows. "I swear, I have no—"

"If you're lying to me—"

"I'm not."

Markard lowered his gun. "Stay right there. Don't move. Don't even *look* in the wrong direction. I'll be back."

Gun still drawn, he ran toward SecFac.

■ ■ ■

The explosion threw Rose into the air. In the seconds before the grenade had gone off, he'd thrown out more tendrils, shoving away more soldiers. *No one has to die. No one has to die!*

The world went white, then black. His hearing vanished, swallowed in the detonation, and when it returned, he was in the air, flying under the closing blast door. Screams assailed him.

When he landed, he went skidding down the hall a good ten or twelve yards before crashing against a wall. Down at the other end of the hall, the blast door had finished closing...almost. A guard was trapped underneath, screaming as the door pressed down on his leg, crushing it. Rose shook his head to clear it. Had he managed to save any of them?

Could he help the man being crushed?

He stood unsteadily; the walls around him dipped and spun. He was out of the cell area, in a wide corridor. He leaned against the wall to keep from collapsing. He was stronger than he had been but still nowhere near full strength. And all around him was steel, concrete, tile. Processed air and artificial light. There was nothing to draw strength from, nothing to use.

The man under the door wailed like a lost baby.

Rose staggered forward. His vision was blurry, his hearing speared with ringing noises that came from nowhere and everywhere.

"Help!" the man cried, and wailed wordlessly before screaming it again: "Help!"

Rose took another step toward him. *No one dies. I will not let anyone die. Not if I can stop it.*

He stumbled forward, collapsed to his knees.

The man stopped screaming. Dead? Unconscious from the pain?

With a slowness that pained him, Rose stretched out to touch the man's neck, feeling for a pulse.

None.

Rose hitched in a breath. This wasn't what he'd wanted. Not what he'd planned. No one was supposed to die.

Lockdown alarms kept up their cry. Lights flashed and whirled in emergency panic. He dragged himself away from the dead man, forced himself to his feet. Off to his right, another hallway splintered off, this one carpeted with threadbare fabric.

And in the distance . . .

Sunlight.

A window. He was sure of it.

The blast door began to crank upward, slowly. Someone must have found the override controls. Smoke purled from the crevice between the bottom of the door and the floor.

Rose pushed himself to his feet. Sunlight. Outside. If he could make it that far . . .

He ran.

■ ■ ■

A cluster of soldiers had joined Markard, and they converged cautiously on the prison building. Deedra watched them, not moving, just as Markard had ordered. She had no idea what was going on and was pleased to discover that *they* didn't, either. The explosion had sped everyone up, then slowed them down as they approached the prison.

It had to be Rose. It couldn't be anything else. No one else in that building could cause such anarchy. She thought of how Rose had infuriated the Bang Boys, then multiplied that by the DeeCees.

Yeah. It was Rose.

And he would need help.

She got up and ran toward the building.

■ ■ ■

He was running through some sort of office area; there were chairs and desks on all sides of him, all abandoned, the workers having fled or sheltered at the sound of the lockdown alarm. The window ahead of him blazed with sunlight.

He nearly tripped. Behind him, he could hear shouts and orders and footsteps.

So weak. But he could get outside…

With his waning strength, he launched a tendril and snagged a chair, then sent it hurtling toward the window. At the same time, he put on a final burst of speed, knees nearly buckling.

The chair shattered the window; fragments of glass exploded outward, and Rose leapt out the window.

■ ■ ■

Deedra paused as a second-story window on the face of the prison erupted outward. A chair tumbled out, falling with broken glass. Below, DeeCees mounting the steps to the prison fell back and scattered. Markard jumped back; the chair crashed right where he'd been.

A moment later a slim figure rocketed through the window. It had flared winglike appendages and for a single instant, it blotted out the sun.

Rose. It was Rose. It could only be Rose.

Deedra realized she was grinning like an idiot.

What are you so happy about? There are still a million DeeCees here….

As if they'd heard her thoughts, the DeeCees opened fire.

■ ■ ■

At the first sound of gunfire, Rose tucked his arms in, withdrew his "wings," and aimed downward. Bullets sailed past him. He rolled when he hit the ground. The concrete around him splintered with the impact of bullets.

"Rose!"

He popped up to his feet. He knew that voice. Deedra. What was *she* doing here?

More bullets. He threw himself to the ground, flattening himself as much as possible, hoping Deedra wasn't in the line of fire.

■ ■ ■

Deedra had edged off to one side as soon as she saw Rose fly out of the window. For a moment she'd been paralyzed with sheer glee.

He was *flying*.

An instant later she realized as he landed that he was actually *gliding*. She couldn't help it; she shouted his name in sheer relief and exultation. She wanted nothing but to run to him.

But she jumped back as more bullets flew.

She had to do something. There had to be *something* to do. She couldn't come this far, and *he* couldn't come this far, only for it to end like this, with her standing on the sidelines, doing nothing more productive than watching.

Time to get your hands dirty, Deedra.

SI Markard was directing the DeeCees. As they fired, Rose flipped and wriggled along the ground. He couldn't dodge forever.

Deedra ran to Markard.

■ ■ ■

Rose was exhausted, his timing impeccable but wavering. As long as he kept moving, they couldn't hit him.

The problem was, he couldn't keep moving. He couldn't keep this up forever. And as long as he was focused on being a moving target, he couldn't figure out where to go next.

He scrambled forward, then to the left, then juked diagonally to the right. More bullets pinged and spat around him.

And he caught a glimpse of Deedra. She was running toward the DeeCees.

• • •

Deedra knew she didn't stand a chance against a platoon of armed Dee-Cees, but Markard wasn't armored. If she could stop him or distract him, maybe that would give Rose a break. All he needed was a second to catch his breath, a cessation in the endless rain of bullets. Then he could escape.

She came up on Markard's side before he even knew she was there. Before she could convince herself that this was a stupid idea, she threw herself against him, knocking him off balance, her momentum sending both of them down the prison steps and into the line of fire.

• • •

Rose watched in horror as Deedra and the unarmored man she'd collided with fell down the steps. The bullets stopped, rifles raised, as they crashed to the ground, tangled in each other.

Without thinking, Rose jumped up and ran to Deedra.

• • •

Markard shoved the girl off him. From his position, he could see only sky. He rolled over.

The kid. Rose. Running toward him. Of course. It had been Rose, just as Markard suspected.

"Open fire!" he screamed. "Big guns! Big guns!"

• • •

Deedra hit her head as she rolled away from Markard. She thought she heard a sound—a voice—and then something like a loud cough. Her ears rang; sound was garbled.

She saw a cluster of DeeCees at the other end of the quadrangle, heaving along something that looked like a gun that had been zoomed in. It had a bulbous, distended barrel and a heavy stock as counterbalance. She'd never seen anything like it.

And she didn't like the look of it. She pushed herself up onto hands and knees. As long as she could move, they weren't going to fire that thing at Rose.

Deedra managed to get one foot under her. She realized she would never make it—she would never get to the DeeCees before they could fire.

Only one choice. One.

She couldn't get to *them*, but she could get between them and Rose. She ran.

■ ■ ■

Rose ran to her. Out of the corner of his eye, he, too, was aware of the big gun swiveling toward them. He put on an extra burst of speed. They would fire right through Deedra if they had to. Her life meant nothing to them.

He strained to his utmost, flipped into the air, and landed near Deedra. He grabbed her by the shoulders and spun her around, pushing her to the ground. "Get down!" he shouted.

For an instant, their eyes met. The joy in hers warmed him more than the sunlight.

■ ■ ■

Deedra couldn't believe she was seeing him. Rattled, she fell to the ground again. He bent over her, shielding her. She thought he was wearing his coat—*They let him keep it in prison?*—but then it flared out and became huge and then it rippled as bullets struck it, poking holes along its length and breadth. She reached up and took his hand to pull him down, out of the line of fire.

Suddenly the world seemed to slow. She had an infinity to stare at him, but in that infinity, she could not move.

She locked eyes with him, their hands clutched.

"Good to see you," he said quietly.

A roar assaulted her. The DeeCees with the massive gun—they'd fired it. She caught the lick of flame out of the corner of her eye.

Rose turned in that direction. Time was still sticky and impossible. She tightened her grip on his hand and pulled.

And then there was a wind. A hard, brutal wind that sucked the breath from her lungs and seemed to drive her ears straight through her skull. Fire blossomed before her, and the wind picked her up and tossed her back. She crashed into the concrete, her entire body rattling with the impact.

She was blind, the world an ever-shifting array of red and black, flashing before her eyes. She could hear nothing but the roar of wind and a high-pitched squeal. She tried to shout for Rose but could not hear her own voice.

After a moment, her hearing began to clear again, and she heard footsteps, shouts, screams. Her vision returned and no more than ten feet away from her was a heap of *something*, something unrecognizable, and she turned to look at Rose, but he wasn't there.

It took a moment for her to realize. She shrieked as she focused—unwillingly, unable to control herself—on the heap.

That was Rose.

He'd suffered the impact from the big gun. His torso was shredded, decorated with pulpy green plant matter and sprays of blood, but he pulled himself toward her, grimacing.

His face was spattered with blood, but otherwise untouched. His eyes provided respite from the horror his body had become.

He made it halfway to her before finally collapsing to the ground, his eyes open and unwavering and perfectly still, a red and green slick trailing behind him, and there was no doubt in the world that he was the deadest thing that had ever once lived.

PART 4

LA PASCUA DE FLORES

CHAPTER 43

*S*hut your damn mouth, you blubbering—"

"Magistrate, please. Hitting her again won't—"

Deedra's jaw ached, the tendons stretched and strained too far, too long. She was aware of a high-pitched lament that went on and on, and she knew that the awful, mournful sound came from her. It roiled her innards; it jostled her very soul, and she wanted nothing more than to stop it, but she couldn't. She was helpless to control her own body. It was as though she'd blinked—Rose, dead, spattered on the concrete, an abstract painting of greens and reds—and then found herself in this darkness, a light shining directly at her, her body making this sound of its own volition, as she watched and listened at a remove.

She was bound to a chair. Her left eye throbbed painfully. She'd been struck. Probably more than once.

"You killed him!" Her wail had taken on the form of words. She felt her lips and tongue move to form them, but she had no control. *"You murdered him!"*

"Shut! Up!" And a hand collided with her face once more. Deedra tasted blood, thought of Rose's blood—and his…chlorophyll?—spilled on the ground before her; she spat into the light, a brief crimson arc.

Something in the latest blow—and maybe in the flavor of her own blood—completed her transition back to the real world. She struggled briefly and fruitlessly against the plastic cords that bound her to the chair. The light pierced her eyes and stabbed at her brain. With a near-violent intake, she hitched a breath into her chest and managed to stop her screaming. Not for *them*. Not to make them more comfortable. For herself. So that she could think.

Her heart pounded so hard and loud that her brain throbbed in sync.

They have you. Rose isn't coming to rescue you—

(She flashed a brief tableau—Rose's eyes looking out at her from that profusion of blood and pulp.)

—so you have to take care of yourself. Which you've been doing forever anyway, so what's so different about now?

(*Good to see you*, Rose had said in that moment of perfection.)

A tear slid down her cheek. The difference was Rose. Yes, she'd been taking care of herself for years, and she could keep doing so for however long she had left (not long, judging by her current circumstances), but...

But she didn't *want* to anymore.

She wanted Rose to take care of her, and she wanted to take care of Rose. She wanted them to take care of each other.

She wanted the impossible. Might as well want the plastic cords to melt, the room to fall away and reveal one of Amory's opulent apartments.

Thinking of Amory recalled to her a line from the book, one that had burned into her memory. She had found herself unable to forget it and now was grateful for it.

There were no more wise men; there were no more heroes, Amory lamented.

This was maybe the only way her world could compete with Amory's. Dr. Dimbali was wise. And heroes...well, she wasn't one. Not yet. But she would be.

They can kill me, she decided, surprised only the smallest bit by how calmly she thought it, *but I won't let them break me.*

"You're going to talk," a voice said from the groping dark, "and you're going to talk a lot."

Markard. She recognized him. His tone was not unkind, but leavened with a determination that bespoke his loyalty to the Territory and the Magistrate over any personal fondness he might have for her.

The other voice—the one she associated with the blunt smack to her face—was familiar, too. She'd heard it on vidcasts her whole life.

The Magistrate. Max Ludo. Jaron's father.

She couldn't see him, but she could feel him hulking in the dark.

"We need to know what you know," Markard went on. "So we're going to ask some questions."

"Stop coddling her!" Ludo barked.

A scuffling sound in the dark. She imagined the Magistrate lunging at her, held back by his security agents and maybe Markard himself.

Come and get me. Kill me, if you want. There's nothing anymore. Nothing left but death. Why keep it waiting?

She laughed.

"Make her talk!" Ludo bellowed.

"Deedra!" Markard came into view, blotting out the piercing light. She blinked, eyes watering. "Deedra, can you hear me?"

Of course I can hear you. You're standing right in front of me.

"You killed him," she said quietly.

"The boy you knew as Rose was an enemy combatant and a murderer," Markard told her. "Now, we're just trying to determine what you knew and when you knew it. I suspect you were an innocent pawn in all this. If that's the case, you'll go home and everything will be fine. Isn't that what you want?"

She thought of "home." Cramped and dirty and too hot. Roach netting. She didn't care if she ever saw it again.

"Now," Markard went on, without waiting for an answer, "the first thing I need to know is this: Who gave you these?" He held out the SmartSpex, enclosed in a clear plastic case with a red tag that said EVIDENCE.

The SmartSpex. Dr. Dimbali. Did they know about Dr. Dimbali? She didn't care what happened to her—not anymore—but there was no reason to let them arrest Dr. Dimbali.

"I found them," she said. "While scavenging. They don't work."

"This kind of tech is very difficult to come by. Where were you scavenging?"

"Why does it matter?"

Max Ludo suddenly loomed before her, eclipsing Markard. His deep-set eyes glowed with rage. "We're the ones asking questions, you drift-rat! You answer them, or you'll be shoved away in the deepest, darkest pit I can find!"

Deedra glanced around at the impenetrable darkness surrounding her. "You mean we're not there already?"

For someone so old, Max Ludo moved with surprising speed—he belted her across the face before she could react. It sounded the same as when she dropped a thawed turkey cube onto her counter—a damp, hollow slap.

One of her teeth was loose. She probed at it, fascinated. She hadn't felt a loose tooth since she'd been a little girl, losing her baby teeth. It was an old sensation made new.

"I don't know anything," she lied smoothly.

"You know *something*!" Ludo insisted, now so close that she could smell his breath, could see the individual crevices and pits on his teeth. "You know!"

"Magistrate, please…" Markard guided Ludo back a few paces. "Please, Magistrate. I'm trained in interrogation. Let me—"

"Get answers out of her, Markard! I don't care if you have to pull them out along with her tongue!"

Deedra took a deep breath and released it slowly. She had a few seconds as Markard persuaded Ludo. She had to take advantage of them to keep herself calm. If she panicked, she would let something slip and things would get even worse.

"Look, Deedra," Markard said, returning to her line of sight, "we know that you were friends with Rose. And we're not saying that you were involved in any of his crimes, but maybe you saw something. Or heard something. Or maybe he said something that you didn't really pay attention to at the time, but now..." He shrugged. "Maybe now it makes sense, hmm?"

"I don't know what you mean." It was only half a lie, really. Markard's question was so broad that it could have meant anything or nothing.

Markard grimaced, the expression of a man chewing something rancid. "We have reason to believe that Rose may have had access to certain...technology. During his prison break, he exhibited certain... Well, the vids aren't entirely clear. Too many bodies, too much motion. Smoke. Confusion. But Rose was doing things that no human being can do."

No human being. And no plant, either. But when you put them together...

"We're not sure exactly what the nature of his, well, I guess *augmentation* would be the best word. We're not sure of the nature of his augmentation." Markard leaned in, urgent. "Deedra, a preliminary examination of his body found no recognizable tech. But there was some strange biological matter. And that makes us think he's been genetically modified."

Like a turkey steak, Deidre thought, and suppressed a sudden, frightful giggle.

"And that sort of modification...it goes far, *far* beyond anything we've ever seen. If other Territories have mastered this kind of technology, well..." He fanned out his hands, helpless. "You want to keep the Territory safe, don't you? You have friends here. Help us, Deedra."

"I don't know anything," she insisted. Rose's body. They had Rose's body. They would learn everything anyway.

"This is a hard world," Markard said to her with some measure of sympathy. "Don't make it harder for yourself."

From beyond Markard, Max Ludo cleared his throat and spoke very slowly and clearly, much more calmly than he had so far.

That calm made it all the more terrifying.

"If you don't start talking," he said, "I'm going to begin cutting things off you."

Deedra nodded as though reminding herself of an errand. "Well, then, you should get your knives," she told him.

■ ■ ■

Markard stepped outside the interrogation room with the Magistrate, under the pretext of giving the threat some time to sink in. In reality, he needed a recess himself—his adrenaline had spiked during the prison break and kept him afloat in the hours after, but he was crashing now. And Max Ludo's ridiculous threats weren't helping at all. The man had no idea how to build a rapport with a suspect, how to insinuate himself into her psyche, how to turn her thoughts inside out. In short, how to interrogate. Markard felt as if he were working not with one hand tied behind his back but, rather, with an extra, third hand. One that did whatever the hell it wanted.

"You're not getting anything out of her!" Ludo complained. "That bitch helped murder my boy and is setting us up for an invasion and you're treating her like a kid!"

"Magistrate, my pardon, but I've cleared a lot of cases." Markard chose his words carefully. "I know my methods may seem slow to you, but—"

"Slow is exactly the problem." Ludo stomped his foot. "We don't have time, Markard. They shot up that Rose kid with some kind of drug cocktail that made him something more than human. Can you imagine an entire army of those creatures coming across the border into our Territory? Because that's what we're up against, I'm sure of it now. Dalcord's been preparing for this all along, and we need to be ready."

Markard had witnessed Rose's physical prowess. The idea of an army of such beings terrified him, but he was professional enough not to show it.

"I understand, Magistrate."

"I mean, don't get me wrong—we're not totally defenseless. I've been stockpiling for years. All sorts of things. Like fossil fuels."

This time Markard couldn't suppress his reaction, but fortunately the Magistrate was gazing upward, lost in his own thoughts. There were rumors of government hoards of oil and gasoline, but he'd always imagined them to be urban legends.

"I had to do it," Ludo went on. "For just such an occasion. Just in case of war." He shrugged. "Ever seen a car, Superior Inspector? A *running* one?"

"No, Magistrate."

Ludo's expression softened for a moment. "It really is an amazing thing, Markard. They're noisy, for one thing. Big buzzing, rattling sounds. And the exhaust! Oh, my, the exhaust..." He shook his head and stared off for a moment before snapping out of it.

"Anyway," the Magistrate said, "my point is this: I will do whatever it takes to protect this Territory. From enemies without *and* within. Do you understand, Markard?"

"I do, Magistrate."

"That girl"—he jabbed a finger at the door to the interrogation room—"knows something. I don't believe in the sorts of coincidence that would land her in our laps innocently. Do you?"

Markard had to admit he didn't. "But, Magistrate, with a little time I'm sure I can connect to her and get her to—"

"We don't have time!" Ludo exploded. "There could be a legion of freaks massing on our borders as we speak!" He flexed his fingers, seeking something to crush. "You want to coddle her and coax answers out of her? We need to *beat* them out of her. Now."

Markard chose his words carefully. Assuming the Ward girl had answers—which he did—the best way to get them out of her was not through random violence. Especially the sort Max Ludo excelled at and preferred. If he let the Magistrate loose in there, the girl would be dead or unconscious within a half hour. She probably had a concussion already, just from the repeated blows to her head he'd witnessed.

"I understand the urgency, Magistrate, but in my experience, physical violence can often lead to misinformation or even to—"

Ludo turned away from him. "Screw this. I'm not wasting time or energy on her. That was the mistake we made with the pretty boy— tried to get him to talk the old way. We'll do with her what we should have done with him all along: Pump her full of SpeakTruth and get her to talk."

SpeakTruth. Markard had heard of it, of course, but had never used it. It was a powerful combination of hallucinogen and antidepressant. The subject more than *felt* compelled to tell the truth; he or she *wanted* to tell the truth. The drug altered moods and brain chemistry in radical, poorly understood ways, which was probably why Ludo hadn't used it on Rose right from the start: In some cases, it resulted in permanent brain damage. In others, death. Either way, Rose would have provided no more information.

Alarmed, Markard spoke up: "Magistrate! That's highly dangerous!"

"These are dangerous times."

"We need an authorized court order to compel self-incriminating testimony."

Ludo grunted in disgust, as though Markard were a small child refusing potty training. He snapped his fingers and held out a hand. An aide slapped a comm into his palm. A moment later, Ludo was speaking to someone on the other end. "Bil? Max. I need to interrogate an insurgent. Want to use SpeakTruth. Is that okay? Great. Thanks." He handed the comm back and beamed at Markard. "Top Justice of the Territory Court. We have our court order. Do it."

CHAPTER 44

When they'd left her alone, they'd turned off the only light in the room, steeping her in darkness. Deedra had become accustomed to the darkness. When she closed her eyes, when she opened them . . . it was the same, no matter what.

Just like the rest of the world. It didn't matter, she realized, what you saw or what you didn't see. The world was the same no matter what. You could imagine something better; you could read a story about something better. But in the end, the world was still the same stinking, hot, clouded-over, dirty, trashy place it had always been.

With a green-red stain where the boy you loved had died.

She struggled briefly and perfunctorily against her bonds. No use. She was theirs as long as they would have her.

The door opened and the lights snapped on, burning red against her closed eyelids. She decided to keep her eyes closed. To hell with them.

Expecting taunts and japes, she was surprised instead to hear only Max Ludo's rumble: "Do it now."

And then hands pushed down on her shoulders and another hand grabbed her wrist. She opened her eyes and saw a man in medical garb at her side, wielding a needle.

"What are you—"

He jabbed the needle into her arm, just below the crook of her elbow. She barely felt it—she'd been dealt more and worse pain today than a little needle prick.

SI Markard stood at the other end of the room, arms folded over his chest, that weird paralyzed grin on his face. Max Ludo stood closer, rubbing his hands together eagerly.

"How long?" Max asked.

"Soon," said the man who'd stuck her.

Deedra blinked rapidly. Her eyes were watering over. The room was swimming in sheer *wet*. She gulped the air like water, amazed that she could breathe it.

From the ceiling, red jewels dripped and sparkled. She caught her breath. They were *beautiful*.

"She's ready," a voice said, musically.

SI Markard approached and sat across from her, leaning forward, elbows on knees. His smile was spectacular. How could she ever have thought it was odd or off-putting? His green eye flashed and his blue eye spun like a whirlpool. She giggled.

"Deedra, can you hear me?"

Of course she could! "Yes!" she exclaimed happily.

"Good. Good. We're going to talk a little bit. I'm going to ask you some questions. To start: Your name is Deedra Ward, right?"

Duh. Why was he asking her something so *easy*? "Yes. That's my name. Deedra Ward. That's my name."

"You're an orphan and a ward of the Territory, correct?"

Thinking about that usually made her sad, but it didn't seem to bother her right now. Waves of light shimmered, and the jewels from the ceiling hung, coruscating, in the air all around her. "Yep! Orphan! No parents. That kind of sucks. No idea where I'm from. Oh well."

"Okay, thanks, Deedra. Now, let's move on. You know the boy named Rose, right?"

"Nope!" she said cheerfully. What a silly question to ask! "He's dead, so I don't know him anymore."

Markard glanced around—when his head moved, she saw multiple versions of it, as if he were caught in slo-mo. "Yes, of course. You *knew* the boy named Rose, right?"

"I sure did! He was my friend! And then you guys killed him." She should have been angry at that, but she couldn't manage to summon the anger. She shrugged instead. "You shouldn't have done that. That was wrong."

"Don't let her babble," someone snapped. "Keep her focused."

"Deedra," Markard said slowly, "I want to talk about Rose. Do you know where he comes from?"

Did she? It depended on exactly what he meant by "where he comes from." Because all she knew was that Rose had woken up in a graveyard and then walked to the Territory.

She wanted to help Markard. She really did. She wanted to tell him *so much*. But she didn't know how to answer that question.

"I'm not sure," she said, because it was the truth. "He was in a graveyard."

The room fell silent. Deedra allowed herself to be distracted by the drifting jewels, which floated here and there on invisible crosscurrents. Occasionally, they would bump into one another and split off into multiple, smaller jewels.

"A graveyard?" Markard asked.

"A graveyard," she confirmed. Up near the ceiling, one of the jewels was spinning now, gaining speed and light. It was like watching a tiny sun being born. "He got up and walked out of the graveyard and came here."

"There are no graveyards anywhere near here," someone said. Markard waved for silence.

"Deedra. Deedra, listen to me. Where was Rose before he came here?"

Ah! Ah! She knew that one! "Across the river!" she explained eagerly. "I saw him out by the old bridge, and he swam across the river."

"So . . . Sendar Territory?" Markard asked.

"Yes. Sendar."

"Impossible!" Max Ludo snorted from beyond. "We have a solid treaty with Sendar; Glorio is scared pissless of me. He's from *Dalcord*."

"He came across the river," Deedra said again. "From Sendar Territory. I watched him."

"She's lying."

"She can't lie," Markard said calmly.

"Then he must have gone around and come through Sendar *from* Dalcord."

"He came from Sendar," Deedra said for the third time. It was the truth, and she would keep saying it as long as she needed to. It was very important to her that they understand the truth, and this was the truth. It was true *and* it was the truth *and* it was a true truth, so she would say it. "He came from Sendar, and I fell in love with him, and then you killed him."

"This is useless. You're not getting anything done." Max Ludo shoved Markard out of the way—the SI blurred as he moved—and hunkered down to fill Deedra's field of vision. "*I'll* get answers out of her." He took Deedra's jaw in one hand and forced her to look at him. "You know who I am, girl?"

"You're Max Ludo, the Magistrate," she said. And then, because it was equally true: "I hate you. You're a horrible person."

"I'll lose sleep over *that*, I assure you," he snickered.

"I hated your son, too. He attacked me and I almost stabbed him, but Rose showed up so I didn't have to."

Ludo glared at her, and his grip on her jaw tightened.

"That hurts," Deedra said. Truth.

"What did you say about my son?"

"I said he attacked me. He tried to—"

"You're lying."

"Nope. I'm not." She sighed. Why on *earth* would she lie? About anything? The truth was *so* important. She just wanted to tell the truth, is all. "We were looking out at the Broken Bubble from the rooftop, and Jaron tried to rape me, and I was going to stab him, but then Rose showed up, and Jaron changed his mind and left."

"Rose killed my son," Ludo said, trembling. The shake traveled up his arm and vibrated her skull, but the truth was still easy to discern.

"No, he stopped me from killing him. Aren't you listening to me?"

"Not then!" Ludo let her go and leaned in closer, shouting. "Not on the rooftop! Later! He killed him later!"

Deedra didn't know if that was true or not, so she didn't say anything.

"He did it, didn't he? He killed my son!"

Deedra shrugged. "I don't know."

"Were you involved in killing my son?"

"No."

"Do you know who did it?"

"No."

"It was Rose, wasn't it? Only he could do it. We found biomass in Jaron's apartment that matches the crap they're hosing out of my court-yard right now."

"He shed that stuff all around the Territory," Deedra supplied helpfully. "Anyone could have found it. Like Lissa."

"Who's—"

"Magistrate…" Markard interrupted. "You need to keep her focused, or she'll ramble on about anything and everything."

Max Ludo gritted his teeth. Deedra watched sparks fly out of his mouth. Amazing. Her head felt like a balloon, tethered to her neck by a thin filament.

"Yes, yes . . ." Max grumbled. "What did the Rose boy tell you about Dalcord and the invasion plans?"

"Nothing."

"So you knew about the plans, but he wouldn't give you any information?"

"No."

"So you're saying Dalcord *isn't* planning to invade?"

"No." She was getting confused. She had to tell the truth—that was so very, very, very, very times a million important—but she didn't know anything about Dalcord. Had she just lied? *Was* there an invasion plan? She didn't know. A buzzing started in her head, and she began clucking her tongue against the roof of her mouth.

"What are they planning, then?" Ludo demanded. "Tell me the truth!"

She shook her head, hard. There was nothing in there. Nothing about Dalcord. She didn't know what they were planning, but that wasn't an answer. Not a *true* answer. He hadn't asked *Do you know what Dalcord is planning?* He had asked for the plan itself. If there was no plan, she could say nothing and be telling the truth. But if there *was* a plan, then she had to say *something,* but she didn't know if the plan was real, so how could she know what to say, but she had to say something and the something had to be true and—

"Whoa! Whoa!" A voice from behind her. Hands on her shoulders again, steadying her. The room spun, the jewels whipping like planets in orbits, the air wet and suddenly rancid. Deedra's eyes rolled and jittered. "She's close to neurotic burn. You have to ask questions she can actually answer, Magistrate. Otherwise, the paradox will burn out her synapses."

"I don't give a dry rat fart about her synapses!" Ludo bellowed. "Tell me about Rose! What is he?"

"He's a plant," she said, and then giggled. It was so strange. Rose was a plant and *a* rose was a plant and she was in love with a plant, but the plant was dead, so was she really in love with anyone anymore? Did love die along with the loved? She had no idea. No matter how much they asked, she would never know.

Ludo gave a triumphant cry. "A plant! I knew it! He *was* sent here. He's a spy." He leaned even closer, which she hadn't thought possible; his face overwhelmed her entire field of vision.

"Now tell me who sent him. Who. Sent. Rose?"

She froze again. She didn't know how to answer the question. It presupposed that someone *had* sent Rose, and she didn't know if that was true or not. And she had to tell the truth. She just *had* to. It was the most important thing in the world to her, telling the truth. More important than her love for Rose, and bigger than Max Ludo's enormous visage hanging before her.

"Who sent him?" Max yelled. "Who? Tell me. Who?"

At last, a question she had a definitive truth for: "I don't know."

Max's face was flushed red and his eyes bulged, but he seemed to be calming down. "Do you know why Rose came here?"

"No."

"Do you know who killed my son?"

"No."

"Do you know what the Dalcord people are planning?"

"No."

Max Ludo sighed, and Deedra almost felt sorry for him.

■ ■ ■

Markard watched the interrogation in despair. The Magistrate was asking all the wrong questions, and even the right questions were worded imprecisely. Assuming the Ward girl knew everything they wanted and needed to know, Ludo would still get nothing but nothing out of her.

As the girl's head lolled back, her mouth open and gasping, Max Ludo shrugged.

"The bitch doesn't know a goddamned thing."

"Magistrate—"

"She doesn't know anything. Get rid of her."

CHAPTER 45

She woke in her apartment, on the bed. The roach netting was balled up in the corner and roaches roamed freely over her mattress. One of them had braved the hill of her left hip and perched there, silent and still, its antennae trembling questioningly, as though demanding answers from her.

Deedra had had enough of demands for answers. She lacked the strength to slap at the roach, but it skittered away when she shook her leg.

She wavered for a protracted moment, stuck on the precipice of sleep. Even though the roaches had free rein right now, she could not summon the energy or the wherewithal to care. All she wanted was to go back to sleep. Darkness wrapped its arms around her and they were warm.

As she sank into that sweet and black embrace, she recalled Rose's tendrils, enfolding her, lifting her.

Her eyes fluttered open. A roach roosted nearby, right where Rose's head had dimpled the pillow the night he'd stayed with her.

Dead.

She had no tears left to offer, so she choked dry sobs for a few moments. Her body ached as though she had a weeklong flu. Had the roach crawled right up to her and begun exploring the contours of her face, she didn't think she would be able to muster the strength to swat it away.

Sinking down into sleep—or unconsciousness, it didn't matter which—she felt the arms again, woke up again, drifted off again, woke up again, a churning cycle of near-sleep and constant waking that lasted for a seeming infinity before her exhausted, battered body finally succumbed.

■ ■ ■

When she woke again, it was morning. Which morning, she didn't know. The roaches were gone, except for two crushed and smeared specimens that had clearly come too close to her sleeping form in the night and paid the ultimate price. There was a greenish ichor from one, and her mind flashed back to the spray of Rose's innards after the explosive bullet shredded his life, and she began crying. Anyone watching her would think she'd been moved to tears by a dead cockroach.

And someone *could* be watching, she realized. Probably *was*, in fact. Before, she'd been one of the anonymous masses. Now she'd witnessed a prison break and an execution. She'd been interrogated by the Magistrate himself. She would be watched for the rest of her life, she feared.

Fine. It didn't matter anymore. *Nothing* mattered anymore. Once, she'd thought Rose meant...

Meant...

Something.

A way out? Out of what and where, she did not know. Maybe he hadn't been a way out but, rather, a way *in*—a way in to a new life, a new way of living. Dr. Dimbali had believed that with Rose he might be able to change the entire world. Not the Territory or the City—the *world*.

It was a nice fantasy. A nice dream. But eventually, no matter how fine the dream, you woke up from it. Sometimes you woke up with every inch of your body aching and protesting and your stomach so tight from hunger that it was almost impossible to move.

But move she did, rolling herself to the edge of the bed, then standing. The room tipped, tilted, and spun for a moment, and her vision fuzzed over. This must have been how Amory felt when he woke after his own brush with horror, imagining he'd seen his dead friend in the night.

She steadied herself with a hand against the wall until the world returned to something like normal. With small, cautious steps, she staggered over to the kitchen area and turned the tap. It seemed to take forever for the rust to rinse out of the water, but when the water cleared, she bent down and drank straight from the faucet, gulping greedily until the auto shutoff kicked in. She waited, chin dripping, until the shutoff disengaged thirty seconds later and repeated. And repeated again.

She was still hungry, though her belly now had something to occupy it at least. In a cabinet, she scrounged an old packet of fruit discs and gobbled them down so rapidly that her jaw hurt and her stomach threatened to return the discs back into the open air.

The metal flower Rose had given her sat near the sink. The sight of it and the sledgehammer of memories it evoked sickened and elated her at the same time.

Behind a folding screen was her toilet and a mirror. Her reflection nearly petrified her—she didn't recognize herself. Her face was swollen and bruised from repeated slaps and smacks; the space around her left eye was almost night black. For the first time she could recall, her scar was not the most hideous thing about her. It was damn near unnoticeable.

I'm alive. At least I'm alive and not in prison.

But even as she thought it, she knew: None of it mattered.

CHAPTER 46

She stayed in her apartment for days as she healed. The mirror she covered with an old sheet, not wanting to see her face.

The comm started bleating on the second day, reminding her that work attendance was mandatory, that shirking her duty as a citizen would have consequences, and so on. She couldn't turn it off, but she didn't have to pay attention to it. She opened the window, even though it was hot and humid outside. Stuck her head outside once an hour on the hour when the comm ran through its gamut of threats and wheedles. Stared out into the endless Territory.

On the third day, the door buzzed. She ignored it. Minutes later someone began pounding on it, and still she ignored it until a familiar voice called, "Ms. Ward! Ms. Ward, open up! I can force my way in, but I'd rather not."

With a sigh and slumped shoulders, she thumbed open the door.

"Ms. Ward," SI Markard began, "I—" He broke off, no doubt at the sight of her bruises. As usual, she couldn't tell from his expression exactly what he was or wasn't feeling. She didn't really care, she realized.

"I'm so sorry for your . . . trials," he said at last, fidgeting in the hallway. "May I come in?"

It was a pointless question—if he wanted to come in, he would do so, no matter what she said. She said, "No," just to see how it felt.

It felt good, she decided.

He surprised her by saying, "Very well, then," and remaining outside. "I just wanted to offer my personal apologies that things got out of hand. The Magistrate was—and remains—quite distraught over the death of his son."

"I don't care," she told him.

"And," he went on, "I wanted to return your personal property."

He handed over Dr. Dimbali's SmartSpex. The pristine lens was still whole, but a new crack had formed in the already-broken lens and one of the stems was bent out of shape. She took them silently and stared at him.

"Again, my apologies," he said. "I hope you—" He shrugged and went away.

Deedra closed the door to blessed solitude once more.

■ ■ ■

Not leaving the apartment meant no way to replenish her food stocks, either from rations or scavenge. She had some food hidden away, and she parceled it out to herself with care, not allowing herself to binge, no matter how hungry she felt.

Each night, she draped herself in the roach netting and tossed in fitful sleep, shifting from dream to dream, nightmares of Rose's death, of her interrogation.

The battery to the SmartSpex was still in the pocket of the pants she'd been wearing the day they'd interrogated her, and it slid into the charging compartment easily. The SmartSpex booted up just fine.

She figured at some point the DeeCees would come to roust her from her apartment. After a week, she had enough demerits that she would receive no rations for a month, meaning a month of starvation and privation. She couldn't summon the energy to care.

The DeeCees never came, though. After her visit from Markard, she was alone and she stayed alone. She'd been written off, she realized. She was in the Territory, but no longer *of* the Territory. Even the bleating of the comm had died eventually.

She was off-ration. A nonperson. She didn't exist.

The big bad Territory forces she'd feared her whole life just didn't care. They weren't paying attention to her anymore.

She opened the window. It was raining, the downpour hissing against the hot concrete as it pelted down. Her water had been cut off entirely, but she couldn't risk drinking the rain, even though it wasn't red; it was too poisonous.

Or was it? Was that, too, a lie? She wondered, but she wasn't willing to test it.

How many of her neighbors had been written off like this? How many of them right now? How many of them in the past?

Eventually she would have to go out. She had some water saved up, but not much. She would have to scavenge, and some dimly lit, quietly churning part of her mind knew that she would need to try to work herself back into the good graces of the Territory. Pure scavenge was no way to live; rations were consistent, at least. Maybe if she went back to L-Twelve, she could work off the demerits and...

But the problem was this: She didn't want to go back to L-Twelve. She didn't want to be a part of the Territory any longer. She remembered Rose saying that he belonged to no Territory—that was her lot, now.

What are you going to do, then, Deedra? You can't go on living here if you're not going to get rations. This Territory can't support you on scavenge alone.

She knew the answer before it actually congealed into discrete chunks of thought in her mind: She would leave. For real, this time.

It saddened her to think of leaving. She'd been prepared to do it before, but it had seemed like a triumph in a way. She would flee to avoid Jaron, and Rose would go with her, and it would have been frightening but exhilarating.

Now...now she was leaving because she had no choice. Because there was nothing left for her but to run.

Still, Rose had wandered and survived, hadn't he? He'd seen other Territories, other Cities.

Maybe this wasn't a sign of defeat. Maybe it was the best way to honor his memory.

She took down the sheet from the mirror. Her face had returned to its normal contours, with only slight discoloration here and there. As long as she kept her scar covered, she would be able to travel without drawing attention to herself.

But first...she would take Lissa with her. Or at least ask her to go. If Lissa had, indeed, killed Jaron, then eventually the DeeCees would catch on. Superior Inspector Markard was cowed by the Magistrate, true, but when Max Ludo wasn't in the room, the man was dogged and smart. He would track down Lissa. Even if she hadn't killed Jaron, her mere possession of one of Rose's tendrils would implicate her and be more than sufficient evidence in the eyes of the Magistrate.

Lissa had family in the Territory, but if it meant her life, she might be willing to leave them. Or they could all go together. It might be safer that way.

Deedra began throwing things into her backpack, including her knife and her gifts from Rose. She put on the drone-avoidance poncho Dr. Dimbali had given her and grabbed the SmartSpex.

She considered going out the window, but she realized she didn't care if the Territory system logged her leaving. She wouldn't be coming back.

...

The rain pelted her as she made her way to Lissa's. It pattered against the hood of her poncho in a rhythm that lulled her as she walked.

Maybe that's why she didn't notice the DeeCees until she was almost among them.

Lissa's building was surrounded by DeeCees, and as soon as she saw them, a memory broke free of its moorings in her mind and rapidly ascended, breaking the surface of her consciousness.

It was Rose, wasn't it? Only he could do it.

That was Max Ludo's voice. From her interrogation. She'd forgotten most of it, being drugged out of her mind and beaten and in shock from Rose's murder. But this bit...

We found biomass in Jaron's apartment that matches the crap they're hosing out of my courtyard right now.

This bit was coming back to her now...

He shed that stuff all around the Territory.

Oh no.

He shed that stuff all around the Territory. Anyone could have found it.

No no no no no!

Anyone could have found it. Like Lissa.

Deedra froze in the middle of the sidewalk. She knew she should bolt for cover somewhere, but her revelation and her guilt stilled her legs. She'd sold Lissa out. Without even realizing it.

It had been a week since she'd been released from SecFac. How long had it taken them to figure out which "Lissa" she was talking about? Probably five minutes.

Gnawing at her bottom lip, she took a step back. She didn't know exactly what was going on here, but she didn't want to walk into it clueless no matter what it was. There might be something on the wikinets or there might not be, but it was a moot point—she didn't have access right now.

Or did she?

She fumbled under her poncho and brought out the SmartSpex. Most goggs could connect wirelessly to the wikinets. She could see if there were any reports of what exactly the DeeCees were doing here and then make a move.

Slipping on the SmartSpex, she turned to sidle into an alleyway, only to bump into a DeeCee.

Oh. Crap.

"Watch it, citizen," the DeeCee snapped, and Deedra could tell from the voice that it was a woman under that riot helmet.

"Sorry," she said, and went to step around the DeeCee.

But the woman held out an arm, blocking the way. "Wait a sec. What are you doing here? This area's off-limits."

"I was trying to take a shortcut," Deedra lied. "Over to the RecFac."

"RecFac is shut down, too." The DeeCee's voice had gone suspicious. "We're still looking for the mother—she escaped."

The mother ... escaped ...

Deedra's breath caught in her throat—she needed to swallow fiercely, but she didn't trust herself to do it without making it obvious how upset she was.

Escaped. So what happened to everyone else? What happened to Lissa?

"You know the family in there? The Stanhopes?"

"No." A whisper. Barely audible. She forced herself to swallow—it felt like a wad of brick going down. "No."

She couldn't see the DeeCee's facial expression through the riot helmet's face shield, but the woman's posture changed just enough that Deedra knew she was in trouble.

"Show me your brand," the DeeCee demanded.

Deedra shook her head, mute and terrified.

"Do it now." The DeeCee adjusted her stance, a hand on her side-arm's grip. "Don't make me tear that poncho off you. Brand. Now."

"Let's go, Spex," Deedra mumbled.

"What did you say?" the DeeCee asked.

The SmartSpex booted up. Deedra shrugged. "Nothing. Did you say you wanted to see my brand?" Stalling during the boot-up. Trying to remember the right murm...

"You heard me the first time, drift-rat." The DeeCee grabbed Deedra by the arm. "If I don't see it, stat, I'm hauling you in for resisting interrogation and refusal to submit to stop-and-frisk. Do you hear me? You want to spend time in SecFac, drift-rat?"

No, thanks. I've spent more than enough time there.

The SmartSpex were online. She ransacked her memory for the correct murm, the one Dr. Dimbali had told her to use only when absolutely desperate. How did it go? Oh, right...

"Did you hear me?" the DeeCee shouted, now shaking her. "You going to answer me?"

"Blow it up, Spex," Deedra said.

For an instant, she was certain that the murm hadn't worked—that either the goggs hadn't understood her or that Dr. Dimbali's "custom script" had gone awry. In the next instant, though, all doubts were erased as the DeeCee howled in shock and pain, both hands coming up to claw at her helmet.

Dr. Dimbali's "custom script" had worked after all. It hacked into the helmet's operating system and sent a five-hundred-decibel burst of static through the speakers. At the same time, it flashed a seizure-inducing pattern of strobe lights along the helmet's heads-up display. The DeeCee went from threatening to thrashing on the ground, desperately scrabbling at the safety catch under her chin, in less than two seconds.

Deedra spun around. An alarm had sounded. DeeCees were

massing back at Lissa's building. She had a head start—she could out-run them. But she couldn't outrun the drones bearing toward her.

Don't panic. Let them get a little bit closer...

She kept her position, waiting. There were six or seven drones—their speed made it tough to tell—closing on her. At least two of them were the armed variety.

"Flashlight, Spex."

Again, nothing happened. Visibly, at least.

But on the infrared band, the SmartSpex emitted an explosive burst of IR light. The drones, blinded, spun out of control, colliding with one another and with buildings.

Deedra didn't stick around to watch the fallout. She ran like hell.

■ ■ ■

Terrorist Family Slain While Plotting, Resisting Arrest

That was the headlink Deedra eventually found on a recent events wikinet. She numbly skimmed for details: *Department of Citizen Services personnel interrogating... Questions about recent murder of Jaron Ludo... Illegal biomaterials in domicile...*

The Stanhope family resisted efforts by DCS personnel to acquire the illegal substances, attacking officers in the course of their sworn duty. DCS officers had no choice but to...

Deedra couldn't read any further. She was hiding behind a phalanx of old shipping crates that had been discarded on a side street. Rainwater dripped down on her. She wanted to scream her pain, but even at the heart of her rage and distress, she knew she couldn't afford to make any noise. She permitted herself a whimper, then another one. She clenched her fists and beat them against the ground until the sides of her hands went numb. Her best friend was gone. Just like that.

Deedra sniffed back her tears. How many stories exactly like this one had she seen in the past? Too many.

How many of them had she believed, word for word?

All of them.

Never again.

It was garbage. It was all garbage. And just as she had thought nothing of it for all those years, so, too, would everyone in Ludo Territory think nothing of Lissa Stanhope and her family's execution for nothing more than the crime of being inconvenient. Lissa and her family weren't terrorists. They wouldn't attack DeeCees. The Stanhopes were the most rule-following-est people she'd ever met.

And now they were all dead. Except for Lissa's mother, who was on the run, if that DeeCee could be believed.

She drew in a jittery breath that did her no good. Blew it out and tried again. This one was deep and true.

Focus. Think. Now what do I do?

A drop of water landed smack on the rim of the SmartSpex and rolled across her field of vision. Despite herself, she laughed. The answer was literally right in front of her face. The SmartSpex. She had to go to Dr. Dimbali. He knew everything. He could help her figure out how to get out of the Territory.

■ ■ ■

She buzzed his apartment for five minutes, receiving no reply. Frustrated, she huddled against the building for as much shelter from the rain as she could steal from the overhangs. She couldn't loiter forever. Even though the rain was letting up, it was too dangerous for her to be outside for long. She'd seen clusters of DeeCees along her route to Dr. Dimbali's and couldn't figure out why. Even the drones seemed thicker overhead. She was nowhere near Lissa's anymore—why were they out in force here?

She had to get inside. Where she could be hidden. Her poncho shielded her from the drones but not from the human eye.

That's when she remembered: During their days and nights planning Rose's prison break, Dr. Dimbali had shown her a hidden way into his building, the old passage from the alleyway. Safe and secure in her drone-resistant poncho, she rambled around the building until she rediscovered the right pile of junk and crawled through.

Dim light ahead reminded her of the bends and turns of the passage. Hands outstretched to touch the walls for guidance, she made her way through a series of switchbacks and turns until the corridor emptied into Dr. Dimbali's workshop.

Dr. Dimbali was not in; the workshop was empty. Deedra's nose wrinkled at a new, unfamiliar smell—something heavy, thick, and unprocessed. It wasn't necessarily an unpleasant scent, but its pervasive presence and unfamiliarity made her uncomfortable.

"Dr. Dimbali?" she called. There were alcoves and shadows down here; maybe she'd just not seen him.

No answer. She tried again. Still nothing.

The smell grew as she crept deeper into the workshop. Her foot collided with something—it was a heavy container of some sort, with a plant growing out of it. Bigger than the ones she'd seen before.

She stepped around it and followed the smell's growing intensity to one side of the workshop, where—she recalled now—she had once found Dr. Dimbali drilling into the concrete wall.

Well, he'd found a bigger drill.

A gaping hole large enough for a child to stand in pocked the wall. The source of the smell lay within, and despite her best instincts, Deedra poked her head in and was assaulted instantly with a wave of the odor. She choked past it and extended her hand into the hole, touching something slightly moist and crumbling.

Withdrawing her hand, she realized: It was dirt. Moist and dark dirt. She sniffed it, inhaling a heady rush of what she now realized was the earthy scent of raw soil. So new and unfamiliar to her.

What was he digging for?

A sound—something halfway between a gurgle and a bubble pop—stiffened her spine and spun her around. There, in an alcove opposite the SmartBoard, was a new piece of equipment she'd never seen before, flanked by more of the heavy pots that grew large plants. The piece of equipment was a large tank of some sort, riveted together from sheets of steel. Hoses ran out of it to a table nearby. On the table...

Deedra had trouble swallowing for a moment. Without intending to, she found herself running to the table—her legs acting independent of her mind, carrying her to—

To—

To his side.

To Rose's side.

CHAPTER 47

It was Rose, and at the same time, it wasn't Rose.

He lay flat on his back on the table, perfectly and wholly still, the three hoses connected to him at painful-looking interfaces along his torso. He was as naked as the first time she'd ever seen him. He looked smaller and more delicate than he'd been before, his limbs loose and gangly. The parts where he'd been shredded by the DeeCee weapon had grown back, impossibly pink.

She looked around—the tank, the hoses. Gurgles and drips. More potted plants, taller and healthier than she'd seen here before. There were small holes drilled into the walls all around her, and she couldn't figure out what any of it meant, but it didn't matter. None of it mattered.

She leaned close to his face. His *face*. That face that she'd last seen when he'd been blasted to oblivion by a DeeCee explosive shell was here, now.

He was breathing. She was sure of it. So slightly that it dipped below the perception of sound, but she could tell.

"You're alive," she whispered. "How? How could you be alive?"

And, she realized, how could Dr. Dimbali not have contacted her?

Later. Figure it out later.

She wanted to touch him. To kiss him. To shake him awake. But the hoses attached to him and the burbling tank at their other ends gave her pause. She didn't know what any of this equipment was for, and she didn't want to mess it up and possibly hurt Rose.

Retreating from the alcove, she paced the length of the basement, this time looking for anything that might possibly help her figure out what was going on. She settled on the SmartBoard, which had been wiped clear of dust at some point.

"Let's go, SmartBoard." It was worth a try.

The SmartBoard stared dully at her, dead. She removed the SmartSpex and tucked them away, trying to remember back to the times Dr. Dimbali had used the board. How had he activated it?

Then she remembered—the goggs used murms, but the Smart-Board used *gestures*. She waved her hands in front of it.

Nothing.

Snapped her fingers.

Still nothing.

She reached out and tapped it.

The SmartBoard flickered to life. There were various images, most of them small icons representing molecules and formulae. She didn't think she would understand much of that. But one icon looked like a miniature tab and had the tag "Lab Notes" attached to it. She tapped it twice, and it expanded to fill the screen.

It was a vid. Of Dr. Dimbali, staring into the camera, slumped in a rolling chair almost exactly where Deedra stood now. He was winded, and his eyes were wild. "Well," he muttered, as if to himself, "that didn't go off quite as planned."

She checked the date of the recording. It was the day before the lockdown, the day before Rose's arrest.

"I shall have to proceed on my own," Dr. Dimbali said, rising from his chair and straightening his tie. "I shall . . ." He drifted off, then blinked as if just realizing the camera was on. He gestured to it distractedly, and the screen went black.

She found another icon and tapped it. This one was more recent. From the day she'd been held at SecFac, she realized.

Dr. Dimbali looked more haggard than usual without his SmartSpex. He was standing near the SmartBoard, apparently, scrutinizing a potted plant, examining its leaves, speaking, but not looking at the camera.

He was talking to the *plant*, she realized. He'd forgotten that the board recorded him whenever he was in the basement. He was on camera and didn't even know it.

"If the reports on the wikinets are true," he said slowly, turning the leaves of the plant to examine their undersides "and that is a substantial hypothetical, as you know…then Rose has been killed by our glorious Magistrate and the DCS." He sighed and gestured helplessly around himself. "All this…worthless. All the work I did on you and on your brethren. *Nothing.* All my efforts have been wasted. My own preliminary biotechnology is too primitive to be efficacious. Only with Rose's…"

Dr. Dimbali drifted off. The camera lingered for long moments as he was lost in thought. Then, without another word, he stood and walked away. The camera followed him as long as it could, but eventually he disappeared.

Deedra frowned and swiped at the vid. It jumped forward—Dr. Dimbali reappeared and she tried to stop the vid by tapping, then tried to rewind with another swipe. Her control was too imprecise and she settled for picking up in the middle of a sentence. Dr. Dimbali held a small potted plant in his arms and danced in and out of frame as the camera tried to track him.

"—allowed my request!" Dr. Dimbali babbled excitedly. "Against all logical assumptions, he agreed! It was a risk worth taking after all. And even though I loathe the necessity of conducting business with him, I cannot quibble with the results."

"I, Suresh Dimbali, swallowed my pride and humbled myself before Max Ludo," Dr. Dimbali crowed. "And just in the nick of time, as well. His dunderheaded scientists were trying to figure out what Rose was, but, of course, I already knew. Rose's unique physiology was—*is*— too important to leave mouldering in Max Ludo's basement. He was appropriately impressed when I 'instantly' discerned things about the specimen that his own people had not noticed. The pig offered me a *job*. I told him I would share whatever I learned if he would give me what I needed." He held the plant high above his head and beamed at it. "And he believed me. Ha! Now, how to begin, considering the necessity of a viable growth medium…"

Dr. Dimbali's ramble took on a scientific bent that left Deedra's head spinning. She swiped at the vid again. Jumped forward at least a day—Dr. Dimbali's beard stubble had grown a bit, and he wore a different shirt.

"—a *sunlamp!*" he shouted, pacing back and forth before the camera. He had a series of plants lined up on a table nearby and lectured them like his students. "I had almost forgotten about it. The technology is still available, but without proper facilities for growing plants, no one really bothers with it. I try to give it—him—*it* a few hours a day. To simulate the rhythm of natural daylight. The photonic response is nearly identical to—"

More jargon. She swiped farther ahead.

"—Rose's body," he said. It was the same day. Or he hadn't bothered with a new shirt. The rank of plants lined up was the same, except for one that Dr. Dimbali nestled in the crook of his arm, cooing to it. "I will thus have access to the crucial human and plant DNA working in concert. And then, well…"

He stepped aside and she could see the table on which Rose lay even now, only it was closer to the camera. On it lay a spindly, skeletal figure, contorted into an almost-fetal ball.

Dr. Dimbali held his potted plant over the body on the table. "You see? You see your brother? When he—when *it* has the proper nutrients, it grows very quickly. I had to mine them from the deep, deep soil. Refine them painstakingly. Our poor planet is not quite dead yet, but it is very, very close. There's little left to support a creature as extraordinary as Rose, to say nothing of the fifty billion of us parasites crawling on its skin."

Just then, the thing on the table—it was Rose, she knew, but she couldn't think of it that way, not yet—reached up and grabbed Dr. Dimbali's wrist. Dr. Dimbali startled and slapped it away. The thing screamed in a high, trembling voice. Deedra's entire body shook, and she stabbed at the SmartBoard, swiping, wiping, and it blurred again, jumping forward some indeterminate length of time.

The camera zoomed in on the alcove. The table was there now, where it still stood. Dr. Dimbali sauntered into frame.

"Better here, yes?" he asked, clasping his hands behind his back and leaning over. "The alcove. Safer that way, I think." He sauntered closer to the camera. He plucked up one of the plants and held it out at arm's length. "Beyond the nutrients, though, was the breakthrough! The blood! Human blood! I spent so much time on his plant side that I neglected the other, but once I began incorporating transfusions into the regimen—"

From back in the alcove, Rose made a high, keening sound that interrupted Dr. Dimbali, who paused until it stopped.

"As growth has continued," he confided, "there have been more and more instances of...awakenings. Compounded by fear-compelled outbursts and vocalizations. I've resorted to a special cocktail of depressants and narcotics. The DeeCees killed his human part, but the plant structures still survived, clinging to life. On a cellular level—"

Her hand on the SmartBoard shook, and she accidentally swiped ahead.

Dr. Dimbali's face loomed large in profile. He was whispering, standing right next to the SmartBoard, blotting out the rest of the basement.

"—possible to imagine subconscious awareness. Still no actual verbal communication, so I believe my suppositions are correct as to psychological construction. When he finally awakens, he'll be a blank slate. And I will write what I choose on it. I believe the popular locution was once *brainwashing*. I prefer to think of it as simply making him, well, pliant, let's say."

Deedra almost gagged. How could she have trusted Dr. Dimbali? She didn't precisely understand everything he was doing down here, but she knew this: It was nothing good. He was treating Rose as an experiment. As a *thing*.

She swiped through another interminable bout of science talk, arriving finally at an image of an exhausted-looking Dr. Dimbali, sprawled in uncharacteristic repose in his chair, staring up at the ceiling.

"I plan to save the world," he said quietly. "No one else will do it. No one else *can* do it. So I will. I must. Regardless of the trauma endured in the undertaking."

He swiveled in the chair and glared at the potted plants. "But more important than that, I want to be *paid* for it. And even more important, I plan to make *damn* sure that the people I save know exactly whom they have to thank for it."

If she'd wondered at Dr. Dimbali's motives before, now she had no doubts at all: The sick light dancing in the man's eyes as he spoke convinced her—he was out for himself and no one else.

"Someone can pay. Someone can *always* pay. When I show the Magistrates the first fresh . . . *orange* grown in ten generations, they will *find* a way to pay."

Dr. Dimbali's gaze wandered, and he leaned back in the chair again. She knew he wasn't looking at the ceiling. Not really. He was seeing the past and his own future at once, as real to him as the smell of the air. She flailed at the SmartBoard, and the vid froze.

She'd seen enough anyway.

She returned to the alcove. To Rose. This *was* Rose. Somehow. She didn't quite understand it, but she didn't really care. Dr. Dimbali had spouted a lot of nonsense, but none of that mattered to her. Rose was here, in front of her now, and she would figure out how to help him back to himself. She reached out to touch him, just to stroke the pad of a finger along his cheek, his reborn cheek, and something grabbed her from behind, wrapping around her midsection so fast and with such force that her breath exploded out of her in an uncontrollable *ugh* as she was lifted bodily from the floor and yanked unceremoniously away from Rose and the table, her hand still splayed to touch him.

Scarcely had the sensation of being jerked off her feet registered than she collided with the wall behind her, smashing into it with such jarring force that she momentarily lost consciousness. When she blinked her eyes open again, the room tilted and spun for an instant before righting itself. Her legs pumped, her feet kicking without purchase, suspended above the ground.

A heavy *something* pinned her against the wall. She thrashed, but it was no good—she couldn't get down. When she tried to pry it away from her body, she realized how familiar it was.

It was a vine. One of Rose's tendrils.

"Rose!" she shouted, trying to wake him. She tugged at the tendril around her waist. "Rose!"

Just then, two more vines snaked out and up from the potted plants around her, enfolding her wrists, pulling them back until she was spread-eagled against the wall, helpless.

"Rose!" she shouted again, bucking her torso, trying to loosen the vines. "Rose, stop it! It's me! Deedra! Wake up!"

"He can't hear you," Dr. Dimbali said, stepping into the alcove. He wore a battered old hat and seemed unconcerned by her presence. "Truthfully, I'm not sure he'll ever hear anything again."

Deedra struggled against the vines. She couldn't be defenseless, not with Dr. Dimbali here. But the vines held her tight.

And just then, she realized—the vines had come from the *plants*. The potted plants all around her. Not from Rose. Not from the boy who lay on the table, perfectly still, barely breathing.

"What are you *doing*?" she demanded.

He adjusted something on the tank. A hose slackened.

"I've been learning to control it," Dr. Dimbali said with a casual shrug. "But without a sentient consciousness such as Rose's controlling them, the vines can be a bit... aggressive."

"What are you talking about? Control *what*?"

Dr. Dimbali doffed his hat and showed her its inside, which was lined with electrodes and wires. "Witness," he said, and donned the hat again. His eyes crunched together in focused concentration, but nothing happened.

"Hmm." He peered over at her, nose pointed down, as though gazing at her over a pair of glasses. But his SmartSpex were still in her pocket. "See? I tried to loosen them a bit. They don't always obey precisely. I can manipulate some of the seeds and sprouts I've grown by splicing his genes with genetically modified vegetables, but my control is crude and imperfect." He raised an eyebrow. "As you can tell."

The vines were as tight as ever. Deedra took shallow breaths. Her diaphragm was constricted by the vine around her middle.

"They? What are you talking about?"

"It's interesting: Actual roses—the extinct plants—don't form vines. They form *canes*, which cannot wrap around structures on their own. I suppose Rose's combination of rose DNA and human DNA has allowed him to manipulate—"

"Get me down!" She regretted shouting as soon as she'd done it; the breath that whooshed out of her would be difficult to reclaim.

Dr. Dimbali stroked his chin. "Get you down? Perhaps. If I can trust you. Can I trust you, Ms. Ward?"

Could *he* trust *her*?

Rose was dead and then Rose was alive. And Dr. Dimbali seemed to be responsible for the resurrection. But he had just abandoned her after their plan failed. And how could he let her believe Rose was dead all this time?

And the holes in the walls. That time she'd caught him drilling one. That had been *a while* ago. The whole time they'd been planning Rose's escape, Dr. Dimbali had been planning something else entirely and had never spoken a word.

Could he trust her? Possibly.

Could she trust him?

"How is he still alive?" she asked, avoiding the answer.

Dr. Dimbali glanced over at Rose. "What's that? How is *who* still... Oh, I see. I see!" He chuckled indulgently. "Rose is not *still alive*. That's absurd. Rose died. Rose was shot through the chest with an explosive ballistic round. You don't survive that, not even with Rose's rather unique anatomy."

He walked over to the tank and adjusted some knobs. One of the hoses surged for a moment. On the table, Rose shifted for an instant, then settled.

"Our first plan failed, Ms. Ward. I don't blame you. You played your part quite admirably. But Rose was impatient and couldn't wait for us to rescue him. It's not your fault he died, and I hope you don't blame yourself."

"I don't," she said defiantly. "What are you doing? Since when can you control—"

Oh no.

Dr. Dimbali turned from the tank and faced her, hands clasped behind his back.

"You killed Jaron." She realized it in the instant before she said it, and it was so strong and true that she couldn't stop herself from vocalizing it, even though some part of her understood that it was unwise to tell him she knew.

Dr. Dimbali said nothing. He flicked a switch and a light hummed to life overhead. Deedra blinked against the sudden brightness.

Sunlamp. That's what he called it.

Deedra thought of the evidence at the crime scene: the vines. She thought of the vine she'd found at Lissa's.

Found it, Lissa had said. *On the way to work.*

I've been learning to control it, Dr. Dimbali had just said.

So he'd been practicing. And maybe he'd left some of his practice vines around the Territory...

"You killed Jaron," she said again, "and made it look like Rose did it."

Dr. Dimbali shook his head. "No, my dear. You're assuming causality where none exists. I did, indeed, kill young Mr. Ludo. Would you like to know why?"

Did it matter? She wouldn't waste a precious breath either way.

"It goes back to the Red Rain, Ms. Ward. And the truth of its origins. Not God. Not aliens. Not the planet rebelling against us, though we richly deserved it. No." He leaned in close enough that his breath warmed her face. "It was *us*," he hissed. "Us, all along."

He stepped back and clenched his fists in outrage. "It was us! *We* did this! We people. The government planned it. They built death machines, Ms. Ward, and used them to murder half the world in secret. I've seen the designs. The spinning blades. The grasping claw-arms. The great chambers with mechanics to process the bodies, stripping them of clothing and jewelry and anything valuable, shuttling the bodies off to be crushed, compacted, reduced to nothing but pulp. Fifty billion, gone. It took a hundred years, but they killed all those people, and their liquefied remains were the Red Rain."

"Don't believe you," she managed.

He laughed, actually doubled over, clutching his gut. When he stood upright again, tears streaked his face. "Oh, your belief hardly matters, but let me assure you: I'm telling the truth. The only problem with the Red Rain was this: It wasn't enough! Fifty billion on the planet is still too many. So you know what, Ms. Ward?" He came close again, whispering in her ear. "They're going to do it again."

I don't think we're building air scrubbers, Rose had said.

Oh no.

"What do you think you build every day at Ludo Territory Pride Facility Number Twelve? I'll tell you, Ms. Ward: You are assembling the motorized chopping mechanism for a murder machine, designed to reduce a human body into easily pulped segments in less than ten seconds. And you are very, very good at your job."

"You're going to kill people," she managed. Now tears glimmered in her own eyes. Dimbali would kill people, yes, but he would do it with a weapon she helped build.

Dimbali shook his head. "I have no desire to kill anyone. Well, anyone *else*. It's not up to me. The machines are built. They lack only a key! One of the activation keys to the ignition and control consoles. In the possession, I believe, of one—or perhaps many—of the City higherups. A key, Ms. Ward, and the proper hand holding it: These are all that stand between us and a second Red Rain. You want to know why I killed Jaron? I will tell you: Jaron had one of those keys. I don't even know how he knew what he had, at first. He must have been paying more attention to the factory specs than I'd thought. Can you imagine such power in such callow, untrustworthy hands?"

She could. She could also imagine it in Dr. Dimbali's. Neither one sounded any good to her.

"He could not be trusted. Obviously. He had to be reasoned with.

I brought a...pet in case he proved obstinate. But the vines are difficult to control even now—they were more so at the time. I nearly died myself as they thrashed and whipped through the room. I fled before I could uncover his key.

"The Red Rain is coming. It's coming back. And I have no intention of being one of its victims! I will do whatever I must to save myself." He turned to the table and leaned on it, staring down at the body in repose. "I want you to hear this, Ms. Ward, and I want you to believe it—I am terribly, *terribly* sorry for all this. I truly am. Do you believe me?"

"I'll never believe a word out of your mouth again. As long as I live."

He sighed. "The entitlement of youth, I suppose. I had no choice in this matter. None at all. Do you know what the world *used* to be like?"

Saving her breath, she managed a shrug instead.

"It was something quite like that old book Rose gave you, I suppose. According to everything I've been able to piece together. And for that, Ms. Ward? For that, yes, I would kill a thousand Jaron Ludos, resurrect a thousand Roses."

"You're willing to kill people to keep people from being killed," she gasped out. "Makes a lot of sense."

He *tsk-tsk*ed. "Think of the scale! Killing thousands or even millions to save billions!"

She remembered what Rose had told her. About every life mattering.

"You don't get to decide," she managed to say. "Not...doing it for the world, anyway. For yourself."

"Does it matter?" he asked.

She gathered her breath. It mattered, she knew. Because he would make the world good for only some people and not for others, and that wasn't just not fair—it was manipulative and evil and greedy.

"Save your breath," he told her. "I have no desire to debate philosophy with you. There's no point."

She thought of the massive hole in the wall, of the dirt spilling from it. She thought of Rose, standing on the small patch of dirt outside her apartment, face tilted to the sun.

"You brought him back to life. You remade him."

"In a manner of speaking, yes." He leaned back against the table, arms crossed over his chest. "I...repaired him. I daresay not another man on the planet could accomplish the same thing. I have managed—in a week's time!—to reassemble and rejuvenate an entire corpus of a singular species. I suppose there's a chance that some residual trace memory—perhaps language or basic cognition—will remain, depending on the way his unique physiology encodes engrams. But, really, I don't care about that. I don't need Rose's memories, only his conscious ability to control his own biology."

Her breath was coming in shallower and shallower gasps. The vine around her midsection was cutting off most of her air; it was beginning to compress her rib cage from below. And the ones around her hands wouldn't budge.

"With a *brain* that has mastered the finely tuned control over Rose's abilities—ah, Ms. Ward, with *that* in my possession—I will be unstoppable!"

"Don't understand...Thought you wanted to save the world."

Dr. Dimbali gazed at her curiously, then clucked his tongue. A teacher disappointed in a pet student.

"Of course I do. Unlike the mass of humanity, which prefers to simply *live* in the world, I seek to better it. And do you know how such people—people such as myself—are treated, Ms. Ward? Do you know what our society does with them? To them? I will tell you. At NatSci, when I learned the truth, as I told you before...when I found those documents, so old and so buried in the bureaucracy that I was lucky to have stumbled upon them. Predating the Red Rain. When I went to my coworkers, my superiors... 'Look! The world wasn't always this way! It wasn't always an abject struggle! We can return to those days.'"

He shrugged and came closer to her. Pinned several inches above the ground, she matched his height and their gazes locked. No intervening SmartSpex. Nothing to blunt the sheer, insane intensity of his eyes.

"They rejected me," he whispered. "Cast me out. Disgraced me and sent me *here*, to this pit of..." His language—for the first time since she'd known him—failed him and he trailed off, staring at her, unblinking for long moments before finally saying, "I will make those who mocked me beg."

"And what about..." She had to stop to breathe. "...the people who never hurt you?"

He shrugged. "Well, I imagine—" He broke off, his eyes dipping below her chin. A momentary chill shivered Deedra. It wasn't quite a Jaron look, but she was completely helpless, and Dr. Dimbali could do whatever he wanted to her.

But he did not touch her. He only—quite carefully—lifted her necklace with one hand, hoisting the pendant from under her shirt.

"I..." He gaped as he stared at it. "Where did you...how in the world did *you*..."

Nothing. She would say nothing to him.

"This is astonishing! To see it here, now..." He smiled with genuine warmth and pleasure. "Ms. Ward! How extraordinary! You—"

He screamed, his eyes and mouth widening in shock and pain. Spittle flecked Deedra's face and she blinked. In the instant it took for her to reopen her eyes, Dr. Dimbali leapt away from her, releasing his hold on her necklace.

No. He didn't leap. He wasn't doing anything at all. He was *pulled*. By *vines*.

They enfolded him from behind and jerked him away from her with a breathless, terrifying ferocity. Dr. Dimbali screamed again, a high, shrill sound that drove into Deedra's head like a nail. He flipped feet over head, and the vines let go, sending him careering across the lab to crash against another wall and collapse into a heap on the floor.

Deedra hardly had a moment to appreciate the luck. A movement on the table caught her attention. The vines were retracting back to that spot, tucking themselves into Rose's body with a slurping sound.

Rose sat up on the table, his eyes flashing with a fury Deedra had never before witnessed. She knew Rose—the old Rose—hadn't killed Jaron or anyone else.

But this one? This new Rose?

He could do it. Her eyes flicked to the heap of Dr. Dimbali. *If he hasn't already.*

"Please..." she whispered.

Rose cocked his head, as though tilting his ear that way would help the sound of her voice fall in. He was expressionless. Did he even understand her words? Or was he a blank, as Dr. Dimbali had said?

A sound. From across the workshop. Dr. Dimbali groaned and pushed himself to his feet.

Rose's head snapped in that direction. Vines whipped out from his back and wavered, casting snaky shadows on the floor. Dr. Dimbali gasped and ran in the direction Deedra had entered from, fleeing the lab. Rose growled deep in his throat and made as though to give chase, but the hoses connecting him to the nutrient tank tugged back at him.

Pain flashed across his face. Deedra felt it—sympathetically and for real. The vines holding her were tightening, and soon she would black out.

As she watched, Rose slowly, carefully unhooked the hoses. He drew them out one at a time, acting with unhurried precision. One by one, three large spikes emerged from him, slick with red blood and greenish plant matter, each one so long that she couldn't imagine how they could have been implanted in him without meeting in the middle.

As the final spike was withdrawn, she saw the flesh around each wound weep for a moment, then close on its own.

"Rose!" she wailed with a precious breath. He had hopped down from the table and started moving in the direction in which Dr. Dimbali had disappeared, his vines now longer and more threatening in their lashing back and forth, almost as though they had minds—angry minds—of their own.

He turned back to her, fixing her with a glare that betrayed no recognition. Standing before her, he came up only to her midriff. Then, his legs extended, lengthened, and his face came even with her own, close enough for a kiss. Or a bite.

If she hadn't been holding her breath out of necessity, the sight of him so close would have compelled it anyway. He was Rose and he wasn't Rose. Those placid, relaxed features were now pressed into the service of a rage she'd never contemplated. No matter all the indignities heaped upon him in the past, she'd never seen him so angry.

Who knows what does or doesn't survive what he's gone through? No one's ever done anything like this before. He could be anything or anyone.

"Do you remember me?" she gasped. Spots swarmed the edges of her vision. Unconsciousness wasn't far off. And death would follow that.

He stared at her, his head cocked again. Confusion flickered in his eyes. Like Dr. Dimbali, he found himself drawn by the glittering of her pendant as it reflected light from the sunlamp. He touched the pendant with the tip of a finger, then traced his way up the chain itself, under the mass of her hair...

Where he encountered the knotty flesh of her scar.

He probed it, ran his finger along it. Lifted her hair to lean in and peer at it, fascinated.

"Do you—" She couldn't speak.

To die like this? With Rose her last sight, her last touch?

There were, she supposed, worse deaths. She didn't want to die, but the decision wasn't in her hands, so she had to make the best of it.

And then he spoke, haltingly at first, as though learning how.

"You're...different," he said. It was like Rose's voice, only rougher, less refined. Coarse from disuse.

"Different," he said again. "Like me."

"Yes." It would be her last word, perhaps. Tears rolled down her face. The voice had changed, but it was Rose. It was Rose and he would be her last—

"You are..." He struggled with it for a moment. It seemed to take him forever, but he finally said: "You are Dee. Deeee-dra."

"Yes!"

And with that, recognition erupted across the height and breadth of his face, from the tilt of his lips to the expanding pupils of his eyes. The recognition—the *remembering*—pounded at her, bursting forth in every line of him, every curve, every angle. Without words, she knew that he knew, and he knew that she knew. He lunged forward, kissing her, locking himself to her, exhaling into her. She tasted the sweet, sweet oxygen as it filled her lungs, lost in him, with him, connected to him, the seal of their lips inviolate, him giving her oxygen, she giving him carbon dioxide, a virtuous cycle that could go on forever.

Forever.

And she would be fine with that. Fine, lost in the heat of his lips and of his breath.

He broke the kiss and that perfect, perfect mouth twisted into a wry grin. A familiar grin.

"You probably don't like being held against the wall, do you?" he asked with solicitous humor.

"Not really."

■ ■ ■

Rose didn't want to harm or kill the plants that grew all around him. They were mindless and under the control of another, with no motivation or guilt of their own. He sent his tendrils between the wall and the vines holding Deedra in place. He tugged gently at first, testing their strength. They felt familiar and unfamiliar at once, as though he were grappling with himself.

"Hold on," he warned Deedra. She nodded, already losing air again. He would have to hurry.

Bracing himself with palms pressed against the wall, he wrapped his tendrils around the vines and pulled. Not as hard as he could—a slow, steadily mounting pressure.

The vines fought back, contracting further. Deedra gasped and made a hiccuping, choking sound. He forced himself to ignore it. He had to concentrate.

It was difficult. Memories were filtering in. From where, he didn't know. But he was seeing flashes of Cities and Territories. The graveyard roses flickered and flared at him. His entire life spun within him, out of order.

He focused on *her*. The river. The rebar. Her apartment. Her bed. Those memories, too, were coming back, and he plucked them from the whirlwind, using them as anchors against his own history.

I lost her before. I lost everything. I won't. Not again.

The vine holding Deedra's left hand came loose. Just a little. She wiggled her hand free, and Rose concentrated on the one around her midsection, the one making it hard for her to breathe.

Eyes closed, he gritted his teeth and focused with all his might. He still felt woozy and tentative from what seemed to have been a long, fitful sleep, the sort that did not refresh, but rather left the sleeper even more tired on awakening. He vaguely remembered running from the DeeCees at the prison, but little else. Save for brief, nightmarish snatches of grandiose speeches from Dr. Dimbali. Laughter. Mumbles. The pain of the nutrient spikes, ruthlessly inserted and manipulated. He struggled and pulled at the vine around her middle, desperate to free her, to do this thing, this one thing he so badly needed to do.

And suddenly the vine came loose, sending him stunned and stumbling backward until he collided with the table. Deedra hung from the wall by the one vine holding her right wrist, but it quickly withdrew almost as if alarmed. She dropped the six inches to the floor and managed to keep her feet under her.

The vine that had encircled her midsection was hacked in two, its bloody, pulpy stumps flailing in pain and shock.

Deedra held up her makeshift knife in her left hand. "Sorry, but..."

"Between you and the plants," Rose promised her, "I choose you."

He reached out to help steady her after the drop. She took his hand, then pulled away after a moment, turning away from him.

"It's me," he assured her. "I just needed to let..." He struggled with the words. For so long, on the table, in torment, his memories and thoughts had been a mash. Until he saw her, bound with the vines, so close to death. "I'm not going to hurt you."

"It's not that," she said, averting her eyes, and letting out an amused little laugh.

He looked down at himself. "Oh. I should probably put on some pants."

■ ■ ■

They scoured the basement quickly, hoping for maybe an old lab coat or smock of Dr. Dimbali's. Instead, Deedra came upon a jumble of material stuffed onto a shelf in a dark corner. She unfurled it to discover a pair of pants spattered with dried blood, as well as something she knew all too well.

344

She shook it out and held it up. "Rose. Look."

His eyes widened in surprised delight as she held his coat up to him. There were slashes and cuts along its length, most of which had been mended or patched. "It's your stuff from SecFac," she said. "They must have given it to Dr. Dimbali along with…" She hesitated to say "your body."

"…along with my remains," Rose said with something like humor. He approached her and took the coat, studying it. "It looks like he tried to fix it. Experimenting on the biomass, maybe…"

She handed him the pants. "They're, uh, not particularly clean, but…"

"They'll do."

He stepped into the pants, then slipped on the coat. It was a bit ragged and worn, but seeing him in it suddenly made everything right again. It made him real again.

"You don't have any shoes."

He smiled. "Don't worry about me. I'll be fine."

Before she could reply, the room erupted in a high-pitched wail.

■ ■ ■

"*Lockdown!*" a familiar, programmed voice bellowed after the alarm wail ended. Deedra almost dropped her knife, still slick with red-and-green-smeared fluids.

"*Lockdown! This is a lockdown!*"

"What in the—" Rose began.

"*This is a block-wide lockdown! Repeat, a block-wide lockdown!*"

Deedra dared to crane her neck around the corner of the alcove. The rest of the workshop was empty and still, save for the screens now lit up with the flashing lockdown logo. Dr. Dimbali was gone.

"He must have reported us—" she began, only to be interrupted by the continuation of the voice, which announced the very block on which Dr. Dimbali's building stood.

"All citizens within two blocks of the location stated are to remain in place until released by the Department of Citizen Services or representatives of the Office of the Magistrate!"

"He reported us, for sure," she fumed. "And now the DeeCees are coming after us."

"He wouldn't report us," Rose said. "Not if he wants to keep me a secret."

"Then how did they..." Deedra gasped as she realized. She fumbled in her pocket for the SmartSpex and slipped them on. In the corner of her eye, a red light pulsed, flashing the words WORM DETECTED!

"They bugged the SmartSpex," she groaned. That was why Markard had returned them. Why she'd been released from SecFac and left alive. Just in case she led them somewhere. She recalled the DeeCees and drones that had shadowed her on her way to Dimbali's basement from Lissa's building. They'd been closing in as she moved and nailed her down when she was still.

"Break them," Rose said.

She took them off and prepared to snap them in half but couldn't bring herself to do it. They were too useful, and she could maybe figure out how to remove the worm. For now, she settled on removing the battery, killing their connection.

Rose scurried to her side and took her free hand. His hand was cool and softer than she remembered, which should have been impossible. New hand; new skin. Untouched, undamaged. "We aren't safe here," Rose said. "It's only a matter of time before they search the place. And find us."

She squeezed his hand. Gently. So fragile. She knew how powerful he was, but he still felt so...breakable. The image of his chest exploding as the shell tore through him lurked at the edges of her imagination. Would she ever forget it?

She thought not.

"We're leaving the Territory, aren't we?"

Rose considered her for a moment. Then: "I don't think we have a choice." He said it with real regret, and she couldn't figure out why. "I know it's your home, but..."

Deedra shook her head fiercely. "No. No, it's okay. I was actually... I was actually getting ready to leave anyway. Before I knew you were alive. There's nothing left for me here." She shrugged. "There was nothing much to begin with. I have to admit—leaving *with* you is a lot better than leaving alone."

He grinned and raised their joined hands so that he could lightly kiss her knuckles. "Then we go. Together." He thought for a moment. "We need to get out of *here* right now. Go somewhere else. The best option to get out of the Territory safely is to move at night, when no one's on the streets. The drones can't see me because my body temperature doesn't fall within their parameters. But you..."

She gestured to her poncho. "Dr. Dimbali was kind enough to make me drone-invisible."

His face split wide into that grin she loved so much, and she had to resist the urge to lean forward and kiss it. There was no time for that.

"I think I know a place we can go. To hide until night."

"Where?"

He clenched her hand tighter and pulled her toward the exit. "I'm pretty sure you call it the Broken Bubble."

CHAPTER 48

Outside, DeeCees were everywhere. Drones thickened the sky. The programmed voice shouted instructions every thirty seconds, reminding citizens to shelter in place, not to leave their current positions, and so on. Deedra's name had been added to the lockdown blast, and she knew photos of her would be flashing on vids throughout the Territory. Her scar alone would make her unforgettable.

If I wasn't planning on leaving before... I'm definitely going now.

Rose and Deedra watched from the roof of Dr. Dimbali's building, ten stories up. The rain had tapered off and the sun was doing its best to burn through the cloud cover. She prayed for it to hold off as long as possible—right now the cloud cover was the only asset they had. That and the fact that the DeeCees and the drones were all focused on the ground. Dr. Dimbali had been right about one thing—no one ever looked up.

They'd had no choice but to run for the roof. Dr. Dimbali's "secret" entrance had been compromised already, with DeeCee robotic cameras positioned at its mouth. (Fortunately, Rose had been in the lead, and he saw them before they could see her.) The block surrounding the building swarmed with DeeCees, like roaches on offal, a slow-moving, oozingly growing sludge of those shiny black helmets and matte black suits of antiballistic body armor. Deedra had never seen so many Dee-Cees in the same place at the same time, except in her nightmares.

The streets were closed off to them. They couldn't stay in the building—someone would see them and report them, or they would be found during a search. And so, the roof.

But now that they were up here, Deedra had to admit that while being outside was preferable to being trapped inside...they were still trapped. The only difference being a slight breeze from the north.

"There." Rose pointed off to her left. Another building, this one a story smaller than Dr. Dimbali's, squatted just off to the east.

"What about it?"

He guided her line of sight. "Once we get to *that* roof," he told her, "we can get to the one on the right over there. And then to the one just past it. That should get us past the blockades, and we can get to street level and make our way to the Broken Bubble."

She could see it in her mind's eye, a series of rooftop hops. It made perfect sense. Except for the part about hopping from rooftop to rooftop.

"It's at least thirty feet from here to that next roof," she pointed out. "We can't jump it."

"I'm not proposing we jump. I'll go over first and then make a bridge for you."

She stared at him, openmouthed. He grinned.

"Don't worry. I escaped from the Blam Boys, remember?"

"The *Bang* Boys."

"Oh. Right." He shook his head. "Some things are still scrambled."

"Are you sure you're okay?" She gnawed at her lower lip. "Can you do this?"

"Watch me."

He stood at the very edge of the building, facing their escape route. His reclaimed coat's ragged hem fluttered in the breeze. As she watched, his arms thickened and lengthened, becoming tougher and more vine-like. Vicious-looking spikes stood out from them. Thorns. To help him grip.

He backed up several paces. Deedra stood aside. She wanted to ask him exactly what his plan was, but before she could form the words, he took off at a dead run, charging full speed toward the edge of the building.

And jumped!

She bit back a shriek of horror. For a moment, Rose's slim form was a green highlight against the lightening sky, and then gravity blinked into awareness and he began to plummet. This time, Dr. Dimbali would not be around to resurrect him.

And then he lashed out with those extended arms of his. Their ends just barely reached the roof of the other building. Running to the precipice, she watched him, one story below, as his body jerked to a sudden and painful halt that made her own shoulders throb in sympathy. He swung against the side of the other building, feetfirst, absorbing the impact with a bend of his knees.

And then—she could hardly believe she was seeing it—he scrambled up the side of the building so fast that it seemed to take no time at all. Some combination of actual climbing and retracting his vines, the thorns studded along their lengths giving purchase, finding support in cracks and fissures along the building's facade. She stared in gape-mouthed astonishment as he hauled himself over the parapet at the top of the building, vanishing behind it for a moment, then popping up to reappear, that infuriating, gorgeous grin on his face.

He gestured to her. It didn't take much to interpret what he was saying:

Jump! I'll get you!

No. Way.

Come on! he mimed.

She risked a look down the side of the building. Not a chance. She had scaled plenty of structures in pursuit of scavenge, and she wasn't terribly afraid of heights themselves. Falling, though? Yeah, she was plenty afraid of falling.

He gestured *Hurry!* and as she watched, a swarm of vines and tendrils protruded from his body, extending out into the chasm between buildings, many of them overlapping. It wasn't quite a net and it didn't cover the entire space, but she supposed it was better than nothing. Like the bridge by the river, it was imperfect and probably unstable, but—like the bridge—it was something she had to do.

Jump and take your chances . . . or stay here and be caught for sure.

She thought of the thorns. Of the night he'd cut her without meaning to.

They've already built the machines. No one knows what's coming. So many people will die.

And hey—at least if Rose misses you, you might squish a DeeCee or two.

One thing she knew for certain: If she screamed, they would hear her down below, and all those faces and robots and cameras currently looking down would look straight up . . . and see her there. And whether she made it or not, they would know where to look for Rose. So before leaping, she wadded up a shirt from her backpack and stuffed it into her mouth to muffle any sounds she made.

She did as Rose had done, backing up a little way. Before she could lose her nerve, she ran full tilt toward the edge of the building. The tricky part was right at the end, where the parapet rose. Time it wrong and she would lose momentum or trip. . . .

At the last moment, she hop-stepped onto the parapet and—

Lost her balance.

And dropped over the edge of the building, arms flailing, legs kicking.

She screamed her lungs out, the sound muffled by the shirt. Desperately, she wanted to close her eyes, but she seemed incapable of doing so. She would get a nice close-up of the shocked DeeCee she landed on. Would it be a squish or more like a wet explosion, she wondered.

Out of the corner of her eye, she caught movement from above. A blur. Rose, she realized, leaping from the other rooftop...

No, no, no! Don't! Not worth both of us dying—

It was all she had time for as her leg jerked, so hard that she thought it might pop out of its socket, driving all thought from her. Still screaming, she twisted in midair, her plunge halted. The fabric of her pant leg ripped, then caught and held strong at the hem. Like a one-way pendulum, she arced toward the opposite building, its face rushing at her with surprising speed. What was worse—smashing into the ground ten stories down or crashing into a building?

Crashing into the building was pretty bad. Her teeth rattled; her entire skeleton felt bruised; her body flamed with pain. But she was alive, panting and moaning into her self-imposed gag.

Above her, Rose dangled in midair, suspended by a vine whose end disappeared up onto the opposite rooftop. Another vine, just as taut, extended to her.

He'd caught her. He couldn't do it from the rooftop, so he'd leapt....

Another vine now, encircling her. Rose's expression was one of almost peaceful agony, acceptance of the strain.

The thorns she'd dreaded were more help than hindrance. They hurt, but they made for a better grip than the smooth surface of the vines. Through her shoe and sock, she felt them stabbing at her. The pain was minor compared with hitting the building.

Only a matter of time, she thought. *Only a matter of time before someone looks up. Or a drone scans this area in visible light, not IR.*

But she couldn't make herself move. The pain was too tremendous, and blood rushed to her head. She was suspended upside down, disoriented, the world spinning beneath and around her.

At last, she craned her neck, looking up. Rose had extended more vines but couldn't reach her with them. They waved temptingly at her.

They couldn't reach her...but maybe *she* could reach *them*. It was a precarious twist, but maybe if she moved just right...

She steadied herself with a palm against the building. Bent double, she couldn't reach far enough. A petulant thought flashed: *Why doesn't he just pull me up???* and she immediately felt ashamed for thinking it. He'd *caught* her. He'd jumped headlong off a building. He could only do so much.

Braced against the building, she tested the limits of her movement. She didn't want to do anything sudden or unexpected that would make Rose drop her or pull him down with her. But she needed to right herself because then she could extend her left hand out and grab one of the other vines. Carefully, she avoided touching the thorns.

It probably took only a minute—perhaps a few seconds less—to reorient herself, gripping the vines around her middle with her right hand, inching herself in a circle to upright with her left against the wall. But it felt like forever. By the time she'd finished, she was exhausted, her body drenched in sweat, her nostrils flaring with exaggerated breaths. Aches consumed her. She wanted (no, *needed*) a break, just a few minutes to rest, but she was keenly aware of the DeeCees below and Rose above, holding her without complaint, surely as exhausted and as battered as she was.

Planting her back against the wall, she reached out with her left hand. The motion pulled her away from the safety of the wall and for a stomach-dropping moment, she was out in the naked air again, but she kept her eyes firmly focused *up* and grabbed the vine.

Now she was more secure. She inhaled as deeply as she could and cursed herself for the gag. Yeah, it had been useful, but right now she wanted it out of her mouth so that she could take a nice, deep breath through her mouth.

Focus, Deedra. Focus.

She steadied herself and adjusted her grip, drifting minutely toward the building again. Guided by Rose? By gravity? Didn't matter.

With her legs stiff, she made contact with the building, facing up, her feet planted.

She stared up. When she'd been falling, it had felt as if she'd been falling forever, but the roof was only two or three stories up. Rose hung in the middle space between her and safety.

Two or three stories. You can do this. Easy, right?

She started to climb.

When she was still ten feet from the top, her whole body jerked once and she was grateful for the stupid gag, which choked off another scream, this one of surprise and delight, not terror. Rose was now pulling her actively, hauling her up into his arms, then dragging them both the last story, over the parapet, where she collapsed onto the rooftop. She rolled away from him, onto her back, yanked out the gag, and gulped in great, huge swallows of air. Rose, his body now more or less returned to its usual slender, bipedal dimensions and form, crawled to her.

"I wish we could rest," he gasped, "but…"

"I know. We have to keep moving." She found her feet and pulled him up. "Let's get going."

■ ■ ■

"Magistrate?" Markard approached Max Ludo cautiously. The Magistrate was huddled with the scientist—Dimbali—on the sidewalk just outside Dimbali's building. A swarm of DeeCees bustled around them, shouting out instructions, warnings.

Max Ludo sneered, his voice laden with annoyance. "What *is* it, Markard?"

"Magistrate, the men have surrounded the building and closed off a perimeter. We're ready to move on your order."

Ludo and Dimbali shared a look. "Well, Doctor?" It was the closest Markard had ever heard to deference or even basic politeness in Ludo's voice.

"Just be careful," Dimbali said. He was a frightened, nervous thing, but something lurked under that skin that set Markard's nerves on edge. There was something powerful hidden under the sniveling and kowtowing. How could the Magistrate not see it? "The..." He paused, glancing over at Markard the way most people looked at cockroaches or dung.

"You can trust him," Ludo said, exasperated. "Markard here had the idea to follow the Ward girl, just in case. He's been working with me longer than you have, Doctor. He's loyal. Aren't you, Markard?"

There was never any question as to the answer: "Of course, Magistrate." What other option was there? "Now, Doctor, let me get this straight: You were conducting experiments on Rose's body, and Ms. Ward just...showed up? Out of the blue?" He hoped his incredulous sarcasm came through; sometimes it was tough to tell.

Dimbali clearly wasn't happy to be spilling secrets and confidences in the presence of a mere cop, but he answered anyway. "Yes, that's precisely correct. She is—was—an acquaintance of mine. She reactivated the creature, and together they overpowered me. It's possible she's a Dalcord sleeper agent. An orphanage would be perfect cover for insertion of a spy."

Markard nodded slowly. He didn't know Dimbali, but the man had a point. It was possible.

"Thankfully you were already in the area when I fled," Dimbali continued, now larding on the sentiment so thickly that Markard felt ill. "The creature is powerful and dangerous. But valuable," he hastened to remind them.

"It killed my boy," Ludo snapped. "I don't care *how* powerful it is—we killed it once before, we can do it again."

With anyone else, that would have been the end of the conversation, but Dr. Dimbali, clearing his throat and flickering a smile, said, "Of course, Magistrate. Of course. Technically, though, I..." He shifted gears. "May I remind you, though, that the creature is infinitely more valuable alive than dead? That, alive, it may hold the key or keys to protecting this—*your*—Territory and defeating your enemies?"

Magistrate Ludo harrumphed. He brought his meaty hands together and rubbed them hungrily. Revenge and pragmatism warred nakedly in his features. Pragmatism—and ambition—won out. "We'll take the creature alive, if at all possible," he finally capitulated. "Plastic bullets."

Dimbali seemed happier than almost anyone Markard had ever seen in his life.

"May I give the order, Magistrate?" Markard asked.

"Do it."

Markard thumbed his comm and held it to his lips. "Commanders, load stun rounds. You may begin your incursion into the building."

CHAPTER 49

The first gap was the widest and the toughest. The next building was only a couple of yards away; getting to its roof was easy compared with that first jump. As they made their way across the cityscape, Rose suddenly paused at the lip of a rooftop, staring off into the distance. Deedra was getting antsy—she didn't like standing still any longer than was strictly necessary. Movement meant life. Safety. The Broken Bubble loomed ahead.

But was he ready to run? After all he'd been through?

"Are you okay?" she asked him. "Do you think you can—"

"My memories are coming back." He shook his head. "It's...distracting, but I can get past it."

"You remember...everything?"

"I think so. And I remember Dr. Dimbali. Standing over me. Talking to himself."

No, talking to his plants. And his SmartBoard.

He blinked and turned to her, eyes wide with memory. "I heard him...I heard him say that...I'm actually a *rose*?"

She nodded slowly. "Yes. That's true. We figured it out after you were arrested. You're a hybrid."

"So I'm not human after all," Rose said.

She couldn't tell how this news affected him; he said it with the same "isn't that interesting?" tone with which he discussed something as prosaic as fruit discs.

"You're part human," she reminded him. "You're something new."

He seemed so vulnerable and tentative, his outline against the gray sky, a single figure backgrounded by the wreck of the Territory's skyline. She took his hand and opened her mouth and realized that she had nothing else to say. Nothing that needed to be said.

I love you, she thought, but did not say. Not because she was afraid to, but because she realized in that instant that it was unnecessary. He knew.

He turned to her and grinned. "Part human is good enough, right? It's *interesting*, at least."

She smiled back. "You're the most human person I've ever met."

"You're the most plantlike human I've ever met," he told her in a joking tone that made her laugh, despite their situation.

"We should get going," she reminded him. "The machines they—we—built…"

"They're still building," he pointed out. "They'll wait until they're all finished, until they have enough of them. Then they'll start. We have some time. To escape. Maybe to warn people."

"How did you know we weren't building air scrubbers?"

He hesitated. "I've seen things, Deedra. I saw the remains of a machine once. Far from here. It looked very similar to what we were building at L-Twelve."

He looked down. They were many stories up and the only nearby buildings they could reach were in the wrong directions—north or west, when the Broken Bubble lay directly to the east.

"Let's get down to ground level. We're out of the search zone, so it should be okay."

She looked around. There was a door nearby, but it was metal, sturdy, and—from the feel of it when she pushed against it—barricaded from the other side. "Well, the stairs are—Whoa!"

Rose had enfolded her in vines and pulled her tight to him, and then—without a word—stepped off the edge of the roof. Deedra didn't have time to yell or scream, as her breath fled her. They dropped a few feet and then stopped, flush against the side of the building. Another vine snaked up and over the rooftop.

"You could warn me before you do that!" She focused all her attention on *not* looking down.

"Sorry." His tone, impish, was anything but apologetic. He was still grinning. "This is going to be the quickest way down."

"Really?"

"I've done this before," he reminded her. He shot a vine out to their left, this one studded with thorns. It lodged into a crevice. Rose pulled slightly, testing it, then released the rooftop vine. They swung gently down and to the left.

"Of course," he admitted when they came to a stop, "I've never done it *holding* someone!"

"Don't remind me!" But even though she felt the need to chide him, she didn't actually sense any danger. She'd never felt safer or more secure than right then, dangling several stories above the hard ground...wrapped up in Rose.

He zigzagged them down the face of the building a bit more, then stopped to catch his breath and reassess their position.

"You didn't kill Jaron after all."

"What?" Distracted, he turned to her. "No, of course not."

"Then how did you get my pendant back?"

He pushed off and dropped them a little. When they caught—a few feet lower—he said, "I went to Jaron's that morning, before light.

To sneak in and take back the pendant. It wasn't really stealing if I was taking it *back*, right?"

It seemed to matter to him, so she nodded.

"But he was dead when I got there. I took the pendant and ran. I was going to explain it all to you, but..."

Lockdown. The gunfire. The arrest. Lissa, shot.... She closed her eyes against sudden tears.

"It was a mistake," he said. "All a mistake. Even trying to fit in. I was tired of being on the road. I was alone all the time. And here was my chance. I knew I would have to have an actual identity to pass among other people, and I knew everyone had brands. I thought maybe I could fake it. I..." He shook his head. "Stupid. Stupid mistake."

"The brands have special—"

"That's not what I mean. That wasn't the mistake. The mistake was trying it at all. Trying to be someone else."

She thought about that. They stared at each other.

"It's an easy mistake to make," she said.

"All the more reason not to," he said, and without preamble retracted his vines. Deedra gasped and fell...

...less than a foot, stumbling on the ground. Rose had lowered them the rest of the way while they had talked.

"That wasn't funny," she grumbled as he dropped into place next to her.

"It wasn't supposed to be," he said. "I was tired."

She looked up. The building seemed infinitely tall, and Rose seemed infinitely small. He was pale and breathing hard.

"You did well." She kissed his cheek. "Do you have a little more left in you? We still have to get there." She pointed off to the Broken Bubble.

"Let's go," he told her, taking her hand.

They stuck to alleyways and cramped walkways. Deedra had never gone so far in this direction before. The Broken Bubble squatted on the very edge of the Territory's boundary in this direction, perilously close to the Dalcord Territory. No one in Ludo would go any closer to Dalcord than was strictly necessary. She lost the path quickly, but Rose had come this way many, many times, and he guided her.

Nightfall was still a few hours away by the time they gained the Broken Bubble.

Up close, it didn't look like a broken bubble at all. It was a massive, oval building, several blocks long, with a domed roof that had collapsed at points along its surface. From here, it looked more like an egg, only this one lay on its side and was cracked along the top.

This far out, the heaps of trash and wreckage were older, less picked-over, more massive.

For the two or three blocks leading up to the Broken Bubble (she still thought of it that way), they had to creep their way over chunks of concrete and mountains of garbage, as well as a profusion of junked cars, the likes of which Deedra had seen before only on wikis. Rats skittered underfoot, unafraid. Blue flashes of fur darted in and out of her field of vision, and she kicked out when she had to.

Eventually they stumbled over the last piece of trash and stood before a massive stone arch that, once upon a time, led inside the Broken Bubble.

Once upon a time. Now it was choked with debris, packed solid and impassable.

She caught her breath and stared at it. The Broken Bubble was immense in a way she'd never encountered. She was used to tall buildings, to skyscrapers, but not something so sprawling and gigantic. Looking left or right, she couldn't see either end of the thing.

Most of the signage on and near the building had long since decayed into illegibility, but Deedra managed to pick out letters that spelled ARENA.

"What was this place?"

"I'm not sure," Rose admitted. "I think people used to gather here. For entertainment."

Deedra couldn't imagine why people would need to commune in such a place to watch a vid.

"Live entertainment," Rose amended. "Contests of some sort, I think. I guess it doesn't matter anymore."

"I guess not." She sniffed the air. There was the lingering, rotted scent of garbage from behind them, but also something else. Something temptingly familiar.

Of course. She leaned in close to Rose. He was redolent of his usual perfume smell, but the smell in the air was different. Similar, but not the same, like different shades of the same color.

"What's that smell?" she asked.

Rose hesitated. "It's probably best to show you."

He took her hand and led her along the right-hand side of the Broken Bubble. The curve of the building became more apparent the farther they walked. Eventually he stopped and looked up.

"Wait here," he said, and before she could speak, he was gone, clambering up the side of the building with his thorny vines. He looked like an enormous green spider, and that image thrilled rather than terrified her.

Midway up, he stopped...and vanished. A moment later, his head poked out and he dangled a vine down to her. She grabbed ahold. It was cool and strong; it wrapped around her arm for support and stability.

And stop thinking of it as "it." It's him.

She started to climb and Rose retracted the vine at the same time. Faster than she could have imagined, she ascended the wall until she joined Rose in a shaft that cut through the building. The new scent was even stronger now, carried on a powerful rush of air from farther in.

"I think this used to be an old air shaft," he explained. "For ventilation. I'm not sure. But this is how I go in and out."

"How long have you been coming here? What have you been

doing?" Another thought occurred to her, completely out of the blue: "Do you ever even sleep?"

"Of course! I just need less sleep than you do, is all. Come on."

Together, they crawled down the air shaft. The smell became more overwhelming. Up ahead, gray light shone through.

And they were out in the open again, Rose helping Deedra climb out of the duct.

She couldn't believe what she was seeing. She began to understand how that DeeCee had felt when the strobing light patterns flashed in her helmet.

She had emerged from the duct onto a concrete platform that overlooked the interior of the Broken Bubble from a height of maybe one story. Above her, the roof was a shattered patchwork of crumbled concrete and a webbing of steel beams, so distant and so wrecked that it might as well have been missing entirely. Clouds clustered overhead, but there was just enough light that she could see something so staggering that Deedra actually lost her balance. Rose caught her, held her upright, as she stared into what was the greenest, most beautiful tableau she'd ever witnessed.

The interior of the Broken Bubble was hollow, with seats and aisles ranged around the perimeter. But below, it was a lush, vibrant carpet of colors, greens, reds, yellows, oranges.... More colors and more intense colors than she'd ever witnessed before. The colors alone assaulted her, battered her deliciously. Her eyes drank them in, as though starved of such hues and desperate for them.

"Beautiful..." she murmured, and then stopped talking, all her energy, her attention, her focus directed on what was before her eyes.

"Welcome to the Arbor," Rose said.

Grass. Not the scraggly, brownish threads that occasionally poked up from sidewalks. But a whole swath of it, green and fresh and swaying in a light breeze. Trees! Slender and raw and young, their branches an explosion of many-fingered hands of multiple shades and colors. Insects buzzed and swarmed, gentle clouds of them migrating from bushes, clotting the air over a cluster of yellow-petaled flowers.

In the middle of it all was one tree that towered over the others, spreading its broad branches wide. A wild, untamed hedge ran around it like a crowd. She couldn't stop staring at it.

"I call that one Big Boy," Rose said. "He was the first thing I saw when I came here. Half dead, but still reaching for the sun. I tended to him and he's grown . . . a lot."

"Did you name every plant here?"

"Just him, so far."

She felt small and insignificant, and in the same moment enormous and magnificent, that she could witness this. The world was alight and alive.

"The smell . . ."

"Flowers," Rose told her. "No roses. Not yet. But others."

She cocked her head at a sound. "Are those . . . birds?"

"Yes."

"How—" There were no birds for miles and miles and miles.

"They were attracted by the insects. And the insects were attracted by the plants. That's how it's supposed to work. That's how it used to work, as best I can tell. It makes sense, doesn't it?"

She nodded, her voice fled again in wonderment. He allowed her to gawk for a little while longer, then asked, "Do you want to go down there?"

To walk among such splendor? She could only bob her head in mute, spasmodic enthusiasm.

He guided her down several turns of broad, concrete stairs, then through a break in an old interior wall. The scent was stronger now, and she could detect different notes to it: Bark and leaves. Grass and flowers. Soil and water.

"We should be safe here until nightfall," Rose said.

They found a spot under an overlap of tree branches and settled in. As she sat down, safe at last, all the panic and terror that had driven her since fleeing her apartment finally drained away, and a surge of emotion broke through the dam she'd built out of fear and necessity.

"They killed Lissa," she whispered. "For no reason at all."

Rose set his jaw, his fists clenched. "I don't know what to say," he admitted. "I'm sorry."

"That's all you can—" And she interrupted herself with a flood of tears. Rose crouched down and put his arms around her, and she realized after a moment that he was crying, too.

"None of this should have happened," he murmured. "I'm so sorry. None of this should have happened."

They held each other and rocked each other until they both fell silent. Deedra would have imagined it to be impossible to sleep after all she'd been through, but she was suddenly exhausted.

"Can we sleep here?" she asked.

"Yes," he said. "This is the safest place I know."

Gratefully, she curled into a sleeping position on the grass, which was softer than she would have thought. Rose lay down next to her. Tucked against him, surrounded by the scent of the Arbor, she fell asleep almost immediately.

Hours later, certain it had been a dream, she feared opening her eyes.

But the Arbor was still there. Even more glorious by a rare, brief glow of moonlight.

Rose had gathered fruit and came to her, arms laden with it. "You did this?" she whispered in awe, looking all around them. "If you can do this, you can change the world."

Rose gave a little half shrug. "The world has to want to be changed," he responded at last.

"But if you can just—"

"It's not that simple. Dr. Dimbali was a big help, too—he helped me figure out how to accelerate things." He pointed up at an angle, and she followed his gesture. Overhead, hanging between old steel beams, were what her squinting eyes told her were panes of filtered glass. "They strengthen the sunlight," he explained. "I sort of made this place into a giant greenhouse."

She didn't know what a greenhouse was, but she was impressed by the effort it must have taken.

"I read about them in a book once," Rose went on.

"Another one? There's more than one book?"

Rose laughed. "There are entire *buildings* of them!"

Rose reached up to rub a leaf between his thumb and forefinger. "I don't just snap my fingers and make this happen. I've always..." He shrugged. "It's funny because I've always had an affinity for plants. I never knew why, but it makes perfect sense to me now. But I don't *control* them. I had to do this the same as anyone else would. Or could. One plant at a time. One seed at a time. It took time just to accomplish this, my little Arbor. And that was with my working constantly."

She touched the tree. The roughness of its bark. Her fingers lost themselves in the channels of it.

A sneeze brought her back to the moment. Her eyes watered and her head felt too full, as though someone had syringed a pound of lard into her sinuses.

"Perfect timing," she muttered. "I think I'm getting sick."

"It's probably allergies," Rose told her. "It's been generations since anyone has been exposed to so much pollen. I'll have to work on that, I guess."

She sniffled. "It's okay. I'll be all right." She turned a slow, lingering circle, spinning the place—the *Arbor*, he'd called it—around her. A montage of greens and yellows and purples and bright colors she'd seen on computer screens, but never in person. She'd never even imagined such colors could exist in the real world. A Broken Bubble full of life in the midst of decay.

"Dr. Dimbali was working with me on it," he said sadly. "Trying to come up with ways to make it easier and faster to grow things. More widespread. Deedra, don't..." He sighed heavily. "Don't think I can save the world. Change the world. I don't know if I can. All I know for sure is that I can do this." He gestured around them.

"Maybe that's enough for now," she said, and kissed him.

That's when Max Ludo's voice boomed out at them, filling the Arbor with its poison.

■ ■ ■

Markard stood stiffly at Max Ludo's side as the Magistrate barked into the portable PA.

"Don't even *think* of moving!" he bellowed. His voice echoed and reverberated within the confines of the old arena's shell. "If you surrender right now, we won't open fire."

That was Markard's cue. He flicked at the screen of his comm and twenty handpicked DeeCees—Max Ludo's most loyal soldiers—stood up from their hiding positions in the upper tiers of the arena. Twenty sniper rifles took aim.

"You're in our sights, you little prick!" Ludo's eyes gleamed. "Surrender and we'll let the girl live."

"Whatever you do," said Dr. Dimbali, "don't shoot the boy. He's—"

"Shut up," Ludo advised.

"My men know what to do," Markard assured Dimbali.

They had spent the past several hours scouring every last cranny of Dimbali's building. When they'd come up empty, the Magistrate had completely lost not just his temper, but also the very veneer of civility. He'd exploded into a rant of epic proportions, cursing with extravagant creativity and vitriol. The DeeCees present had made themselves scarce, returning to the street as Ludo rampaged through the basement of the building, knocking over screens and furniture, bawling to the ceiling at the top of his lungs. It was a tantrum the likes of which Markard had never before witnessed and—knowing the Magistrate's moods—he would have feared for his job, and possibly his life, had not the focus of Ludo's anger been so obviously Dr. Dimbali, who had led them inside with promises of a murderer and a weapon delivered.

In those moments, Markard had instead feared for Dimbali's life and, if asked, would not have given the man even odds on surviving the day. But Dr. Dimbali—with his trembling and obsequious manner—somehow had the skills and the savvy to calm the Magistrate. Markard watched silently as Dimbali slowly talked Ludo down from his inchoate rage.

"There is one more place," Dimbali said with confidence. "A place he would go to hide."

It had been a hustle to get ready and assemble a group to mount an assault on the old arena near the Territory border. Markard had almost forgotten the place existed. And when Dimbali led them there, the mountains of debris and trash surrounding the place convinced him that no one in his right mind would flee there. Not even two kids on the run from the Magistrate's ruthless brand of personal justice.

And then he'd seen the inside.

Agog and gape-mouthed, he'd stared at the heaven nestled within the innards of the decrepit arena. His mouth watered at the sight, the smells.

"If you or any of your men speak of this," Max Ludo said pleasantly, "I'll have you hanged. With your own intestines for rope."

It didn't need to be said twice.

And now Markard's men had drawn beads on the figures down below, the kids doing what Markard himself longed to do—walking on that grass, touching those leaves...

Markard had seen Rose shot dead in person, had chased the kid through the factory, and had seen him perform some damn-near-impossible acrobatics. So he was surprised to see him up and walking, but not *too* surprised. This whole setup that Ludo and Dimbali had cooked up was obviously way, *way* beyond him. He wanted to know how the kid had come back to life. He wanted to know how the hell the old arena had become heaven on earth.

But asking questions was an easy way to end up on the wrong side of Max Ludo's favor. So he tamped down his curiosity and accepted the microphone from the Magistrate.

"Ms. Ward!" He tried to make his voice soothing and reasonable, but the amplification and the echoes made it mechanical and harsh. "Ms. Ward and... Rose. This is Superior Inspector Markard. We have marksmen with you in their sights. No one has to die today. Just lie flat on the—" *beautiful, gorgeous, endlessly green grass* "—ground and no one will be hurt."

He peered at them through his binoculars. They were frozen in the middle of the arena, clinging to each other. He zoomed in to the maximum magnification, but he couldn't make out their facial expressions.

"Hurry it along!" Ludo snapped.

"Magistrate," Dimbali said in a low, comforting tone, "if it means recovering the Rose creature without losing the work I've put in, it's worth a couple of minutes—"

"We're using plastic bullets. He shouldn't be hurt too badly. And even if he is, you can just bring him back again," Ludo said carelessly. "Or you can do things with the corpse, right?"

Dr. Dimbali sighed. "Magistrate, I remind you that the processes required to 'resurrect' Rose were and remain extremely difficult, the materials arduous to obtain. There's no guarantee that a second time—"

"Wait," Markard told them. "They're moving." He blinked. "Oh, hell." He thumbed his personal comm. "Fire!" he yelled.

■ ■ ■

"What do we do?" Deedra murmured, her lips against Rose's cheek. As soon as Max Ludo's voice had boomed out at them, they'd gone still. Moving only their eyes, they confirmed that there were DeeCees high up above them, aiming rifles from multiple angles.

They were at the bottom of a well, with guns ringing them from on high. Cross fire would kill them.

Deedra didn't want to die. But she also didn't want to surrender. Surrender, she knew, meant putting Rose back in the hands of Max Ludo. Who would just hand him over to Dr. Dimbali for more experimentation. Dr. Dimbali would use Rose to figure out how to regrow parts of the world for people who could pay, people like Max. Sure, the world would be greener, but it would be no better off. It would just have beautiful scabs on its wounds.

Surrender would mean she would die, anyway. Once they had Rose, they didn't need her. She was nothing. No one. They didn't care about her. Just Rose. What he could do. What he was.

What he represented.

Then again, wouldn't she die no matter what? If Dr. Dimbali was right, someone could turn the key to one of the death machines and then it wouldn't matter. The Red Rain would come back, and the people with the keys would control it.

"You need to escape," she whispered.

"*We* need to escape," he whispered back.

"No. I'll run left; you stay still." The plan formed itself as she spoke it. "They'll all focus on me, since I'm moving. Wait until the first shots, then run to the right."

He held her tighter. "That's a pretty stupid plan," he murmured.

Around them, the Arbor filled with the sound of a new voice—

370

Markard, she thought. It was tough to tell, what with all the echoes. "It's the only chance we have to keep you alive," she told him.

"Well, it ends with you dead, so I'm not into that plan."

"Rose..." She couldn't move her hands, so the tear gathering in her eye spilled down her cheek unblotted. "I'm nothing special. You are. You have to live—"

"You're special to me," he said very, very calmly. "So we *both* have to live." He tilted his head; his eyes were even with hers, and she saw no fear in them. "Do you trust me?"

"With my life."

"Good thing." She felt vines extending around her, and then he said, "This might get rough."

And then—without warning—sepals flew up into the air, as though caught in a sudden updraft. They flared around them, blocking out the sky and the moon, and an instant later, the bullets started flying.

■ ■ ■

Rose winced as bullets shredded his sepals. But their sudden blooming had done the trick, providing a small bit of protection and also distracting the snipers.

In the same moment that he flared his sepals, Rose reached out with a vine, wrapping it around the closest of Big Boy's branches. He pulled with all his strength, hoping that the branch was strong enough to support them.

Birds exploded from the undergrowth, ascending in a ferocious welter of squawks, twitters, and panicked music.

With Deedra tightly bound to him, he yanked them both to one side, zipping them at top speed through a thicket of bushes and then underneath Big Boy. The dull, echoing crack of gunfire overlapped itself in the confines of the Broken Bubble, merging with the birdsong to fill the Arbor with a discordant, half-mechanical, half-alive throb of sound.

He hissed in a breath as he and Deedra collided with Big Boy. A bullet had creased his shoulder. Red blood welled there, bubbling like thick syrup. It captivated him, entranced him, and the spell was broken only by a groan from Deedra.

Releasing her from his vines, he leaned her against the tree trunk. A bullet had hit her, too. In her hip.

"How bad is it?" she asked, biting out her words against the pain.

"I was about to ask you the same thing," he told her. He examined her hip, careful not to touch too close to the wound. "It's a bruise. I think they're using plastic bullets. It doesn't look bad."

She nodded, her face pallid and slick with sweat. "I would hate to feel one that looked bad, then."

"Might have a bone fracture," he said. He couldn't be sure. His own shoulder throbbed; the plastic bullet must have fragmented upon firing to cut him like that.

Her eyes refocused on his shoulder. "Damn. We're a matching pair."

"They don't know what they're in for," he told her with a confidence that surprised him. "Can you move?"

She tested her weight on the wounded side. "Yeah, a little, but there's nowhere to go. They—"

"There are *many* places to go," he told her. "And we're going to go to them. But first..."

■ ■ ■

"Where the hell are they?" Max Ludo cried. "What the hell is going on down there?"

Markard licked his lips as he stared down into the lush and vibrant greenery of the arena. The two kids had just *vanished*. The trees offered excellent cover. He thought maybe one of his men had hit someone, but there was nothing to see, no way to tell. The plant growth was messing with the infrared drones he had hovering above the arena—they'd never encountered such abundant foliage and had never been calibrated for it.

"Send the men in there!" Ludo bawled. "Get their asses down there *now* and have them search under every goddamn *branch* if they have to!"

"Magistrate," Markard said tentatively, "my men have never encountered jungle warfare before. No one living has—"

"Your men are very capable, I'm sure," Dimbali interrupted.

Markard ground his teeth together. "Your opinion is noted, Doctor. But—"

"He's right," Ludo snapped. "Send them in. And…" He trailed off, then his eyes lit up. "Give me a comm. I have an idea. If the plants are a problem, let's get rid of the plants, eh?"

Markard commed his men: "Abandon your posts and regroup on ground level for a sweep of the arena."

Off to one side, Max Ludo was shouting into his own comm, and Markard couldn't believe what he was hearing.

■ ■ ■

"They're moving down," Rose said.

"What do you mean?" Deedra's mind was clearing after the shock of being shot. She felt as if she were hearing him for the first time, even though he'd been talking for the past minute or so.

"The men who shot us." He gestured up. "They were up there. Now they're moving down. Coming down here."

"After us."

"Yes."

Her hip pulsed with pain. She could put weight on it, but even taking a single step lanced a hot bolt up that side. Walking would be difficult; running was impossible.

"You're only shot in the shoulder. You can run. Go."

He grinned at her. "That's ridiculous. Then they would catch you."

"And they won't catch you. Better than nothing, right?"

"Worse than both of us getting out of this."

"Don't be an idiot. You can't—What are you doing?"

He was staring up into the branches above them. "Can you climb?"

"I've been climbing my whole life. What do you mean?" And then she got it: the tree. He wanted her to climb Big Boy.

Unreal. She followed his gaze. It was possible, she figured. Her hip hurt, but she would mostly use her arms. The branches appeared sturdy and crisscrossed one another. It would be no more difficult than scaling a mountain of debris. Probably a good bit easier.

"I'll give you a boost." He squatted down, and once again she was reminded that he was so much stronger than he appeared or let on. In moments, she was perched on a low branch.

"Go as high as you can," he told her. "Stay quiet. Hide among the leaves."

"What are you going to do?"

"You have to trust me."

She shook her head. "Whenever you say that, you end up getting killed."

"Not this time. I've been thinking like a human this whole time. No more. Now it's time to think like a plant."

CHAPTER 50

R ose strode into the middle of the Arbor.

For the first time in his life, he felt *connected*. Connected to Deedra, yes, but also connected to the Arbor, to this place he had grown. He imagined he could feel through every flower petal, every blade of grass. Could sense motion in the tilt of a branch or stalk.

Not true. None of it true. But he felt it nonetheless.

They were coming for him.

They would want him alive, if at all possible. That was his only advantage. They'd shot at him from a distance because they feared him. They'd tried to wound him. And they had.

Now they would try to weaken him further. And take him down.

That wasn't going to happen.

The first men spilled out of a doorway to his left. He didn't even look their way as an amplified voice broke the new stillness of the Arbor:

"Lie down on the ground, hands on your head! Do it now and no one gets hurt!"

A lie, like all the others. Humans lied so easily.

He didn't lie down. He didn't move at all.

"Where is the girl? Down on the ground! Do it now!*"*

More men, now—from the north. He was being surrounded. Twenty of them that he could see, all armed, all crab-walking as they fanned out in a circle around him.

It was the stupidest thing they could do. Were they really going to shoot at him while directly across from their comrades? Had they thought of this at all? Even with plastic bullets and body armor, they would be risking injury to one another.

"You will not take me!" he called out to them. "I will *not* be moved!"

"Get your ass on the goddamned ground!" the voice wailed in a near panic.

They knew what he could do. Or thought they did.

They respected his power.

Good.

"Come for me," he whispered, and it began.

CHAPTER 51

Maybe they thought he would attack. Maybe that's why they were so slow in moving in on him, content to keep their distance. Maybe they were realizing that they couldn't open fire in their current configuration.

He didn't plan on allowing them to rearrange themselves.

Raising his arms to the sky, he closed his eyes.

"Get down, you freak! We won't ask again!"

That was fine by Rose. Something else was already in motion.

The background hum of the Arbor intensified. Rose opened his eyes and looked all around himself. The men in the black body armor were advancing on him with slow, cautious steps.

One of them—just one—stopped for a moment, looking around.

Hey, Rose imagined his muttering, as though to himself, *hey, do you guys hear something?*

If they didn't, they would in just a few seconds.

The buzz built in intensity. Behind and above the DeeCees rose a great, fragmented black cloud.

And then a swarm of insects overtook the DeeCees and descended.

The DeeCees were swallowed by a wave of buzzing, darting bees, flying cockroaches, and airborne stinging ants.

On their own, the insects couldn't—or wouldn't—do much of anything. Rose was counting on the men to panic, because that's what humans did.

He'd been right to rely on them.

They immediately and predictably freaked out as the bugs swarmed them. If they'd stayed calm, the insects probably would have drifted away as the breeze shredded the cloud of perfume Rose had emitted. But once the men began to jitter and slap at the bugs, the bugs responded. They slipped into the crevice between the neck and the helmet. Yelps and cries of pain rang out as bee stings took hold on sensitive flesh.

The distraction was enough—the stings, the crawling, the bugs under the armor, the mass of them shrouding the air. Rose took advantage of the moment of chaos to whip out vines, snaking them along the ground and wrapping around ankles. He tripped half a dozen DeeCees who were flailing at their helmets before anyone realized what he was up to.

"Subject attacking! Flank him! Flank him!"

One gun went off. The shot went awry amid the hail of insects. Rose concentrated on his skin. He'd never tried this before, but then again, he hadn't known until recently that he was Rose in more than name.

Some roses were delicate and fragile.

Others were not.

He thickened his skin to an almost bark-like consistency. He took on a woody appearance, his flesh mottling and deepening in color. His sepals, in tatters after the fusillade of bullets from before, grew and filled in, wrapping around him for an additional layer of protection.

Another bullet. This one chipped off an edge of his hip and whined off. He barely felt it.

Someone else did, though: *"Man down! Man down!"*

Followed by: *"Cease fire! No firearms!"*

Rose took no pleasure in knowing that their violence had downed one of their own.

Then again, he didn't regret it, either.

CHAPTER 52

"What are they *doing* down there?" Max Ludo shouted. He grabbed Markard's arm and practically shoved him through the opening that led to a plunge down to the floor of the arena. "Shoot him already!"

"Magistrate—"

"Shut up, Dimbali! You can grow another one from the corpse! I'm not waiting any longer. Markard! Kill the damn thing!"

"Magistrate..." He extricated himself from Ludo's clinging grasp. "They can't fire without risking hitting one another. But don't worry— these men are well-trained in melee combat. They'll catch him. We've done it before—at the factory, at SecFac."

Just then, the Magistrate's comm bleated for attention. As he checked the screen, Max Ludo momentarily forgot his ire, and a wicked smile refolded his features. "Excellent," he said. "The Truck is here."

■ ■ ■

Deedra watched from midway up the tree as Rose stood his ground and fought with the DeeCees. The insects were still buzzing and spinning around, providing a distraction. One DeeCee was down, possibly for good, hit by a ricochet.

The ache in her hip prevented her from going any higher, but the foliage was thick enough that she felt safely concealed. Parting a fan of leaves, she could watch.

Rose didn't move at all. He just stood there, his skin thick and armored, as the insects choked the air around him and his vines whipped this way and that. Thorned, the tendrils ripped through body armor. The force of his blows lifted the men bodily and tossed them like discarded refuse into the air, arcing high before crashing into the ground or slamming against another tree.

It was quiet and violent and somehow beautiful all at once.

They came at him with bludgeons and blades, raised fists, pepper sprays. But it was like fighting a wall or a building. Rose remained in his spot, feet planted stolidly, and fended off every attack. The formerly pristine blanket of grass was now littered with specks of blood, torn pieces of body armor, discarded weapons.

The DeeCees—as though all bound with a common string—retreated in the face of Rose's wrath, stumbling back and away, expressions of terror and disbelief evident through the cracks in their riot helmets. They ran or dragged injured comrades between them, and they didn't look back.

It was over.

Or so she thought.

For just then, there was a rumble that nearly shook her from the tree, and she grabbed a branch and held on for dear life.

■ ■ ■

At the controls of the Truck, Markard experienced thrill and dread in equal measure. He'd played around with vehicle simulators back in his cadet days, but he'd never actually driven one before. Personal vehicles were outlawed and too expensive to maintain anyway. The power of the roaring engine under his control was intoxicating. He gunned it and crashed through a thicket of shrubbery, casting leaves and branches in all directions.

The dread receded a bit. He'd worried about being able to control the Truck, but it was dead easy—two pedals for stop and go, a wheel for left and right. A child could do it. He hit the gas, and the engine howled in what Markard imagined to be pleasure. His tires cut furrows into the ground as he lurched forward.

The Truck was sturdy and plated with armor, the glass bulletproof. Mounted on the roof were massive speakers, and he hit the button for the PA system now as the boy—Rose—came into view through a patch of crushed bushes.

■ ■ ■

Deedra watched the mechanical monstrosity tear a dirt-spewing path just below her. It was as if the thing had teeth and had chewed its way through Rose's beautiful Arbor. There was a curved window at the front of it, and she recognized the DeeCee inspector—Markard—through it.

He passed beneath her, slowly guiding his machine toward Rose. For a moment, she thought he would keep going until he trundled right over poor Rose, crushing him, but he stopped about twenty feet away, right at the edge of the clearing in which Rose stood.

Markard's voice boomed out from the vehicle:

"Rose! Stand down! You can't win! You can beat my men, but you can't beat the machines."

Deedra's hip throbbed, but that wasn't going to stop her. She began to make her way down the tree.

．．．

Rose didn't move except to turn his head in the direction of the voice. It came from a large-wheeled construct that vibrated the ground and spewed forth a noxious gray-white cloud that made Rose want to choke even at a distance.

"*Surrender,*" the voice went on, "*or we'll use this truck to wipe this place out. This place means something to you, doesn't it?*"

He wasn't sure if the man in the machine could hear him or not, but he answered anyway: "Every place means something to me. And it's sad that nowhere means anything to you."

"*Like before—down on the ground. Hands on your head. No one else has to get hurt, and this place can go on.*"

Rose clenched his jaw.

．．．

Deedra eased her way out of the tree, favoring her hip. She was behind the Truck and to the left. She didn't know if it was possible or not, but she figured she could sneak up along the left side…somehow get that door open…disable Markard…

Her knife rested comfortably against the small of her back. "Disable" him for good, if need be.

She crept forward. The grass was soft, the ground giving and generous to her injured hip.

And then it happened.

．．．

A new voice, one Rose knew from broadcasts and his time in prison. This one not amplified, but loud enough to be heard, even over the Truck's engine:

"Hey! Hey, look what I have!"

Coming around the Truck was Max Ludo. He had one arm wrapped around Deedra's neck and was prodding her to limp forward. He held a gun to her head.

"It's simple, Rose!" Ludo called out. "Go back to the lab, or you can watch me turn her head into—"

And Deedra twisted. Something flashed. Her knife. She plunged it into Max Ludo's thigh, and the Magistrate screamed.

At the same instant, Rose shot a prickled vine in Max's direction. It hit him in the face at full force and turned Max Ludo's head into a mass of bloody pulp.

Magistrate Ludo's body slumped to the ground.

■ ■ ■

Deedra, relieved, shaking with adrenaline, hopped to one side. Her hip was about to give out; she leaned against a nearby tree.

As she gulped in a huge, relieved breath, the door to the Truck opened and SI Markard tumbled out. He cast a panicked glance at Rose, at Ludo's body, then back to Rose.

For a long, silent moment, no one moved or spoke. Then Markard, slowly, raised both of his hands above his head. "I'm not going to hurt you," he called out, his voice quavering.

"You can't hurt me," Rose said. Not bragging. Just stating a fact.

"Look, maybe we—"

"You should go," Rose said very calmly. "You should go now."

Markard hesitated for just a moment, then glanced over at Max Ludo's body again...

...and then ran in the opposite direction as fast as he could, disappearing back along the Truck's path and vanishing through one of the exits from the Arbor.

Deedra closed her eyes and laughed.

It was over.

She thought that for a good five or six seconds.

■ ■ ■

Rose startled at the sound of the Truck's engine gunning. He'd seen Markard run off, so what could—

"Rose!" It was Deedra, screaming to him. "Run!"

The Truck lurched forward, then gained steam. Through the windshield, Rose could make out Dr. Dimbali. The man's expression was twisted into a rage unlike any Rose had ever seen. The rage of a man who has held infinity in his hands and watched it slip through his fingers.

"Run!" she shrieked again, but he couldn't. He couldn't run because—

The Truck bore down on him. Rose stood perfectly still. It was close enough now that he could count Dr. Dimbali's teeth between his peeled-back lips, gritted in determination.

The Truck collided with him, full force. Dead on.

And—

And the entire front end crumpled like cheap foil, the windshield shattering into a million glittering fragments.

Rose didn't move.

His roots. When the fight began, he'd sworn not to go.

You will not take me! I will not be moved!

And he'd meant it. Here, in the Arbor, in his place of power and peace, he could not lose. He'd sent his roots deeper than ever before, deep into the rich soil he'd cultivated. He'd thickened his skin, made himself like an oak.

The destroyed Truck bore testimony to the strength of not moving. He hadn't fought back. Not this time. He'd stood his ground and let the world move around him.

And he was alive.

The Truck, sputtering and coughing out its last black clouds of noxious fumes, squealed as a door opened. Dr. Dimbali stumbled out, then collapsed to the ground. He was bleeding profusely.

The man could harm him no more. Rose walked to Dr. Dimbali, who could barely move, barely breathe. The impact had thrown Dr. Dimbali into the steering column, crushing his ribs. His face was a mask of contusions, abrasions, and dozens of gashes from flying glass.

Rose knelt next to him. Despite all Dr. Dimbali had done and planned to do, he felt no anger or hatred toward him. Only sadness. Confusion.

"We were going to do it together," Rose said. "Like building this place. You didn't have to try to control me. We could have helped *everyone*. With my powers and your knowledge, we could have—" He broke off. Rage threatened to overwhelm curiosity, and he tamped it down. "Why, Dr. Dimbali? Why?" He took the dying man's hand in his own. "You could have helped the entire world, *changed* the world. But you got greedy. *Why?* I need to understand."

Dr. Dimbali coughed. Blood welled up in the corner of his mouth, but he managed a weak smile. "I don't expect a plant to understand human nature."

And then he leaned up with obvious pain, reaching out for Rose's face. Rose put an arm under him, helping him move. Dr. Dimbali touched Rose's cheek and smiled. Then he leaned in farther and whispered in his ear.

■ ■ ■

Deedra limped over to where Rose crouched on the ground with Dr. Dimbali, her knife drawn. She didn't trust Dr. Dimbali, who had his lips close to Rose's ear. She didn't trust death at this point. She only trusted Rose.

She needn't have worried. By the time she made her way over to them, Dr. Dimbali's body had gone slack and still. Rose gently laid him back on the grass. He didn't need to tell Deedra that the man was dead.

Standing over the two of them—Dimbali's eyes unblinking, Rose's head tilted down over his former mentor—Deedra rode a wave of cresting, incompatible emotions. Dr. Dimbali had tried to enslave Rose and steal something that could have helped the world. But he'd also taught her so much, helped her.

"I don't know what to feel," she admitted. "I think I'm glad he's dead, but..."

"All I wanted was to learn," Rose said, and the distress in his voice stabbed at her. "I just wanted to learn what I could, then use it to help people. That's all I wanted. And this is what happens."

It took a minute, but she managed to work around her hip and get on the ground with him. She put her arms around him.

"None of this is your fault," she whispered. "And he can't be the only one who could figure out how to use your powers to make things better. If there's *one* person like him, there have to be more. We have to find someone else, someone *good*, who can really make a difference."

"And we need to warn people. Warn the world. The Red Rain is coming."

They sat like that for she knew not how long, just holding each other. She became aware of the silence, then of the nonsilence—the insects, the birds. The rustle of leaves in the breeze.

Had the whole world really been like this, before? Could it be again?

She didn't know the answer to either question. She only knew this: She would *get* the answers.

"We should go," she said. "More people will come. We can't stay in Ludo Territory. It's too dangerous. Markard will come back with more DeeCees. The next Magistrate will still want to control you."

"I know." He stood and helped pull her to her feet. She took one last look around the Arbor. Its pristine green was now marred by the wreckage wrought by the Truck, the ground abused and furrowed and gouged. Max's body and his splattered blood and brains. Dr. Dimbali. Shards of plastic and glass and fabric and armor. Dropped weapons. And the great, hulking, smoking wreck of the Truck.

As though the Territory had exploded inside the Arbor.

"It's not beautiful anymore," said Deedra. "It's not perfect."

Rose touched her cheek, then gently stroked his fingers down to her scar. "They're not the same thing," he told her.

As they walked toward the exit, she leaning on him to support her tender hip, she asked, "What did Dimbali say to you? Right before he died?"

Rose paused, as though deciding. Then he shrugged and touched her scar again, this time to loop his finger under her necklace. He pulled gently, lifting the pendant out from her neckline. The circle with the protruding cross.

"It was about this," he said.

"This?" She looked down at it. "My pendant?"

"He said . . . it's not a pendant. It's a *key*."

"A key?" She lifted it so that it hung between them. "You know the interesting thing about keys?"

"What?"

Her eyes widened and she grinned at Rose. "They can turn things on, but they can also turn things *off*." She gestured toward the world beyond the Arbor. "Let's get out there and see what this one's good for."

CHAPTER 53

They made their way out of Ludo Territory as dense clouds the color of old, grease-stained concrete roiled overhead, as though shielding them from the sky's gaze.

Deedra wondered what color the rain would be when it fell.

ACKNOWLEDGMENTS

The authors would like to thank the many, many people who made this book possible: our editor, Alvina Ling, and her crew: Bethany Strout, Nikki Garcia, and Pam Gruber; Annie McDonnell and the entire Managing Editorial team, including copyeditor Tracy Koontz; all of Sales, Publicity, and Marketing, including but not limited to Andrew Smith, Melanie Chang, and Victoria Stapleton; publisher Megan Tingley; and everyone else at Little, Brown, for their faith and their hard work.

Also, of course, we must tip our hats to our agents and managers and sundry other folk without whom we could not survive: Kathy Anderson, Steven Fisher, Barry Littman, and Carlos Carreras.

And, individually:

Barry would like to thank his wife and early reader, Morgan Baden, for keeping him sane (well, as close as possible!), as well as moral supports Libba Bray, Paul Griffin, Sarah Maclean, and Eric Lyga. You all rock, both individually and collectively. I couldn't get anything done without you guys.

Robert would like to thank Barry Lyga for embarking on this journey with us; Joseph and Alice DeFranco for their loving support: his brothers and sisters, Christina, Joe, Chris, Mike, Rich, Steve, and Barbara; the Drayton Family; David DuPuy; and Peter Facinelli for everything you all have done for me.

Peter would like to thank, first and foremost, Rob DeFranco, whose vivid imagination sparked the idea for this book, and Barry Lyga, for the countless hours of conversations we spent hashing out this world in order to put it on paper. The experience was beyond my expectations. Thank you.

I'd also like to acknowledge my sisters, Joanne, Lisa, and Linda, for their unwavering love and support, and my parents, Peter and Bruna... Thank you for teaching me at a young age to use my imagination. Thank you also to Jaime Alexander for being my sounding board and best friend... ES.